Queen's Chess

by

Brenda Huber

Queen's Chess

Cover Art by *Rae Monet, Inc. Design*

The Wild Rose Press, Inc.
PO Box 708
Adams Basin, NY 14410-0708
Visit us at www.thewildrosepress.com

Publishing History
First Crimson Rose Edition, 2018
Print ISBN 978-1-5092-2032-8
Digital ISBN 978-1-5092-2033-5

Published in the United States of America

The sight of that all too familiar envelope dropped Jesse's stomach straight to his shoes.

Shit. Not already.

No, he corrected himself just as quickly. The message had been delivered late. Somehow, he didn't think the Chess Master would take that into consideration.

We don't even have a fighting chance to save this woman now.

Knowing the Chess Master's prints would be all over this thing, following protocol to preserve evidence, Jesse held the envelope by the corner between his fingertips and carried it back to his desk. Dropping the envelope on top of the clean piece of paper DeMarco helpfully supplied, Jesse snapped gloves on and opened it. He should be turning this over to the FBI, but something was riding him. Frustration? Curiosity? Resentment? He'd been drawn into this sick game by a monster and then shuffled to the side by Anderson and the rest of her crew.

He didn't particularly care right now. Right now, he was only worried about what was inside this envelope and the imaginary clock that seemed to have kicked into a faster countdown.

DeMarco leaned over his shoulder, conveniently blocking any view the Feds might have, and swore aloud as a white piece of paper slipped from the envelope. One piece of paper, and no photo. A single, precise, damning word was neatly scripted on that startlingly bright and otherwise blank sheet.

Checkmate.

Praise for Brenda Huber

"Brenda Huber is an author to watch. The way she paints a scene [in *SHADOWS*] is fantastic…"

~*Catherine Bybee, New York Times and USA Today Bestselling Author*

~*~

"Huber's serial killer is truly twisted and readers will be guessing the person's identity until the last pages of the story…Huber's engaging characters and winsome town [in *SHADOWS*] will have the reader yearning for a sequel."

~*Romantic Times*

~*~

"[Brenda Huber's] ability to infuse romance, action and humor…will certainly keep me coming back for more. Reading Chronicles of the Fallen Series is a must for any PNR fan."

~*The Jeep Diva*

~*~

"Author Brenda Huber has crafted a tale that will ensnare the mind and enrapture the heart…"

~*Long and Short Romance Reviews*

Dedication

I dedicate this book to one of my best friends
and her prince charming biker,
Angie and Doran Moore.

~*~

May every day together feel like your first date.
May every storm only bring you closer together.
May every memory be precious.
And may you spend the rest of your life
happy that you chose to look at each other
across the breakfast table every morning.

Prologue

The Chess Master surveyed the elegant dining room with a critical eye. Everything had to be just right, no element was too small, no detail unimportant. He stopped beside the long mahogany table one final time to inspect his tools, making certain they were arranged in precise order. He'd sterilized every last blade. Surely the Rook, a surgeon by profession, would appreciate his efforts.

It really was the least he could do. He, being the gracious champion that he was, liked to afford his players what small comforts he could.

He'd probably let himself into the Rook's house a little too early, but the anticipation had been more than he could stand. He had an opponent now.

A real opponent. Finally!

He barely resisted the urge to clap his hands in glee. Instead, he picked up a scalpel, tested the edge against the pad of his thumb. A thin bead of crimson burst from his skin. Pleased, the Chess Master cleaned the blade with due diligence once more, then replaced the shiny tool in the proper grouping.

He'd noticed his blades had begun to dull a bit while he'd been maneuvering the last chess piece into play. So last night, filled with restless anticipation, he'd taken the time to give his tools the sharpest edge possible—everything from the smallest utility blades to the large hunting knife with a blade nearly as long as his forearm. He'd even purchased a new blade for his bone saw. The freshly polished pliers, clamps, chisel, and claw hammer gleamed beneath the golden glow of the chandelier.

He caught his breath and hesitated, his focus falling on the small gray pouch in the center of the table. His stomach clutched. He'd put this off long enough.

It's time.

Gritting his teeth, he ignored the slight tremor in his hand and reached for the pouch. The suede material slid against his skin, smooth as butter. Benign. But the pewter pieces inside, rolling and clanking against each other, weighed his hand down like an anvil. The drawstring gave way with ease, and he gently spilled the Florentine chess pieces onto a towel he'd carefully folded and positioned earlier.

As the small figurines rolled and glinted in the early morning light, memories he'd never quite been able to put behind swept him back.

An eager little boy, a beautiful, stern woman, and a chessboard in play between them.

"It's your move," she prompted, cold and impatient.

With shaking hands, he reached out and positioned his piece into play.

The woman brushed her long hair over her shoulder and then reached for the board, her pale narrow hand confident. She picked up a polished pewter queen, her pinkie elevated with delicate precision before placing the piece back on the board in a new position.

"Checkmate," she said, her tone clipped.

The little boy's head dipped, and his shoulders drooped as he tipped his little pewter king over. "I'm sorry, Mother."

She stared down her nose at him, her lips compressed in a thin line. "Were you even trying?"

"Yes, Mother."

"I don't think you were."

"I'll do better next time, I promise. I can be a good player."

Silence stretched out between them, broken only by the steady tick tock of the grandfather clock down the hall. He wanted to squirm on the hard-wooden seat. Desperately, he wanted to squirm. But he didn't dare. He knew better. She'd never raised a hand against him. She didn't need to. Cold disappointment and aloof displeasure were the only tools of punishment she'd ever needed. And those she'd wielded with expert precision.

"Good isn't enough. If you are to play, then you must excel." She peered at him as though he were a bug, or worse, a speck of dust on her tidy chess board. "No. I don't believe you'll ever improve. You fail to strategize, every time. You leave your most valuable pieces open to attack, and you fail to capitalize on even the most obvious weaknesses in your opponents defenses. You'll never have anything beyond a rudimentary grasp of the game." Her chin elevated, and she shook her head. Her shoulders rose and fell. "I'm just going to have to face the fact that you'll never live up to expectation. This is a waste of my time."

He almost bounced out of his chair in protest. Almost. But he caught himself just in time. Still, he couldn't quite filter the needy pleading from his voice.

"Please, Mother! I can excel. I'll keep practicing. I'll—"

The moment she lowered her chin a notch and fixed a narrow-eyed stare on him, he fell silent.

Filled with shame, he let his gaze drift to his lap. He clutched his hands tight together and blinked away the tears blurring his vision.

"I'm sorry, Mother," he whispered.

A fine sheen of sweat peppered the Chess Master's brow, and his belly churned as he shook himself free of the recollection. That was a long time ago. He'd proven her wrong, hadn't he? He was a master now. A true Chess Master.

Determined, he set the Rook piece aside, positioning it next to the small torch with great care, and then he poured the rest of the pieces back into the pouch. The rest would get their turn, in due time. For now, it was the Rook's moment to shine.

Frowning, he stretched a little farther along the table and repositioned the handle of a fillet knife, just a tiny bit. He'd precut the tape and evenly spaced the pieces along the edge of the antique mahogany— nothing worse than trying to peel and tear duct tape with wet hands—and his ropes were prepped and ready to go.

The shades had been drawn to block prying eyes. He'd even cleared the necessary wall space. He took a moment to tug on the stakes he'd hammered into the wall studs earlier in preparation. Nodded approval when they'd held firm. The only thing left to do was wait for the Rook. He hoped this piece might appreciate his efforts more than the last had.

Pleased all was as it should be, he moved deeper

into the house. He considered all the possible countermoves his opponent might make. And he ran through his own plan, hatching new plays, cataloging them in anticipation. Strategizing.

Each move had to be weighed with care, each countermove planned out with meticulous concern. After all this time, he'd finally found an opponent worthy of the game. Detective Reid. A true challenger.

No worries, Detective. I won't let you down.

The Chess Master headed toward the Rook's bathroom to freshen up a bit. Her shift at the hospital wouldn't be over for at least another two hours. He had plenty of time. A shot of adrenaline spiked through his system, sending a shiver down his spine. The excitement of the game was building, and the Chess Master let the smile tugging at his lips bloom fully.

What a rush!

He paused for a moment on the way to the Rook's bedroom as came upon the study. Curious, he moved through the study to examine the titles on the Rook's shelves. Twain and Melville, Hawthorne and Poe. So many classics to choose from, though Poe tended to be a little dark for his tastes.

Ah, what's this?

Jules Verne's *The Mysterious Island* had captured his interest. He balanced his selections in one hand as he scanned the shelves. He couldn't resist choosing a few more volumes. Reading gave him a great amount of pleasure—almost as much as the game. Almost. Satisfied he hadn't missed anything noteworthy, he returned to the kitchen to drop his pilfered treasure on the table near his backpack. That was it. He couldn't fit anything else in his bag.

He'd found a lot of useful items among the Rook's things, including a roll of cash in an unmentionables drawer, but there was no use weighing himself down too much. He still had the duffel bag with his tools to carry as well.

Returning to his previous mission, he cut through the master bedroom and entered the attached bath. It had been a long time since he'd had the luxury of a hot, uninterrupted shower, so he savored the hard beat of scalding water against his flesh. The flowery shampoo and body wash wasn't something he'd have picked for himself, but he'd learned to make due long ago. As he stepped from the shower and began drying off with a thick, white towel, his stomach rumbled, reminding him it had been some time since he's last had a good, home-cooked meal as well.

Those strawberries he'd observed the Rook picking over at the market last night had made his mouth water. French toast topped with fresh strawberries and whipped cream with just a dusting of powdered sugar sounded divine. Bacon would have been a wonderful accompaniment, but alas, the Rook was Vegetarian. Ah, well. At least there were some excellent coffee selections.

Dressed now and smelling of the Rook's scented body wash and shampoo, he picked a pumpkin spiced coffee pod. After positioning a short, fat red cup with white polka dots in the coffee machine, he collected fruit, eggs, and heavy cream from the fridge and spread out the items on the counter.

Now where would she put that loaf of French bread?

He recalled the mouth watering, yeasty smell that

had painted the very air a wonderful shade of delicious, and decided to go back to that little bakery again. Maybe right before he left town, a celebratory feast of sorts.

Oh, now. But that's not being very fair, he scolded himself. *Detective Reid is very good. He could triumph.*

If anyone stood a chance of beating him, it was the good detective. The very idea sent a wave of exhilaration racing through his bloodstream.

With a pleased murmur, he found the loaf of bread in a large wooden box with an old-fashioned roll-top lid. He then dug out a cutting board and took a moment to admire the Rook's kitchen knives. A sudden, inspired grin split his face, and he set one long shiny blade aside for later. He turned the small kitchen radio on, adjusted the volume so he'd be able to hear if anyone came to the door, and hummed along as he began cooking. Before long, his supper was sizzling away on the griddle and the delicious aroma of coffee scented the air.

Just as he positioned the last sliced strawberry atop a fluffy mound of fresh whipped cream, the crunch of gravel alongside the house drew his attention. His brows snapped together, and he glanced at the enormous clock on the far wall. His eyes narrowed.

He hurried to a side window and drew the curtain aside just enough to peep through. The Rook's tan SUV had already pulled into the garage. The overhead door was, even now, slowly lowering, blocking the red glow of tail lights. An hour early. He shot a scowl at his feast on the counter, gritted his teeth, and drew a deep breath through flared nostrils.

And here he'd worked so hard to make things nice

for the Rook. Well, there was no help for it. He'd have to tie the piece to a chair or something. He was hungry, and he fully intended to finish his supper before they could get started. The Chess Master pursed his lips. He dusted his hands on a kitchen towel and turned the radio off.

Awfully inconsiderate.

Chapter One

"Excuse me. If I can have your attention, please?" a cool, female voice called over the cacophony of voices.

Homicide Detective Jesse Reid set his coffee cup aside and turned his focus toward the front of the room. As FBI Supervisory Special Agent Anderson's clipped tone cut through the chatter, an oppressive silence descended over the small, crowded conference room. Jesse, along with every other law enforcement officer present, regarded the slender, middle-aged woman standing behind the podium in grim, expectant silence.

"As you can see, ladies and gentlemen," SSA Anderson continued, pointing to one of the large whiteboards taking up the entire west wall, "we've been tracking this particular subject for quite some time. To date, he's stuck to large cities—easier to get lost in the crowd. He surfaces to make a seemingly random number of kills, then goes dormant for months at a time, only to resurface somewhere else to begin the cycle all over again."

She stepped from behind the podium and made her way down the row of pictures, pointing to each one in turn as she spoke.

"Laura Avery was our first known victim. Kansas City. Twenty-six, single, a veterinarian. She coached pee-wee baseball in her free time." SSA Anderson pointed to the next photo. "Trisha Conner, also from Kansas City. Twenty-eight, lived with her boyfriend of two years. She was a dentist who volunteered at her local women's shelter teaching self defense classes. Next, we have Cora Salazar, KC as well. Twenty-five, single, a physical therapist. Cora moonlighted as a singer at a nightclub."

On and on she ran down the list, making certain the room at large knew each face had a name, and a life. And that everyone present took each woman's loss personally.

"And finally, we have our most recent victim. Catherine Skogdell, thirty-five, single, an ER doctor at Hennepin County Medical Center." SSA Anderson returned to her post behind the podium. "We've tried to build an UNSUB profile based on victimology, the identified similarities of the victims, but the demographic is pretty widespread. Our UNSUB's not making it easy for us. So far, the only thing linking these victims is that they were highly successful in their chosen careers. Dedicated. Ambitious."

Jesse hooked a finger in his collar and tugged. It didn't help. He struggled to focus on the moving speech, but he—like so many others in the room—was dragging himself through one of the low points of this adrenaline rollercoaster on which they'd all found themselves trapped.

The claustrophobic effect of eighteen overworked, overstressed bodies crowded into a conference room roughly the size of a jail cell sure as hell wasn't helping matters. It had to be a hundred and ten in here. Sweat dampened his hairline and beaded on his lip. He tugged at the knot in his tie again and then flicked open the top button of his gray dress shirt, gaining himself a precious bit of breathing room. Jesse rubbed his gritty eyes and squinted at Anderson once more.

"In a nutshell," she went on, giving no outward indication that she even noticed the restless shifting around her, "we believe we're looking for a white male, most likely aged thirty to forty-five, acutely intelligent, narcissistic and highly resourceful.

"These women were not taken impulsively, nor were these murders crimes of passion. They were coldblooded, premeditated slayings. Each woman was studied, followed. Stalked, if you will. He knew her routine, knew her interests, knew intimate details of her day to day life. And he knew exactly when the perfect moment would present itself for him to make his move. And, once he had her, he spent a lot of time with her." She glanced toward the second row of macabre pictures filling the board, frozen mementos of brutal mutilations, and she murmured, "A *lot* of time."

SSA Anderson let her gaze touch upon every face in the room, lingering, it seemed, on Jesse's for a moment longer than any of the others. He didn't have to wonder why. He'd been thrust front and center into the middle of this investigation, whether he liked it or not, whether he'd asked for it or not.

SSA Anderson returned to addressing the room once more, "Given the vast range of his killing field, the petty theft at each scene and the erratic time frame for the killing sprees, he is most likely transient."

Jesse glanced around the room, taking in the stoic expressions, the anxious fidgets, the caffeine jitters, and the random exhausted yawn. He could sympathize.

The investigation was being led by a small task

force from the FBI's Serial Killer Division that specialized in apprehending the most violent of offenders. Their track record was supposed to be outstanding, though they'd had pitiful poor luck catching this particular nut job. Everyone else in the room made up their local backup. His fellow Homicide Detectives, the Minneapolis Violent Criminal Apprehension Team or VCAT, the Violent Offender Task Force, VOTF, and Forensics. Department heads from each precinct were present. Even a handful of beat cops. In short, the FBI's foot soldiers.

Nearly every square inch of the four huge whiteboards lined up along the far wall were covered with maps, diagrams, timelines, lists of names bulleted with personal data, and a whole hell of a lot of graphic pictures no one in their right mind should ever have to see.

"While he is careful to take nothing that would throw up a red flag or leave a trail to follow," Anderson said, "he helps himself to whatever else he wants, cash, clothing, food, books. Completely random items every time. Portable and disposable."

"Excuse me," a voice called from the rear of the room. Jesse glanced over his shoulder to see a hand in the air.

Jesus, what is this, kindergarten?

Mazetti, a young beat cop stood up. Eager. Level-headed and observant. Had to know everything about everything. The captain had been eyeing him for a promotion already. "How do you know he took food? Or books for that matter?"

"Thank you, officer?"

"Mazetti."

"Thank you for paying attention, Officer Mazetti. We found many instances of cupboards and pantries being...well, rifled through, for lack of a better term. And that, combined with Misty Greenville's and Joey Callaghan's grocery receipts in correlation to items missing from the grocery bags still in the trunks of their cars, we feel we can safely deduce our killer helped himself to their shopping.

"In the case of his most recent kill Catherine Skogdell, the ER doctor, he not only took books—as we've deduced from the empty spaces in her library and the plethora of fingerprints he left behind, but he also showered and made himself supper as evidenced by the wet towel, dirty dishes and coffee mug with his DNA and prints on them, and the absence of said food in the contents of Miss Skogdell's stomach per the autopsy."

A murmur and a shuffle met this new bit of information.

"The guy showered at the victim's house?" Chief Emerson sputtered from just behind Jesse. "*And* made himself a meal? Freakin' creepy bastard."

Jesse was inclined to agree.

SSA Anderson cleared her throat. "Our guy doesn't appear to care about being identified or tied to his crimes. Aside from his particular brand—pardon the pun—of calling card that he leaves at each kill sight, the prints and DNA are how we've been able to positively link him to each murder. We feel, given his narcissism, that the leaving of prints and DNA is most likely his way of laying claim to his kills. A stamp of ownership, if you will."

Jesse's long-time partner, Detective Christian DeMarco leaned close and whispered, "More like it's his way of flipping us the bird."

Jesse grunted in agreement.

Grimacing, he leaned back in the hard metal folding chair and crossed his arms. The chair squeaked and groaned beneath him, threatening to dump him on his ass should he shift the wrong way. Jesse stretched his legs out beneath the table and worked his neck from side to side. He'd long ago given up rubbing at the persistent knots in his muscles, knowing it would do no good. They weren't going anywhere, not while this killer was on the loose.

"Although his M.O. stays pretty consistent with every kill, he changes his appearance drastically according to the few credible witnesses that have come forward. Our guy's a regular chameleon. A handicapped, aged man. A homeless bum of indeterminate age. A middle-aged businessman—the business suit, I might add, stolen from a previous kill sight. Shaggy brown hair. Bald. Well groomed. Scraggly beard. Clean shaven. Always something different," SSA Anderson said, holding her hands out at her sides, palms up. "No evidence of sexual assault on any of the victims, though the repeated slicing and stabbing could indicate a high level of sexual frustration. Perhaps he's impotent or struggling with his sexual identity. Regardless, the guy's definitely got a type."

Anderson directed their attention to clusters of pictures affixed to the second whiteboard in the line. All head shots of young, vibrant women. And each of those pictures had a corresponding snapshot pinned next to it of the same subject on a stainless-steel morgue table, eyes closed, lips bloodless, skin ashen.

Jesse had already seen the autopsy reports. Well, most of them anyway, before he'd lost the stomach for it.

He'd been having trouble sleeping ever since.

Seven separate clusters of photos. Twenty-seven women in all. Twenty-seven victims that they knew about.

Who knew how many more were out there, unidentified and waiting for justice.

Incredible. How can this guy still be on the loose?

Jesse caught himself shaking his head as he counted the faces once more, appalled that this monster hadn't been caught yet.

"Our guy likes his victims young," SSA Anderson went on. "All of them so far have been in their twenties or early to mid thirties, long hair, slight build, fair skinned. Relationship statuses range from single to dating to divorced. Within each group of killings, the victims are all acquaintances in some way, though not necessarily with everyone in the group. And there are no definitive common denominators. Group to group, there's no connection at all. He likes to get up close and personal with his blades. That or he's got some major anger management issues. And, of course, the one detail we've managed to keep under wraps, the chess piece branded on each victim's body."

Silence held reign for a long moment as every man and woman in the room absorbed the cold hard facts SSA Anderson had laid out for them.

Beside Jesse, DeMarco scratched his fingers through the thick, dark stubble on his chin. The man had a five o'clock shadow at seven o'clock in the morning. Demarco pitched his voice low as he leaned close to Jesse. "Thing I don't get? Why the brand? Why a chess piece?"

"Crazy's got its own set of rules." The muted words popped out of Jesse's mouth before he had time to realize he should have kept it shut. DeMarco snickered and began tapping his pen on the edge of the table.

"We believe the branding of each victim is his way of paying tribute to the players in his twisted version of a chess game. Living chess, if you will. And yes, Detective Reid," SSA Anderson added, her emotionless gaze drifting slowly over the crowd until it zeroed in on him, "you would also be correct. As you so succinctly put it, crazy has its own set of rules."

Chairs squeaked and scrapped as nearly every other face in the room turned his way. He wanted to bang his head on the table in front of him. Instead, he angled his chin and stared back at the FBI agent, his attitude reeking of defiance. No way was he going to let her make this about him.

Anderson turned her attention back to the room at large, her cool smile not quite reaching the frost in her eyes. She thanked everyone for their time and cooperation. The clang and clatter of folding chairs and the shuffle of feet filled the room.

As Jesse joined the group spilling from the conference room, the commander called out to Jesse's partner, motioning him over. With a silent nod at Demarco, Jesse veered toward his desk, confident anything important would be passed along. Yawning, he made a pit stop in the break room where he filled a Styrofoam cup with the usual stationhouse sludge.

Back at his desk, Jesse dropped his tired body onto the same lumpy chair he'd been assigned nearly six years ago when he'd first made detective. He didn't even have time to pretend to look busy. The very businesslike click of heels was all the warning he got. A tired sigh escaped him. He should have known he wouldn't be able to dodge this bullet.

"Detective Reid, can I have a moment of your time?"

Jesse leaned back in his seat. "For you, Agent Anderson? I got all the time in the world."

The FBI had immediately and completely assumed the lead on the Chess Master case, almost before the first Minneapolis victim had made it to autopsy. And Jesse—whether he liked it or not—had become the department's unofficial point man during the ongoing serial killer investigation.

Every muscle in his neck, shoulders, and back slowly tightened. "What can I do for you?"

He knew he wasn't being Mr. Congeniality, knew this woman had the power to make his career—and his life—damned difficult, but right now he couldn't find it in himself to give a flying rat's ass about his insubordinate attitude. He was all out of nice for the day, his reserve tank bone dry. Besides, what were they going to do, fire him? Put him on administrative leave? They couldn't afford to lose him. He was their MVP.

The Chess Master himself had made sure of it.

Yippee-freakin'-do-dah.

SSA Anderson leveled one of those looks at him. One that suggested she was above his petty snarkitude.

"Given the Chess Master's…" her voice trailed off, as if she were considering a diplomatic way to present her case, "*fixation* on you, we'd like for you to meet with one of the Bureau's psychologists. At this point, we think it best to take a closer look at the connection between you—"

"Connection?" He barely managed to stop himself from shouting as he came forward in his seat. Barely. Just like he barely managed to stop himself from snarling at all the curious faces turning their way. Just by the skin of his teeth. He fisted his hands on the top of his desk, narrowed his eyes at her, and hissed, "How the hell can you think I would have *any* kind of a connection with this sick bastard?"

"Facts speak for themselves, Detective Reid," SSA Anderson replied, her tone hard as steel. "This guy's got twenty-seven murders under his belt. Twenty-seven we can positively tie to him beyond a shadow of a doubt. Only thing keeping us from pinning a name on him is the fact he has no priors and isn't in IAFIS. A killer doesn't typically burst from the starting gate with his technique so well perfected. Considering the sheer confidence displayed at each kill site, more likely than not, there are a whole hell of a lot more bodies out there we don't even know about. The guy likes getting his hands dirty. And he's not showing any signs of slowing down, or stopping.

"Right before the last three murders, he's communicated directly with *you*, Detective Reid. Addressed *you* specifically. Given *you* clues and pictures of the intended victims, given *you* the chance to stop him before he commits the act. To date, he hasn't reached out to anyone else that we are aware of. *Ever*. So, whether or not *you* like it, whether or not *you* think there's a connection between the two of you, *he* does. And with all due respect—"

"Oh, I'm sure," Jesse growled, unable to muster up

even the thinnest veneer of a civilized response.

SSA Anderson continued as if he hadn't uttered a sound, "*With all due respect*, what *he* thinks is what matters." Perched on the corner of Jesse's desk, arms folded over her black blazer, SSA Anderson stared him down like an old Western gunfighter at high noon. Her face was impassive but for the steely glint in her eye. "In my book that qualifies as a connection, *detective*."

Leaning back in his squeaky chair, he mirrored her body language, crossing his arms. He knew he shouldn't do it, had been on the force long enough to be a seasoned pro at keeping his own thoughts and emotions under wraps. To play it close to the vest, so to speak. But the woman knew how to push all the right buttons.

Then again, maybe she was just taking advantage of the buttons this serial killer had already exposed.

He let his emotions have full reign in the mutinous glare on his face. "In *your* book his little riddles might be some necessary step in a psychotic version of catch-me-if-you-can. But in *my* book, they're nothing more than taunts. You know, a big, fat, collective screw you. He's yanking our chain, sidetracking us. He doesn't give a crap about me or anybody—any*thing*—besides the sick high he gets from killing. You're wasting time bringing in some shrink. Wasting time analyzing the wrong damn person. You guys are playing right into his hands, letting him turn your focus away from him and putting the attention on me."

She stared at him for a long moment, silent and unmoved. He refused to be the first to blink.

"Dr. Richards will be here tomorrow sometime after three," SSA Anderson said, a dog with a bone.

"We expect you to make yourself available."

She rose and tugged at the hem of her blazer. And then, as if the thought had just occurred to her—and he damned well knew it hadn't, SSA Anderson was nothing if not prepared well in advance—she shot him one last tough-as-nails look. "And, Detective Reid, we expect you to cooperate, *fully*."

The smile she sent him was ice. Pure, brittle ice.

Chapter Two

Jesse ground his teeth as he watched SSA Anderson stride away. He glanced down when something wet splashed the back of his hand and scowled when he found his half-finished cup of coffee clutched tight, Styrofoam beginning to crumple, ready to be thrown. Heaving a disgusted groan, he took a big gulp instead, set the cup aside and wiped the back of his hand against his trouser leg.

What the hell did I do to deserve this crap?

A thick manila folder landed on the battered desk, and Jesse glanced up. Demarco let out a slow whistle as he checked out SSA Anderson's backside. When the woman disappeared inside the chief's office, he finally turned an appreciative smile on Jesse.

"With a body that hot, you'd think she'd have a warmer personality," Demarco lamented. The man was a player, one who happily wallowed in his easy-come-easy-go, love-'em-and-leave-'em, confirmed bachelor status.

Jesse snorted. As far as he was concerned, it didn't matter what a woman's ass looked like when she was a stone-cold bitch. He was a firm believer in the old saying, ugly is as ugly does.

His partner eyed him and quirked an eyebrow. "Saw you rated a special conference."

Jesse grunted and snatched up his coffee cup once

21

more, an addict looking for a fix. He choked down another swallow of the now lukewarm mud along with the bitterness brewing inside him. By his best calculations, since this killer had surfaced, he'd consumed roughly enough caffeine to keep a small third world country floating for the better part of a decade. Jesse reached up, tugged his tie the rest of the way loose and flicked another button open.

"What'd she want?" Demarco pressed.

"I'm supposed to meet with some Bureau shrink tomorrow. Apparently, I have a *connection* with this killer," he said, unable to conceal his disgust.

Questions boiled inside DeMarco's dark eyes. Despite his lackadaisical, playboy attitude, Jesse's partner never missed a detail. Thankfully, DeMarco knew him well enough not to push. Not right now, at least.

Later in the car without all the little ears around it would be a whole other ballgame.

"Autopsy report's back on the Navarro homicide," Demarco said, motioning to the file he'd just dropped on Jesse's desk as he took his own seat, reminding Jesse they still had other cases to work. "COD exsanguination."

Was anyone surprised given the nature of the crime scene?

Wife had come home early to find hubby doing the neighbor lady. Said wife had then gone bat-shit crazy with the hubby's hunting knife. The neighbor lady— and Jesse used the term *lady* loosely—had gotten away…carved up a bit, but alive. The hubby, well, he hadn't been so lucky. Jesse pulled the file closer, only to push it away again. He'd had enough of blood and gore to last him a lifetime thanks to the Chess Master.

He gave in to the urge to rub the back of his neck after all.

"I don't know which one is worse, the Chess Master or Anderson. Hell, this whole case is getting to me."

"Ya think?" DeMarco reached for his coffee, took a slug, and grimaced. "Ugh. This crap is probably giving us cancer or something. You know that, right? Can't you feel it eating a hole in your stomach?" After taking another sip, he set the cup aside, scrunched up his face, and clutched his gut while he groaned in dramatic misery. "I swear it's like the scene in Aliens where it's trying to claw its way out."

Jesse snorted, resisting the urge to roll his eyes. "We'll be sure to stop at Starbucks for one of your sissy lattes later."

DeMarco grinned, flipped him the bird, and sat up to dig through a stack of files on the corner of his desk. Jesse drained the last of the swill in his own cup, licked his lips with feigned gusto, and tossed the cup with all the rest overflowing the can under his desk.

This serial killer case had them all twisting in the wind. It was hard to focus on anything else. Not even the job he *should* be doing. Nevertheless, he didn't need to review the ghastly photos of Gina Navarro's handiwork. They'd been first on the scene after the beat cop and had gotten a good look at the real deal, up close and personal. Nor did he need to review any of the other homicides he was working. Every one of them had been indelibly etched into his memory.

But none of them held a candle to the Chess Master. That bastard was a real piece of work, on a level all by himself. Jesse and his partner had been diligently working in the FBI's shadow for the last three weeks.

But the Chess Master's handiwork here in Minneapolis hadn't been the only file Jesse had gotten his hands on. As the MPD liaison, he'd had an all access pass to the complete file on the Chess Master. Access to *all* the photos. Even the ones not tacked up on the white boards.

Kansas City, Omaha, St. Louis, Des Moines, Davenport, Peoria, and now Minneapolis. Each city had hosted this killer's sick game. The Midwest's own homegrown killer.

But this time things were different, as SSA Anderson had pointed out. The killer had made contact. Provided clues. Maddening notes delivered twenty-four hours prior to each murder, and along with those notes a seemingly innocuous snapshot of a smiling, unsuspecting, nameless young woman. All personally addressed to Jesse. The Chess Master had turned killing into a demented version of living chess, designating Jesse as his unwilling opponent.

Jesse shuffled through the file until he found a copy of the last note, and a candid, grainy snapshot of a pretty young woman. Catherine Skogdell. Pretty and so full of life, so unsuspecting, presumably in the hours before she'd fallen prey to a monster. Pulling the photocopy closer, he leaned back in his chair and studied the enigmatic clue. How many times had he stared at it? Twenty times? A hundred?

The Rook is isolated. Don't blunder again. It's your move...
                        The Chess Master

"It's your move," Jesse whispered.

The notes from the Chess Master always ended with that phrase. *"It's your move..."*

Did the warped bastard truly believe he was playing a game? With living, breathing human beings as pieces on some fantasy chessboard?

Jerking out the copies of the other two notes he'd received from the Chess Master, Jesse scanned the words of first one, and then the other.

Is your battery enough? Is this Knight to be a desperado? It's your move...

The Chess Master

The end game draws near. Protect your Bishop. Your Queen is in peril. It's your move...

The Chess Master

What was it supposed to mean? He leaned back and ran both hands through his hair.

"Maybe the chess pieces branded on the victims aren't just his signature. Maybe they're literal," he theorized aloud, his gaze narrowed on the notes in his hands. "Not just part of his torture, but actual symbols of the women themselves. They were pieces in his game, the pieces themselves, and the brand indicates exactly *which* piece. It's like a...a label. A literal label."

"You really buying into what they were saying, about this being a game?" Demarco rubbed his fingers across the creases in his brow as he nodded toward where the FBI clustered around a conference table conversing in hushed tones.

Jesse watched as Mazetti skirted that table like it was surrounded by an invisible force field, his attitude reflecting that of nearly every other local uniform and detective here.

The Feds weren't going out of their way to be sociable. No matter what company line they'd spouted about working together to bring this killer down, lines had clearly been drawn. And no matter what SSA Anderson or any of the other Feds claimed, they were taking the Chess Master's continued reign of terror personally.

The hell of it was, that's exactly how Jesse was taking it too. Like all these deaths were riding on his shoulders now.

Bastard.

Jesse turned his gaze back to his partner. "Sick as it is, I think they're right."

A wave of utter exhaustion washed over Jesse from just saying the words out loud. He could probably pass for a zombie in one of those horror TV shows right about now. Oh, yeah. Exhaustion was taking over all right, exhaustion and the true horror of the situation, and the coffee wasn't making a dent anymore. This went beyond his experience, beyond anything he'd ever seen on the streets, and he'd seen a lot.

"The women here in Minneapolis, they were pieces on the board. Just like in all the other cities. Pawn, Knight and Bishop, Rook. But not the Queen. Not *the* Queen. He said the end game was near. That the Queen was still in peril. But how the hell are we supposed to save her if he hasn't sent his damned clue yet?" Jesse leaned back in his chair, squeezed his eyes closed, and pressed his fingertips against his eyelids, rubbing hard until points of light swirled.

"You suppose he hasn't sent it because we ran the last two photos on the news? Maybe he thinks we cheated or something."

"It didn't matter anyway, did it?" Jesse pinned his partner with a hard stare. "Nobody came forward, at least not until it was too late, and he still got to them."

Doing his best to squelch the boiling anger seething in his veins, Jesse dropped his fists to his lap, tilted his head back, and closed his eyes. All around him phones rang, computer keys clacked, chairs scraped, voices droned. But the only sound that registered was the big clock on the far wall ticking away. Some innocent woman's time was running out, and they were no closer to stopping this monster.

Jesse heaved a weary sigh. As Demarco had pointed out, they had other cases to work. Other crimes to solve. And, technically, his involvement at this point was only peripheral, but he just couldn't shake this sense of impending doom. What it was, or why he was feeling it, he couldn't say.

The fate of an innocent, unknown woman maybe?

Hell, yeah. The Chess Master had made this personal.

His skin was too tight, and antsy energy hummed in his veins. Another sign he was headed for another energy crash. But instead of being able to take a much-needed nap, he was stuck at work, chasing killers. Jesse shot to his feet. "I'm hungry. Let's get the hell out of here."

DeMarco arched a black eyebrow and shrugged. "I could use a bite. Coffee and donuts?" He grinned at his own sad cop joke that wasn't all that funny. When Jesse failed to laugh, Demarco cleared his throat and tugged his jacket on. "Wanna try that barbeque shack over on Grand?"

"How about Vinnie's?" Jesse asked. The Italian

27

restaurant most of the precinct frequented was small and dated, but the pizza couldn't be beat, and the calzones were to die for.

"Sure." DeMarco adjusted his shoulder holster. "Afterward, we can pay a surprise visit to Dee-Wayne and Ice Dog; see if they've come up with any more info on the Parkway robbery or the shooting over at Ridgewood. That shit's got gangbanger written all over it."

"Shotgun," Jesse called, smiling to himself at DeMarco's answering groan.

"Aw, man, come on, I drove yesterday."

"Hey! What can I say? You snooze, you lose."

Jesse half turned as they reached the precinct door, ready to do some serious ribbing about Demarco's late-night activities, until he caught sight of something that made his blood run cold. Harvey, the officer assigned to the front desk, hurried toward them, a harried expression on his face and a small manila envelope clutched in one hand.

"Detective Reid, hold up. Delivery service just dropped this on my desk. Guy apologized, said there was a mix up of some kind in their office. It was supposed to have been delivered yesterday." The older man held up the envelope and grimaced as the phone began ringing. "Been a busy one. You'd think it was a full moon or something." The officer hurried back behind the counter and lifted the receiver to his ear.

The sight of that all too familiar envelope dropped Jesse's stomach straight to his shoes.

Shit. Not already.

No, he corrected himself just as quickly. The message had been delivered late. Somehow, he didn't think the Chess Master would take that into consideration.

We don't even have a fighting chance to save this woman now.

Knowing the Chess Master's prints would be all over this thing, following protocol to preserve evidence, Jesse held the envelope by the corner between his fingertips and carried it back to his desk. Dropping the envelope on top of the clean piece of paper DeMarco helpfully supplied, Jesse snapped gloves on and opened it. He should be turning this over to the FBI, but something was riding him. Frustration? Curiosity? Resentment? He'd been drawn into this sick game by a monster and then shuffled to the side by Anderson and the rest of her crew.

He didn't particularly care right now. Right now, he was only worried about what was inside this envelope and the imaginary clock that seemed to have kicked into a faster countdown.

DeMarco leaned over his shoulder, conveniently blocking any view the Feds might have, and swore aloud as a white piece of paper slipped from the envelope. One piece of paper, and no photo. A single, precise, damning word was neatly scripted on that startlingly bright and otherwise blank sheet.

Checkmate.

DeMarco raked a hand through his hair. "*'Checkmate?'* What the hell's that supposed to mean?"

Jesse stared at the note and frowned, his sense of dread growing with every passing second until he was smothering beneath the weight.

No photo.

What. The. Hell?

"*Checkmate*," he repeated aloud as a churning ball of nausea formed in his gut. The answer screamed at him.

Either the Queen had fallen…

Or she was about to.

****

Jesse climbed from his unmarked cruiser and staggered across the darkened yard. Stifling a wide yawn, he fumbled with his keys, so tired he was seeing double. He'd probably flunk a sobriety test at this point and he hadn't touched a single damned drop of alcohol. Christ, he was dead on his feet.

And the shitty thing was, he knew he wasn't going to sleep. Not since receiving that last note from the Chess Master.

Checkmate.

He'd be sleeping with one eye open now, waiting for the phone to ring, waiting for the call to tell him they'd found another body.

Sick bastard.

He stumbled a bit as the toe of his shoe caught on an uneven crack in the sidewalk. A square of golden light illuminated a patch of grass near the sidewalk. Jesse glanced up to the second floor. The light in their bedroom was still on. Molly liked to wait up for him sometimes. Not often, considering she had to get up early to get to her classroom before the kids did, but once in a while. Whenever she knew he had a particularly taxing case bugging him, or if she'd had a tough day with one of her students.

His pulse picked up despite his fatigue. Sometimes his girlfriend would wait up for him wearing one of those skimpy little nightie things he liked so well. Then whatever had gone down during the day didn't seem to matter so much. At least, not while he was in her arms.

Either way, the mere thought of showering off the day, stripping down and climbing into a warm bed—into his Molly's welcoming arms—was enough to put a little more pep in his step.

Turning the lock on the front door, he let himself in. One glance over at the keypad on the alarm system told him what he already knew, and he gritted his teeth.

Damn it, Molly.

She was forever forgetting to set the alarm. It was like she thought she was still living on that small farm in rural Iowa where she'd grown up. For a woman teaching inner city kids in a youth offender's program, you'd think she'd have lost something of her trusting nature. But she hadn't, giving everyone she met the benefit of the doubt.

Then again, maybe that was why Jesse loved her so much. She was just so stubborn about seeing only the good in people, himself included.

After easing the front door closed behind him with the flat of his hand, he relocked it and set the security alarm. In an absent motion, he dropped his jacket over the back of the sofa. The distant tick tock of the Grandfather clock in the living room was the only sound in the darkened first floor.

He toed off his shoes on the mat near the door, stripped his tie off, and dropped it on top of his jacket. Jesse shuffled through the dining room, glancing at the bag on the table on his way by. The enormous canvas tote overflowed with folders, binders, books, and papers.

Semester tests are this week, aren't they? Forgot all about that. Must have stayed up late grading test scores.

Jesse stopped in the kitchen and snagged a bottle of water from the fridge. He leaned against the counter, unscrewed the lid, and took a long, long draw. His entire body ached, and the softness of his bed, the softness of Molly's body, called to him. His gaze wandered to the coffee machine. Yep. Coffee mug in place, just the tip of the spoon barely visible over the rim of the travel mug. Toaster pulled forward, ready for her bagel.

She was a creature of habit, his Molly.

He grinned, groggy around the edges. Another ten bucks said she was upstairs right now, reclined on the bed with a romance novel in her lap and those sexy, horn-rimmed reading glasses perched on the tip of her nose.

After emptying the bottle, he tossed it into the recycling bin under the sink, and then made his way upstairs. At the top of the landing, he paused out of habit, reaching just inside the doorway of the bathroom to shut off the light. The familiar scent of body wash and shampoo lingered in the air, and his tired body began to stir to life. The bedroom door was slightly ajar, soft yellow light spilled out onto the blue hall carpet.

That would have been an easy ten bucks.

Smiling now, anticipation growing, he slowly began unbuttoning his shirt. Maybe he could talk her into taking another shower. With him.

"Baby, I'm home," he called softly, not wanting to startle her. He tugged his shirttails from the waistband of his pants, and reached out to push the door open.

And there, in the threshold of the bedroom, Jesse froze, his mouth going slack as his eyes widened in shock.

At first, he couldn't comprehend what he was seeing. His eyes were looking, but his brain refused to engage. Everything around the periphery of his vision dimmed. His throat closed, and something sharp and vicious squeezed his chest in an unforgiving vice.

His gaze found the fragile form staked to the wall like a butterfly spread out and pinned to felt. Jesse's legs gave way, and he dropped to his knees. His hands fell limp at his sides as he shook his head in denial.

He stared up, dimly registering the blood—oh, God, so much blood—and he locked on Molly, on the livid mark branded in the middle of her chest.

The brand of the Queen.

Chapter Three

Almost a year later…

Jesse pulled his motorcycle alongside the gas pumps, jerked the keys from the ignition, and jumped off. The minute his boots hit concrete, he stretched and let out a wide yawn. While he waited for the tank to fill, his gaze scanned the front of the gas station and its adjacent lot. A neon ATM sign flashed in one of the dingy windows.

The pump shut off, and he made his way inside. He ignored the clerk's apathetic stare as he walked down one of the short aisles to the big red arrow at the back of the store and the ATM beneath it. The machine spit out his cash request and a small stub of paper. Jesse scowled at the balance on the receipt in his hand. Oh, he had enough to go on for a while yet. But a cop's savings didn't hold up all that well after almost a year of sporadic employment.

Almost a year spent coming to grips with the fact that he'd ruined a once stellar reputation by obsessing over the sick, twisted bastard who'd gutted his girlfriend and gotten away with it.

He'd been chasing after the Chess Master, dogging the Feds every step of the way. Three killings in Davenport. Then a couple more in Dubuque. But the trail had gone cold after just one killing in Eau Claire,

Wisconsin. Same MO, but no follow up. Like the guy kept getting bored and moved on without letting the whole game play out. That last murder had been nearly a month ago.

For a while Jesse had burned up the highway, trying to get inside the bastard's head. But it had been no use. He couldn't figure out where to go, or how to get a step ahead. And he'd come to the realization that circling the Midwest aimlessly wasn't going to get the job done.

So, with nowhere else to go and no new leads, Jesse had done the only thing he could. He'd stopped in the first town he'd come to and rented a little, one-room shithole for dirt cheap while he waited for the Chess Master to surface again.

He couldn't go home. He had no home left. He'd put the house in Minneapolis up for sale and most everything he owned right along with it. Couldn't face the thought of living where Molly had lost her life because he hadn't been good enough at his job.

But even with SSA Anderson's most recent threat to throw his ass in jail for obstruction of a federal investigation still ringing in his ears, he'd kept right on hunting. He monitored police reports where he could, tuned in to national news segments, and ruthlessly pumped every last law enforcement contact he had for fresh sightings.

His stomach growled. Jesse picked up a bottle of pop, a candy bar and a pack of gum and stopped at the counter. He dropped one of the crisp twenty-dollar bills from the ATM beside the bottle of soda and let his gaze wander to an old hole-pocked bulletin board hanging beside the register while the attendant rang up his gas and lunch. Bright flyers and pamphlets covered the board, but one particularly bold notice caught his eye. Reaching over, he plucked the neon pink flyer free.

Help Wanted
Full-time Bouncer/Bartender needed.
Must be willing to work nights and weekends.
Experience preferred but willing to train.
Apply in person at the Irish Rose.
Ask for Charlie.

He held the flyer up for the clerk to see. "You know where this Irish Rose place is?"

"Hmm? Oh, yeah. Nine miles down the road in Badger Creek, south on Highway 27. Pub's on the far side of town, right on the outskirts. Real hoppin' place. Great food. Live bands on the weekends."

Nodding his thanks, he folded the flyer and shoved it into his pocket. Although he had zero experience at bartending, he could fill the role of bouncer easy enough. He needed an income, couldn't keep depleting his savings the way he was or he'd be lucky if he could even afford his crap apartment much longer, much less gas for his motorcycle.

Besides, he needed something to do. The sane part of his brain—what was left of it, at least—recognized that fact, even if his heart wasn't in it. And a job with whatever they had around here for local law enforcement probably wasn't in the cards for him. Not after the bridges he'd burned.

After collecting his change, he stuffed the gum in his pocket, picked up the candy bar, and twisted the lid off the pop on his way out the door. Looks like he was headed to the Irish Rose to find this Charlie guy and get himself a job.

Traffic was nonexistent as Jesse followed the highway signs to Badger Creek, population 857. He drove through the small town, a real blink-and-you'll-miss-it kind of place, before pulling into the pretty-much-empty parking lot.

He surveyed the building as he got off his motorcycle and sauntered across the fresh gravel. The wood siding was aged, but he'd be willing to bet that was from artistic design rather than neglect. Large whiskey barrels with flowers spilling from the tops flanked the double doors.

He fingered the folded flyer in his pocket, hoping this worked out. Getting a job this fast sure would make his life a damned sight easier.

At least, until he got word of the Chess Master again.

He was nearly to the pub door before he noticed the closed sign. Checking his watch, he cursed beneath his breath. Half an hour yet till opening. He thought about heading back into town, maybe stopping by that little diner he'd passed for a quick bite. But he was already here.

Oh, what the hell. Taking a chance, he tugged on the door handle.

To his surprise, the door swung open. He eased inside, absorbing details as he went. A corkboard just inside the door held an array of flyers advertising everything from a *Party in the Park* to raise funds for playground equipment to a number tear-away printout for Domestic Violence. Reaching up, he plucked down another neon help wanted poster advertising the Bouncer/Bartender position.

As he stepped inside the main taproom, he was

honestly impressed by what he saw. Everywhere he looked, wood was polished to a high sheen. The massive, embellished mirror behind the bar gleamed, and the glass in the dozen or so chandeliers overhead sparkled with a warm and welcoming golden glow.

Big, arched wooden knockouts on either side of that huge mirror held row upon staggered row of alcohol bottles. Authentic Irish bric-a-brac filled strategically placed shelves, nooks and crannies around the enormous taproom. Stained glass pictures, the ends of oak barrels, and framed vivid landscapes from what could only be the Emerald Isle covered the walls.

Upon entering, he'd expected to be overwhelmed by the scents of stale beer, old cigarette smoke, and grease. Instead, the pleasant scents of lemon polish and some kind of simmering stew caught him by surprise.

In the far corner, a band was noisily setting up beside a massive fieldstone fireplace. Two waitresses in khaki's and emerald green shirts were filling napkin holders, ketchup bottles and salt and pepper shakers. Behind the bar, an average sized Joe with flaming red hair was tinkering with a blender.

At the far end of the bar, another guy with dishwater-blond hair, a goatee, and dark rimmed glasses sat pouring over some kind of spreadsheets. He had management written all over him.

"Sorry," the Joe behind the bar called as Jesse approached, "We aren't open for another half hour."

"I'm looking for Charlie," he said, holding up the flyer, his gaze going to the guy at the end of the bar.

The man finally glanced up. A shrewd gaze skimmed Jesse from head to boot and back again. He rose and approached Jesse, a polite but reserved smile on his face as he held out his hand. "Hi, I'm Caleb Westmore, assistant manager."

Not Charlie. Jesse shook his hand. All right then. "Jesse Reid."

"Looking for a job, huh?" Westmore scrutinized Jesse, testing his grip in the way men do when sizing up the new guy.

"That's the idea."

Jesse squeezed right back, letting his cool gaze challenge the assistant manager. If he was going to be working here, best get the posturing out of the way, let management know he had no intention of being a pushover right out of the starting gates.

"Well then, welcome to the Irish Rose, Mr. Reid. Hey, Eli, you wanna go get an application for him to fill out? Let Charlie know there's somebody here about the bouncer job."

"Sure thing." The bartender disappeared through a door behind the bar. He returned a moment later and handed Jesse an application.

"If you'd like to have a seat, Charlie should be out in a few," Westmore offered. Apparently, Jesse had passed first round inspections. Nodding, he moved to a table to fill out the forms while Caleb returned to his work.

Jesse had just finished the paperwork and turned in his seat to watch the band as they adjusted mikes and speakers when the unmistakable click of a woman's heels approaching drew his attention. Turning, expecting to see another waitress, Jesse froze.

The half-smile slid off his face as adrenaline shot through his system. A jolt of unwanted lust arrowed straight to his groin.

For one long heartbeat she stood beside him, a friendly expression on her beautiful face as she extended her hand. He couldn't move. His mouth went dry.

And then he managed to pry himself from his seat, and took her fine boned hand in his. Damn, had he been gawking at her? Was his mouth hanging open, drool running down his chin?

"Good afternoon," she said, her grip firm, businesslike.

Her honey-smooth voice wrapped around his senses. Her scent—the faintest hint of flowers, something exotic and delicate—made his head swim. The zing that went through him at the feel of her fragile hand in his had him clamping down on the urge to draw her closer. He couldn't remember ever reacting to a woman like this.

Not even with Molly...

And that was a cold slap of reality right in the face. One he desperately needed. After the brutal murder of the woman he'd loved, he'd figured that part of his life was over. He hadn't experienced so much as a stirring of interest in another woman in all this time, assumed he'd buried those emotions when he'd buried Molly.

It looked as if he'd been wrong. And the realization did not please him. Not one bit.

Chapter Four

Charlie smiled as the man stood up. He had a presence that was larger than life, and a body that would draw the ladies like flies. That was her first impression. Her second was that he had sad eyes. Why she thought that, she couldn't say.

The moment his hand, strong and confident, closed over hers however, an unexplained fluttering swooped through her stomach. As if she had something to be nervous about.

Ridiculous. He was the one looking for a job, not her.

She couldn't explain it, but Charlie was suddenly a kid with stars in her eyes. What was *wrong* with her? She was all but moonstruck, tongue tied to be sure. Scrambling for some self control, she forced a brighter smile to her lips and reminded herself that she was a professional businesswoman and, as such, she was more than capable of behaving accordingly.

She still had to clear her throat before she could speak. "I'm Charlotte McKenna, but everyone just calls me Charlie."

As she stood there, shaking his hand, her confidence faltered, just for a moment. He hadn't uttered a sound yet, simply stared at her as if…

Well, she wasn't exactly sure. The intensity of his stare unsettled her. She could usually read people pretty well.

Him? He was a vault, locked up tight.

Finally, he broke the silence. "Charlie, huh?" Pure exasperation laced his voice as he held up one of her flyers. "This Charlie?"

She nodded, puzzled by her strange reaction to him. Confused by his tone. He huffed out a short grunt, a strange half-smile curling one corner of his mouth upward. Charlie could all but feel Caleb's gaze skewering them, as well as those of her waitresses and Eli. But the only gaze that seemed to matter was his. This stranger who continued to—albeit gently—hold her hand captive while glaring holes through her hide.

Self-conscious, Charlie tugged her hand from his and mustered her most businesslike tone. "If you'll follow me, we can interview in my office."

She took his application in hand and used it as a convenient excuse not to have to meet Caleb's piercing stare. Taking for granted that the heretofore nameless stranger would follow, she turned on her heel and measured her steps back around the bar, staring blindly at the papers in her hands. For one mortifying moment, she wondered how to handle the situation if he didn't do as she'd suggested. If he decided to waltz out instead.

That moment was blessedly short lived. The sound of heavy boots on hardwood trailed behind her. She could almost feel his eyes drilling holes in her back. It unnerved her.

He unnerved her, and she couldn't figure out why.

Aside from the fact that he was, quite possibly, the most attractive man she'd seen in…well, ever.

Charlie stepped inside the office and motioned for

him to take the seat in front of her desk. She closed the door behind him, firmly blocking out the prying eyes, appreciative glances, and intrusive ears the kitchen staff had aimed their way.

Charlie turned to find him standing in the middle of her small office, making it seem a whole lot smaller. She took a deep, steadying breath and eased around him as she offered him a tentative smile.

"Won't you have a seat?"

She simply stared up at him now, determined to be cool, determined not to let him fluster her again, patiently waiting for him to sit down as she'd asked, half hoping he wouldn't.

He dropped onto the seat she'd indicated earlier. Charlie folded nervous hands in her lap below her desk. Where, hopefully, he couldn't see them tremble.

He shifted his attention to the flowers and balloons on top of the filing cabinet in the corner, then to the cheerful card propped up on the corner of her desk. "Your birthday today?"

She smiled. "Yesterday."

"Happy belated."

"Thank you."

He was staring at her lips again, making her wonder what he was thinking. Slowly, he looked up, met her stare.

And there it was again, that heavy tension settling in the pit of her stomach, making it hard to breathe. Charlie tore her focus from his face and made a show of reading through his application. She cleared her throat, took a deep breath, and looked him straight in the eye.

Normal. Act normal.

"So you're looking for a job, Mr. Reid?"

"I am," he said, nodding. "And it's Jesse."

"And you've just moved to Sackville?" She asked, referring to the next town over. Nine miles wasn't bad for driving distance, except in the winter of course. And then, during or after the right storm, it could just as well be a million miles away. Still... "I'm assuming you have reliable transportation?"

He said nothing, simply nodded.

"Says here you lived in Eden Prairie before moving to Sackville." She flipped pages, and blinked in surprise. "You listed you were a homicide detective with the Minneapolis PD. But that was almost a year ago. Where were you between then and now? What have you been doing?"

"Here and there"—he shrugged—"this and that."

Short and sweet.

And not very helpful.

Charlie eased back in her chair and crossed her arms, determined to act natural despite the way he had her nerves humming. "There isn't much to draw somebody to this area. What brings you here?"

For a split second, his placid expression cracked, and she caught a glimpse of something dark in his eyes. But then he blinked, and it was gone.

"This is where I ended up," was all he settled on saying.

"Why not go back to law enforcement?"

He took a moment to respond, his face impassive. "That's not in the cards for me anymore."

She barely resisted the urge to grind her teeth. "Are you planning on sticking around?"

Again, he shrugged. "Depends."

"On what?"

"On whether or not I get a job." A little dimple flashed in his left cheek. There and gone again.

She pressed her lips together, struggling to remember standard questions that had once come easily to her. "Why did you leave your last place of employment?"

"I moved."

"You don't have any place of employment listed in the last three months." She flipped through his application. "Why is that?"

"I chose not to."

"Not to list it?"

"Not to work."

She raised a brow. Okay, she'd kind of walked into that one. She chewed on the inside of her lower lip as her supply of patience began to dwindle. There was a pattern developing here, one she usually showed to the door with a polite smile and a clear dismissal. Usually.

But this man was...*different*. She just couldn't put her thumb on why. She'd never been one to let her hormones influence her decisions, particularly her business decisions. Yet she found herself cutting him all kinds of slack she otherwise wouldn't.

"Any character references?"

"Not really."

"Do you have any previous experience bartending?"

"No."

A tiny frown tugged her eyebrows together. "Do you have family in the area?"

Just like that, his expressive eyes became distant, closed off. "No."

"No," she repeated, took a breath and waited. And

waited. "Jesse, I think we can safely say you're not much of a talker, can't we?" When that failed to elicit a response, she pressed on, determined. "Look, you have to help me out here. Perhaps you can tell me a bit more about your previous work experience? What makes you think you'd be a good fit for this position, and for the Irish Rose?"

He heaved a sigh, finally releasing her from the spell of his steady gaze. "I have extensive experience with security. And I've worked in a bar before, back when I was in college. I can pour a beer, that's not all that hard. And I know how to card someone," he added with a wry twist of his lips.

"We do more than '*pour beer*' here, Jesse." She moved her hands to the arms of her chair. She gave him a brief rundown of the pub's history and reputation, as well as what she was looking for in an employee.

When she wound down, he sent her a long, measured look. "This was a mistake," he said at last. "I'm really only looking for something temporary anyway. Not a big deal. I just needed something to get by for a little while. Thanks anyway."

As he stood up, the pit of her stomach dropped. Some inexplicable sense of panic caught her by surprise. What it was, and why she was feeling it, she couldn't quite say. Only that it was there, and that she always went with her gut. It hadn't led her wrong yet.

But good Lord above, where had her common sense gone?

"Wait," she blurted, rising too. "Okay? Just..." she heaved a sigh, "just wait. Please?"

He paused, his hand on the doorknob. Closing her eyes for a second, wondering what the hell she was thinking, she motioned for him to return to his seat.

"You have experience with security?" Should she be asking which side of the law his experience leaned toward given his comment about law enforcement not being in the cards for him any longer?

"Yeah," he eyed her, but sat back down. "Are you having trouble?"

"No more than any place that serves alcohol," she quickly assured him. "Maybe a few customers that can't hold their liquor and need to be shown to the door. *Politely.* A few coming in already looking for a fight. Nothing out of the ordinary." She toyed with her pen and weighed her decision. It was a stupid decision, and it made no sense, was completely out of character. But she was going to go with it nonetheless. "We're both in a position to help each other."

His gaze heated, swept over her, lingering on her lips. She was sure of it this time, as a woman is aware of a man's interest.

Choosing to ignore the way her heart jolted, determined to convince herself that she was seeing things that weren't there, she shifted in her seat.

"Our bouncer recently moved back to his hometown to be closer to family. Eli, our bartender, will be taking family leave soon. His wife is expecting their first baby. You need a job, and I need help. We're willing to train you. I understand you view this as only a temporary situation. I can accept that. All I ask is that you give me sufficient warning before you pack up and skip town."

He frowned at her. "What about character references?"

She stared him down now, determined. A

businesswoman shrewdly negotiating for something she wanted. Something that would be good for her business. She hoped.

"I'll be your character reference."

He considered her for a long, uncomfortable moment. His eyes narrowed and, for a moment, he seemed almost...angry. "You don't know me from Adam. You got some kind of do-gooder complex going on? Giving jobs to every stray that walks in off the street? 'Cause the only other option I can think of is you're hopelessly naïve."

"I am neither." She leaned back in her seat and forced her temper down. Meeting his unwarranted anger with cold reserve. "Let's just say, I usually have a good gut instinct for this kind of thing. And my gut tells me to take a chance here. Besides, I run a tight ship. If things start disappearing, I'll know before the end of your shift. I've known the local police since I was old enough to walk...every last one of them...and I have no qualms about pressing charges."

She quoted him pay and hours, told him she'd supply uniform shirts for him, all of which he agreed to.

She eyed him then, moistened her lower lip, and once again went with her gut. Sackville had fallen on hard times and had gone to seed. As such, the population had grown sketchy over the years. Very sketchy. Besides, having him on premises not only would assure her that her bouncer/bartender wouldn't be missing any shifts due to weather related issues, it would also give her the added advantage of knowing he wasn't into any extracurricular criminal activity. It would also add an extra layer of security for the bar, not that it really needed it. But one could never be too careful.

"There's one other thing, a perk of the job you could say. There's an apartment upstairs, fully furnished. Hasn't been used in a couple years, so it's a bit...ah, dusty." She'd lived there until she'd moved to her cabin just outside city limits. "It would be mutually beneficial to have my head of security living on premises, don't you think?"

"I told you, I'm not planning on sticking around all that long."

"I understand that. But there's no reason to pay for someplace else when you could be living upstairs rent free. Plus, I won't have to worry about you not making it to work because of bad roads," she added, ruthlessly turning the screws. "Besides, it's a good reason for me to get the place cleaned up again. I can always rent it out to somebody else after you're gone."

Why did she find those words so disappointing? *After you're gone.*

His expression told her he was wavering, and so she pressed, "Look, I'm offering you a job and a better place to stay. You want it or not?"

His gaze moved around the room, lingering on this and that, his expression thoughtful. Designed, she was certain, to make her squirm. He was doing a damned good job of it. And then he pinned her with a hard stare.

She suffered a sudden and driving urge to confess—she wasn't even certain what she should come clean about—but that look...that look made her *need* to confess to...something. Anything.

He must have been one hell of a detective.

And that sparked her curiosity.

Why did he leave the force?

He leaned back in his chair and crossed his arms. "When do I start?"

Chapter Five

Charlie glanced up from the pint she'd been building and grinned at the short, stocky man climbing onto the barstool.

"Well, hey there, Sean. Haven't seen you in a month of Sundays. Where've you been hiding yourself?" Sean had been a regular as far back as she could remember. She reached behind her for a bottle and a glass.

"Here and there, my girl. Here and there." Sean eased his jacket off his lean frame and draped it over the back of his seat. "Been making the rounds with the children out east, we have. Stayed a full week in Albany with the middle two. Spent part of a week in Plymouth with my oldest, and the rest of it with my youngest in Winchester."

"Has Eliza had her baby yet?"

His chest swelled as all proud grandfathers did when asked about his ever-expanding brood. "That she did. A bouncing baby girl. Pretty as her mama was when she was born. Nine pounds two ounces and dimples in both sets of cheeks. They named her Abigail."

"Congratulations, Sean." Charlie topped off the liquor with a shot of club soda and slid the glass in front of him with practiced ease. "That one's on the house."

"Lord love you, girl." He sighed in pleasure before

taking a long, appreciative sip. Then, leaning to the side, he elbowed John Carroll, the thin-as-a-broomstick man occupying the barstool to his right. "Got to appreciate a fine girl like our Charlie, now don't ya? She's got a glass in your hand nearly before your ass— er, forgive the language, Charlie—bottom hits the seat."

"Excused," she said, playing along.

Smiling to herself, she turned her attention back to the pint she was working on. It never ceased to amuse her how some of these gruff old men still treated her like a fragile daughter that might wilt away if spoken to with a crass tongue.

Charlie slid the pint onto a serving tray alongside four other mixed drinks and glanced around the packed room. Then she nodded to the nearby waitress who'd been stealing a much-needed breather. "Looks like we're in for a workout tonight. Not usually quite so busy this early."

"I sure ain't gonna complain." Georgia Ann patted the bulging pocket of her abbreviated apron before reaching for the tray, her toe tapping in time to the energetic music. "Tips are good."

With a cheeky grin, the leggy redhead balanced the serving tray and sauntered over to the table in the far corner with a graceful finesse Charlie couldn't help but admire. Though saunter might not be an apt term when it came to the way Georgia Ann moved, Charlie mused, all long legs and swinging hips. That walk belonged on a runway. And those sultry smiles were downright lethal. Charlie stole a peek at the group of frat boys Georgia Ann was currently mesmerizing, and she shook her head.

Poor saps don't even stand a chance.

"I'm back from break." Eli came up beside her, drawing her attention. He nodded to a patron who'd just taken a seat at the end of the bar.

"How's Kendra?" Charlie reached for a bar towel and then rolled the kinks from her shoulders as she wiped her hands dry.

"Tired and cranky." Eli frowned as he filled another tray with longnecks. "She hasn't been sleeping all that well lately. I read that's normal around this point in a pregnancy, but she just looks so worn out and miserable. I'm never getting her knocked up again."

Spoken like a frazzled first timer. He'd taken to checking up on his wife at every break, physically jumping whenever the pub phone rang, expecting *the call*. Charlie filled a shot glass to round out the next order that Paula, one of the other waitresses, had dropped in front of her. Despite the fact she wasn't that much older than Charlie and had a body to give even Georgia Ann a run for her money, Paula had somehow fallen into the role of Mama Bear to the rest of the staff. To know Paula was to love her.

"Sure you won't," Paula teased Eli as she slipped behind the bar to grab a sip from the glass of Dr. Pepper she habitually kept stashed out of sight. "Right up until she starts gettin' a hankerin' for another one. You know that girl's got you wrapped around her little finger."

Eli shook his head, but his grin gave him away.

Charlie studied his face a little closer. From the shadows under his eyes, it was a pretty safe guess that Eli hadn't been sleeping all that well either.

"You sure you don't want to take off early tonight?" Charlie brushed a loose curl behind her ear and shifted her weight from one aching foot to the other. "I'd be happy to cover for you."

"Naw, but thanks, I appreciate it." With a smile and a nod, he passed a Screwdriver to a customer, and then made change from the register. "When's the new guy start?"

Charlie shot a glance at her watch. "Fifteen minutes."

If he shows up.

Despite her wishes to the contrary, she'd been on pins and needles all evening wondering whether he'd report for work or just say screw it and skip town without so much as a goodbye. She'd gotten the feeling he'd been reluctant to ask for the job in the first place. But, then again, a couple of times there she could have sworn he'd been thinking about kissing her too, which was probably just wishful thinking on her part.

That man was a tough nut to crack.

"Good," Eli said, drawing her attention. "Once he's trained in I won't feel so bad leaving you for a while when the baby comes."

"I don't want you to worry about anything, Eli. We'll be just fine till you come back."

Movement near the door caught her eye. Turning, Charlie caught her breath.

Jesse filled the doorway, taking it all in with those crystal clear blue eyes. One of the emerald green button-down shirts she'd given him earlier showcased his broad shoulders. His damp hair curled around his collar. And he'd changed into a pair of faded blue jeans. Jeans that made her mouth go dry.

As if sensing the weight of her stare, he turned unerringly her way. Those entrancing eyes locked on her, and Jesse strode toward the bar with a kind of confidence that left a woman a bit breathless.

"Speak of the devil." She laid the bar towel aside. "Got this?"

"Sure thing, boss lady," Eli piped up, already focusing on the next order.

Hyper aware that Jesse was watching her every move, Charlie met him at the end of the bar with a calm smile on her face. A calm smile that belied the jittery butterflies swarming in the pit of her stomach.

Professional, Charlie. Be professional. You're his boss, for God's sake!

"I wasn't sure you'd be back." She had to shout to be heard over the wail of the band and the noisy crowd. The dinner patrons and the laid back, grab-a-drink-after-work crew had pretty much thinned out. The clientele was fast transitioning over to those looking to let their hair down and have a boot-stomping good time. He tilted his head down and leaned closer to hear her. The scent of a man fresh from a shower, soap and leather and a hint of cologne turned her muscles to rubber.

"I wasn't either," he admitted with one of those heart-stopping half grins of his. His breath caressed her cheek, sending goose bumps rippling over her skin.

Shooting him a lopsided smile, she motioned toward the door behind the bar. He nodded and followed. They moved into the kitchen—Doris's domain—where the noise level didn't threaten to shatter eardrums.

Doris, the pub's head cook glanced up from her labors at the sink. With bright orange hair and a roadmap of premature wrinkles attesting to a hard life, Doris could take nearly as much credit for Charlie's upbringing as Charlie's dad could.

In the beginning, after Charlie's mother had lit out, Doris had reluctantly stepped into the role of part-time babysitter. It hadn't taken Charlie long to wrap the ex-biker chick around her little finger. And before long, the tattooed, slightly abrasive Doris had slipped easily into the role of the beloved, doting, slightly-racy aunt every girl dreamed of having.

Glancing over, Charlie nodded at Doris where she stood scouring the last of her huge soup pots. Like the sun rising in the east and setting in the west, you could always count on Doris…and her penchant for saying exactly what was on her mind.

According to Doris, who'd made certain to weigh in with her take on the new guy the moment Jesse had left after his interview, Jesse looked to be just the kind of excitement Charlie's life had been lacking.

The speculative gleam in the older woman's pointed stare had Charlie double-timing the pace. Leading Jesse into her office, Charlie flipped the light on and closed the door behind them with a sigh of relief, blocking out the wiggling eyebrow and the merry twinkle in Doris's hazel eyes.

Charlie had no intention of letting Doris—much as she loved the older woman—or anyone else for that matter, dictate how she should lead her life. She had everything she wanted. Everything she'd worked so hard for. If and when she decided to take on the kind of excitement that Doris had implied she needed, well then, Charlie would be the one to decide the when. And the where.

And the *who*.

While Jesse might very well fit the *who* part,

Charlie had already made up her mind that *now* definitely wasn't the right *when*. And the pub certainly wasn't the *right where*. He might be able to make her entire body light up like a Christmas tree with nothing more than a single glance, but she had other things on her radar. The pub was her top priority.

A deep breath brought another delicious wave of his scent her way, and Charlie barely resisted the urge to fan herself. Nope. Not the right time, she reminded herself. She had a plan in place, for herself and for the pub. A plan that didn't factor in time for a boyfriend, and most certainly not for a temporary lover. And that's all Jesse would be, all she was sure he'd let himself be. Temporary. He came across as that kind of guy. He'd admitted as much. This was just a pit stop for him.

She'd do well to remember that.

Clearing her throat, and those oddly depressing thoughts from her mind, Charlie turned a sunny smile his way. "I know we went through company policies and your duties earlier, but do you have any questions before you start?"

Unable to stifle a wince, she leaned on the edge of her desk but resisted the urge to take her shoes off and rub her sore feet. She hadn't had time to run home to change this afternoon after her appointment with the banker. And if she took her heels off now, as swollen as her feet were, she'd need a crowbar to get them back on. She really needed to remember to leave a pair of tennis shoes in her office for occasions such as these.

"No, I think you covered everything." He reached up without warning and tucked that pesky loose strand of hair back behind her ear. Startled, Charlie froze, staring up at him like a deer in the headlights. His gaze was on her mouth again. She moistened her lower lip before she could stop herself.

He blinked, sucked in a sharp breath. Jesse shoved his hands into his back pockets and took a healthy step back. The gesture was not lost on her.

"I'll move my stuff upstairs in the morning if that's all right."

"Sure, no problem." Smoothing her hands down the hips of her pencil skirt, she straightened and put the safety of the desk between them before digging in the top drawer. "Umm…here you are." She stretched her arm out, dangling a lone silver key on a red keychain between her fingertips. "The stairs for the apartment are out back. This will unlock the door. If you don't mind waiting till after ten tomorrow morning, I've got someone scheduled to come in to clean."

"Thanks." He took the key from her.

Unsettled, unsure whether to be offended or relieved by his obvious effort not to touch her as he accepted the key, she crossed her arms and wished once again that she'd had the chance to run home and change clothes before the pub opened. The silk of her shirt and the form fitting skirt were a little too thin, a little too revealing beneath his steely-eyed scrutiny.

"Well then, if you don't have any questions, I'll turn you over to Eli. He'll be showing you the ropes behind the bar till you get the hang of things. I'm not too worried about security for right now. I'd rather you get the bartending part down first. I want to ease his mind that his backup will be ready and able before he leaves."

"And if I'm not ready?"

"Then I'll cover until you are."

He frowned. "You bartend?"

Why did he look so surprised? "And cook when needed. And wait tables, and bus those same tables. I've even been known to take out the trash on occasion." She smirked at him. "Both literally and figuratively. A responsible owner, a good manager should know firsthand every aspect of running his or her business. I don't ask my staff to do anything I can't or won't to do myself."

His gaze swept down over her, then drifted back up. Slowly. Appreciatively. Even so, there was a definite note of skepticism lacing his tone. "In those heels?"

"No, not in these heels." She walked around him and opened the door, flat out refusing to show how excruciating every step was. "The heels I usually wear are much prettier than these."

Then she left him to follow or linger at his own discretion.

****

Jesse flipped a bar towel over his shoulder and deposited a customer's money in the till. He wasn't used to standing on concrete floors for so long, and his feet were aching like a bad tooth already. He glanced at his watch. Two hours till closing time.

Even as that thought crossed his mind, he caught sight of Charlie chatting with a group of people in one of the booths, a tray of empties propped on her slim hip and a wide smile on her beautiful lips. The crowd had thinned some, and her laughter drifted across the short distance to him. He liked the sound of it a little too much.

He liked the way she looked in that skinny skirt

and those mile-high shoes a little too much too.

Those heels had to be next thing to killing her by now if his own feet were anything to judge by. He hadn't missed the wince of pain earlier in her office. Yet she hadn't spoken a word of complaint. And she hadn't gone to hide in her office, letting her employees do all the dirty work as he'd often seen others do. She'd told the truth when she'd said she didn't ask her workers to do anything she wouldn't do herself. He'd witnessed that for himself firsthand tonight.

The woman seemed to have an unending supply of energy, and he'd caught himself a time or two...or ten...watching her when he should have been paying better attention to Eli's instructions. She'd helped Paula clear tables, and she filled endless baskets of pretzels and peanuts for Eli. She'd also served drinks with Georgia Ann and worked shoulder-to-shoulder with both him and Eli to pour those same drinks whenever business spiked. Her supply of patience and her good humor with her staff and customers was boundless.

If it weren't for her naïve, too-trusting attitude, she'd be damned near perfect.

A naïve, too trusting nature, just like someone else he used to know.

With gritted teeth, he shut that train of thought down fast. Nope. Not going there. Not now.

A customer at the end of the bar caught his eye, holding up an empty bottle. Giving him a nod, Jesse reached into the cooler for a replacement. After serving the beer, he caught his gaze scanning the crowd once again for a glimpse of Charlie. But she was gone.

He told himself not to go after her. She was his boss and he had no business flirting with her. And yet, for the first time in almost a year, something new and intriguing burned inside him, something besides the bitter hatred and crippling need for revenge.

Fascination. Curiosity.

Raw desire.

And all of it centered around a beautiful woman he'd known less than twenty-four hours.

Feeling strangely a bit like that proverbial moth with its suicidal attraction to flames, Jesse picked up a tub full of empties.

"Hey, Eli. I'm gonna go dump these."

"Sure thing," Eli called over the roar of the blender. "Hey, tell Charlie to take a break while you're at it. I think she went out back to take the trash out."

Jesse's gut gave a weird little tug when he thought about the dark, fenced off area on the side of the pub opposite the parking lot. He'd noticed earlier that the light out there was crap, and had meant to say something to somebody. Those were the kind of spaces that, as a cop, he'd cautioned women and children about avoiding.

He gathered up a couple more empties as he went, dropped them in the tub, and carried the whole lot to the back. The kitchen was dim, only the recess security lights on now that Doris had gone home for the night, but he didn't see Charlie. The lights in her office were off too, and the freight door was closed. Frowning, he nearly turned to go back to the taproom, but a slight scratching sound and a muffled voice caught his attention.

Stepping farther into the kitchen, he rounded a counter and drew up short. There, kneeling on the floor, pert bottom thrust up into the air, was the woman he'd been looking for.

"Damn it, come on," she hissed softly as she stretched her arm beneath a deep chef's rack. As she stretched, her waist twisted this way and that, and Jesse couldn't help the slow, appreciative grin spreading across his lips. Damn, he liked that skirt.

"Lose something?"

"Oh!" Startled, she turned, thumping her forehead against the edge of the rack. "Umph…" Charlie sat back on her heels and, pressing her palm to the side of her forehead, she blinked up at him. "Oh, Jesse, I didn't hear you come in.

"You were a little preoccupied." He nodded toward the rack.

"I put some papers down before I took the trash out. The draft caught them, and they slipped between the rack and the cooler. Now I can't reach them." She turned back to glare at the thin crack.

"Here," he knelt beside her and bent to peer into the sliver of space. He could just make out the very tip of the corner of paper in the shadows. "I think I see them."

Edging down farther until he was lying on his side, he wedged his arm under the rack and stretched, sliding his fingertips along the floor. Focused on his target, he froze as she leaned above him to peek into the narrow opening. The silk of her blouse was close. So very, temptingly close.

"There it is," she exclaimed. "I see it. Reach to your left a little. No, your other left."

As far as distractions went, she rated right up there, somewhere between earthquakes and volcanoes. His eyes were level with her cleavage, and he couldn't drag his gaze away. The light scent she wore tantalized his senses, nearly putting him straight into a stupor. A tiny tug, he told himself. That's all it would take to topple her onto his chest. It would be only a simple matter from there to taste those sweet lips. A simple matter to wrap his arms around her and roll her beneath him.

Forcing a swallow, shaking those tormenting thoughts from his head, he slid his hand farther to the right and trapped the smooth paper beneath his fingertips.

After pulling his arm back from the dark space, he held up two printouts. "How many were there?"

"Just those." She smiled, leaned back, and took them from him. "Thank you so much."

Jesse sat up and propped his elbows on his bent knees, clasping his wrist in the opposite hand. "Welcome."

"I just couldn't reach that far back." Becoming color, filled her cheeks. Her gaze dipped to the pages in her hand. "They're very important."

"Hmm."

"Yes, well..." Clutching the paper, she braced her hand against the rack and struggled to rise, hindered by the confines of her slim skirt.

"Here, let me help." He hastily rose and offered her a hand.

"Thank you," she said, face flushed, as he pulled her to her feet. "Let me just put these on my desk so I don't lose them again." She hurried away before he could reply.

He stood there for a moment, grinning after her like a fool. Stirring himself, he reached for the tub of empties and began dumping them into the receptacle.

The ratta-tat-tat of her heels echoed behind him. Finished with the empties, he turned to face her.

Her smile went straight to his groin. "So what do you think so far?"

What did he think so far? What he *thought* was that she was far more appealing, and far more dangerous to his peace of mind, than he'd first realized. What he *thought* was he'd like nothing better right now than wrap his hands around her waist, drag her close and lay a kiss on those delectable lips that neither of them would be likely to forget anytime soon.

What he *thought* was he was in a hell of a lot farther over his head than he'd originally feared.

And what he suddenly realized was that he hadn't thought about Molly, not one stingy thought, since he'd first set eyes on this woman. That realization brought a befuddled scowl to his face.

Her smile slipped a bit, turned uncertain, and she prompted, "It's not that bad, is it?"

Making an effort to smooth his features, he forced a smile to his lips. "No, its fine," he said. "Things are going just fine."

"Good." She eased her hand along her lower back, kneading and massaging unobtrusively, and all the while she kept that easy smile in place. "Eli likes you. You should take that as a high compliment. He doesn't usually like working with anyone else behind his bar."

"He doesn't seem to mind having you there."

She laughed. His mouth went dry, lust warring with guilt. "That's because I'm his boss and he doesn't have a choice."

No, it was because she knew what the hell she was doing back there. And she looked damned fine doing it.

But he didn't voice that thought out loud.

Several tempting tendrils of that long golden hair had worked themselves loose again. He'd observed her all evening as she'd absently tucked them either behind her ear or shoved them in annoyance back into the loose bun at the back of her head. Every time had been like a punch in the gut. Now she pulled a couple bobby pins from her hair and absently released the bun. The muscles low in his gut clench tight as he watched that long, honeyed mass bounce and unfurl down her back. His fingers itched to touch.

"Why don't you take fifteen? You've earned it." It took a moment for her words and their meaning to register.

Seemingly without giving it a thought, she smoothed her hands along her scalp, scooping up all that glorious hair, twisting it with practiced ease back into a tight bun once more. She ruthlessly shoved the bobby pins back in place.

He didn't want a break. What he wanted was to take those bobby pins and toss them where she'd never find them again. He wanted to take all that hair down and wrap it around his fist while he trapped her in his arms and laid claim to those luscious lips.

He rocked back on his heels.

Where the hell had that *come from?*

Nope, he shook himself. Not going to happen. Even if the line in the sand hadn't already been drawn by his need to keep a certain amount of distance between him and anyone else, *everyone* else, technically she was his boss. While the idea held an added amount of excitement, she didn't strike him as a one-night-stand kind of girl. And honestly, could he really offer her anything more than a few weeks at best?

No, sleeping with her was a bad idea all the way around.

Forcing a swallow, he drew in a steadying breath. And then he frowned as he remembered Eli's last remark. He regarded her through narrowed eyes. "When did *you* last take a break?"

She shrugged, unconcerned. "I had a break when I ate supper."

"Inhaling a bowl of stew in ten minutes while you work on the next truck order isn't exactly a break."

"It's called multi-tasking. I'm quite good at it."

"A little too good, I bet," he grumbled beneath his breath.

"Excuse me?"

For reasons quite beyond his understanding, a sudden wave of protectiveness swept through him. Before he gave himself time to think about it, he stepped forward and closed his hand gently around her elbow. "You need a break too."

She opened her mouth, no doubt to argue, but he ignored her and pulled her along to the freight door. Darkness and blissful quiet descended as the door banged closed behind them.

As soon as the cool, autumn air hit him, Jesse sighed. He hadn't realized how hot it had been inside the pub until just now.

"You should put some chairs or a bench or something out here," he observed, glancing around the empty space.

"Everybody usually takes their break in the breakroom. Nobody comes out of this door except to unload truck or to take out the trash. In fact," she said with a light laugh, "you just locked us out."

He glanced to the door and groaned. Still, instead of suggesting they return to the noise, unwilling to analyze *why* he'd rather stand out here in the cold with her, he searched for something to say. That was when he noticed the small fenced in area some fifty feet away, and he remembered his earlier intentions. "You need to have some security lights installed out here. It's too dark. At a bar, anywhere really, that's not safe."

Tilting her head, she seemed to assess his comment for a moment. "You're right," she conceded. "The girls come out this door just as often as Eli and Caleb. I'll call somebody tomorrow."

"What about you?"

"Hmm?" She turned those big blue eyes on him. "What about me?"

"You just came out here a few minutes ago."

She frowned, clearly puzzled.

"Your safety is just as important as Georgia Ann's or Paula's or Doris's."

"Nobody's going to bother with me," she scoffed.

Molly had been the same way, and the reminder stung.

Jesse scowled, grinding his teeth. It wasn't his place to lecture her about her safety, no matter how badly he wanted to. Her shoulders stiffened, and she glanced away, letting her gaze drop to the toes of his boots. "You're catching on fast behind the bar. You've impressed Eli."

Pursing his lips, he stared at her for a long moment. Heaving a frustrated sigh, he let the subject drop. Really, he didn't have any right to lecture her, but a cop's instincts were hard to ignore. Yeah, lame as that excuse was, that was his story, and he was sticking to it. His concern was purely professional. Not personal. Not in the least. And yet…

Nope. Not going there.

"Thanks. Eli suggested I take the mixed drinks manual under the bar with me tonight to study."

She murmured approval.

He thrust his hands into his pockets, toying with his spare change to keep from reaching for her. "Is it always this busy?"

"Weekends usually are. Though tonight seems to be a new record. The live bands really draw the crowds. Week days are a lot slower."

"Do you know everyone here?" He'd noticed she'd greeted many customers by name.

"Quite a few of them. Of course, there are always new faces too." She shivered and wrapped her arms around herself.

"Have you lived here long?"

"Pretty much. I moved away for college. Got a few years experience at other establishments, but you know what they say. Home is where the heart is."

Unless your heart had been ripped out and staked to a wall.

Taking a deep breath, he pushed those dark thoughts back, refusing to let them suck him under. Somehow, surprisingly, the process was easier tonight, standing under the stars with this woman by his side.

"Eli mentioned your dad owns the place. I haven't seen him yet. The great Quinn McKenna," he said with a chuckle. "Eli talks about him quite a bit, as do your customers. They make him sound larger than life."

"Larger than life?" That earned him another of

those astonishingly sexy smiles. "Yes, I guess he probably is. You won't see him for a while, though. He's taking a much deserved vacation with some of his buddies. If he knows what's good for him, he'll be gone for several weeks."

"And he just left you in charge?"

Her eyes narrowed at that. It didn't take a genius to figure out he'd unintentionally pushed a button.

"I'm in charge even when he *is* here. I've worked here, in one capacity or another for as long as I can remember. After graduation, I went away to college as I mentioned earlier, spent a few years working in and then managing a couple bars out east. Got some experience under my belt, made some valuable connections. I learned the hard way what it takes to not only make a business a success, but how to put that business on the map, a real go-out-of-your-way attraction.

"I assumed operational control of the pub from my father two years ago. I'm buying the place from him now. Dad says he's easing me into ownership, but in reality, he's easing himself into retirement." She chuckled then, relaxing a bit when, he could only assume, he must have looked suitably impressed. "I think he's afraid he's going to run out of things to do and get bored."

Regardless of his careful expression, he couldn't help but be a little surprised. She was so young for all the responsibilities she shouldered on a daily basis. He was also surprised to realize he was more than a little disapproving of a footloose father that could dump so much on her slim shoulders and then run off without regard for her welfare. From what he'd seen tonight,

Charlie was working herself into an early grave.

Then, unbidden, the protective way Doris had treated Charlie when she'd made introductions earlier came to mind. "Has your dad always let other people take care of things for him?"

A frown wrinkled her brow again, a darker one than before, and a defensive light crept into her eyes. Her tone chilled enough to rival the air surrounding them. "My dad has never pawned his responsibilities off on others."

"Look, I meant no disrespect." He held his hands up, palms out, between them. "Running a place like this, one as obviously busy as this one is, just looks like a lot of work for one person. It just seems like you have an awful lot on your plate. I would think he would realize that and not be so quick to dump it in your lap and run off."

Her eyes narrowed even more, and her lips thinned. "For the record, he didn't 'run off.' Believe me, I know the difference." She crossed her arms, hugging tight. "And as far as dumping the pub on me, I worked for years to convince him he could trust me not to run this place into the ground. He's stood beside me, supporting me every step of the way."

"Okay! Okay. Look, I'm sorry for jumping to conclusions." The heat with which she defended her father left no room to question the depth of their relationship and her loyalty. It also left him to wonder who, exactly, had "run off" on her. "I'm sorry," he said again as she continued to glare at him. "I put my foot in my mouth. I do that once in a while. I'm sorry, all right?"

Making a visible effort to calm down, she nodded.

"So you've lived here all your life? I would think that has to have its drawbacks too?"

"It can at times." She conceded, turning to stare off into the distance. The alley was heavy with shadows and darkness. They seem to fit her mood now, and he couldn't help feeling he was to blame for that. "Winter's going to come early this year." She rubbed her hands up and down her arms.

What a fool he was. He hadn't even given the temperature outside a second thought. She was probably freezing in that whisper thin shirt, and he hadn't even thought to offer her a moment to grab a jacket. But he also wasn't ready to go back inside yet. Wasn't ready to relinquish her to the demands of all those other people in there.

"Come here, you must be freezing." Without giving her time to object, without giving himself a chance to fully consider his actions, he pulled her into a loose embrace. She stiffened at first, but she didn't fight him. In a heartbeat, he wanted to kick himself. How stupid could he be? Not only was he torturing himself, but she'd probably think him some kind of opportunistic perv.

Just when he thought to release her, she gave a grateful sigh and burrowed into his chest, fisting her hands in his shirt between them. She tucked her face against the side of his neck and shivered.

Her skin was cold beneath the silk. He splayed his hands on her back, rubbing for a moment before slipping his arms all the way around her, closing them tight. She fit against him like she'd been born to be there.

For a moment, he could almost pretend she

belonged to him. Jesse closed his eyes, savoring the feel of Charlie pressing against him. Guilt crept in around the edges of the pleasure, but he refused to give in to it. This was the first time in almost a year, the first time since Molly had been murdered that he'd truly felt alive.

He just needed a few more minutes of this. A few more minutes that would have to last him a lifetime.

And there they stood, wrapped up in shared warmth as not a word passed between them. He wasn't sure why she allowed the embrace, wasn't sure why she didn't push him away and insist on going back inside. Just as he wasn't sure why he preferred to stand out in the cold, with her in his arms, rather than returning to the warmth inside the pub.

Then again, perhaps that was exactly the answer. She was in his arms. Out here she'd allowed it. Once they were back inside, he had no doubt she'd put that employer/employee distance between them once more.

And so he would stand here and be content in the cold.

But all too soon, contentment faded in the face of growing need, and the pleasure of the moment, the freedom of feeling alive again squeezed out the guilt. The scent of her teased him, as did the feel of her smooth hair against his cheek. Her body was warming beneath his hands, supple in his arms. Enchanting against his body. The curve and the delicate skin of her neck called to his lips. The heat between their chests brought an answering heat much lower, and he grew hard—uncontrollably, demandingly hard—against the softness of her stomach.

But what floored him, what stunned him immobile

and nearly senseless was that she wasn't moving away, wasn't putting distance between them, between her and his unmistakable erection, or what that erection meant.

Instead, she tipped her head back and looked up at him with those beguiling, deep blue eyes. His gaze dipped to her mouth, to those lush, kissable lips.

And all good sense was lost.

Chapter Six

Charlie's head swam. Her blood surged and crashed, an ocean in her ears. A giant weight pressed down upon her chest, and yet she was floating, the only thing keeping her from drifting to the heavens was Jesse. Drunk on the desire in his eyes, she let the warmth of his body and the pure masculine scent of him surround her, muffle all else. The pub, her responsibilities, the people on the other side of that door all faded into nothing. She had no business being in his arms like this. But right now it was just her and Jesse and the tension between them. Nothing else mattered.

"Charlie." Her name slipped from him on a tormented groan.

His head dipped, closing the distance so slowly she had plenty of time to deny him, plenty of time to evade what was coming and slip from his arms. If she wanted to.

But she didn't.

She didn't want to stop this, whatever was happening between them despite her earlier resolve. Just as she hadn't been able to resist allowing him to draw her into his embrace. She wanted this kiss. Wanted it as she'd wanted little else.

He hesitated a moment longer, his lips a hairsbreadth from hers, the puff of his breath a soft caress upon her lips. And then he brushed his mouth over hers, the soft whisper of a butterfly's wings. Twice more he feathered his lips over hers. Twice more he tormented her with the unfulfilled promise of bliss.

She couldn't take anymore. She pushed up on her tiptoes, pressed her lips to his in silent demand, and slipped her arms up around his neck. Charlie tunneled greedy fingers through his hair. Her body leaned against his, leaned into his, chest to knee.

A flood of desire broke free. His groan was muffled against her lips, but it went through her like a shockwave. His strong arms, already wrapped tight, crushed her to him. His erection, hot as a brand, hard as granite, surged against her stomach, igniting a blaze in her veins.

He tilted his head, slanting his mouth over hers. His tongue rode the seam of her lips, demanding entrance. And she granted it. Happily.

He claimed her mouth, laid siege to it, his tongue dipped and danced and dueled with hers, rolled against hers. Charlie lost touch with reality. He mastered the kiss, sweeping her deep under a tidal wave of need. His hands were by no means still. He caressed and teased, kneaded and massaged, staking claim to her body as his lips branded her soul.

She'd been kissed before, of course. Sweet kisses. Stolen kisses. Even passionate kisses, or so she'd thought at the time. But this was a new experience for her.

This wasn't just a kiss. This was...*ravishment*.

He somehow managed to wrap his body around hers, caging her in an unbreakable hold. But she didn't feel trapped, or the least bit threatened. In that moment, she was wanted, desired above all else. It was exhilarating. He moved his mouth over hers with such raw, unrestrained hunger. Almost as though he thought if he didn't hold on to her with everything he had, didn't kiss her with every ounce of his need, he'd die.

As if kissing her were the only reason he drew his next breath.

But then, without warning, Jesse ripped his mouth from hers. His chest heaved against her, his breath coming in fast ragged pants. He closed his eyes and pressed his forehead to hers, the tip of his nose brushing hers. But he still held her tight, thighs to thighs, hips to hips, chest to chest. Shocked, she peered up at him. His forehead puckered against hers. Was he grappling for control, just as she was?

Or was he already regretting kissing her?

His eyes popped open, and she caught her breath. His crystalline, aquamarine stare glittered dangerously.

"Charlie," he growled low in his throat, both frightening and thrilling her. His tongue snaked out, swept across his lower lip as if desperately seeking her flavor. "Tell me to let you go," he whispered. A desperate man at the end of his rope.

She'd never experienced this before, this shivery current of awareness and need arcing between them. She was nearly incoherent, dazzled speechless.

"My God, Charlie, say *something*," he growled, part hoarse plea, part harsh demand.

She stared up at him, wide-eyed. Stunned. She was balanced on the edge of a cliff, dangling over a dangerous precipice with no safety net and no idea what awaited her should she fall. Her heart in her throat, she blinked up at him and did what she'd never before done in her life. She threw caution and all good sense to the wind and leaped without looking.

"Don't stop."

He sucked in a sharp breath. His eyes flared, and he searched her face for a split second. A low hungry growl escaped him, and he seized her lips once more, dragging her under wave after wave of sensual hunger.

Steel suddenly pressed against her back, unyielding and so cold it burned her skin right through her clothing. But everywhere else an inferno raged, writhing, coiling even more tightly around her than before, consuming her. His greedy hands were everywhere. Her hips, her face, her breasts, her hair. Lifting, caressing, molding, kneading.

His breath was ragged when he tore his mouth from hers. But he didn't stop this time. Instead, he moved to her jaw, her earlobe, her neck, and she gasped for air. He grazed his teeth along her skin, leaving behind only the tiniest of stings, stings immediately soothed by the arousing lick of his hot tongue. He nipped and nibbled her earlobe with deft lips. He delved into the hollow of her throat.

"So sweet," he murmured against her skin.

Jesse tangled one hand in her hair while the other fumbled with the top button of her shirt as his lips claimed hers once more. Helpless, she clung to him. She tugged at his hair, and whimpered against his lips, desperate for him to hurry. She was so hot; she wanted the shirt off. Wanted the crisp night air to cool her before she completely incinerated. She needed, more than anything, skin on skin contact until they both erupted.

Her own heartbeat pounded in her ears. Abruptly, Jesse stilled in her arms.

No, someone was pounding on the door behind her.

A familiar voice, muffled by thick steel, joined the pounding. "Charlie? You out there?" Eli cursed. The doorknob by her hip rattled, and the door bumped against her back. "Is something wedged against the door?"

Dragging in one shaking breath after another, Charlie fought to clear her head. "Just a sec, Eli."

Hating the way her voice shook, hating even more the cold emptiness that suddenly chilled her to the bone as Jesse drew back and released her, she straightened and struggled to smooth her clothing back into place. Her gaze lingered on Jesse, on his lips and his passion-drugged stare.

He was breathing hard, his hands fisted at his sides. Against her will, her gaze dropped. The huge bulge in the front of his jeans was unmistakable. Her breath snagged in the back of her throat, and she caught her lower lip between her teeth.

Oh, God, had that pitiful little moan come from her?

Jesse's eyes flared, his chin dipped, and he took a determined step forward. He slowly reached for her, and there was no misunderstanding the look in his eyes. He had every intention of picking up right where they'd left off.

"Is Jesse out there with you?" Eli called from the other side of the door. Jesse jolted back, letting his hands fall to his sides once more. A strange disappointment swept through Charlie.

It took two tries to get her voice to work. She couldn't drag her gaze from his. "Yeah. Yeah, he's here. We're coming right in."

Embarrassment warmed her cheeks. Her legs were like rubber. She glanced down as a particularly biting gust of wind swept against her bare chest, only just realizing her top three buttons were undone, revealing the ivory lace beneath. Too numb, perhaps still too aroused to be completely mortified, she set about redoing the buttons on her shirt. Her fingers were shaking too badly to be effective.

Long, competent hands brushed hers aside. She watched, utterly absorbed, as he pushed the recalcitrant buttons back through their tiny slots. And then he lifted those hands slowly to brush her hair back before gently cupping her face. A small part of her actually wanted to giggle when his hand trembled. Thank God she hadn't been the only one affected.

He held her immobile. With his hands. And with his unwavering stare. And then he lowered his mouth to hers once more, placing a lingering, gentle kiss upon her lips. One so at odds with the wild, unrestrained passion of just moments ago, that she was left dazed and confused once again. Releasing her, he stepped back.

She gaped up at him, unable to move. Unable to form a coherent thought.

"We should go in," he prompted, his expression bleak.

"Yes." She blinked. Cleared her throat. "Yes," she repeated more firmly.

Turning, she fumbled with the knob, only remembering at the last moment that it was locked from the inside. "Eli, we're locked out."

The door opened, and Eli stepped out of their way. A subdued Jesse followed her back inside.

She could barely meet Eli's puzzled look. And then, Eli's stare dipped to her mouth, moved to the side of her neck where the skin was still a bit tender from the stubble on Jesse's jaw, before skating sideways to scrutinize Jesse's grim expression. Slowly, Eli turned back to Charlie, and his eyes widened with one of those ah-ha looks.

Lifting her chin, determined to brazen it out, she arched an eyebrow and stared back in defiance. "Can I help you with something, Eli?"

He blinked at her, amusement twinkling in his eyes. "No. No, I, ah, I'll just head back up front. I was, ah, just making sure Jesse hadn't decided bartending was too much work and skipped town already."

"I'm still here." Jesse's deep voice came from behind her. Too close behind her.

Eli's unintentional reminder of Jesse's temporary position made her stomach clutch. A fresh wave of embarrassment heated her cheeks. Charlie was a little surprised her head hadn't exploded from all the blood that seemed to be rushing there.

"I'm sorry. I should have told you I was sending him on break. That was my fault."

"No big deal." Eli began backing toward the door to the front of the pub, his hands splayed before him. "Like I said, I'll just head back out. No rush. It's starting to slow down anyway. Take your time. Take all the time you need."

With a sly wink, Eli spun on his heel and beat a hasty exit, leaving her alone once more with the man who'd just upended her world.

She'd been propositioned before. A couple times, in fact, though never here at this particular pub. She knew better than to get involved with a coworker, and most certainly *never* with an employee. Let alone one she'd only known such a short time.

Those incidents had all happened when she'd been away at college and after college while she'd been gaining experience managing other bars in other towns. The few times someone had expressed an interest, she'd always handled the situations with a cool head, polite but unwaveringly firm, making it unmistakably clear that an intimate relationship—be it long term or a one-night stand—was something she could not allow. A non-negotiable line she'd never, *ever* allowed herself to cross.

Until now.

This was so not like her. Not like her at all.

What was I thinking?

Screwing up her courage, she turned to face Jesse, but the smoldering heat in his eyes, the grim set of his mouth, and the rigid way he was holding his body flustered her. She couldn't find the words, couldn't form the firm set down she desperately needed right now to put things back on an even keel.

After all, what was she supposed to say here? That what just happened between them outside in the dark shouldn't have happened? That he shouldn't have kissed her? That she most certainly should not have kissed him back? That it was inappropriate? Crossed some moral line? That it could never happen again?

How could she say those things when her blood was still thrumming through her veins? How could she say it when her knees were still weak and her hands were still shaking?

How could she say those things when all she could

think about was doing it again?

"I better get back out there," he murmured after a long, tense moment of silence. His gaze flickered to her mouth, and he let out a long ragged sigh. Jesse eased around her and walked away without a backward glance, not giving her the chance to speak at all.

Snapping her mouth closed, Charlie stared after him. The man was impossible to read. A moment ago he'd all but taken her up against the door. And now he walked away without discussing what had just happened between them…without so much as a second glance. As if what he'd just done—what *they'd* just done together, she reminded herself—was nothing out of the ordinary, a perfectly natural occurrence.

Absolutely *nothing* about that kiss had been ordinary for her.

Shaking her head, the taste of him still fresh upon her lips, she went to her office, closed the door, and dropped heavily onto the chair behind her desk. And there, trying to sort through her unruly emotions, she did something she'd never done before—yet another thing in a long line of firsts for her all since she'd met Jesse Reid.

She hid until last call.

Chapter Seven

Jesse put the last shot glass on the shelf alongside the others and reached for another. Three days had passed. Three days of lust and confusion. Three days of doubt and desire, weighted glances, and avoidance. The memory of Charlie's yielding body pressed against his, her mouth soft and greedy beneath his, twisted his insides into tense, hopeful knots.

He waited for some suffocating mix of emotions—disgust with his own lack of self control maybe, or guilt over betraying Molly—to surface. But those crippling emotions didn't come, didn't hit him like a ton of bricks as he'd expected they would.

That more than anything left him uneasy.

He shouldn't even be worrying about it. He had enough on his plate to deal with as it was. Just getting through the basics of day to day was hard enough. Knowing that the Chess Master was still out there somewhere, free to kill again, drove him crazy if he thought about it for too long. No, he hadn't given up the hunt for that sick bastard. The moment he caught wind of another victim, Jesse would be gone. Hot on the trail.

Jesse had vowed to bring the killer down if it was the last thing he ever did. He had every intention of keeping that vow. Nothing was going to get in his way.

Laughter and soft voices broke the almost eerie stillness of the closed pub. Jesse slowly turned to face the room in time to see Georgia Ann and Paula depart for the night. He watched Charlie lock the door behind them.

They were alone now.

All. Alone.

Something she'd been vigilant to avoid ever since they'd kissed. He knew it. Hell, he'd been trying to avoid her too. She was a complication he hadn't expected or planned on. He was still struggling to figure out what he wanted to do with her.

Well now, that wasn't entirely true.

He knew perfectly well what he *wanted* to do with her—in infinitesimal, erotic detail.

What he didn't know was what he *should* do with her.

Tucking his hands in his front pockets, he watched Charlie move across the room, her gaze flitting over tables and upturned chairs, over the freshly mopped hardwood floor before coming to rest on him. He watched the emotion play over her face and knew by the color staining her cheeks and the shy way she had trouble making eye contact that she was thinking about their kiss too. The same way he'd been thinking about it.

Hell, he hadn't been able to *stop* thinking about it for the last three days.

Though he'd found it annoying...and uncharacteristically comforting, he'd taken Eli's brief but brotherly warning in stride. In short, don't mess with Charlie if his intentions weren't aboveboard. He'd seen the same protective attitude from Charlie's cook and her waitresses, as well as a few of her regulars ever since the night of the kiss.

He'd also gotten the impression from Charlie's rather large circle of friends that the times she'd allowed herself to become romantically involved were few and far in between. Hell, it seemed the very idea of Charlie having a wild fling was unheard of.

So, to say her friends were protective of her was rather an understatement. That's why it was especially unsettling when he'd also gotten the *very* strong vibe that those same friends were now breathing a collective its-about-damned-time sigh of relief.

He was no fool. Ten to one said within five minutes of Eli backing his way out of the kitchen that night, with that screwy-assed grin, every waitress and patron in the joint knew where Charlie and Jesse had been, and exactly what they'd been doing out there.

Or they had a damned good idea, at least.

Apparently, he'd gotten the collective stamp of approval. Whether he wanted it or not.

Whether he deserved it or not.

Charlie cleared her throat. "Um, do you have a minute?"

He nodded, shifted his weight from one aching foot to the other, and hoped to high heaven she wasn't going to go where he thought she was going with this. After that moment of unguarded stupidity out back, he knew if he had any kind of sense whatsoever, he'd quit right now and stay as far from her as humanly possible.

"About what happened…about the kiss—"

Yep. She'd gone there.

"Look, you don't have to say it," he interrupted, holding a hand up. "It was a mistake. A bad decision all around. It won't happen again."

Charlie came to a stop with the bar between them.

One fine brow arched, and she tilted her head the tiniest bit. "My thoughts exactly. I'm glad we're on the same page. No misunderstandings that way." She offered him a tentative smile.

He'd been about to turn away when he remembered overhearing a snippet of conversation. "Everyone left for the night. Is something wrong with your car? I thought I heard Paula ask if you needed a ride home."

"Oh, well, um…" She was blushing, and her gaze dropped to the tips of her shoes. "My vehicle's at Ed's. I had a little, ah, accident this morning on the way to work. No big deal. But I guess there's a hole in the radiator. So Jerry's gonna see what he can do with it. Caleb loaned me his car for the night."

Something sharp and unwanted punched him in the gut. She'd been in an accident this morning? And no one had thought to mention it to him?

But then, hot on the heels of that stab of concern, came an unwanted kick of jealousy. She was driving Caleb's car. Mr. Cool and Collected with his spreadsheets and his iron grip of warning. Caleb had had the weekend off. Jesse hadn't even noticed Caleb stop by to drop off the keys to his vehicle. Nor had Jesse had any interaction with the assistant manager beyond that initial meeting before his interview.

Why was Charlie driving the guy's car? Was there something beyond just a working relationship between them?

And if so, then why the hell was she kissing *him* out in the alley?

Not liking where that train of thought seemed to be heading, he reminded himself it wasn't any of his business. Except for the fact she'd been just as hot for Jesse as he'd been for her out there in the dark behind the pub.

Those nasty suspicions served as another reminder that he needed to put space between them. They knew next to nothing about each other. What had happened between them had been...crazy. Crazy and stupid.

Besides, he might be in the middle of forced downtime, but he was still hunting a killer. A very active, very twisted killer.

And it was only a matter of time before the hunt resumed and he would have to take off again.

He could quit this job, no skin off his nose, and spend the rest of his time cooped up in some shithole apartment until another body turned up. But time wasn't his friend. Time allowed him to think, to overanalyze. To wallow in blame and guilt.

Been there, done that. Every day of his life since the night Molly had been taken from him. No need for rehashing.

Or he could suck it up and exercise a little self restraint. Something that had never been a problem for him before Charlie.

"You can go ahead and go," she said. "I'll lock up."

He thought about arguing with her, considered insisting on walking her to her car. It wasn't safe for her to be in the pub alone in the wee hours of the morning. He knew all too well the things that could happen to an innocent woman. But it wasn't his place. And it wasn't like he was going far. He'd be right upstairs if she met with trouble. Besides, she wouldn't appreciate him telling her how to do her job. He did know that much about her.

Against his better judgment, he nodded. "All right then. See you tomorrow."

He strode back to the break room for his jacket and keys, lecturing himself with every step that he would keep his hands—and his mouth—to himself, even if it killed him.

Preoccupied, he stomped back into the kitchen, and nearly ran Charlie over. She was just stepping out of her office, wrestling on her own jacket.

Muttering a curse, he grabbed her waist to steady her. Her hair became dislodged from her bun and bounced down her back in wild disarray.

"Sorry," he mumbled, releasing her just as quickly.

"Um, no problem. Good night," she murmured, mustering a smile. He watched as Charlie tugged her hair loose from her collar, finished pulling her coat on, and jerked up the zipper.

Go! Just walk away.

But he couldn't do it.

"At least let me walk you to your car."

"Oh, that's all right. You don't need to—"

"Hey, it's my job, remember? Security?"

"It's really not that big of a—"

"No arguments."

"Fine." She rolled her eyes and heaved a sigh. "Okay, fine."

Not knowing what else to say, feeling like he was treading on eggshells to avoid talking about their kiss, Jesse followed her from the building. She punched in the alarm code on her way out, flipped the lock on the door, then tugged on the handle to make sure the door had latched. Each motion was practiced, if absent.

At least she understood *that* aspect of safety.

Jesse frowned as they crossed the gravel parking lot side-by-side. "I never thought to ask before. Do you live in Badger Creek?"

"I have a cabin a few miles out of town. It's back in the woods, right on the river." She stopped by a vehicle he assumed was Caleb's and clicked the button on the key fob. "Don't get me wrong, I love the pub, love the crowd and the noise. But it's peaceful by the river, quiet out there, you know? A good place to take a step back and recharge the batteries. I love it."

"You live out there alone?" He scowled, all sorts of criminal scenarios flooding his overactive cop mind.

"Mmhmm." She nodded, oblivious, as she studied the keys in her hand.

"No neighbors?"

She shrugged. "Not for, oh, probably two or three miles."

Did she have no common sense? Did she not realize the kind of danger she could be placing herself in? He opened his mouth, actually opened it, to tell her exactly what he thought of her living arrangement. Then snapped it closed just as quickly.

Nope. Not my business.

It might not be his business, but he was still ready to pull his hair out. A movement in the tree line at the far edge of the parking lot flickered in the periphery of his vision. Jesse tensed, instinct sending his hand flying to his hip...where his gun should have been. A split second later, a coon dropped from the lowest branch on a sapling, went scampering along the ground a few feet, and then disappeared into the undergrowth. Jesse eased up, his heart pounding.

Too many dark thoughts about the Chess Master tonight had Jesse's nerves on edge. He glanced over to Charlie. She been a few steps ahead, her back to him, and hadn't even noticed.

She slipped behind the wheel, adjusted the seat, and started the engine. She seemed awfully comfortable driving Caleb's car, no momentary pause to orient herself the way most people do when faced with driving a strange vehicle. Much too comfortable for this to be a first-time experience. Grinding his teeth, he stood near the open door and waited for her to snap her seatbelt into place, oddly reluctant to part company.

"So, where did you grow up?" she asked. Maybe she was as reluctant to go as he was to let her leave? She reached up to adjust the rear-view mirror.

Still, he hesitated. These were the kinds of questions he tended to avoid.

Aw, hell. What harm would it do? It wasn't as if he'd be sticking around all that long anyway. "Crystal, Minnesota. It's a suburb of the Cities."

"Do you have any brothers? Sisters?" She kept up the innocuous chatter seemingly oblivious to the cold. Truth be told, when he was with her, he didn't seem to notice it all that much either.

"One brother," he allowed, kicking at loose gravel with the toe of his boot. He caught himself easing closer to the open door, drawn against his will.

"Younger or older?"

He chewed on the inside of his cheek before admitting, "Younger."

"You're gonna make me work for every little scrap, aren't you?" She gave him a sideways, cheeky grin. "Does this younger brother have a name?"

He shifted from one foot to the other, uncomfortable with the twenty questions. "Billy."

"Jesse and Billy. Your middle name wouldn't be James by any chance, would it?"

He nodded ruefully and shrugged. "My mom had a thing for western folklore."

A burst of laughter erupted, but then she caught herself and pressed her lips together. After a moment, and Jesse's good-natured grin, she cleared her throat and said, "I always wanted a brother or a sister. Didn't really matter which. I hated being an only child."

He knew what she was doing, trying to build some kind of rapport with him in a misguided attempt to develop some semblance of relationship parameters. Or it could be simply so she didn't have to live with the fact that she'd made out with a complete stranger in a dark alley.

Unable to placate her bruised conscience, unwilling to deliberately mislead her into believing there could be something permanent between them, he let the silence stretch.

And yet, he couldn't walk away.

"Are your parents still in the Cities?"

"No, they're both gone now." Somehow, he'd angled himself so he was completely wedged in the door opening, leaning intimately closer, with his forearm braced along the top of the door frame.

Her contrite gaze cut to his. "I'm so sorry, Jesse."

Uncomfortable with her sympathy, he sought to divert the focus. "What about you? Everybody's always talking about your dad, but I haven't heard anyone mention your mother."

Her carefully blank gaze swerved to the dash. Just

91

like that, an invisible door slapped closed between them. Normally Charlie was as easy to read as an open book. But in that moment, her face didn't register an ounce of emotion.

"My parents are divorced." Even her voice had changed.

Now his curiosity was truly piqued. His instincts were shouting for him to press for answers. There was far more to the story than a simple divorce. Charlie's feelings were locked down tight, and chilly enough to freeze water. He didn't like seeing her this way.

Part of him, the cop he used to be, wanted to dig for answers, find out what had happened. The other part of him, this stranger he'd become since the night he'd lost everything, sensed the pain buried deep inside her and couldn't bring himself to rip open those old wounds.

"Nice pictures of you behind the bar, by the way," he said, searching for some safe topic.

A long sigh seeped from her, and the tension charging the air slowly drained away. She released her death grip on the steering wheel and dropped her hands to her lap.

"Thanks." He wasn't sure if she was thanking him for the compliment, or grateful for the change of subject. No way in hell was he going to ask. "Dad's idea," she went on. "He's a sentimental sap, but I'll deny saying so with my dying breath if you tell him you heard it from me."

"My dad was like that too," he admitted before he thought better of it.

She hesitated a moment, licked her lips. "What happened to your parents, if you don't mind my asking?"

He turned his face to look beyond the parking lot, beyond the highway and the field in the distance. He hadn't talked this much about himself in years. Even with Molly, it had taken forever for him to open up this much. What was it about Charlie that had loosened his tongue so quickly?

"Mom was diagnosed with breast cancer almost fifteen years ago," he said at last, filled with equal measures of consternation and admiration.

Oh, she was good. He heaved an exasperated sigh. He could have used her a time or two in interrogation. One look at those big blue eyes and that innocent smile, and every last one of his perps would have fallen all over themselves to spill their guts.

"Oh, Jesse," she murmured, sorrow flooding her face.

"By the time they found the mass, it was too far gone, metastasizing to her lungs…all over really. After that, she went fast. After her death, my brother started getting in to trouble. It was just too much strain on my dad. He had a massive heart attack, died two years after she did. I'd just turned 21. Billy was 17."

Even after all this time, the pain of it still had the power to steal the breath from him.

Charlie peered up at him from the darkened interior of the SUV. He caught the shimmer of tears swimming in her eyes by the light of a passing car, but she blinked them away and turned back to the dash.

Silence fell between them. She picked at her thumbnail, her steady gaze locked on some point beyond the windshield.

"My mom ran out on us when I was four," she said,

her voice so subdued, so quiet he almost missed it. She was calm, held herself perfectly still, but for that nervous picking. Her voice betrayed no emotion whatsoever.

"She woke me up one morning, told me I was a good girl and said she'd love me always. She made me breakfast—my favorite at the time, pancakes with maple syrup and strawberries. Then she tied bows in my hair and sent me off to preschool." Charlie paused, glanced down at the steering wheel. "That was the last time I ever saw her. She was gone by the time I got home. I remember dad just sitting in this big old overstuffed rocker in the living room, staring at a piece of paper for what seemed like forever. Eventually, he got up, threw that paper in the trash and made supper for us, read a story to me, and tucked me into bed.

"But I got back up after he went to bed, and I dug that paper out of the garbage. I stared at it so hard, trying to figure out why it had made my dad cry. I could make out some of the letters, but I couldn't really read yet." Her voice grew even more quiet, almost a whisper. "It was the only time in my life I've ever seen him cry." She cleared her throat, and her voice gained strength. "After that, it was just him and me."

Jesse remained silent, knowing nothing he could say would change a thing, nothing would bring her mother back or heal the pain.

She drew a deep breath. Her voice was unnaturally bright when she chirped, "Well, I suppose that's about enough of those depressing topics. I better let you go on upstairs. The temperature is dropping, and you're starting to shiver."

"Yeah," he said, tapping his thumb against the cold

metal trim as he hunched his shoulders against the wind. Still, he didn't want to step back and let her go. Not yet. "I suppose," he murmured, just to break the silence. But he couldn't find a safe subject to pursue, and he noticed he wasn't the only one shivering. As he straightened, he made the fatal mistake of glancing at her face.

Her smile was entirely too bright and didn't come anywhere near reaching her eyes.

"Damn it."

His lips were on hers before he even realized he'd moved. But by then it was too late. Her mouth was warm beneath his, yielding and oh so sweet. Her hair was silk against his skin. The curve of her cheek fit perfectly in the palm of his hand. And the taste of her upon his tongue was the most delicious, most intoxicating flavor he'd ever experienced.

She clutched his wrist, but she wasn't pulling it away, wasn't trying to end the kiss. That was just fine. He wasn't finished with her yet. He slanted his head, taking her deeper, feeling himself spinning out of control.

The bite of the steering wheel digging into his ribs reminded him of where they were, and what they should *not* be doing. Should *not* be, but *were*. Again.

He finally managed to pull back. She was breathless, blinking up at him in a daze. His own breathing was a little too erratic. Her reaction to his kiss affected him far more strongly than he liked. Tempted by that well-kissed, pink lower lip and too damned turned on by how sexy her mussed hair looked, he swore again and eased back, slamming the door a little harder than he'd intended. He could feel her gaze on the back of his neck as he stomped across the barren parking lot, heading toward the stairs at the back of the pub.

Don't do it. Don't.

He looked back.

She was still sitting there, clutching the steering wheel, staring after him.

It took every ounce of his pitiful self control not to march back to that vehicle, rip the door open, and take her right there in her precious Caleb's SUV.

He broke into a trot before taking the steps two at a time. Running away with his tail tucked between his legs. As if the hounds of hell were nipping at his heels.

Chapter Eight

The Chess Master and his bags occupied the last seat in the back of the Greyhound bus. He stared at the small figurine in his hand, rolled the pad of his thumb along the sturdy pewter. Restless dissatisfaction churned in his gut, made his skin crawl.

A sneer played at the edge of his lip, but he was quick to smooth his expression. He even smiled at the elderly woman across the aisle. She smiled back at what she must assume was a man around her own age, mid to late sixties, balding, wrinkled, with slightly stooped shoulders and just a bit of a paunch. This was one of the more difficult personas to maintain. Much too easy to forget to hunch over just right, or walk with too much spring in his step. It was a challenge, but he liked challenges. He touched the edge of his finger to his forehead to mime tipping a hat at her.

As the bus lurched forward, rocking over potholes and dips in the road, the Chess Master went to that place he often visited, that place deep inside where he replayed his matches and analyzed his moves and those of his challengers. He even, on occasion, considered the players themselves...the Pawns, the Knights, the Rooks, the Bishops, and the Queens. How *they* had affected the game. Could he have maneuvered them more efficiently? Neutralized them more creatively?

He tried to think about those things tonight. But he

97

couldn't quite get there.

Was it because his latest match had been so…well, lacking? With no real challenger, the game had lost its luster.

A little kernel of resentment boiled inside him, burning like acid. It wasn't *his* fault that his most recent opponent had been so inept. In a city the size of Waterloo, one would think there would be a detective *somewhere* who could live up to expectation.

How was I to know Detective Idiot would fail so miserably? Honestly, it was like he couldn't read a simple clue.

The Chess Master had followed the rules, played the game as it was meant to be played. The only other way to point the man in the right direction would have been to write SSA Anderson's phone number on the wall beside the Pawn. And that would have been cheating. After all, there was no point playing if your opponent was too inept to realize the game had even begun.

He'd used all his signature tools, the piece's insignia, all of it, and still that moron Detective Summers hadn't even bothered to call in the Feds. What a disappointing let down he'd proven to be.

I miss matching wits with Detective Reid, the Chess Master mused. *Now there was a true adversary. Nothing like that last bumbling schmuck Summers.*

The Chess Master called to mind Detective Reid's Queen, the way the piece had screamed and sobbed so sweetly. There had been something…*special* about that Queen. He had to give his most revered opponent credit. Detective Reid sure knew how to pick them. So sweet. So innocent.

Turning the pewter piece in his hand end over end, he considered the pieces that had come after. None of them nearly as much fun. He frowned, trying to puzzle out why. He'd followed the same methodical steps. Used the same tools. Followed the same rules. But these last matches had left him...deflated. He knew in the way a true player trusts his instincts that there would be others. More pieces on the board.

And another Queen.

Was he looking at this all wrong?

What had made his checkmate against Detective Reid memorable and exciting? Perhaps it had been Detective Reid himself. The man had an added sense of urgency and intimacy to the game that the Chess Master's previous games had lacked. The knowledge that he'd been *inside* Detective Reid's *home*, that the man could have returned at any moment had certainly added a fair amount of excitement.

He was left to deduce that, while the Queen was crucial to the game—otherwise, why would it be called *Queen's Chess*—maybe it wasn't *completely* about the Queen after all.

No. Changing his strategy now would not benefit the game. Utilizing the Queen improperly wouldn't challenge the players to put forth their best efforts, would it?

Hmm? But what, then?

Maybe he needed to challenge the King more. Force moves. Push the envelope. But to do that, he needed another worthy opponent.

And that's when it hit him. The *real* game might not be over yet.

No! Of course it's not. Not till the final checkmate.

Not till one of the Kings *had fallen. How could I have been so shortsighted?*

The Chess Master had known *something* was keeping him from moving on. Always before, after the Queen had fallen, he'd set the old game aside and been eager to start looking for a new opponent.

But Detective Reid had done what none of the others had. He'd challenged the Chess Master, forced him to think outside the box. He'd utilized the media as the others had not. He'd taken each piece's elimination to heart, as a true player should, more so than any of the other had. Detective Reid had pursued him, even after the Queen had fallen. He'd intrigued the Chess Master so much that he'd had stuck around after the game had ended, however briefly, to check up on the good detective. Quite out of character.

Imagine his surprise to learn the detective had been inconsolable after his defeat. So much so that his superiors had removed him from the field, placing him on administrative leave.

The Chess Master had even gone out of his way to draw Detective Reid out of his grief. He'd given the detective another piece to focus on. But that last move had been a blunder, despite his good intentions. The waitress hadn't been a true Pawn. What was the point of a Pawn, after all, if there was no higher purpose to serve, no Queen to protect?

And Detective Reid's heart just hadn't been in the game. Not yet. It had been too soon.

That Pawn had been the Chess Master's one and only mistake to date, a mistake that had almost cost him dearly. The Feds had been too close, and he'd been careless in his attempts to console Detective Reid from his loss.

And that, in and of itself, the Chess Master found surprising. Somehow, he'd grown fond of an opponent. How odd.

How novel!

Strange, but nevertheless true.

He'd grown *fond* of the good detective. But how could he not? The man was just so fascinating. His dogged determination, even to the point of self destruction. His moral code, his complex relationships with those around him, and his devastation, and grief over the loss of their last match. To be honest, the Chess Master still had trouble processing the range of Detective Reid's emotions.

Ah, but Detective Reid had proven himself a fine opponent, regardless of his emotional vulnerability. Then again, perhaps that's what made him a good adversary in the first place. He'd come much closer than any of the others had in stopping the Chess Master once the game had begun. Some of his other opponents, like Detective Summers, had been so dense they hadn't even realized they'd been part of the game.

But Detective Reid had known, right from the beginning, that he was a player…and that he could affect the outcome of the game. He'd known, and he'd kept the Chess Master on his toes. Detective Reid was a true Master, coming closer than anyone else to capturing him.

Once again, he congratulated himself on taking the initiative to track down Detective Reid. A man's credit cards often paved a trail easier to follow than a neon sign.

By now he should have had sufficient time to

compose himself. Perhaps he's ready to engage in another game?

The bus jolted, bringing the Chess Master back from that happy place he'd finally found. Calmly, he peered around the dim interior at the groggy people rousing from travel induced slumber. He turned his attention to the window to his left, and peered into the night, black as pitch, all around them. The highway was deserted. They hadn't met a single pair of headlights for miles and miles. The bus started slowing, wobbling along like a limping old man with an uneven walker.

An annoying tap-tap-tap came over the scratchy PA system.

"Sorry, folks. Looks like we're in for a slight delay," the driver announced as he angled the bus toward the side of the road. "Roadside services are on the way. It's probably best if we all stay on the bus for the time being, but if you'd like to stand up and stretch your legs a bit, that'd be fine."

A small child suddenly poked her head over the seat in front of the Chess Master. All blonde ringlets and big blue eyes, the toddler grinned at him, displaying two tiny pearly white teeth.

"Hi!" The toddler squealed with glee and pitched a tiny plastic horse over the seat. "Hi!"

Smiling, the Chess Master bent to retrieve the toy from the floor by his foot. As he straightened and handed the toy back, the toddler crowed, "Hi!"

She accepted the toy with slobber covered fingers, only to toss the horse right back on the floor.

Chuckling, the Chess Master scooped the toy up once more. This time, instead of handing it back, he made a show with the little plastic beast, trotting it along the back of the tall seat between them. He made shuffling, snickering sounds and tapped the horse's muzzle gently against the tip of the toddler's nose.

"My horsey." She giggled, delighted by the new game.

"Oh, Janie, no! Don't bother the nice man," her mother said, twisting in her seat to blink blearily at him. "I'm so sorry if she troubled you."

"I don't mind," he assured the mother with a benevolent smile. He turned to the little girl. "Makes the time go faster, doesn't it?"

The mother stretched and yawned. "I wonder how long this will take?"

"Hard to say." He handed the toy back to Janie, pleased when she bounced the horsey along the top of the seat, mimicking the sounds he'd made.

Such a smart child.

"Where are you headed?" Janie's mother asked, angling in the seat to watch her daughter play.

"Wisconsin," he said, letting his smile grow. "I'm on my way to see an old friend."

"Isn't that a nice coincidence? We're headed in the same direction."

The Chess Master murmured a pleased sound. "Well then, I'll have good company for the long ride." He returned his attention to the child. "Do you know what goes with little horses, Janie?"

The little girl's brow knitted for a moment as she blinked big blue eyes back at him. When the Chess Master lifted the pewter figurine he'd been absently rubbing up for her to see, her eyes lit up. "Pretty tower!"

"No, sweetie, this isn't a tower. This here is a

Queen. She's one of the most valuable players." He offered the antique piece over the seat to the toddler, but her cautious mother caught the child's hands at the last second.

The toddler's face screwed up, and she demanded, "'Ween! 'Ween!"

"Oh, no, honey. No touching." She smiled apologetically at the Chess Master. "I'm sorry, that's very nice of you. But little hands don't always appreciate heirlooms, and that chess piece looks very old."

"Ah yes. Right you are. Didn't think of that." He shrugged in a what-can-you-say kind of way. "I'm not used to little ones, I'm afraid. How old is she?"

"She'll be three next week."

"She's very sweet."

"Thank you."

He caught the horse when the girl tossed it, snatching it right out of the air this time. The toddler collapsed in a fit of giggles. He offered the horse back to Janie. "You know what, Janie? I bet your mama would make a fine Queen."

After giving the mother a quick wink, the Chess Master settled back in his seat and closed his eyes for a short doze. He linked his fingers around the chess piece and propped his joined hands on his artificially plump middle.

He slicked his thumb along the figurine with renewed purpose as hope swelled in his chest, his mood much improved. He had a great deal of work ahead of him. Orchestrating a game, after all, took a lot of attention to detail. He had to find just the right players, and that took time. Each move had to be meticulously plotted out.

It was all about strategy.

And then there was the matter of drawing Detective Reid into the game. The Chess Master quelled a shiver of anticipation.

It was time to set the board once more.

Oh, this is going to be so much fun!

Chapter Nine

"I got it. Thanks." Jesse nodded to the delivery driver. The man dipped his chin and made his way to the cab of his truck. After closing the pub's heavy freight door—the same door he'd pushed Charlie up against when he'd lost his mind and kissed her—Jesse turned to the stack of white boxes.

Don't go there, he reminded himself. *Just don't.*

He checked the last two cases of salad dressings off the sheet attached to the clipboard. He was just signing the bottom of the slip when a flash of movement caught his eye. He glanced over. Charlie—looking just as sexy in a pair of faded jeans and an old baseball T-Shirt as she did in her skinny skirt and silk top—stepped out from the walk-in cooler where she'd just put away a crate of peppers.

Okay, maybe not *quite* that hot. That skin-tight skirt of hers had done some freaky shit to his libido. But this was damn close.

"Oh, wait! Let me get one of those." She hurried toward him, but he was already picking up the cases.

"That's all right, I got 'em."

"You shouldn't take both of them. Those are really..." he hefted the crates with ease, "heavy." Clearing her throat, Charlie leaped to open the stainless-steel cooler door and chirped, "Well, that didn't take long at all. Caleb and I are usually at this a good hour when the truck comes. I can't believe we're done already."

He mumbled an inarticulate sound as he edged around her, all too aware of her. The scent of her perfume tempted him to ease a little closer than necessary. He very nearly groaned aloud.

Once inside the big walk-in, Jesse braced one case of dressings between his hip and the shelving unit while he maneuvered the top case onto one of the metal racks. But as he did so, he bumped a head of lettuce which started rolling toward the edge of the shelf. Instinct had him stretching for the lettuce, which caused him to bobble the case he'd pinned with his hip. Before the case could slip any farther, Charlie jumped into action to steady it.

Every muscle in his body tightened as her forearm brushed his abdomen. Jesse returned the lettuce to the shelf along with the others, and then took care of the last case of dressings.

She was so close it wasn't much of a stretch for his imagination to nudge her a little closer. He only needed to ease forward a little, mere inches really, to feel those luscious breasts pressed against his chest once more. And if he did, would she step away? Or would she—

Overcome by the memory of the last time he'd had her this close, he found himself leaning in before he'd fully considered the consequences. A soft sound escaped her, heating his blood.

His gaze dipped from those beguiling blue eyes to her lips—pink lips slightly parted and oh so inviting— and lingered there. For one slim moment, her body swayed toward him. The tantalizing whisper of her breasts brushed his chest.

But then, with eyes gone wide, she jolted back. Disappointment washed over him, colder than the steady stream of refrigerated air circulating in the small confined space.

"Lunch!" Her voice rang out an octave higher than normal. "You haven't had anything to eat yet, have you?"

He blinked, the moment lost. "Ah, no. Not yet."

"Good," she called over her shoulder as she popped the door open and hurried from the walk-in as though it were on fire. "I'm headed to the diner. You can come along, my treat."

"That's all right. I'll just grab a quick bite upstairs, maybe catch a catnap before for my shift tonight."

She turned to him with the distance of a kitchen island safely between them. "Really?" She arched a fine brow. "Do you even have any groceries up there? I wouldn't imagine you'd be able to fit much in your bike saddlebags. What do you have up there? A candy bar?"

He said nothing, just stared at her. Couldn't she see what she was doing to him? Didn't she realize that the two of them spending any more time together than absolutely necessary was a really, *really* bad idea?

"Come on. I hate eating alone. We can stop at the grocery store when we're done and grab some stuff to stock your fridge."

He opened his mouth to protest, but she quickly cut him off. "Boss's orders."

"Still have Caleb's SUV?" He couldn't help the disgruntled tone, anymore than he could understand the reasoning behind it.

"No," she called over her shoulder as she headed toward her office, apparently oblivious of his rancor.

"Georgia Ann loaned me her car for the afternoon."

Placated for reasons he didn't even want to consider, Jesse waited for her by the door separating the kitchen from the main taproom. "Is it running all right now? Last I heard, it was in the shop too."

She frowned up at him and tilted her head in an unspoken question.

"I met Jerry, the mechanic from Ed's, the other night here at the pub. Mentioned to him my bike was making a funny sound. So he told me to drop it by. Anyway, he was working on a little orange car yesterday when I stopped in. He mentioned it belonged to Georgia Ann."

"Oh," Charlie murmured, a small smile tugging at her lips. "I'm sure it's running just fine."

He eyed her speculatively. "You say that like you know something."

"Jesse, *everybody* in town knows something." She grinned now, ear to ear. "Well, everybody but that thickheaded idiot Jerry. Ready to go?"

Crossing his arms over his chest, he tried one last time. "You know, this isn't necessary."

"Sure it is," she said, blowing off his attempts at looking intimidating. It usually worked with everyone else, why not her?

Damn it.

She was doing a real number on him. Every time she smiled at him, it was like a direct hit to the gut, knocking the wind from his sails.

"Can't let my bouncer starve, now can I?"

"I hardly think I'm going to starve. Your cook kept eyeing me last night like she couldn't wait to fatten me up."

That brought a burst of merry laughter from those tempting lips. There was a definite twinkle in her eyes now. "With anyone else, I'd say that's exactly what she was thinking." After tugging her coat on, Charlie flipped her hair out from under the collar. "With you, I'd be willing to bet she was plotting."

"Plotting? Plotting what, exactly?"

For a split second, her smile slipped. Just a tiny bit. He'd nearly missed it. But then she was flashing pearly whites in a smile wide enough to split her face. "It's not important. All set? Don't you want a jacket?"

He was at a complete loss as to how to respond to her obvious evasion. A snort escaped him. Jesse stepped back, holding the door for her. He followed her to the little, unusual colored car and folded his large frame inside the cramped interior.

A short while later, Charlie skidded the tiny vehicle into a parking spot in front of the diner. Forcing his white knuckled grip to loosen from the door handle, Jesse made a mental note to never let her behind the wheel again.

The huge plate glass windows on the front of the diner gleamed in the afternoon sunlight. Jesse followed her inside, all too aware of the speculative gazes tracking them down a side aisle to the counter at the back of the restaurant. They placed their order, picked up their soft drinks, and then chose a booth at the front with an excellent view of the street.

Pulling the paper wrapper from her straw, Charlie dropped the clear plastic tube into her soda. "So now that you've had a chance to settle in, what did you think of the apartment?"

"It's fine." He took a drink. The cold sweet bite of

soda hit the spot.

"Is there anything you need up there? The bedding's old, but it's clean. I'm not sure what's left for towels—"

"Don't worry about it. It's not like I'm gonna be there long."

A shadow passed over her face. Her smile slipped, and her subdued gaze dropped to the straw wrapper in her fingertips. With focused concentration, she began pleating the slim strip of paper.

He caught himself reaching for her hand and firmly squelched the urge to comfort her. Instead, he watched as she nibbled at her lower lip. Though she was careful not to vocalize, her face was easy to read. She might not say anything, but she clearly didn't like the idea of him leaving. And that knowledge had him twisting in the wind.

He forced himself to look away before he gave in to the urge to reach out and touch her after all. Jesse blinked against the glare of bright sunlight glinting off the chrome of a passing car and let his eyes adjust.

From his seat, Jesse surveyed the tidy row of business fronts running down the opposite side of the street. A quaint little movie theatre advertised a new release. The aged marquis sign was missing a few letters. The narrow pharmacy across the way displayed an old-fashioned soda fountain in the window. Suds 'N Duds Laundromat was all lit up. A woman stood inside folding towels while a couple of kids raced circles around the row of machines.

The spiffy little hair salon had a huge chalkboard anchored near the front door advertising half price men's haircuts on Wednesdays. At the end of the block sat a long, low building with massive bowling pins decorating the sign overhead. Badger Creek was a thriving little community. Small, but self-sufficient for the most part.

"Did you have time to study the manual Eli gave you?"

"Hmm?" He turned to her again. "Oh, yeah, the mixed drinks book. I'm getting there. I can safely say I know the difference between a Strip and Go Naked and Sex on the Beach now."

As soon as the words were out of his mouth, he could have kicked himself. *Duh!* Suggestive sexual names. Not a good topic to discuss when one was trying to avoid…well, er, sex.

She licked her lips and glanced away. Apparently, her mind had gone straight to the gutter too, which made him want her all the more.

"So, um, tomorrow afternoon we're having a get together at my place." She held up a hand the minute he began to decline, cutting him off. "It's just a barbeque Dad and I do every year for the employees and their families, and a few close friends, sort of an appreciation dinner thing."

A few close friends? That probably meant half the damned town had been invited.

He bit back a groan as she forged on. "Gives us all a chance to hang out away from the pub. Well, dad usually helps, but he's on a fishing trip with some old Army buddies this year…it just didn't work out timing-wise." She shrugged. "Anyway, I'd really like for you to come, too."

He hesitated. He really didn't need an employee appreciation barbeque, nor did he want to bond with his fellow employees. And he sure as certain didn't need to spend any more time with his boss than necessary. She was already under his skin as it was. But something in her hopeful gaze strangled the denial before the words could march past his lips.

"Okay," he found himself agreeing. And immediately wanted to kick himself.

Please don't give me the smile. Not that one. Please.

"Great!" She beamed at him, and fire rushed straight to his groin. *Yep. That's it. That's the one.* "I'll have Georgia Ann pick you up on her way over if Jerry doesn't have your bike finished yet."

"Here you are," said a plump waitress with frizzy gray hair and wrinkles. She slid loaded plates in front of Jesse and Charlie, and then glanced at their still nearly full soda glasses. "Get anything else for ya, sweetie?"

"No thanks, June," Charlie replied, peeling the top of her bun from her thick burger. She took off roughly half the onion, and then stacked the huge pile of pickles that had been on the side of the plate—probably double the amount as had been placed on Jesse's plate—on top of her sandwich. "I think we're good for now. How's Amy?"

"Fine, just fine. Got transfer orders last week. She's being stationed in Oahu." The waitress grinned and gave her plump hips a spry twist. "Gonna have to get me one of them fancy grass hula skirts when I go out to visit her in a few months. Maybe one of those coconut bras, too." June wiggled her eyebrows.

Jesse bit back a groan, trying to mentally scrub that image from his mind. Across the table, Charlie broke into peals of laughter. June, planting work-reddened fists to generous hips, leaned back and hooted right along with her.

"I bet she can't wait to have you come see her," Charlie said after they wound down. "What's it been now? Two years?"

Jesse sat quietly, observing the easy interaction between Charlie and the waitress. There was a lot of comfortable familiarity here. Not something you saw everyday where he came from.

"Three," June said, shaking her head. "Lord, I miss that girl. I remember you two running in and out of here, thick as thieves in those short little cheerleading uniforms, to grab a burger before heading off to cheer at this game or that. Which reminds me," June leaned over and grabbed the nearly empty bottle of ketchup from their table. She quickly switched it out with the full bottle from the next table. "There you go, honey."

June gave an abbreviated head jerk in Jesse's direction, shot Charlie a meaningful wink, and bustled off, humming along with the 80's rock pouring from a radio in the back.

Shaking her head, Charlie picked up the bottle of ketchup and proceeded to dump nearly half of it on her plate. Jesse watched with growing amusement as she picked her cheese and pickle burger up and dunked it in the pond of ketchup like one might dunk a donut in coffee.

Charlie leaned over her plate and bit into the juicy burger, closing her eyes and moaning her appreciation aloud. She caught the extra ketchup at the corner of her mouth with her thumb before popping it, too, into her mouth. Jesse laughed out loud.

"Eat," she encouraged, picking up a fry. After

dredging it through the ketchup, she pointed it at him. "I don't care where you go. You'll *never* find another burger as good as that one right there. Henry makes *the* best burgers, hands down."

And, just like that, he could see her there, just as June had described. Young and innocent, dressed in a cheerleading uniform, hair up in a ponytail, her whole life ahead of her and not a care in the world, her pretty blue eyes glowing with excitement. Unexpectedly warmed by the image, he let one side of his mouth curl up on a grin. Jesse added a small dash of ketchup to his own burger and poured a little on his plate for his fries.

He picked the burger up, leaned over his own plate as burger juice dripped onto his fingers, and took a big bite. Flavor exploded in his mouth, and he had to admit she was right. This was one of the best he'd probably ever had.

Then again, maybe it was just the company.

They exchanged small talk over lunch. Charlie gave him a brief overview of the town's businesses and their owners. Periodically, Jesse would interrupt with a question for clarification, but for the most part, he was content to just sit back and listen to the sound of her voice.

It was obvious, both from her knowledge of the town as well as her tone, that she loved Badger Creek. The small Midwestern town and its occupants were integral to the fabric of her life, just as, from what he'd observed of those around her, she was an important part of their lives.

Somewhere in the middle of Charlie's prose, June wandered back with fresh glasses of fountain pop. With a mystifying little smile, she gently slid the full glasses onto the table, picked up the empties, and disappeared without a word.

Charlie smiled absently in her direction, never missing a beat in the story she was telling as she swabbed up the last of her ketchup with one of the fries left on Jesse's plate. He grinned, positive she hadn't even realized what she'd just done. She was just winding down when June came back with a green slip of paper.

"Can I get you two any dessert? Henry made peach cobbler this morning, and he just whipped up a batch of fresh turnovers."

Charlie groaned aloud, leaned back in her seat, and clutched her hands over her stomach with dramatic flair. "Are you trying to kill me, June? I'd explode!"

"Awe, come on," June coaxed. "How about one piece, two forks? Half the dessert, half the guilt."

Jesse watched as Charlie's gaze flew to his face. She blushed, and his heart lurched. The unexpected vision of him slowly licking peach cobbler from Charlie's very naked body made his mouth go dry. His gaze dipped to the base of her throat where her pulse fluttered, and he imagined lapping fresh whipped cream from her skin.

She stared right back at him, and licked her lips. Her voice cracked as she spoke to the waitress. "No, um, no thanks, June. Not, ah, not this time."

Jesse caught June's smirk as she turned to walk away.

Jesse reached for the green diner check at the same time as Charlie. She got there first, but his hand closed over hers. "Let me."

She shook her head, her wide-eyed gaze locked on

his. He couldn't help it. Her skin was just so soft beneath his. He rubbed small circles with his thumb over the back of her knuckles.

"No. I insisted that you come along, so it should be my treat." By the time she finished speaking, she sounded a bit breathless.

"All right," he said at last, reluctantly letting her withdraw her hand from his. "But I'll cover the tip."

Catching her bottom lip between her teeth, she dropped her gaze to her purse. God, she drove him crazy when she bit her lip like that, leaving behind tiny indentations from her teeth. He wanted to draw her into his arms and suckle that lip, lick at it, and sooth it until the marks disappeared. Shaking himself from that ludicrous notion, he dug for his own wallet.

She left her money on the table with the diner ticket and climbed out of the booth. She was halfway to the door before he remembered what it was he was supposed to be doing. After dropping a generous tip on the table, Jesse stalked after her, his eyes following the sway of her hips like a heat seeking missile.

They climbed back inside Georgia Ann's car. He'd been so distracted, he completely forgotten to suggest that he drive until she was already behind the wheel. Thank God it was only a short trip to Ed's. Jesse's knuckles were white, his fingertips numb on the seat as she rounded the corner fast enough to make the tires squeal. By the time they pulled into the auto shop, any thoughts of lust in his head had been replaced by prayers for a safe arrival at their destination.

He was more than a little surprised his legs weren't shaking by the time he climbed from the car. Shaking his head, he hurried to catch up to Charlie as she ducked inside the building.

"Hey, Charlie, Jesse," Jerry called, turning from where he was working beneath an old Ford pickup hoisted up high on a huge hydraulic lift.

The scents of old motor oil, fresh grease, and dirt surrounded them as they stepped farther into the garage. Jerry finished tightening a bolt, tucked the wrench in his back pocket, and withdrew a stained shop rag. Wiping his hands, he ambled toward them.

"Just got your radiator done about an hour ago, Charlie. Probably gonna wanna think about bringing her in to have the brakes changed pretty soon. Ed'll be back in a few if you wanna wait, otherwise, the keys are hanging up in the office. He said you can settle up when you have time."

"You're done with it already? I figured it would be a few more days yet. Man, you're fast!"

Blushing, rocking back on the heels of his oil-stained, scuffed boots, Jerry shrugged and muttered, "Wasn't that big a deal. We tend to keep most parts on hand for your car."

Shuffling his feet, Jerry glanced up, his gaze going to the parking lot, Jesse suspected, in an effort not to look Charlie in the eye.

Irritated for no apparent reason, Jesse crossed his arms over his chest. But then thunder clouds rolled into Jerry's expression. Consternation wrinkled his forehead as his attitude did a complete one-eighty.

"Did she bring that damned thing back *again*? Where the hell is that infernal woman?"

Startled, Charlie's eyebrows flew up. "What? Who?"

"Georgia Ann. Why'd she bring that damned car

back this time?" After shoving the shop rag in his back pocket beside the wrench, Jerry waved an agitated hand toward Georgia Ann's car. "What does she think is wrong with that blasted thing this time?"

"Ah, nothing." Charlie held her hands up, waving them defensively. "Georgia Ann didn't bring it, she just loaned it to me for the afternoon. It's fine. Everything's fine."

That seemed to mollify the mechanic, but then his eyes slowly narrowed. He turned a shrewd gaze on Charlie, and Jesse found himself moving closer, looming protectively beside her, scowling an unspoken warning at Jerry.

The mechanic didn't seem to notice. "You drove it?"

Charlie nodded, wary now.

"How did it ride? You hear any knocking? Any strange sounds?"

"No." Charlie shook her head, bewildered.

"Did it pull one way or the other? Shimmy or shake?" Jerry propped his fists on his hips. "Smell funny? How are the brakes? Sticky? Squealing?"

Shooting a confused glance at Jesse, Charlie shook her head. She faced Jerry and gave a helpless shrug. "It ran just fine."

Jerry turned his attention to Jesse, gave him one of those man-to-man looks and arched a brow.

"Ran fine," Jesse confirmed, relaxing somewhat now that Jerry wasn't glaring holes through Charlie anymore.

"I knew it," Jerry suddenly whooped, jerking the shop rag out of his pocket once more to snap it over his palm. "I *knew* it! Ain't a *damn* thing wrong with that car. It's all in that blame fool woman's head. Stubborn, hard-headed, cussed…" His agitated voice trailed away as he stomped over to a white car in the next stall. The hood was already up, and Jerry ducked beneath it. The sound of his furious swearing accompanied angry metallic clanking and banging.

Clapping a hand over her mouth, eyes wide, Charlie whirled to face Jesse. Her shoulders shook as the muffled sound of her laughter slipped free. Grinning, feeling his own laughter rising up, he grabbed her by the shoulders and pulled her outside and around the corner, well out of Jerry's earshot.

Gasping, giggling like a couple school kids, they huddled close together. Charlie's forehead brushed Jesse's chest, and his hands clutched her shoulders. His cheek brushed her hair, and her hands gripped his waist. Charlie peeped up at him, laughing over Jerry's temper tantrum until tears gleamed in her eyes. Jesse's own eyes were damp, and he was beginning to get a stitch in his side.

When they finally wound down, Charlie groaned. "Oh, no! We forgot to ask about your bike."

"I saw it in the corner. It's still in pieces." He drew a deep breath, easing the ache in his side. He hadn't laughed like that in longer than he cared to remember. It felt damn good.

"I don't want to go back in there after the keys to my car," Charlie whispered in mock fear.

Puffing out his chest like he was preparing to beard the lion in his den, Jesse announced with feigned grim determination, "I'll do it."

Charlie bit her lip and giggled again. But then the sound of a dropped wrench and a loud cuss echoed from inside the dim building. Her eyes shot wide, and Jesse cringed.

"No," she gasped over a laugh and clutched his shirt. "Don't! Ed'll drop it off at the pub. Come on." She took him by the hand and dragging him over to Georgia Ann's car. "Let's head over to the grocery store. We better get this poor car out of Jerry's reach. He might do something he'll only have to fix later."

Laughing, they crawled inside the much-maligned car and quickly drove off like a couple of bandits. And once again, Jesse held on for dear life. Only this time, he was laughing too hard to care.

****

Taking the first gravel road he came to, the Chess Master turned north and drove on. Mile after mile of dust flew by. He glanced at the little plastic horse propped carefully on the dash, and he smiled.

What a charming little girl. So bright, and so generous to share her little toy with him. He'd been so taken with the child that he'd given the mother his special book, Jules Verne's *The Mysterious Island*, extracting the promise from the woman that she would read it to Janie.

It was more than a fair trade. Surprisingly, the horse brought as much pleasure to look at and remember as the book had. Perhaps, someday, Janie would love books as much as he did. Maybe her mother would keep the book for her, and Janie would remember the nice man on the bus who had given it to her.

Time was moving quickly, and he was getting antsy, eager to see Detective Reid again. He surveyed the road ahead, looking for a good place to ditch the stolen car. He needed a new set of wheels, had been bumping along in this little car for far too long. Sooner or later, an APB would be issued, if one hadn't been already. The last thing he needed was to be tossed in the slammer for grand theft.

Wouldn't that be a kick in the shorts?

A little farmhouse came into view about a mile and a half up the road. Slowing down, pulling off to the side of the road, he hung back, checking things out. That tractor wouldn't get him far. He wouldn't even know how to start it, much less drive the thing. But the old beat'em up pickup truck beside it ought to do him just fine.

He squinted through the glare on the scratched windshield. There looked to be a decent sized pond behind that big old barn on the other side of the farmhouse. Might be a good place to dump the little car he was driving now...if he could get it back there through all those weeds.

He surveyed the yard with a critical eye. You could tell a lot from a person's yard. Kids, he surmised, by the swing set and the array of discarded toys and bikes littering the neatly clipped yard. Pretty flowerbeds. Freshly painted house.

Kids *and* a woman, he thought with a predatory smile, judging by the nightgowns and bras fluttering amid men's blue jeans and worn plaid work shirts hanging on the line. He idled the car closer and checked his watch. Two o'clock. Kids were probably still in school. But mama should be home. His smile grew.

It had been a long time since he'd had a decent, home-cooked meal. *French toast*, he remembered with a smile. Suddenly a medium sized dog came barreling down the short lane barking like there was no tomorrow.

Jerked from his pleasant musings, the Chess Master held his breath, waiting for someone to come and investigate. When no one came out from the house or peered from the barn he let out a long sigh. Lady Luck was smiling on him. Easing the car closer to the house, he took a better look around.

"Some Midwestern hospitality here," he grumbled. "Doesn't look like anyone's even home."

Parking the car, driven by a sense of urgency, he opened the door and climbed out.

"Hey there," he called to the barking dog, holding his hand out. "Hey, come here." But the dog only hung back, just out of reach, snarling and baring its teeth.

"Stupid mutt," he muttered, kicking dirt at it.

After deciding the dog was all bark and no bite, the Chess Master made his way to the house first. He walked right in as if he owned the place, confirming no one was at home with a quick glance around and another shout. He made short work of finding something suitable to wear. The man who lived here was close enough to his size that the clothing fit relatively well. He even found a heavy work coat and a stocking cap. A bonus since the weather would be edging into winter soon.

Sadly disappointed by the poor offerings—not a decent book in the whole house—he pilfered two hundred forty dollars and sixty-nine cents from two piggy banks and a colored glass mason jar.

Next, he grabbed a loaf of bread and a plastic container of cold cuts and tossed them into a grocery bag he found in a closet in the kitchen. Snagging a half gallon of orange juice, he took a long swig, then recapped it and hooked a finger through the handle. He looked around one last time for a book, an iPod, anything, but found nothing more interesting than a deck of cards and an old VCR. The cards he took. The VCR, he didn't waste his time on. Carrying his plunder, he went outside and crossed to the old truck.

The rusty door screeched when he opened it. As he climbed inside, dust rose up in a cloud from the seat. After a few minutes searching beneath the dash and trying to connect the necessary wires in vain, he got back out to check under the hood.

And there he stood, mouth pursed to the side, hands on his hips, staring at a yawning hole where the engine should have been.

Should have been, being the operative words there.

Well, then. He lifted a brow as he weighed his options. The little car might have a great big, albeit figurative target painted on it, but it didn't look as if he had any other choice. He'd been here too long as it was, and he needed to hightail it. His gaze went to the kids' bikes, then the tractor, but he turned away just as quickly.

Guess him and the little car were stuck with each other for a bit longer. He'd drive it till he found something else, or it ran out of gas. Whichever came first. Then he'd ditch it and move on.

Like a scavenger hunt, he thought, nodding to himself, well-pleased with the analogy.

Well, that was just fine. The Chess Master loved games. Nothing put him in a better mood. He just hoped Detective Reid was up to the challenge.

Chapter Ten

Charlie brushed a stray lock of hair behind her ear with the back of her wrist. Saturday nights were usually hopping at the pub and tonight proved to be no exception. It was just after midnight, but the band was going strong and the empties were piling up faster than the girls could get them cleared.

She stole a peek toward the bar. There he stood, a towel draped over one shoulder as he worked the taps like a pro, a smile on his handsome face while he joked with one of the customers. Jesse had been with them for two weeks now. And she still caught herself watching him like a schoolgirl with a crush. Shaking her head, she glanced around to find the next recently vacated table.

After picking up the half empty tub one of the waitresses had left behind, Charlie weaved her way around sturdy tables, moving chairs, and wobbly customers. She grabbed empty bottles and glasses as she went.

"Honey!" Large hands captured her hips from behind, and a solid wall of muscle pressed up against her back. Charlie stiffened.

Oh shit!

"Dylan, no." Wiggling away, she spun around, anchoring the bus tub between them like a shield.

"Just look at you! Sexy as ever. Baby, I've missed

you. I've been dreaming 'bout those sweet lips. Come over here and plant one of them dee-licious welcome home kisses on me," he slurred.

Oh, no. No way in hell.

The only thing she was willing to plant on those lying, cheating lips was her fist. But she wouldn't lower herself to cause that kind of scene. Not here. Not in her pub. Instead, she eyed him as one might eye a wad of gum stuck to the bottom of a new pair of shoes.

"When did you get back to town, Dylan?"

"Yesterday. I'll be here for a couple weeks, sweetness." He wiggled a suggestive eyebrow at her.

A couple weeks? Dear God! She was going to jail for sure. Murder in the first. Maybe she could plea bargain to Manslaughter. Then again, everyone in town knew Dylan. Maybe they'd let her go, rule it as justifiable homicide.

Once she might have found him handsome and charming. All broad shoulders and square jaw. An all-American jock. Now he was just a pain in the neck. A mistake she blamed on youth and inexperience.

Resting one hand on the back of a chair, bracing the toe of his huge boot on the opposite side of his other foot, he leered down at her, effectively blocking her path to the kitchen and safety.

"Had to come on down and see my girl."

She recalled the last time Dylan had come home while on leave from the Army to *see his girl*. He'd tried to rekindle the old flame then too. Damn near succeeded, until she'd caught him cattin' around with Gina Bixby, one of the town's two hairdressers. Gina was popular with the ladies due to the steady stream of gossip whistling through her salon. She was also popular with the men because of her *special discounts* on men's haircuts. The only thing in town that saw more action than Gina's salon chair was the bed at Gina's doublewide trailer.

A couple weeks?

Ugh! Heaven help her.

"I am so not your girl, Dylan." Charlie rammed a loose strand of hair into the bun at the back of her head, but it wouldn't stay. He obligingly reached out to help, and Charlie bobbed, batting his hand away. The glassware in the tub she was holding rattled.

"You used to be." Despite the blatant rejection, he aimed that wide, heart stopping, breath stealing grin her way. The one he'd used all too often to weasel his way around her. "You could be again."

Now that just pissed her off.

How could I have been stupid enough to fall for a loser like him?

"I haven't been your girl for quite a few years now," she hissed. "Not since high school. Remember? Finding you and Leslie in the back of her car sort of killed it for me, Dylan. It's over. Done. Move on. I have." Scowling, she turned to skirt around the table to her left.

"Hey, Dylan," a slurring male voice called from a nearby table. "Leave Charlie alone, she ain't interested no more."

Whipping his head around to glare at the interfering patron, Dylan told little Jeff Jones what he could do with his suggestion. Loud and crude.

Charlie eased back another step, shaking her head. She flicked a glance around the room to see who else had overheard. Her gaze connected with Jesse's, and she couldn't look away. He stood behind the bar, all his attention locked on her, and on Dylan. The forgotten makings of a Screwdriver squeezed in his fists, his body stiff, his expression grim.

"Oh, now, don't be like that," Dylan said, drawing her attention to him once more as he grabbed her by the hips. He tugged her back and rubbed against her, making her skin crawl. "I'm a changed man, baby," he purred against the side of her neck and she cringed away.

Fed up at being manhandled, embarrassed by the situation in general—and oddly nervous about the look on Jesse's face, Charlie jerked away and turned to confront Dylan. With an ice-cold smile pasted on her lips, she ordered, "You need to leave, Dylan."

"Oh, but the band's just warming up, sugar lips, and so am I. I haven't danced with my best girl yet." He stepped forward, reaching. She'd forgotten what a damned octopus he could be. Charlie jumped back, the tub bobbling in her hands as bottles and glasses rolled and clanked together hard enough that she wouldn't be surprised to find a few broken later.

A slow, seductive grin spread over Dylan's handsome face as he dogged her step for step. "You know how it always turned me on when you played hard to get."

"I'm not playing anything." Charlie stole a quick glance over her shoulder. If she kept going, maybe she could lead him outside, avoid a bigger scene.

Avoid witnesses if she had to drop his sorry, philandering ass on the ground like he deserved.

"I'm not dancing with you, Dylan. And I'm not doing anything else with you except asking you to leave."

Forty feet. Thirty. The bright red exit sign was a finish line she'd never been so anxious to get to.

But there were far too many obstacles in her way. Someone bumped into her from the side and mumbled an apology, momentarily halting her progress. Dylan took advantage of her distraction and swooped in, closing the distance. Under cover of the milling crowd, he snatched the bus tub from her and deposited it onto a surprised woman's lap. Just as smooth as the snake he was, he slipped an arm around Charlie's waist and tugged her into his arms.

"Baby, you smell so good," he murmured, burrowing his nose against the side of her neck, bowing her backward over his arm. "Makes a man just wanna eat you up."

"Dylan, let me go." She pushed at his chest, struggling, fighting down panic.

"Yeah, that's it, baby," he slurred. His free hand strayed down to her bottom, squeezing as he ground his thickening erection against her. "Rub up on me. You know how I like it."

Turning her head to the side, she scrunched her face up in disgust as she struggled desperately to get free. Movement caught her attention, and Charlie's eyes flew open. She froze. She couldn't even breathe. Jesse was charging around the end of the bar, the bar towel and a bottle of liquor flying in his wake. His expression was thunderous, to say the least.

Someone was about to end up bloody.

Before she could think of something to avert what she knew would be a huge scene, Dylan went down. Jesse caught Charlie to him at the last minute, preventing Dylan from dragging her down with him. Dylan landed on a table, tipping and knocking it over. Beer bottles, glasses, and Dylan crashed to the floor. Chairs skidded. Men and women leaped back, shouting and screaming in shock. Jesse gave her a quick once over with his eyes as his hands skated down her arms, steadying her.

"You okay?" His voice was harsh, his question terse.

Swallowing, too stunned to speak, Charlie bobbed her head, owl-eyed.

Jesse eased her to the side and slightly behind him as he faced Dylan. She was almost surprised he didn't pat her on the head and tell her to be a good little girl and stay out of the way. Jesse leaned down, fisted his hands in the front of Dylan's shirt, and hauled him off the floor.

Charlie gasped, ready to shout a warning as soon as she saw Dylan's expression. But she was too late. Dylan, larger than Jesse in build and no stranger to a barroom brawl, was already swinging. A beefy fist connected with Jesse's cheek, snapping his head back.

Dylan might have had more than a few pounds of muscle on Jesse, but Jesse was faster and not hampered by alcohol.

And he fought dirty.

Dodging a second blow, Jesse jabbed a hard fist to Dylan's middle, doubling him over, following up with a shot to the kidneys. Then Jesse grabbed a handful of Dylan's tousled blond hair in one hand and slammed his knee into Dylan's face.

Dylan went down like a ton of bricks. And there he stayed.

"Who'd he come here with," Jesse shouted, though there was no need. The band had long since trailed off on a discordant note, and the rest of the bar had gone still as a graveyard.

Two nervous men stood up. One managed to clear his throat. "Um, us?"

"Get him out of here," Jesse barked, glaring at them as he pointed to the door. "*Now.*"

The two men rushed forward, all but tripping over each other. Charlie stood back watching Jesse as he, in turn, watched the men drag Dylan's unconscious body from the bar. His chest heaving, his face set in stone, Jesse's gaze finally swung to her. And the look in his eyes took her breath away.

The look in his eyes quite simply declared, *Mine*.

Someone started clapping. Pretty soon a few more people joined in. And then the room at large was applauding.

Exasperated, temper starting to boil, Charlie caught the band's attention and gave them a curt nod to get them playing again. Next, she snagged Paula's eye and the ever-efficient waitress, along with Georgia Ann, hurried over. With the help of a few of the patrons, they began cleaning up the mess.

And all the while, Jesse's intense gaze remained riveted on Charlie, making her want to squirm. But she refused to bow to the accusation, or acknowledge the possessive claim in his unwavering gaze.

"Office," she snapped as she stalked by him. "Now."

She didn't stop or glance over her shoulder as she stormed toward the end of the bar, a woman on a mission. The look on her face must have been one to behold because everyone in her path, eyes wide, stepped back or moved out of her way as she passed.

The moment Jesse entered the dim kitchen, Charlie whirled on him, barely allowing time for the door to close behind him. "What the *hell* do you think you were doing out there?"

"My job." His eyes narrowed, and he crossed his arms over his chest. A bluish smudge was already beginning to form on the ridge of his cheekbone.

"Your job?" She could all but feel the steam rolling from her ears. "*Your job*? Your job is *not* to cause a scene. Your job is *not* to brawl in the middle of the pub. *Your* job is to prevent such…scenes. *Your* job is to keep the peace and ensure the safety of the customers."

"I was ensuring *your* safety," he shot right back. "Which I take as part of my job as well."

"I was fine! I had the situation in hand."

"Really? 'Cause from where I was standing, it looked like *he* had *you* in hand."

"I was dealing with it until you came along and started a fist fight in my pub!" Her voice had steadily gotten louder with each word until she was yelling.

Jesse snorted his disagreement, further infuriating her.

Something bumped the door between the kitchen and the taproom. Without saying a word, she stormed over and smacked the door, causing it to swing outward and crash into a body. The muffled "Oow!" was quite satisfactory.

The lack of privacy was not.

Grabbing Jesse by the wrist, she towed him behind her to the freight door and outside. The door slammed shut behind them. Spinning around, jabbing a finger at his chest, she snapped, "That kind of...of...of *Neanderthal* behavior is not acceptable. Do you understand me, Jesse? This is a respectable, well-run establishment. We do not need Stanley running down here every time I turn around."

He scowled at her. "Stanley?"

"The town's Chief of Police."

Lord, she was mad. Mad at Jesse for overreacting. Mad at herself for not being able to do something to stop it. Mad at Dylan for starting this whole mess in the first place. Crap, she was yelling again. And she'd grabbed him, poked her finger at him! This wasn't her. She wasn't physically aggressive. What was happening to her?

Making a colossal effort to calm down, she raked her hand through her hair as she paced away, paced back, dislodging pins, sending them flying. Her hair bounced down her back and flapped in the wind.

"Look, I don't want that kind of confrontation in the pub again."

"I took care of an unruly drunk who was mauling my wo...my *boss*. I did my job." He stood firm, glaring at her.

"No. More. Scenes." She crossed her arms over her chest, belligerently glaring right back, ignoring the biting wind that raced around the side of the building and stirred the leaves at their feet. And she ignored his slip. Or tried to. At the sound of him calling her his woman, her pulse had begun tripping double time.

Suddenly, Jesse's eyes narrowed, and he cocked his head. "Who is he?"

She frowned. "He's just a customer."

"Bullshit!" Jesse snapped, leaning closer until their

noses brushed. "I haven't seen any of your other customers handle you that way."

"He wasn't handling me."

"You're right. He wasn't *handling* you. He was all *over* you. You think that's good for business? You think you two weren't already causing a scene before I got involved? Think again." His brows were drawn so tight they nearly touched. "You're defending him. So, I'm going to ask one last time, who the hell was he?"

"My ex, all right," she blurted, angry because he was right. Partially right. They had been causing a scene. But she most certainly was *not* defending Dylan. "It was a long time ago. And I'm not defending him. He's an ass."

"Another one. Christ, what is it about you?"

Something in his tone cut her, offending her on a bone deep level. "What are you talking about, another one?"

"You...*ugh!*" Now it was his turn to storm away, raking his hands through his hair, and then stomped right back. "You make me nuts. Men drop at your feet like flies."

"You're crazy," she scoffed, shaking her head. "Nobody falls at my feet."

"They do." He pointed an accusing finger at her. "And you...you don't even realize it. You're oblivious. So goddamned naïve."

He loomed over her again, and she braced herself for another angry outburst. But he froze, his expression suddenly bleak. He dragged in a deep breath. His mouth fell open, and his eyes widened. Then Jesse rolled his eyes, and his sigh nearly knocked her over.

"Christ, I'm no better than they are," he muttered

beneath his breath.

Confused, she glowered up at him, "*What* are you talking—"

Without warning, he snaked his hand into her hair, fisted it and tugged her close. He seized her lips. Slanting his head, Jesse wrapped his arm around her waist and dragged her up against him. And just like that, her anger turned into something else, something hot and wild and overwhelming. Where Dylan's groping had left her cold and disgusted, Jesse's embrace set her on fire.

Her arms shot around his neck, and she pressed closer still, absorbing his heat, absorbing the voracious desire in his kiss. His tongue slid along hers, gliding, stroking, tasting. His mouth slanted, again and again, and he devoured her. His breath was ragged. The unmistakable evidence of his need for her shoved against her belly. Moaning, she let her head fall back as his hungry lips sought her neck. He feasted on her, branding her as he tracked sensual kisses down her throat.

"Oh, my God, Jesse," she gasped as he nipped at her pulse where it beat wildly at the base of her throat. "This is…so unacceptable," she moaned again as his hand closed over her breast, kneading it, rubbing his palm against her nipple through her shirt. Shivers of need wracked her body. "I shouldn't…we shouldn't be—"

Her words were cut off on a strangled groan as his lips claimed hers once more in a soul searing kiss. Then she was kissing him back, mindless with hunger. Jesse reached behind her, and he gripped her bottom with both hands. Then he hoisted her up, and crushed her back against the door. Pinning her with his body, he ground himself against her, and growled low in his throat as he slipped one knee between her thighs.

"Jesse," she panted, clutching at his shoulders, pulling him closer, angling her head to the side so he had better access to her throat. She pulled her legs up and wrapped them tight around his waist. "We have to stop."

His teeth rode the ridge of her jaw, and he growled something against her skin, though she couldn't tell if he was agreeing with her or arguing.

"We shouldn't be standing out here in the cold, necking like a couple of horny teenagers." She shivered as he nipped the sensitive skin below her earlobe, and it had nothing to do with the autumn chill in the air.

"I know," he rasped, his lips racing over her cheek until he nibbled and sucked at her bottom lip. "This is a bad idea." His lips left hers, and he pulled back, just a bit, to stare down into her eyes.

Charlie blinked up at him, dazed, aching. Her lips parted, and his name spilled from her, part question, part plea. Did she truly want him to stop?

She didn't even know anymore.

Groaning, Jesse dropped his forehead to hers, the very tips of their noses touching. She watched, mesmerized, as his eyelids sagged shut. When his eyes opened, there was a new light in them. The spark of something that made her wary, something that threatened to consume her whole.

And yet that same spark excited her, made her want to jump into the fiery temptation of his passion, made her want to burn alive.

"Go inside, Charlie," he ground out, slowly setting

her on her feet and pulling away from her. "Go back inside right now."

"Jesse," she whispered, reaching a trembling hand up to cup his cheek. But he jerked back out of reach, avoiding her touch.

"When I—damn it, *if,* if I make love to you, it's not going to be outside in the cold, in the dark, up against the back door of a bar."

She stilled at his words. Her eyes went wide, and her ragged breath caught in the back of her throat.

"Damn it, go!" He took another step back. As badly as her knees trembled, she dared not pursue him.

She wanted to say something. Anything. She wanted to reprimand him for kissing her. Again. She wanted to beg him to kiss her again. She wanted to make sure he understood that scenes like what happened with Dylan were not acceptable. And she wanted to thank him for protecting her.

But she couldn't seem to form an intelligent, articulate sound. So instead, her wary gaze locked on his, she fumbled with the doorknob behind her until she realized they were locked out. On a strangled curse, Charlie fled, racing around the side of the pub until she reached the front door. And there she stood for a moment, her hand on the door handle, her head hung low, remembering the way Jesse had looked at her.

Shivering, Charlie went inside.

Chapter Eleven

Humming along with the radio, the Chess Master absently reached up and aimed the rearview mirror toward his face. Fingering the beginnings of a beard, one eye on the road, he smiled at his reflection. Funny how a few small changes could alter a man's whole appearance. He pressed an experimental finger to the large mole by his nose. He'd run out of the adhesive he normally used and had been forced to use an off brand. But the latex was holding, so far.

Good. Very good.

Give somebody a focal point like a big mole or a gaudy hat, and, more often than not, they had trouble looking beyond it to remember with any accuracy the true features of the face.

After pushing the rearview mirror back into place and readjusting his thick, horn-rimmed glasses, he turned his attention back to the road. The beard he could handle; facial hair itched for a while, but then you got used to it. The glasses, however, were driving him insane. But he refused to take them off. He had to adjust to them now so that when he was in public they would appear natural to others. As if he'd been wearing them for years.

A fleeting glimpse at the speedometer on the old Buick sedan told him he needed to slow down. He eased his foot off the accelerator. He was too close to his goal, and the fake ID in his wallet was good, but he wasn't sure how well it would stand up to close, professional scrutiny. He'd rather not find out the hard way.

Settling back in the seat, he got comfortable...but not *too* comfortable. He had a full belly and several hours—according to the map—before he made it to Badger Creek. Wouldn't do to fall asleep behind the wheel either. In fact, he had one very important stop to make before he got to Badger Creek. And a very special message to construct for Detective Reid, one the Chess Master was sure only the good Detective could appreciate.

His only regret was that he wouldn't be able to see the look on Detective Reid's face when he realized the Chess Master was back on the board.

It hadn't been all that difficult to track the detective down. A simple stop at a convenience store and the purchase a couple of disposable phones. A few well-placed calls, a believable story, the right questions...and hello, Detective Reid! A little disappointing, actually.

A brief frown tightened his forehead. But then the tightness eased. An oversight on the detective's part, he was sure. Besides, they hadn't truly started the match yet. So, inattentiveness at this point could be overlooked.

Narrowing his eyes against the sun, the Chess Master squinted at the road sign as it drew closer and made a mental note of the mile marker. He slowed and made the turn, humming softly, tunelessly. A few miles down the road, he reviewed his plan of action one last time.

The game had changed this time. No more big crowds to blend in with. No more anonymity. He'd need a base of operation this time. And a cover. A solid one. It was much more difficult to blend into a small-town atmosphere. But he looked forward to the challenge.

A thought suddenly occurred to him. One so surprising, so pleasing, he laughed aloud. Detective Reid had just added an extra element of difficulty to the game. So, perhaps the ease of finding him had been merely a ruse. A lure to draw the Chess Master out. His grin grew, and his happy humming morphed to a jaunty whistle.

So exciting.

Clever, Detective Reid. Very clever.

****

The morning dawned sunny and unseasonably warm for late October. As the pub was closed on Sundays, Charlie allowed herself her one "*Charlie Day.*" Usually, she slept in, but not today.

Today there would be no leisurely walk in the woods, no catch-up housework waiting for her, no relaxed baking just to enjoy the scents of cinnamon and spice heavy in the autumn air. No pot of soup or stew simmering on the stove, and no lazy Sunday afternoon nap.

Not today.

Today she was up with the birds, wrapped in a warm robe with big fuzzy slippers on her feet. She took her coffee out to the back porch, her one allowance of leisure. Seated in one of the Adirondack chairs facing the river, she slowly sipped the strong brew, savoring the way the sunlight bathed the autumn meadow on the far side of the narrow ribbon of river, setting the foliage aflame.

Later, her house and her yard would be overflowing with people. Men, women, children, and probably a few dogs if Doris decided to bring her "kids" along. Noisy laughter and merry chaos.

Picnic tables had already been delivered, but coolers filled with soft drinks and bottles of beer would soon join them. Insulated dispensers would be filled with hot cocoa and apple cider, and the grill would be working overtime. One last hurrah before winter descended. The pub's annual employee appreciation dinner. Only this time, instead of hosting the party at the pub, Charlie had thought it might be nice to get away from the business.

The muffled sound of a 70's rock song buzzed through the open kitchen window. Grinning, Charlie set her coffee on the rustic little table beside her and hurried back inside to snatch her phone from the charger.

"Mornin', Dad."

"Good morning, baby. How's my girl?"

"Good. How's my pops?"

"Alive and kicking," his deep voice responded. She laughed at his time-honored comeback. "I didn't wake you, did I? I forgot about the time difference until after I heard the first ring."

"No, I was just enjoying a cup of coffee on the porch." She went back outside and sat down. After transferring the phone to her left hand, she picked up her coffee and took a cautious sip of the hot brew. "Now you can keep me company."

"We'll have coffee together." His deep chuckle

filtered through the phone line. "How are plans for the party coming?"

"Everything's ready. Caleb and Paula will stop by the pub and pick up all the food and drinks. Eli and Tom came by yesterday and set up the tables. And Doris's going to come over a little later to help decorate."

"Sounds like you have everything well in hand."

"You know me." She paused a moment, toying with the handle of her mug. "I hired a new bouncer/bartender. He'll be filling in behind the bar when Eli goes on leave. He's never bartended before, but he's learning quickly."

"Good. I was worried you'd be shorthanded. Who'd you hire?"

"Well, that's the thing." She paused again, not because she worried about his reaction. But because she was still struggling to define the odd situation she'd found herself in with Jesse. "His name's Jesse Reid. He's…new to the area."

"And?"

She didn't detect any censure in her father's tone, only curiosity.

"He used to be a homicide detective from Minneapolis. He was just passing through. I guess he decided to stop in the area for a while. His bikes at Ed's. Bad fuel injector or something. Anyway, it's only temporary. Who knows for how long? But it should be enough to get us through till Eli gets back."

"Homicide detective, huh?"

"Yeah," Charlie said, holding her breath. What would her father make of it? Lord knew, she was still dying with curiosity over why a man like Jesse would leave a career like that.

"Well, I suppose it'd be easy for a man to get burned out from that sort of job. I would imagine he saw a lot of things that wouldn't sit too well."

That hadn't occurred to her. Charlie took a long sip of coffee and rolled the idea around in her head. It made a lot of sense. It would also explain why he wasn't eager to discuss his reasons for leaving.

"How's he working out?"

"Good! Great!" Charlie chirped, trying not to think about the incident with Dylan, or the kiss. *Kisses*, she silently corrected. *Kisses. Plural.*

"I gave him the key to the apartment. He's a quick learner, and he's good with the customers." Well, good with everyone but Dylan.

"Good to hear. I have to say, I'm glad you gave him a chance, Charlie. Everybody needs a helping hand now and again."

She didn't know exactly how to respond to that. What would her father think if he knew about the things that had been going on out back of the pub? Would he be so glad then?

"How about everybody else?" Her father changed the subject, much to her relief. "Eli? Georgia Ann? Caleb?"

"Everybody's pretty much the same as when you left."

There was a slight hesitation, then her father asked, "How's Doris?"

A slow, mischievous grin curled her lips. "Oh, didn't I mention? She's making plans to run off with Henry Peterson from the diner. He started calling on her the day after you left. He's been bringing her flowers and candy every day, swept her right off her feet."

"*What?*"

A tiny shot of guilt lanced through her at her father's panicked tone. Just as quickly as it flared, she squashed it. Doris and Quinn had been dancing around their attraction for one another for as long as Charlie could remember. They were locked in a tragic stalemate and both too stubborn to make the first move. It was about time somebody lit a fire under one of them, and Lord knew she'd hit a brick wall with Doris. That woman gave new meaning to the word hard-headed.

"Gotcha," she gloated.

"Charlotte Elizabeth, that's not funny." His breath hissed across the connection. "I, ah, I thought she might leave you high and dry."

"Mmmhmm. First, just so we're clear on the subject, you and I both know that was *not* your first worry. Second, you also know Doris would never do that, to either one of us. Third, and most important, when are you going to quit being such an obstinate old goat and tell her how you feel? *Before* somebody else does? You know Henry's been sniffing around for years now. Why do you think she's never said yes to him?"

She paused meaningfully, but when her father refused to take the bait, she rolled her eyes. "Dad, if you don't step up to the plate, sooner or later she's going to start to believe you actually *don't* care."

"Now Charlie—"

"No, Dad, don't you '*Now Charlie*' me in that tone. You know I'm right. For once, just go for it. Stop second guessing everything." Then, her tone softening, she added, "Doris isn't Mom. Give her the benefit of the doubt, Dad. Give yourself another chance. You deserve to be happy too."

A long silence passed. If she didn't know her father better, she would have looked at the display on her phone to make sure he hadn't hung up. She waited.

"The guys are getting ready to head back out on the lake, Charlie. I've gotta go."

Her shoulders slumped. "All right. Have a good time."

"Tell everybody I said hello."

"Will do. Hey, Dad?"

"Yeah?"

"She's not going to wait forever."

Another long pause met her declaration. "I love you, kiddo."

"Love you too."

Glaring fondly at the phone, she shook her head and set the cell phone aside. Charlie curled her legs beneath her, tucked her robe close against the chill, and clasped both hands around her cup. All too easily, the memory of Jesse's lips on hers, and how good it was to have his arms wrapped around her, came back to haunt her. Frowning, she took a big gulp of the cooling coffee and watched the river carry fallen leaves downstream.

Maybe Dad isn't the only one being stubborn.

Chapter Twelve

Charlie glanced at her watch and snuck a quick peek through the front window one more time. The day had gotten away from her. Her guests had begun to arrive almost before she was ready, and she was still bustling about to make sure everyone was enjoying themselves. Chewing her bottom lip, she ran a hand over her hair, smoothing it along her ponytail. Jesse and Georgia Ann should have been here by now. What was keeping them? Had Jesse changed his mind? Refused to come?

Ugh! Why can't I get that man out of my head?

Charlie had been on edge all morning. She'd taken great pains last night to avoid Jesse after *the incident* with Dylan. But wow, the way he'd spoken to her, tersely ordering her back inside the pub last night had shaken her to the core.

He would have taken her right there behind the pub, up against the side of the building. No holds barred. She had no doubts about that. None whatsoever.

What shocked her though? She would have let him.

She knew that now.

And, never having done anything so impulsive in her life, she didn't know how to react. What was she supposed to say to put them back on an even keel?

"...if I make love to you, it's not going to be out in the cold, in the dark, up against the back door of a

bar."

Those words seared through her memory, left her feeling...hunted. And more than a little excited by the chase. As if he'd already been thinking about taking her, already been scheming over the how and the where. A delicious chill rippled through her.

Just the thought of it, the very idea of him making love with her, caused her heart to beat just a little faster, made her breath come just a little quicker.

What really set her blood to racing was the memory of the way he'd continued to watch her the rest of the night. The raw heat smoldering in his eyes as his stare had followed her around the pub. It had been so intense, she'd caught herself staring right back on more than one occasion, whatever task she'd been in the middle of completely forgotten.

Jesse had looked as if he'd been waiting for one look of invitation, one unguarded move on her part, so he'd have just cause to pounce.

The back-screen door slapped closed, drawing her from her thoughts. Hurrying to the kitchen, she picked up two pies, elbowed the door open, and stepped out into the dazzling sunshine.

Laughter and noisy chatter replaced this morning's serene quiet. The pleasant aroma of grilling meat mingled with the crisp scents of autumn. Three small, giggling children chased a Golden Retriever with a tug rope dangling from the side of his mouth around and around the tables and across the yard. Another Golden Retriever, almost an exact replica of the first only slightly smaller, chased after the children, barking excitedly. Doris scolded them all when they came too close to the grill, and sent them on their way with a fond smile. A large group of women fluttered around the picnic tables, setting out platters and huge bowls piled high with food.

Farther down the yard, closer to the river, eight guys were engaged in a game of touch football, fallen leaves flying around their ankles. A handful of men stood off to one side critiquing each play, a beer in one hand, the other tucked inside a pocket.

Charlie paused on the back porch, drinking it all in. Though she missed her father, an overwhelming sense of peace filled her, bringing a huge smile to her lips. She was so blessed. Technically, she may be an only child. Technically, her father was the only blood relation she had left, at least the only one she was willing to claim. But this right here—these people—they were her family.

The only family that mattered.

"Hey, Charlie, you gonna stand there all day with that silly grin on your face, or are you gonna bring those pies over here?" Kendra, Eli's wife, stood at the end of one of the picnic tables, one hand pressed to the small of her back, the other fondly smoothing over her huge belly. "You wouldn't tease a pregnant woman like that, would you?"

Laughing, Charlie bound down the steps. "I wouldn't dream of getting between a pregnant woman and her pie. How are you feeling, Kendra?" Paula took the pies from her with a smile and lined them up on the table. Charlie turned to rub the back of Kendra's shoulder. "Can I get you anything? Shouldn't you be sitting down?"

"I'm fine, just fine. And no, I don't want to sit down. I can't get comfortable sitting anymore. Or laying down. Or standing, for that matter. I'm as big as a blimp. So, I might as well be up and moving around. Get a little exercise before Eli realizes I'm on my feet again. I love that man to death, but he hovers. He's driving me crazy."

"Hey!" Caleb sauntered over, popping a handful of trail mix into his mouth. Nodding to Kendra, he motioned with his beer toward the tables. "Need help with anything?"

"No, I think that's the last of it. I'm just going to go check on Doris," she excused herself with a smile.

"I'll come with you," Caleb said, falling into step at her side.

She glanced to the autumn sky. "I'm so glad the weather held for today. Not a cloud in sight."

Caleb murmured agreement before shooting her a sideways glance. "Weather's not the only thing that's beautiful today."

Laughing, her hands tucked in her front pockets, Charlie nudged his shoulder with hers. "You're such a goof. How many of those have you had to drink?"

Caleb blinked at her, smiled slowly as he tipped his beer to his lips, and shrugged. But then his gaze grew somber. "Listen, I heard about what happened with Dylan. I'm so sorry, Charlie. I should have been there to—"

"Don't." She shook her head as she took hold of his elbow and pulled him to a stop, gazing earnestly up at him. "Okay, Caleb. Just don't. It would have happened whether you'd been there or not. You're entitled to a weekend off now and again too. It's over and done. Besides, I can handle myself. You know that."

"Sounds like Reid handled it." Why did he sound so angry? Or was it frustration lacing his voice, she couldn't tell.

Despite her confusion over Caleb's disgruntled attitude toward Jesse, heat flooded her cheeks at the reminder of how her night had ended. Resettling her scarf, she ducked her head and muttered, "Yeah, well, like I said, it's done and over."

"Still, I should have been there. Dylan shouldn't have gotten anywhere near you. Not after the way he behaved the last time he was in town. I would have—" Caleb bit the words off, and Charlie glanced up to see what was troubling him. He was glaring at the little orange car that had just pulled up alongside the house.

Or, more accurately, he was glaring at the tall, handsome man unfolding himself from the passenger seat.

"Caleb, please." Charlie shot a swift glance at Jesse, working to dim her giddy smile to reasonable proportions. Butterflies took flight in the pit of her stomach at the sight of Jesse. Stepping in front of Caleb, she gently placed a hand on his chest. "I don't want you beating yourself up over Dylan. All right?" She waited till his gaze met hers, and he nodded before she went on. "And I don't know what you have against Jesse, but whatever it is, you need to let it go."

"Who said I have anything against him?" Caleb arched a brow.

"Mm-hmm. Every time anyone even mentions his name, you get all stiff. If you were a cat, all your hair would be standing straight on end, and you'd be hissing."

"I don't like him, Charlie. There's something about

him…" His voice trailed off as his earnest gaze locked with hers. "He's hiding something."

"Caleb." She shook her head, disappointed. "If you don't trust him, then trust me. He needs work, and we need him, especially now that Eli could be leaving at a moment's notice. If Jesse screws up, then it's on me. Just try to make an effort, please?" She reached up and squeezed his shoulder when he didn't respond. "Please, Caleb? Can I count on you?"

"You're a soft touch." He sighed in defeat, but a muscle began to twitch along Caleb's jaw line. Finally relenting, he nodded. "Okay. For you, all right. I'll lay off. But only for you."

"Thank you." She offered him a radiant, grateful smile. "Could you give Doris a hand at the grill? The dogs and kids are distracting her, and I don't want my burger burned."

Caleb shot one more narrow-eyed glare at Jesse, who was crossing the yard toward them. Georgia Ann had already flittered off to watch Jerry running with the football tucked firmly under his arm.

"Caleb," she hissed the warning beneath her breath when her friend didn't budge.

Shaking his head, heaving another beleaguered sigh, Caleb stalked away. Charlie watched him go with a frown tugging at her brows. She ground her teeth.

What is his problem?

Usually the very epitome of calm and collected, Caleb had never behaved this way before. She was at a complete loss. Couldn't he see Jesse was no threat to the pub?

"Hi."

Turning at the sound of Jesse's voice, Charlie faced

him, her troubles with Caleb forgotten.

"Hi, yourself." Fiddling with the bottom button on her vest, Charlie tried to look nonchalant. She had the uncomfortable feeling she looked more like a blushing teenager with stars in her eyes. "I wasn't sure you'd come."

He smelled of soap and aftershave. His still-damp hair curled around the edges. His jaw was smooth, and his tanned skin held that slightly pink, freshly-scrubbed look. The collar of a white T-shirt peeked from beneath his blue plaid button-down. His pale jeans were worn and faded, and he had on his ever present thick-soled black boots.

"It's probably not a good idea, but I'm here anyway," he said.

She kicked at a clump of leaves with the toe of her tennis shoes. "Don't be ridiculous. You belong here, same as the rest." Then, a little more softly, as if testing the waters, she added, "I'm glad you came."

His lips curled up on a hint of a smile, and he glanced away. Jesse nodded toward the game unfolding by the river. "Tackle?"

"It was supposed to be touch football." She, too, looked over, and then smiled ruefully as the group of men got all tangled up and went down like a stack of bricks. "As you can see, it's devolved into tackle. It usually does. Eli thinks he's playing pro level."

Jesse grunted, his gaze on the men wrestling on the ground like a pile of little kids.

Okay, so they were going to avoid talking about the kiss, both of them. Again. She didn't know how to feel about that. Relieved? Disappointed?

Irritated?

She glanced up at him, right on the verge of speaking. She didn't exactly know what she'd been about to say, something about kissing, surely? After all, they couldn't keep going at each other behind the pub like horny teenagers every time they happened to be out there alone together. And though it might prove uncomfortable, they needed to address the issue like grownups.

But she caught him staring at her mouth. And he had that look in his eye again. That look that made her breath catch and tension knot deep in the pit of her belly. She reflexively moistened her bottom lip and caught it between her teeth.

His eyes narrowed, and he took half a step closer, his gaze smoldering now.

The children came running between them, one of them holding the tug rope aloft in one hand, giggling and whooping. The dogs were in hot pursuit, barking up a storm.

Holy crap!

He would have kissed her again. Right here. Right now. Right in front of everyone.

I would have let him. Right in front of everyone.

Wow.

And there was her answer. The one she'd been trying to puzzle out without even realizing it. Did she want a relationship with him? A serious relationship?

A *public* relationship?

Asked and answered.

She just wasn't sure where *he* stood on the subject.

Clearing her throat, Charlie searched for a safer topic. "Got your costume ready?"

He raised both eyebrows. "Costume?"

"For next weekend? You know? Halloween?"

"We're supposed to wear a costume?"

"It's a tradition at the pub. Employees and customers alike, we all dress up." Tucking her hands in her vest pockets, she tilted her head, studying him as if giving the matter deliberate consideration. "I could see you as a pirate." Narrowing her eyes, she tilted her head. "Or a gangster. You'd make a great Capone."

"You see me as a bad guy, huh?" He chuckled, but his humor was short-lived. "I thought Caleb was the only one who thought that."

"No, you're definitely not a bad guy. At least, not in my book." She was surprised when color filled his cheeks. He glanced away. "What is it with you two anyway? You and Caleb?"

Jesse shrugged as if Caleb's attitude didn't bother him. But his narrow-eyed gaze cut to her, and he had a strange, considering expression on his face. "Maybe he feels threatened."

"I don't know why that would be." She frowned up at him, genuinely puzzled. From the beginning of Jesse's employment, she'd told Caleb that Jesse would only be with them temporarily. Why would he feel his job might be in danger? Besides being an invaluable employee, Caleb was one of her best friends. Surely, he knew she'd never dismiss him so casually?

"That's just ridiculous," she reiterated softly, shaking her head, her gaze following Caleb as he laughed at something Doris said. Positive she could figure out a way to reassure Caleb his position was not in jeopardy, she set the matter aside. Charlie turned a bright smile Jesse's way. "Anyway, back to the costume choice. Halloween is all about dressing up, you know? Spooky decorations. Gruesome treats. Getting scared. Adrenaline rushes."

"I haven't seen any costume shops in Badger Creek, and I must have misplaced my prison jumpsuit somewhere." He shrugged.

"I bet," she chuckled. "Not to worry. We have a trunk full of costumes at the pub. That way no one has to go without. We might not have any prison orange for you, but I'm pretty sure you can find something else just as exciting in there."

"What are you going as?"

Determined not to act the part of a school girl with a crush, she flippantly replied, "You'll just have to wait and see."

"Food's done," Doris shouted.

Charlie looked over. Caleb was juggling a huge platter of barbecued chicken and another one filled with burgers and hot dogs as he made his way to the table designated for the buffet. Doris's Golden Retrievers danced around Caleb's feet, focused solely on an entirely new game of keep away.

"Oh, man, we better go help Caleb before Buddy and Bear get it all," she said, grabbing Jesse's hand and tugging him into the thick of the chaos.

Chapter Thirteen

Jesse finished the last bite of his apple pie and set his fork on the side of his plate. All around, voices and laughter filled the air. Despite his earlier apprehension, he'd thoroughly enjoyed himself. The food had been terrific, the company even better. Everyone had gone out of their way to make him feel welcome.

Well, everyone with the exception of Caleb. Caleb had avoided him like the plague…when he wasn't glaring holes through Jesse's hide. Which was nothing new.

Caleb needed an attitude adjustment.

Jesse and Eli were in the middle of a lively discussion over hopefuls for the next Super Bowl when Charlie slipped back into her seat beside him, distracting him. She'd been doing that a lot this afternoon, distracting him.

Oh, who was he trying to fool?

She'd been distracting him ever since he'd walked into the pub that first day. The hell of it was, the longer he stuck around, the less it bothered him.

"There you go." Reaching over, her shoulder brushing his, she set an ice cold can of soda in front of him. Then she settled back and popped the top of her own.

"Thanks," he murmured.

God, she smelled good. Crowded around the table

as they were, hip to hip, shoulder to shoulder, had been a special kind of Heaven and Hell all rolled into one. If it weren't for all the other people around, he would have caved hours ago and dragged her across his lap. Shown her exactly what all that lip chewing and laughing of hers did to him. As it was, all he could do was sit there in frustrated silence and take it.

Kendra, sitting across the table from them, said something—Jesse didn't catch what, he'd been too busy imagining what he'd do with Charlie when—*if*—*if* he got her back in his arms again—and Charlie burst out laughing. It must have been about Eli, because the bartender's face flamed bright red.

"I've said it before, and I'll say it again," Doris drawled from his other side, drawing his attention. "That boy is slow as molasses in January when it comes to women."

Jesse followed Doris's nod at the next table over.

"It's just plain painful to watch," Doris added, tsking as she shook her head. Georgia Ann all but sprawled across the table in front of Jerry, contorting herself in a transparent bid to get his attention. Rather than gawking at the goods on display for his personal consumption—as any other man in his right mind would do—Jerry was solely focused on balancing the football on the tip of his finger and spinning it.

"Maybe somebody ought to clue him in," Jesse said. His gaze flickered to Caleb, and he frowned. The assistant manager was watching Charlie. Again. Was Jesse the only one seeing this?

"Jerry isn't the only one that needs clueing in," he muttered beneath his breath and gritted his teeth.

All afternoon it had been like this. Caleb and his

damned puppy dog eyes. It was obvious the guy had it bad. A small part of Jesse—a very stingy, miniscule part—almost felt sorry for the guy.

But a bigger part of Jesse just wanted to punch the prick's teeth down his throat. Charlie wasn't some grand prize at the bottom of a cereal box or the monster stuffed bear at a carnival game.

"Maybe somebody should," Doris said softly, for Jesse's ears alone. He darted a look at her and blinked, surprised to realize she, too, was watching Caleb. But then shrewd gray eyes turned Jesse's way and narrowed pointedly. "Then again, seems like a lot of men around here need clueing in. Just because something makes sense doesn't mean it's a good fit."

Jesse stared at Doris, unsure of how to respond as she slowly lifted a can of soda to her lips and took a long drink, her gaze holding steady on his. She set the can down and her head tilted to the side. All of a sudden, Jesse knew what a bug beneath a microscope might feel like.

"Sometimes things that don't make a lick of sense at first end up clicking together like pieces of a puzzle," she added with a slow, calculating smile edging the corners of her mouth upward.

Jesse blinked as Doris's gaze slid from him to Charlie and back again. His lips parted, but he didn't utter a sound.

Had Doris just…

Is she clueing me *in?*

Nonplussed, he closed his mouth so he didn't look like an idiot sitting there with it hanging open. Jesse leaned back and let his gaze wander over the faces around him, and the sense of…of community hit him.

He'd experienced it before, much as he'd tried to ignore it. But it was there all the same, and it wasn't going away. He could belong here, with these people.

If he let himself.

But Doris's words had kindled something else in him as well. Or, maybe more accurately, they'd put the spotlight square on something Charlie had kindled. Charlie and all these damned emotions churning around in his gut.

What if Doris was right? On paper, Caleb made perfect sense for Charlie. He was a long-time resident of Badger Creek, somebody she'd known for years. He was already part of her business, and part of her life. He was a nice guy—well, nice to everybody but Jesse. He was good-looking, if you liked that sort. Smart, charming, dark good looks. And he treated Charlie with respect and affection.

And the more Jesse thought of Caleb and Charlie together, the more Jesse wanted to jump over the table and strangle the guy.

But then he considered the rest of Doris's sage advice. He'd also been watching Charlie when Caleb was around. Charlie treated Caleb the same as she treated Georgia Ann or Eli. The same as she treated Doris. As far as Charlie was concerned, Caleb was a friend, nothing more, nothing less. That thought eased the jealous violence simmering in his veins.

Caleb might be perfect in some ways, but he wasn't a perfect fit. Not for Charlie.

But was Jesse any better for her? He was a complete stranger. Well, sort of, if you took out the fact that he'd come this close to having sex with her. He'd walked away from a career he'd once thought he'd have till the day he died and a deeper sense of justice by which he'd defined himself. He'd turned his back on everyone he'd ever cared about to chase after a sick obsession, all to assuage his own guilt, ease his grief and seek vengeance.

And then there'd been Molly. The way he'd let her down…

Crossing his arms over his chest, he frowned. How could he even think that *he* might be a better fit for Charlie?

He, who hadn't held a steady job since he'd left the MPD over a year ago? The guy that had let his own girlfriend die at the hands of a vicious monster? All because he hadn't been smart enough to figure out the clues and stop the madman before it was too late? He'd run away from the pitying looks and well-meaning friends. Run away from life.

Sitting here, surrounded by people who so obviously cared deeply about each other, Jesse could admit now—at least to himself—that he'd had an unhealthy fixation over finding Molly's murder. Still had it, if he were being totally honest. He'd been focused on revenge, hung up on death and retribution. There was more to life than that. The proof was all around him.

He was damaged goods, and Charlie didn't need that in her life.

But when he held her in his arms? He was whole again. She made him *feel* again. Hope. Anticipation. Like he had a future. A real one, not just this empty, sorry excuse for an existence.

And the chemistry between them was scorching. Hotter than anything he'd ever experienced. Not even—

God forgive him for thinking it—but not even with Molly.

Why not me?

That insidious thought kept creeping up on him, no doubt encouraged by Doris's pointed "clueing in."

Why not me?

Charlie made him feel other things too. Emotions he hadn't experienced in so long. Protective drives. Possessive desires. Contentment and happiness. Aggravation and intrigue. Hell, she made him half-crazed with lust most of the time. She made him *want* to look forward, not back at a past he couldn't change.

She made him feel alive.

She made him *feel*, period.

And then, maybe just as important, were the things she *didn't* make him feel. When he was with her, when he held her in his arms, he *didn't* feel like he was suffocating. He wasn't paralyzed with guilt. He didn't feel dirty, like he was betraying Molly's memory, cheating on her.

Letting her go, maybe. But not cheating on her.

But the monster that had murdered Molly was still out there. Still hunting and killing and...*playing*. Serial killers aside, so many other bad things could happen out there. How was Jesse to protect Charlie from all the things that went bump in the night? He didn't have a badge anymore. And they'd taken his gun too, put him on administrative leave because he'd become too unpredictable. Suicidal, they'd feared. A danger to himself and those around him, they'd accused.

Was he still a danger to himself? A danger to others?

And what happened when the Chess Master

surfaced again? It was just a matter of time. A guy like that didn't just quit cold turkey. The only thing that would stop him would be prison bars...or the Chess Master's own death. Could Jesse give up the hunt at last? Or would he, someday soon, walk away from Charlie in order to seek vengeance for a woman who was dead and cold in the ground?

As Jesse sat there, with noise and laughter flowing all around him, he glanced to the animated woman at his side. Something tightened inside him, seizing up until he could barely breathe.

He had a decision to make. And now was the time to face it.

He could continue in this state of limbo indefinitely, one foot in the grave with Molly, and the other set on the path of his own destruction.

Or he could choose to live. Maybe even build a life he could be proud of again. With a woman who was vibrant and full of life and love. Charlie must have realized he was staring at her. She angled a questioning smile at him, but before she could speak, someone down the table called her name, drawing her attention.

Jesse had let the Chess Master rule his life for far too long. First, while he'd obsessed over stopping the animal before he could claim another victim. Then, after he'd killed Molly. Jesse had lived for nothing more than to bring the Chess Master down.

And, in doing so, he'd let the Chess Master own him. Every time he'd drawn back from people he'd once held dear. His brother, Billy. Demarco. Even Molly's sister, Kelly. Every time he'd hopped on his bike and put another town in his taillights.

But that was over.

Here and now, that was over. He refused to let the Chess Master have power over him anymore.

Why did he have to run again? Why couldn't he put it all behind him and start over? Let SSA Anderson and her crew hunt that bastard down and bring him to justice. Let the Feds do their job. Didn't Jesse deserve another shot? Another chance to be happy?

Why not *me?*

"Hey," Charlie whispered, leaning close enough that the scent of her shampoo teased him. Her shoulder bumped his. "Earth to Jesse."

"Huh?" He blinked and made an effort to smooth his features. "What?"

"You keep scowling at Jerry like that, and pretty soon Georgia Ann is going to take issue with you." Angling her body toward him, leaning close, she considered him with a concerned frown. Beneath the table, Charlie gently, tentatively touched his knee. He knew she meant the contact in a purely nonsexual way. But that wasn't how his body was taking it.

"What's up? One minute you were laughing and joking, the next you're looking like you want to choke somebody. Where'd you go?"

He didn't give himself time to over-think it, or time to talk himself out of it. Instead, beneath the table, he reached down and slipped his hand along hers, palm to palm, lacing his fingers through hers.

Her eyes widened in surprise before dipping to their joined hands.

"Sorry. My mind wandered a bit," he offered. When her frown deepened and her lips parted on a half-formed question, he smiled and shook his head. "Not important anymore. I'm here now."

He lifted their joined hands above the table and brushed a kiss across her knuckles. Then, with a deliberate show of possession, he placed their clasped hands in his lap, forcing her to sidle a little closer and lean into him. It seemed perfectly natural to have her there, just like that.

Charlie blinked up at him, questions rife in her eyes, her lips slowly curving upward. A feather would probably have knocked her over. Judging by the sudden silence that fell over their table, he'd shocked a few others as well.

Turning back, he made a disparaging remark to Eli about his team. The bartender, grinning ear to ear as his gaze darted between Jesse and Charlie, crowed, "Five bucks says your team won't even make it to the playoffs."

"Five," Jesse sputtered, half distracted by the weight of Charlie settling her head against his shoulder. A wide grin split his face. He was feeling lucky. Awfully lucky. "Make it twenty, and you're on."

Slowly conversation resumed, though he was aware of sly glances being cast their way. Turning to Doris, Jesse arched an eyebrow and smirked.

Some people took "clueing in" very well, thank you very much.

Doris reached up behind him and gave his shoulder a little squeeze and pat, nodding obvious approval. Jesse was content, relaxed as he hadn't been in longer than he cared to consider. Not even the thunderous scowl on Caleb's face could dampen his spirits.

****

Charlie snapped the lid onto a plastic container filled with macaroni salad, and passed it off to Doris with a dreamy smile. "That's the last of it. Did you send some of that pie with Kendra?"

"Sure did. And some chicken and a big bowl of calico beans too."

"Good." Charlie tucked her hands deep into her vest pockets, and rocked back on her heels, surveying her vacated yard. The afternoon's golden glow had already started to fade, and the air had turned chilly.

Giddy despite her resolve to act like a mature adult, Charlie waved as Jerry backed Georgia Ann's little car from the lane. A beaming Georgia Ann waved back from the passenger seat.

"You sure you don't want me to stick around and finish cleaning up?" Doris asked.

"Hmm? Oh, no, you go on home. Jesse's going to give me a hand with the last of it. I'll take him back to his apartment later. Jerry brought my vehicle back."

"Oh? Then I suppose you have all the help you need." The smile on Doris's face was a little too knowing as she glanced around the empty yard. Heat rushed into her cheeks. "Speaking of, where is that handsome boy?"

"He went inside to wash up after he got rid of the dead squirrel Bear dumped in his lap. Did you get enough leftovers?"

"Oh, heavens yes," Doris assured her, chuckling. "Honey, nobody went home empty handed, and ain't none of us gonna have to cook for a week."

A frown tugged at Charlie's brow. "Caleb was pretty grouchy when he left. Actually, he was kind of grumpy all day. Or was it just me?"

"Charlie, honey, don't you worry about Caleb." Doris narrowed her eyes, looking serious all of a sudden. "He's a big boy, and one that's been chasing a dream that was never going to happen for far too long. He just got his eyes opened today is all. Best thing that could've happened to him, if you ask me, even if he wouldn't agree right now. He'll come around. Just give the boy time."

Charlie's frown deepened. What was Doris talking about? What dream? Why hadn't he talked to her about whatever it was that was bothering him?

"Maybe I should call him," she murmured, staring down the now empty gravel road.

Doris shook her head. "No. That'd be the worst thing you could do."

"But—"

"Now you trust me on this. Let him deal with this on his own. If you go calling him, it's only going to make things worse for him."

"Worse? How?" Confused, she turned to the older woman who'd been, for all intents and purposes, a mother to her. "Doris, I don't know what's—"

"Honey," Doris said in that no-nonsense tone she'd used while Charlie was growing up, gentle but firm. She cupped Charlie's cheeks and peered into her eyes. "Trust me on this. Promise me you won't call him."

Charlie pressed her lips together. She scowled, but eventually nodded agreement. "Oh, all right. I promise. But you're going to explain what this is all about."

"I will. I will. Just not today. Walk with me." Releasing her, Doris hefted a stack of odd shaped plastic containers onto her generous hip. Charlie fell into step beside her as they walked toward Doris's old station wagon.

"Now that young man in the house is another

matter."

"Doris!" Ducking her head, Charlie shot a swift glance toward the window to make sure Jesse hadn't overheard. Scuffing the toe of her shoe in the leaves, Charlie stood by the open car door as Doris leaned into the back seat to situate the leftovers on the floor.

Straightening, the older woman turned to her and grinned. "I've been nagging on you for years. This time I'm just gonna step back and let nature take over."

Charlie blinked up at Doris. She'd never, not in all the many years she'd known Doris, *never* known her not to meddle when she believed something was important.

Doris shook her head and slipped an arm around her shoulders. "Trust me, baby, some things you can't fight. Nor should you. Just go with it."

"Well, you're just brimming with all sorts of cryptic comments today, aren't you?" Annoyed, Charlie wrapped her arm around Doris's waist.

Doris simply smiled.

Knowing Doris had no intention on elaborating further, Charlie asked, "I think everybody had a good time, don't you?"

"Everybody had a ball. You did good, honey. Real good." Doris squeezed her shoulder. "Your daddy would be proud."

"Thanks." Pleased with the praise, she smiled. "I'll have to call him later and tell him how things went."

"Tomorrow," Doris said glancing over as the back-screen door slapped closed. A moment later, Jesse came strolling around the side of the cabin. "You go on and enjoy the rest of the night, kiddo. I'm gonna hit the road." She gave Charlie one more squeeze, pecked a kiss to the side of her forehead, and released her to climb into the driver's seat.

"Drive careful," Charlie called, stepping back from the car. She stood there, arms crossed against the chill, watching as Doris drove away.

Turning toward the back yard, Charlie paused. Jesse was standing there, hands deep in his pockets, watching her, his expression far too serious.

"Well, that's the last of them." Smiling, she closed the distance. At the last moment, suddenly nervous, she skirted him and returned to the back yard where she picked up a small cooler. Jesse followed her in silence. "Give me a few more minutes to finish putting the last of this away, and I'll take you back to town."

"No rush. Here, I got this." He gathered the remaining remnants of the party and turned to follow her inside, leaving nothing but barren picnic tables in their wake.

She held the door for him, inwardly cursing because things were suddenly awkward between them. "Jerry and Eli will come out tomorrow to pick up the rest of the tables. It's getting too dark now."

She carried the small cooler inside and placed it on the counter. Charlie positioned the cooler's nozzle above the sink and flipped the plug on the bottom so the melted ice inside could drain. Turning back to Jesse, she motioned toward the island. "You can put those things here."

"It turned cold out there really fast tonight," he said letting the load in his arms spill onto the counter.

"Yeah, I'm actually kind of surprised we don't have snow yet."

"Snow." He gave a rueful grunt. "That was

something I hadn't really considered. Snow and a motorcycle. I should know better. Guess I wasn't thinking too far ahead when I sold the car last spring."

She couldn't help but address the elephant in the room. Nor could she hide the dismay in her voice. "I suppose you'll be leaving soon?"

Jesse watched her now, a guarded expression on his face. "You know, I've been meaning to talk to you about the apartment."

Here it comes.

She picked at one of the decorations Jesse had just dropped onto the island and focused on it instead of his face. Disappointment settled like a cold, slimy rock in the pit of her stomach. He was going to tell her he was leaving.

She'd known this conversation was coming. Why was it hitting her so hard?

"You don't have anybody else lined up for the apartment yet, do you?"

Frowning, she tilted her head to look at him again. "No?"

"Good. I'm thinking, with winter coming, it might be a good idea to settle in for a while, you know? That whole motorcycles and snow thing? I'd like to rent the place…indefinitely. If that works for you? And stay on at the pub, of course."

She sucked in a breath at the sharp spear of pleasure his words had brought. She wanted to punch a fist in the air like a triumphant athlete. She wanted to dance around the room, shaking her hips and sing. She wanted to fall onto the floor and giggle. And then she realized he was still staring at her, waiting for a response.

Oh, God, Charlie, wipe that stupid grin off your face.

"Yes. I mean, the place is all yours. For as long as you want. And so is the job." And now she was babbling.

Jesse smiled that slow melt-Charlie-where-she-stands smile of his, and he let his gaze wander down the length of her, leaving a trail of scorched, needy flesh in his wake. By the time his stare met hers again, something hot and dangerous smoldered in the depths of his clear blue eyes.

"Good. Something tells me leaving would have been a lot harder this time around anyway."

She couldn't help it. She stood there staring at him, her lips parted, unable to make a sound. Like a complete and utter moron.

Grinning, Jesse swept that sinfully erotic gaze over her one more time. Then he turned his attention to his surroundings as he wandered from the kitchen, cool as you please. "Nice place. I can see why you like it so much."

"Uh-huh." Shaking herself from her stupor, she blinked. *Get a grip!* "Thanks, I like it." On autopilot, she closed the kitchen window, flipped the light off, and followed him into the rapidly dimming living room.

She made short work of closing the rest of the windows in the living room against the chill. But when she reached for the lamp on the end table, he nodded toward the fireplace. "Wait. Does it work?"

"It does."

She was flustered. Him. Her. Alone in a cozy cabin. With a fire blazing in the fireplace. No one around for miles. No distractions this time.

It didn't take a roadmap to see where this was heading. She met his steady gaze, and made up her mind. She wanted this to happen. Right here. Right now. With him. Whatever tomorrow brought. She'd have this.

The tension in the room amped up another notch.

His deep voice, when he spoke at last, sent shivers racing through her. "Would you like to start the fire, or should I?"

Chapter Fourteen

A swarm of butterflies took flight in the pit of Charlie's stomach. She could barely breathe as Jesse knelt in front of the fireplace and took a few logs from the basket. After carefully arranging the kindling, Jesse drew a long match from the holder and patiently coaxed the fire until he had a cozy blaze going.

Turning, forearm braced on his knee, Jesse looked up at her. His expression as hot and just as dangerous as the flames crackling behind him. Slowly, he got to his feet. Jesse dominated the room, and she couldn't look away.

"Um," she cleared her throat. "I think I still have some wine left. Would you like a glass?"

"No, thanks. I'd rather have a clear head right now." His lips curled up at the edges. He crossed to the sofa and took a seat, stretching his arm along the back.

"Okay." Charlie shifted from one foot to the other, fingers fidgeting with the bottom button on her vest.

His gaze dipped to her nervous digits, and his smile grew. "Come over here."

She eyed the sofa beside him, and forced a swallow. Never before had the prospect of being with someone filled her with such nervous excitement. She recognized that look in his eyes, knew what it meant, what he wanted.

She stood at a crossroads. The point of no return.

No take backs and no changing her mind.

No protecting her heart.

Then again, if she were being truly honest, her heart had already crossed that line long before her mind had even realized she was in the race.

Telling herself to calm down before she made a complete fool of herself, she closed the distance and eased onto the cushion, careful to leave a modest amount of space between them. Not so much that he would think she wasn't interested. But just enough that it wouldn't make her look desperate.

She hoped.

Gah! She was over-thinking again.

Stealing a peek, she studied his profile. She'd give just about anything to know what he was thinking right now. Without taking his gaze from the fire, without uttering a sound, he shifted. Natural as you please, Jesse slipped his arm around her, drawing her snug against his side.

Surprised and off balance, Charlie dropped her hand to his thigh to balance herself. Before she could recover and draw it back, he captured her hand and laced his fingers through hers, keeping it anchored right where it was. On his hard thigh. She couldn't seem to get beyond that focal point, their joined hands.

And his thigh.

Great! She'd turned into one big raging hormone. Next, she'd be drooling. Tearing her gaze from jean clad muscles, Charlie stared at the fire.

They spent the next several minutes in silence. Jesse watched the fire, casually smoothing one hand up and down the side of her arm. She tried to relax, desperately tried, but her gaze kept bouncing between the fire and their joined hands. Ever so slowly, he angled the hand holding hers, and he began tracing tiny patterns with his thumb on her palm. An uncontrollable shiver coursed through her.

Every muscle in her lower belly slowly tightened. Relax? She didn't even know what that word meant anymore.

"So, you host these employee appreciation dinners every year?"

She'd been so lost in the moment, every bit of her attention focused on that slightly rough thumb and the tingling sensation it invoked, that she jumped at the rumble of his voice. And still his left hand kept stroking over her arm, soft and gentle, as one might do to calm a skittish animal.

Embarrassed to realize how tense she was, hypnotized by his touch—one of his hand soothing her, cocooning her in a bubble of intimacy, the other pinpointing sensation into tiny, erotic caresses—Charlie forced herself to focus on the conversation.

"Yep."

Wow, there was an intelligent response.

"That's really nice. A lot of places wouldn't do something like that. You know, most employers just hand out a voucher for a free turkey or something at Christmas and call it good."

"We're a family business. We want our people to feel appreciated because they *are* appreciated." Tearing her gaze from his thumb, she blinked up at Jesse, feeling dazed. As if all the air had been sucked out of the room, leaving her lightheaded. Why was it so hard to think, so hard to form coherent words? "The pub wouldn't be what it is without them."

"Don't kid yourself. The pub wouldn't be what it is without *you*."

Was that admiration in his gaze? He was looking so serious now. Entirely *too* serious. Heat flooded her cheeks.

"You are an amazing woman, Charlie."

He released her hand and reached up to capture a lock of her hair. His fingers combed through her ponytail, drew it over her shoulder, and he rubbed the strands between his fingertips. Then he skated those same, slightly callused fingertips from her temple to her chin before cupping her cheek.

It was dark in the room now but for the warm glow of the fire. When his crystal blue eyes met hers, Charlie caught her breath. She'd never, never had anyone look at her like that before. As if he couldn't stand another moment without touching her. Like he'd cease to exist if he couldn't kiss her…right that very second.

"Charlie," he whispered her name, his voice hoarse with need. "I want you so much."

He shook his head slightly as his gaze searched hers, as if he couldn't believe what was happening between them, the suddenness of it, the sheer power of the attraction between them. Then again, maybe she was projecting.

She could barely form a coherent sound. Just a murmur of assent, really. But his lips were on hers so fast her head spun. His hand tunneled into her hair, cupping the back of her head, holding her for his sensual onslaught. His mouth was hot, branding her to her soul.

Charlie laid her hand flat against his chest. His heart beat a wild tempo against her palm. That fast beat was for her, was *because* of her. Entranced, she reached up, easing her arm around his neck, and pulled him closer.

She didn't know how long they sat there like that, mouths mated, tongues rolling against each other, tangling. It could have been minutes, or hours. Time spun out as she lost herself in him.

But then it wasn't enough. Itchy need took over. She wanted, more than anything, to feel his bare skin on hers. To feel his weight pressing down upon her.

She trailed her fingers over his chest, eagerly flipping buttons open. Without breaking the kiss, he eased away from her long enough to strip off his plaid shirt.

But that wasn't good enough either. His T-shirt hindered her, hugging all those rippling muscles, yet impeding her from stroking the smoothness of his flesh. Tugging at the hem, she pulled the soft material upward until she'd managed to bare his midsection. Charlie flattened her hand on the ridges of his abdomen, and she let her fingers trace, knead and stroke. His skin was smooth, just as she'd imagined, taut and oh so hot. The muscles beneath her fingertips flexed as he moved, hard as steel.

Twisting, leaning away from the sofa, lips still locked on hers in greedy demand, he pulled the shirt up, tearing his lips from hers for only a split second, only long enough to whip the shirt over his head and toss it aside. And then his mouth was back on hers, even more demanding than before.

Jesse leaned back, drawing her with him by nothing more than the power of his kiss. He grasped her hips with both hands, guiding her up and over until she straddled his lap.

Kissing him was addictive. She couldn't stop, couldn't get enough. Not as he tugged the scarf from around her neck. Not as he worked the buttons on her vest open and dragged it from her body. Not as he wrestled her long-sleeve mock-neck shirt up until it was bunched around her neck.

He tore his mouth from hers again and, the same way he'd discarded his own shirt, he whipped hers over her head and tossed it. This time, though, instead of sealing his mouth back over hers in urgent demand, he leaned back and studied her through hooded eyes, as if committing to memory every single detail.

Jesse's focus lingered on the lavender lace encasing her breasts. His expression was almost frightening in its intensity. A muscle along his jaw twitched. His nostrils flared and his muscular chest lifted as he dragged in a deep, deep breath. His chest came so close—but not quite close enough—to brushing her breasts.

It was sweet, delicious torture. She murmured his name. That small sound seemed to shatter his restraint. On a groan, he surged forward and wrapped both arms around her.

Without any warning, Jesse suddenly stood up with Charlie wrapped tight in his embrace, startling a gasp from her. He clutched her thighs urging them higher around his waist, until she locked her ankles at the small of his back. His hands cruised along her jean clad legs until they cupped her bottom. Then Jesse carried her to the deep pile rug in front of the fireplace. With his steady gaze holding hers, he eased down to one knee, before slowly lowering them both to the soft rug.

His hot lips sought the hollow at the base of her throat, and his deft tongue delved. He nipped his way along her collarbone as his nimble fingers freed her from her bra. And when his hand covered her breast, callused fingertips to sensitive flesh, Charlie moaned.

The ridge of his erection strained against the cradle of her thighs, and he pushed his hips into her, rubbing. Fire erupted in her core. Charlie let her legs fall to the sides, planted her heels in the thick rug, and used the leverage to arch her hips into him for better contact.

Jesse groaned and rubbed against her, harder now. His breath ragged against her skin as he trailed kisses across her chest, and his lips sealed over her nipple. The things he did with his mouth then…

Oh, God.

Her eyes all but rolled back in her head.

The hot swirl of his tongue lapped at her, spearing sharp sensations through her, drenching her in pleasure so sharp and so pure that when his teeth scraped over her pebbled nipple, she arched her back and cried out. Charlie tunneled both hands into his hair as Jesse licked at her breast, soothing the sting.

He pushed his free hand down the outside of her left thigh, and he hooked it behind her knee, tugging it up and around his hip. The weight of him, his hips pressing against her at this angle was delicious torture. His hand kept moving, trailing down her calf until he swept off her shoe. Shifting his mouth to the other breast, he eased his weight onto his left elbow and smoothed his free hand down her right thigh now. Lifting it as he had the other, hooking her knee over his hip and freeing her of her last shoe.

Then, centering his weight, he eased up over her,

wedging his hips tighter into the cradle of her thighs, and he captured her lips once more. Jesse pushed his erection along her core, their jeans a nerve-racking barrier between them. Charlie moaned into his kiss, trembling beneath him as her body ached and wept for relief. She moved her legs restlessly, squeezing his hips, digging her heels into the backs of his thighs as he pumped his hips in a slow rhythmic mimicry of sex. Heat raged low in her belly, growing and churning until it consumed her.

"Jesse! Oh, God, please," she gasped, pleading for something, anything to ease the ache he'd ruthlessly kindled to life.

His lips claimed hers again, his tongue sinking into her mouth, thrusting faster now, more urgent, another sensual teasing of what was to come. His bare chest pressed against hers as his lower body moved, the friction and pressure on her naked breasts and shielded feminine core drove her out of her mind.

As his lips cruised across her cheek, and he nipped at her earlobe, Charlie shoved her hands over his broad shoulders. Reaching down his back, she clutched at him, urging him closer, digging her fingertips into his rippling muscles. Her hips rose to meet each stroke, begging for more.

Much more like this, and she wouldn't even need to get fully naked before she reached climax.

"Jesse," she begged, whimpering now as desire took on a painful, sharp edge.

He groaned into her ear, the sweetest, most erotic sound she'd ever heard.

"Say my name again," he growled. "Say it again, just like that."

His name had no more than slipped from her lips, a tortured plea, and he was suddenly gone, jerking himself up and away from her. Charlie cried out in confusion as cool air swept over her.

But then he unbuttoned her jeans and began dragging and tugging them down her hips with crazed urgency. With her blood singing in her veins, she didn't wait for an invitation to help. They moved together in a tangle of arms and legs, knees and elbows as they worked first on her jeans, and then on his. They rolled on the carpet, wrestling his boots and his boxers off.

Charlie sucked in a sharp breath at the first sight of him, fully aroused, straining, pulsing, begging for her touch, the very tip of his erection moist with his body's demands. But before she could reach for him, he pulled her up onto her knees and moved behind her. His thighs on either side of her, Jesse pressed up against her back. He pulled her hair to the side, over one shoulder, and buried his face against the side of her neck as he wrapped her tight in his arms, caging her for a moment as if he feared she might slip from his grasp.

His big body shuddered around her, and he whispered her name against her sensitive skin. Gliding his hands over the curve of her hips and across her stomach, angling for her breasts, Jesse kissed his way along her shoulder and up the side of her neck.

Charlie turned her face to him, and he captured her lips. Jesse cupped her breasts fully in his hands, his erection pressed urgently against her bottom, rubbing, pulsing. The thin barrier of her panties was the only thing left between them. And it was driving her crazy. The feel of his hands on her, of his body caging hers, of his mouth mastering hers was overwhelming and sinfully decadent.

Still kneading one breast, rolling her nipple between his fingers, tweaking it, Jesse slowly eased his other hand down over her stomach, trailing the tips of his fingers along the top edge of her lace panties.

Using just the tip of one finger, he traced the pattern of the lace, over and over, every swirl, every scallop, every edge, every dip. So. Slowly. Her hips arched into his hand, and she whimpered. Charlie shivered as her muscles clenched deep inside. She had no control over her body now. She was completely at his mercy. His captive. His to command.

He released her breast, reaching across her body to capture the other breast. And all the while that fingertip kept moving, tracing slow, whisper light, erotic patterns over the lace between her legs.

And then, finally, his fingers dipped inside the lace, gently tracing over slick, aching flesh. Unhurried, deliberate strokes. Charlie shuddered, gasping for air. She was coming apart at the seams. Melting in his arms. A hairsbreadth away from exploding with pleasure.

Her nails scored his hard thighs as she rocked against his hand. Silently urging him to move faster, push deeper. But he refused to cooperate, holding back what she most desperately needed. Gasping, moaning his name aloud, Charlie let her head fall back against his broad, strong shoulder. It seemed to be what he'd been waiting for, her complete surrender to his touch. Charlie was poised on the brink of climax when Jesse withdrew his hand all together, denying her that much needed release.

Shocked, outraged, she cried out.

Jesse spun her around, jerked her up, and slammed

her against his body. All semblance of gentleness gone. Her hands flew to his shoulders, gripping, unmindful of her nails. She was strung out on desire, painfully aroused. Jesse slanted his mouth over hers, again and again, pouring fuel on an already out of control blaze. He tipped her back, bringing her down to the floor, and roughly dragged her panties off before following her down.

Charlie's head spun as he moved over her. Leaving searing kisses in his wake, he worked his way down her body. She was trapped in a world of sensory overload. Every shred of her awareness was locked on him. On what he was doing to her body.

He pushed his hands over her thighs, urging them farther apart. And then his mouth was on her, his tongue flicking, lapping, delving, and Charlie lost her mind.

She was a feral creature of desire. Her hips rocked up to meet his mouth. Her head thrashed, side to side. He slid one hand beneath her bottom, lifting her higher, angling her to his liking. And then he slipped one finger deep inside her, then another. He worked them ruthlessly as he suckled the tiny bundle of nerve at the apex of her thighs until her world exploded, and she flew into a million pieces, screaming his name.

On and on he pushed her, until she cried out, begging for him to stop.

When Jesse finally released her, Charlie collapsed back against the floor, staring up at the ceiling through half closed eyes, unable to move. But he wasn't done with her. He continued to lavish the sensitive flesh along her inner thighs with tiny nips and nibbles and butterfly kisses.

Her mind was completely blank, her body still vibrantly alive, trembling with the aftershocks of the mind-boggling orgasm he'd just given her. His lips gentle now, Jesse trailed feather kisses up over the crease of her hip, across her lower abdomen, and along her stomach. The sensation was so delicious, so decadent she moaned aloud.

The sound of fabric sliding over carpet pricked her ears. But her brain had drifted away for a moment, and she couldn't understand why she was hearing that sound.

And then the crinkle of foil broke the silence. A condom. Thank God he, at least, was coherent enough to think about protection. Heaven knew she couldn't even remember her own name right now. She glanced down between her legs to where he was kneeling. And she watched him unroll that thin bit of latex slowly over the pulsing rigid length of his penis. The whole time, every heart stopping second, his steady stare held hers. It was the most erotic thing she'd ever seen in her life.

And then, like a predator focused solely on his prey, poised to attack, Jesse crawled up her body, his deliberate progress belying the tense, reckless need etched on his face.

Gently, he eased his strong body down on top of her once more. His lips captured hers as he braced his weight on his elbows and cradled her head in his hands. His mouth moved over hers with seductive intent. The steely ridge of his erection slid languidly along the drenched cleft of her womanhood, back and forth, back and forth, swiftly bringing her receptive body back to life with every shift until her hips rocked in time with his.

Charlie clasped his wide ribcage with splayed fingers. Then she slid her palms along his sides, down, down, until she grasped his hips and silently urged him on. Lifting her knees higher, she tilted her hips, angling them in an attempt to draw him inside, deep and hard so that he might quench the burning ache he'd so deftly rekindled.

Arching his back slightly, Jesse poised the tip of his pulsing erection at her threshold, the thick head just barely inside her, and he paused, easing his lips from hers. The heat of his body seared her from head to toe. He waited until she opened her eyes. Waited until he had her complete, undivided attention. Blinking, Charlie struggled through the haze of desire until his face came into focus.

He didn't say anything. He didn't have to. His expression said it all. He wanted her to know who was taking her. He wanted her to know he was staking his claim. That she now belonged to him.

"Jesse," she whispered, both acknowledging his claim, his demand, and pleading with him to end the torment.

At the sound of his name upon her lips, he drove himself inside her in one sure, deep thrust. She watched as his eyes went cloudy and his lids slid closed. The look of exaltation on his face as he paused there, buried deep inside her, caused her heart to flutter.

And then his blue eyes slowly opened. The intense burning need in their crystal depths swept her back into the intoxicating maelstrom of his desire. He began to move, long powerful strokes, his body rocking inside hers with a confidence and driven purpose that left her breathless. Charlie lost touch with reality. The feel of him stretching her, filling her to her limits sent pleasure cascading through her system.

Desperate to get closer, she raised her legs higher, wrapping them tight around his waist, locking her ankles, squeezing. He continued to cradle her head with one hand as he alternated scorching kisses and murmurs of encouragement along the side of her throat. His free hand skated down her side, pausing here and there to caress, to touch, to explore. And all the while, he kept up a steady, powerful rhythm that drove her closer and closer toward the edge.

Charlie arched beneath him, her movements becoming frantic, as she whimpered and moaned. The tension in her body was unbearable. As if sensing her need, Jesse slid his hand beneath her. He gripped her bottom tight and tilted her even more. At the same time, his thrusts increased in intensity. Jesse rotated his hips and ground against her, pushing deep.

Incapable of containing the conflagration ripping through her for even a moment longer, Charlie shattered. She cried out, unable to muffle the sound as her body shivered and spasmed around him, clutching him tightly.

"Charlie!" He groaned, his voice hoarse, his forehead pressed to the side of her neck as his body bucked and shuddered in her arms. His orgasm pulsed over and over, prolonging her pleasure. His body had tightened around her, caging her in his steely strength as that one perfect moment held them both captive.

Charlie floated back to reality, and she slowly became aware of her body. Aware of the continued pressure where he erection still filled her. Aware of Jesse's muscular chest heaving against hers as he struggled to catch his breath. The warm masculine scent of him surrounded her, imprinting itself on her consciousness. He'd moved to brace his weight so he wouldn't crush her, but still, he held her as if he'd never let her go.

At length, he leaned up and gazed down upon her. Jesse didn't say a word at first. He stared down at her with a deep and gentle yet all consuming possessiveness. A man who'd been wandering alone for far too long; a man who'd finally found his home and would never willingly give it up again.

Dipping his head, Jesse swept her into a kiss so intimate, so tender, that her heart stuttered. His tongue moved against hers, sensuous, seductive. With heartbreaking need, and yet with such desire that her body began to respond before she fully had time to realize what he was doing, he swept her away once more. And then his hips began to move. Slow and steady, he began to slide in and out of her, still rock hard. Still wanting her even though he'd just had her.

And had her *very* well.

She followed his lead, rocking with him in an age-old rhythm. The urgency, the desperate need, was gone now. This time, as they moved together, it was a soft exploration. No longer a driven dash to the finish, but a sensual, erotic journey of soft murmurs and unhurried touches.

And when that slow burn built to a crescendo, it was no less powerful, no less stunning than the first time. Jesse was left gasping her name against her skin, while Charlie clung to him in wonder.

When they came back to earth the second time, Jesse finally moved away from her. For one moment, as the cool air touched her overheated flesh—flesh Jesse had kissed and touched and worshipped with such fierce need—Charlie was bereft.

But he only disposed of the condom, and then he returned to the sofa. After gathering up throw pillows, he quickly fashioned a nest for them on the floor, and tossed another log on the fire. Then he drew her back into his arms and covered them both with the blanket he'd pulled from the back of the couch. He cradled her to his chest as if she were the most precious thing in the world and smoothed the hair from her brow before pressing a soft kiss there.

And in that bright shiny moment, Charlie knew beyond the shadow of a doubt.

Her heart hadn't stood a chance.

Chapter Fifteen

The Chess Master yawned, arching his back to ease the stiffness. He readjusted his grip on the steering wheel and tilted his head from side to side, shrugging his shoulders.

He liked to drive, always had, though he didn't always have the opportunity. Driving gave him time alone to think. He needed information, but he didn't like to rely on anyone but himself. After all, everyone was just a piece in the game, including himself and his opponent. Pawns, Knights, Bishops, Rooks. Even the Queen was disposable.

Anticipation for the upcoming match had been growing steadily inside him until he was giddy. This would be the best game yet! But he didn't want to leave even the smallest detail to chance.

As such, he had one final call to place. Picking up the disposable phone from the seat next to him, he punched in a series of numbers, one eye on the road, then held the phone to his ear and waited.

"Yo. I don't recognize this number so don't be wastin' my time, feel me?" The gruff voice answering the phone was heavily weighted with the threat of violence.

"Santiago," the Chess Master said, unimpressed. "It's Malloy."

A long pause met his greeting. The scrape of metal

chair legs against concrete echoed through the line. And when the voice returned, it held a layer of cautious respect. "Mr. Malloy. It's, ah, a surprise to hear from you."

A wide grin split the Chess Master's face. He'd found the young thug a few years back on the mean streets of the Windy City. Rescued him, really. Santiago had met with an unfortunate accident involving a rival gang, the discharge of a certain unregistered firearm, and a dark alley. The Chess Master just happened to be in the right place at the right time. At first, he'd considered just letting the gangbanger bleed out. But then he'd become intrigued with the possibilities.

And now Santiago owed him a life debt, one the Chess Master had rarely called upon, but one that he never let the young thug forget. Seeing potential in the boy, the Chess Master had even allowed Santiago to accompany him—the one and only time he'd ever let anyone observe his game—during a checkmate. The memory made the Chess Master smile. His opponent at the time had been almost as good as Detective Reid.

Almost…but not quite.

He'd considered grooming Santiago, coaching him in the game. But, alas, it turned out the boy hadn't had the stomach for it.

Literally.

"How are you, Santiago? I trust your family's doing well?"

"My family?" Santiago asked, his voice squeaking. "They're, ah, they're doing fine."

"I'm glad to hear that, Santiago. Such a sweet little wife you have, and that pretty sister. How old is

Camille now? Seventeen? Eighteen? Why, if I had someone in my life like that lovely, innocent girl, I think I'd do just about anything to protect her. But I'm sure you'd agree, Santiago. Wouldn't you?"

An audible gulp slipped across the phone line.

"Yes," the thug rushed to assure him. "Anything."

The Chess Master paused for a moment, letting the weight of Santiago's burden weigh heavy upon his slim, pale, tattooed shoulders.

"Um, what can I do for you, Mr. Malloy?" Good. The boy's voice held a new understanding, and a willingness to help an old friend. The Chess Master fed off the fear he detected in Santiago's voice, a junky given unrestricted access to an unlimited stash. That the fear came from someone like Santiago—someone with enough brain power to hack into even the most secure of financial institutions—made it all the more addictive. Too bad the boy didn't have the ambition to go with all that brain power.

"You remember that account number I asked you to track?"

"The cop? Yeah, yeah." Eagerness flooded Santiago's gruff voice. "You want me to drain his accounts? Or better, I can register some big deposits, make it look like he's on the take." The clatter of computer keys fired off in the background.

"No, no. Nothing like that, but I do appreciate your eagerness." The Chess Master glanced up, checked his rearview mirror before turning back to the road ahead.

The keystrokes died. Caution crept into Santiago's voice once more. "What do you need me to do?"

"I just want to make sure his card hasn't registered any new transactions in a different location."

"Sure, sure," Santiago mumbled as clacking filled the airwaves once more. "Ah, looks like the same place as last time. Four consecutive transactions all in Badger Creek, Wisconsin. And, hey, a deposit now too. From an Irish Rose Pub and Grill."

Four transactions in one location. And a deposit. Hmm, had the Detective Reid decided to dig in for a while?

"Thank you, Santiago."

"Sure thing, Mr. Malloy." The hint of a hesitant pause. "Uh, anything else I can do for you?"

"No, Santiago. I think that will be all. For now." He'd carefully considered the angles before placing this call. As such, he held no reservations about making the next move. Useful as the boy had proven to be, the Chess Master could always head back to Chicago later to tie up that loose end, if need be. "Have a pleasant weekend, Santiago."

"Yeah, ah, you too, Mr. Malloy."

The Chess Master disconnected the call. Using a disinfectant wipe, he carefully polished the phone with one hand while he drove. Normally he didn't care so much about leaving a bit of himself behind. Enjoyed it, actually. After all, he took pride in his work. But it wouldn't do to tip Detective Reid off too quickly.

Wouldn't want to spoil the surprise.

Rolling down the window, he checked his mirrors and then looked down the road ahead of him. Not a car in sight. He tossed the phone out the window of the moving car and watched in the rearview as it smashed into tumbling bits and pieces, small parts exploding everywhere. He briefly turned his attention to the road map spread out on the seat beside him. He located the

191

red line he'd carefully traced out yesterday. Over the next rise in the road, he checked the road sign coming into view.

"Welcome to Wisconsin."

The Chess Master grinned. He'd been able to review Detective Reid's movements through the use of his debit card transactions. And what a trail that had been. The Chess Master certainly had to give Detective Reid points for creativity. The man had left a long, zig-zagging trail behind him. How considerate! How fun!

And some of those locations had even been close, if not in the same city, as the Chess Master had been, suggesting that, perhaps, the detective had been looking for him.

The Chess Master was flattered. He hadn't realized it at the time and, quite frankly, was a little ashamed of himself for his own remiss in not contacting the detective sooner. Well, he was answering Detective Reid's call now.

Excitement bubbled in his chest, like a bright-eyed child opening a mountain of presents on Christmas morning. He was near to bursting with excitement.

Would that precious child Janie feel like this when she woke up Christmas morning?

What a beautiful image!

Then and there, the Chess Master made up his mind. He'd find that precious little Janie when this match was over. He'd give her a whole box full of little horses like the one she'd given him. Maybe a doll or two as well. Little girls liked dolls, didn't they?

But why should they have to wait till Christmas?

A strange feeling flooded his chest. Odd enough that he found his foot easing from the accelerator for a moment. Frowning, tilting his head, he tried to sort through the strange sensation.

He'd experienced it while thinking about that fascinating child. He'd also experienced it while in her presence as well, come to think of it. He'd never been intrigued with children before. They were often unpredictable, and therefore did not make for good players in his game. Not that he thought Janie would either. Her mother, maybe. But not the toddler.

What, then, is the child's significance?

A muffled thump from behind the back seat of the sedan he'd picked up in a shopping mall parking lot distracted him. The sound of frantic movement soon followed, and then a muted scream.

Distracted from his musings, he grinned at the noise. There was his little stocking stuffer now, just waking up. His opening salvo in his upcoming match with Detective Reid. Ah, but this impatient Pawn would have to wait a bit longer, he didn't have time to play just yet. He had at least another hour of drive time ahead of him, and the eagerness to reach Detective Reid was pushing him relentlessly onward. He'd have to make sure to stop well before he grew too tired, though. He wanted to make certain he could devote the proper amount of energy to all the details.

With every move, after all, it was *always* about the details.

He'd made sure to consider his previous match with Detective Reid with great care. He'd been too straightforward. Too direct. Almost insulting Detective Reid with the simplicity of his messages. He was sorry about that, he truly was. He should have given the detective more credit. But he'd do better from here on out, starting with the Pawn in the trunk.

Oh, how he wished he could be a fly on the wall to see Detective Reid's reaction to this first move. How thrilling would that be? He chuckled, just imagining it. The dawning understanding and the horror. The panic.

Would he feel helpless? Or would his characteristic determination take over?

Oh, yes. Detective Reid would be on a veritable rollercoaster of emotion once he realized the game was back in motion. The Chess Master was sorry he would miss it. But he had to keep moving this time, had to stay on his toes.

The Chess Master was so grateful to Detective Reid for making this match so exhilarating, particularly after months upon months of stagnating, attempting to draw out a real challenger to no avail. It was only fair that the Chess Master make this just as exciting for the detective. Just as invigorating.

Another loud thump came from the back.

Reaching down, he gently tapped the button to turn on the CD player. The disc whirled to life. Country music, not something he typically listened to. He picked up the CD Case and examined the cover. *Hmm.*

The Chess Master cocked his head to the side. No, judging the CD by its cover, he certainly wouldn't have chosen this music. But as the words of the first song began to pour forth, he slowly began bobbing his head, making a mew of his lips. He could listen to this.

The game was about evolution, after all, learning to adapt with the changing tides.

Yes, he liked that. His grin stretched wide.

Evolution.

Survival of the fittest.

Once he neared his destination, the Chess Master checked his map one last time, tapping a finger on the tiny dot. He glanced to his rearview mirror before smoothly guiding the car to the side of the road, taking the next gravel turnoff. He drove an extra few miles, just to be assured of privacy. After shifting the car into park, but not shutting it off, he leaned over and dug through the duffel bag on the passenger seat.

He extracted one of the slim syringes already filled with a premeasured sedative courtesy of a Vet Clinic he'd visited late last night. He scanned the barren road, turned and glanced behind him. The broken, pale yellow corn stubble in the empty field on one side of the road was bathed in silvery moonlight as far as the eye could see. And to his left, a deep, dark forest filled with shadows and secrets.

While those woods held a certain...*allure*, he wasn't overly tempted. He was a city kid, after all. He preferred concrete and amenities. He liked his work out in the open. Where it could be appreciated.

And this little Pawn was meant for greater things. His message would be lost, wasted as it were, buried out in these woods.

But what a playground it could be, he supposed. *For someone else.*

He opened the door and climbed from the driver's seat. He'd driven a little longer than he'd intended, and he was beginning to feel a bit sluggish. Standing, the Chess Master stretched and took a deep breath of cool night air. He turned this way and that, loosening muscles and limbering up.

It smelled different here. Cleaner. Crisper. With just the hint of wood smoke from somewhere far off. A night ripe with promise.

Catching his second wind, he popped the latch on the trunk and then rounded the end of the car. He smiled down at the bound and gagged figure now illuminated by the bright trunk light. The Chess Master reached into the trunk to gently brush the matted hair from the Pawn's wide brown eyes. She jerked back, straining away from him.

"Don't struggle so," he counseled gently. "Save your energy, it isn't time for that just yet."

Reaching farther into the trunk, he put his hands on the Pawn's hip and pulled, ignoring frantic attempts to resist. Rolling the piece onto her stomach, he checked her bindings. The cords securing her ankles were firm. The rope around her wrists was intact, as secure as when he'd first tied it, but blood had begun to seep from her skin where she'd fought against her restraints.

"Oh, no," he tsked. "Look what you've done."

Pulling a kerchief from his pocket, he carefully tucked it under the cords, wrapping it around her wrists to protect her delicate skin from further abrasion. He preferred to work with a blank canvas, not one marred by imperfections before he even got started.

Then he considered the state of her clothing. Shaking his head, he tugged her trouser leg back down so it was no longer twisted halfway up her calf, pushing the cuff beneath the rope binding her ankles for added padding. He smoothed her powder blue silk blouse back down as well, carefully tucking the side into her waistband, preserving her modesty.

"There now, you must be more careful. You'll only hurt yourself further," he told her as he rolled her to her side once more. "You're freezing! My goodness, I'm so sorry. How thoughtless of me." He stepped around the car to open the rear door and retrieve a throw blanket he'd noticed earlier.

Returning to the trunk, the Chess Master carefully tucked the soft material around the Pawn. "There now, comfortable? Or would you prefer to stay on your stomach for a while?"

Her forehead wrinkled and bewildered eyes blinked up at him. She began mumbling, her words a garbled mess behind the gag and duct tape.

"Shh. Shh." He smoothed long brown hair from her eyes once more. "So many questions. I have something very important planned for you." He tsked again as he considered the intelligence in her wide eyes. "You would have made an excellent Bishop. Maybe even a Queen, given the chance.

"Ah, well. Too late to reposition the pieces now, isn't it?" Smiling apologetically, he drew the syringe from his pocket and uncapped it. "Now, we can't have you making so much noise once we get to town, so I'm going to give you another shot. Just a little something to take the edge off. Here we go, just a tiny sting."

She began shaking her head, her huge eyes wide and hysterical, welling with fat tears as she whimpered and mewled.

How unbecoming. Well, perhaps not a Queen after all. Not enough courage. Not even enough for a Knight. But certainly, a Rook. He leaned into the trunk and injected the sedative into her shoulder.

"There now." He carefully rubbed the injection site with the pad of his thumb and watched as her eyelids slid closed. Patting her shoulder, he eased the cover a little higher, tucking it beneath her chin.

And then he stilled, his head cocked to the side. The pawn reminded him of someone.

Coolly analytical, he dissected her behavior and her appearance. She'd behaved in a purely circumspect manner, not flirting with him or behaving in a shameless way. She had the look of a professional. A businesswoman. Or a doctor.

And then it hit him. A doctor. The long hair. The wide brown eyes. Doctor Blair, the child psychiatrist his affluent parents had made him visit twice a week for nearly eight years. She'd been…kind. Gentle.

The Pawn reminded him of Doctor Blair.

Nodding, satisfied, he set the conundrum aside, recapped the syringe and tucked it inside his pocket. Stepping back, he closed the trunk on the sleeping Pawn and took his seat behind the steering wheel. After clicking his seatbelt back into place, he consulted the roadmap one last time and then shifted the car into drive. He glanced briefly at the small plastic horse propped up on the dash, and he smiled.

The miles flew by, and before he knew it he was pulling into a pothole-riddled gravel parking in front of a little roach motel on the outskirts of a small town.

Sackville, the town sign had announced. *Population 700.*

The Chess Master parked the car, got out, and walked toward the large neon sign advertising the office. Stepping inside the cramped room, he closed the door and smiled at the woman behind the counter.

Early to mid forties, he'd guess. Bleached blonde hair. Makeup applied with a heavy hand and nails that couldn't possibly be real. Forcing the bile that had risen in his throat back down, he averted his gaze from the ample cleavage on display.

"Hi'ya, sugar," she drawled, then snapped a wad of gum. "Need a room?"

The hair on the back of his neck all but stood on end. A cold, slimy ball of disgust began churning in the pit of his stomach.

Nevertheless, he pasted on a polite smile. "Yes. Please."

"Rates are charged by the night, or by the hour." Her smile held a decidedly predatory light as her bold gaze skimmed over him and came back to his face. Once more she snapped her gum. Only this time she tossed in a lewd wink for good measure. "What'll it be, hon?"

"The full night, please. And a very quiet room, if you have one. I'm a light sleeper, I fear. The slightest noise wakes me."

He swallowed the bile rising in the back of his throat. Cheap whores like this always generated this reaction.

"You bet. That'll be forty-eight dollars, hon. And I'm gonna need to see an ID."

God, he wished she'd stop looking at him like that, like a vulture eyeing fresh road kill. It made his skin crawl.

He dug the wallet from his borrowed pants and handed her the ID he'd forged. Then he began counting out the cash as she typed his information into a computer so ancient he was surprised it still functioned.

"There you are, Mr. King." She slid his ID and a brass key attached to a large black tag labeled 18 across the counter. "To the left and down toward the end. Got nobody on either side of you so you should have a nice quiet night."

Her long, painted nails lingered on the key.

He waited until she removed her hand completely before reaching for the key chain. "Thank you."

As he turned to leave, she called out, "Oh, sugar?"

He turned back.

"If you need anything—*anything* at all, mind you—you just dial zero. My name's Melanie, and I'll be here *all*-night long. All by my lonesome." A gaudy painted nail trailed along her cleavage.

Try as he might, he just couldn't hide it. He shuddered. Turning quickly, he suppressed the reflexive gag as he hurried out the door. It was all he could do not to run for the car.

Don't draw attention.

Deliberately, the Chess Master slowed his pace. He climbed inside the sedan and pulled across the dark parking lot, guiding the small car around the side of the motel where he backed it up near the door to room 18. Climbing out, he glanced around. The nearby highway was barren, as was the parking lot. Only one lone rusty pickup occupied a stall on the other end of the long, low building. The huge neon sign at the edge of the parking lot blinked, buzzing like a great big bug zapper.

Satisfied there wasn't a soul in sight, he reached into the back seat and grabbed his duffel bag. He considered leaving his backpack right where it was. He wouldn't need it, after all. He wouldn't be staying that long. But then, after a brief glance at his surroundings, he changed his mind.

This rundown town screamed poverty. He wouldn't risk some filthy criminal stealing from him. They could have the car. He could always find another. It was probably about time to do that anyway. He reached inside to gather his belongings, and then made certain to grab the little horse from the dash. Some things could never be replaced.

He whistled as he made his way to the door of his room and went inside. After carefully propping his bag on the rickety table near the window, he flipped on the light switch and glanced around the small room.

Green shag carpet. Gold flecked laminate paneling on the lower half of the walls. Water stains on the ceiling. An old nineteen-inch TV with rabbit ears sat at an angle on a beat up dresser in the corner. One dresser leg had been replaced with a chunk of aged, splintered two by four. The air in the room was musty.

It would serve his purpose just fine. He'd worked in far worse conditions.

He returned to the sedan, glanced around the darkened, nearly vacant lot one last time, then popped the trunk and hefted his Pawn onto his shoulder. He quickly closed the trunk and strode inside the motel room to deposit her on the remaining empty bed. He took the time to hang the *Do Not Disturb* sign on the door handle for the morning cleaning crew…if they even had one here. He wanted to give himself as much of a head start as he could.

The Chess Master returned to the bag and drew the long zipper open. First, he took out a thick roll of plastic. After covering the bed to preserve his tools— God only knew what kind of bodily fluids covered that ratty old duvet—he reached inside the bag once more for the duct tape and his box of box cutters and knives. He positioned them with care on the plastic. Next, he extracted a couple of bottles of rubbing alcohol, a needle nose pliers, a bread knife, and a length of rope, placing them all just so. He turned back to the bag, took out the rest of his implements and carefully arranged his items on the bed before standing back to make sure he hadn't missed anything.

All was in order.

He set to work clearing wall space and took out his stud finder. Anchoring the stakes in the wall was second nature by now, and only took a few moments. He extracted the proper chess piece from the soft draw string pouch, positioned it beside the torch, and returned the pouch to the duffel bag.

Are you ready, Detective Reid?

Rubbing his hands together, the Chess Master turned his attention to the unconscious woman lying on the bed.

Let the game begin.

Chapter Sixteen

Jesse loaded a tray with drinks and pushed it across the bar.

"Thanks," Georgia Ann said, offering him a saucy smile as she hefted it up and sashayed off toward one of the booths on the far wall. Paula, one of the pubs other regular waitresses slid up to the bar to take Georgia Ann's place.

After rattling off her next order, Paula propped her elbows on the bar to wait. She watched him fill her order. "Hey, you're getting pretty good at that."

He glanced up from the Long Island he was putting together. "Thanks."

He liked Paula. She was friendly and helpful, hardworking and no nonsense. She had a good head on her shoulders and seemed to have the knack of reading people pretty well.

She'd figured out early on where his interests lay, and she'd made it clear that although she considered him attractive, she wasn't into chasing after a man who was interested in someone else. Hadn't even tried to test the waters, which earned points in his book. He didn't want to cause any trouble for Charlie. She ran a tight ship and the last thing he wanted was to poke holes in her boat.

"Picked out your costume for tomorrow yet?" Paula asked, popping a cinnamon disk into her mouth.

She glanced around, then snuck behind the bar and took a drink from the half empty glass of soda she perpetually kept stashed there whenever she was on shift.

"Not yet." He grinned, his gaze focused on the glass he was filling. "Charlie says she thinks I'd make a good gangster."

"She's right, you would. But..." Paula deliberately dragged that last word out, waiting till she had his full attention. When he stopped pouring and glanced up, she shot him a mysterious little smile. "You'd make a much better gypsy."

"A gypsy?" He frowned and followed her gaze as it slid to the door opening behind him. Charlie walked through the doorway with Eli close on her heels.

"Yep. A gypsy," Paula whispered, tipping her head and winking meaningfully.

"Is that so?" A grin tugged at the corner of his mouth. He finished filling her order and slid the tray toward her.

"Trust me," Paula assured him. She picked up the tray and strolled away.

Eli came up beside him as Charlie skirted the bar. Her gaze slid to Jesse, lingered, and becoming color filled her cheeks.

He'd ended up spending the night at her place on Sunday, and she'd given him a ride to Ed's this morning to pick up his bike. While Charlie, he'd soon gathered, didn't seem to feel the need for official announcements or sloppy PDA, that hadn't stopped him from dragging her out back behind the pub, sneaking into her office, or stealing her away to the walk-in cooler for an illicit kiss here or there. Completely out of character for him—for her too apparently—but he couldn't seem to keep his hands to himself. The woman turned his mind to mush and tore his self control to shreds.

And, since she wasn't putting up much of a fight, he didn't see any reason to stop.

Charlie had finally begun to relax, no longer slipping into a carefully polite demeanor whenever the topic came up of Jesse leaving town. In fact, the issue had pretty much died away all together, and he wasn't looking down the road anymore. Tomorrow was tomorrow. All that mattered to him was the here and now.

Despite their efforts to keep things, if not a secret, then low-key, everyone and their brother seemed to know anyway. Know, and approve. People weren't blind. They'd witnessed the way he looked at her.

And the way *she* looked at *him*.

He grinned.

Besides, he was pretty sure their clandestine meetings weren't very clandestine. But he agreed with Charlie, what was happening between them was between them and should stay that way.

Jesse happened to glance over in time to catch a brief flash of longing tightening Caleb's expression. The assistant manager stood at the top of a ladder near one end of the bar re-hanging one of the long furry legs attached to a massive spider that spanned the ceiling.

Jesse gritted his teeth. Caleb had till the end of the night to get on board with Jesse and Charlie being an item. Get on board, and get the hell over his crush on Charlie. Or Caleb was about to get a big "*clueing in*" via Jesse's fist.

"Did you catch the scores?"

Wiping the scowl from his face, Jesse turned to Eli. "Naw, not yet."

Eli picked up the remote and aimed it at one of the angled flat screens in the corner. The TV flashed on, but the scoreboard was already blipping out to a commercial.

"Crap," Eli muttered as he began channel surfing.

Jesse stood there, his eyes on the TV screen, but his mind was wrapped up with his seemingly-unavoidable, upcoming confrontation with Caleb. As such, it took a moment for him to register the brief picture of yellow crime scene tape affixed to a motel door. What shocked him to attention was the few seconds of audio clip.

"—handiwork of the very same serial killer that claimed twenty-nine victims throughout the Midwest last year. The most recent victim, Patty Scott, was found this morning by housekeeping staff—"

"Sick bastard," Eli muttered and flipped the channel again.

"Wait," Jesse yelled, "go back!"

"Dude, what's wrong?"

"Turn it back! Turn it back now!"

Eli blinked at him, a confused frown on his face, but he started clicking the controller. "Man, I'm sorry. I don't know what channel that was on."

Jesse snatched the controller from Eli and furiously scrolled through the channels. But it was too late, the news clip had already played out, and he had no idea what channel it had been on either.

Cold unease slithered through him.

Can't be. He couldn't catch his breath, couldn't

slow his wild thoughts. *It just can't be.*

Calm down, he told himself. *Breathe. Don't freak.*

Eli was staring at him now as if he'd lost his mind. He didn't care.

He still had Special Agent Carver's card in his wallet. Carver, a member of SSA Anderson's task force, had taken pity on Jesse after Molly's murder and slipped him a tip a time or two. Jesse was sure he could count on the agent one more time. Jesse dropped the glass he was holding into the tub beneath the bar, and snatched up a towel to wipe his hands. He'd just run to the back and make a quick call, just to put his mind at ease.

The phone behind the bar rang, and Jesse, strung tight, jumped.

His alarmed gaze still locked on Jesse, Eli reached for the phone. "Irish Rose?"

Jesse watched as all the blood drained from Eli's face. "Oh, Jesus! Are you serious?"

Without another word, Eli dropped the phone and ran toward the door, digging in his front hip pocket. Halfway to the exit, he skidded to a halt, spun around, dodged behind the bar, and bolted into the kitchen.

"Eli! What's wrong?" Charlie dashed after him, ignoring the commotion they were creating.

"Kendra," he shouted over his shoulder. "She's at the hospital. It's time."

"Slow down," Charlie advised. "She's not going to have the baby before you get there. Eli! Slow down, you can't drive like this!"

"I have to get there now! What if something happens? What if something goes wrong?" He was already running back through the kitchen toward the taproom, keys in hand, but he'd forgotten his coat.

"Stop," Charlie insisted, planting herself squarely in his way. He damned near plowed her over. The only thing stopping him was the fact that Jesse stood directly behind her.

"Move," he shouted.

"Okay." Charlie soothed, throwing her hands up between them in a conciliatory manner. "But getting yourself or somebody else killed isn't going to get you to Kendra any faster. Let one of us drive you over, okay?"

Eli raked a trembling hand through his hair. "Okay, whatever, let's go."

He tossed the keys to Jesse. Eyes wide, Jesse blinked at Charlie. How the hell had *he* gotten involved in this? He had to call Carver.

"*Go,*" she insisted, turning to push Jesse ahead of her. Eli crowded them from behind.

As soon as the inhabitants of the pub pieced together the reason for Eli's mad dash, cheers went up, and congratulations were called, one over the top of the other. Charlie shouted at Jesse over the din as the three of them crashed through the crowd on the way to the door, every patron eager to slap Eli on the back. "Take the highway, head south out of town. Stay on the Twenty-Seven, it'll take you right to Viroqua. Once you hit city limits just follow the signs to the hospital. It's about twelve miles from Badger Creek."

"But—"

"Don't worry about the bar," she insisted, pushing him from behind. "We can handle it. I'll come as soon as I can. Go, now, before he changes his mind about letting somebody else drive."

Eli darted around them in the taproom and shot through the door toward the parking lot.

"Go!" Charlie shouted. Jesse, his call to Carver pushed to the back burner, sprinted after Eli.

Once they got to Eli's car, Jesse slid behind the wheel and Eli jumped into the passenger seat. In seconds, they were tearing down the road. Eli dug in his pocket and flipped his phone open.

"Shit! Three missed calls. Reception inside the pub sucks shit. Kendra must be terrified. Go faster!"

"We'll get there, Eli. Take a breath, man, you're turning blue. There'll be plenty of time for her to cuss you before the baby comes."

A nervous laugh escaped Eli. "I'm gonna be a dad."

Then, without warning, his expression turned horrified. He almost looked like he was going to toss his cookies. Eli reached over and clamped a death grip onto Jesse's forearm. "Oh, God! I'm gonna be a dad! What if I drop the kid? What if I swear in front of it? What if I don't—"

Jesse smacked the back of his hand against the middle of Eli's chest and chuckled. "Breathe! Eli, you're going to be fine. Trust me. You're going to be a great dad."

Eli dragged in a shuddering breath. "Okay. Okay, I can do this. It's going to be fine. Breathe. Just have to keep breathing." He stared out the window ahead of them as if comatose, repeating Jesse's command to breathe. And then Eli began Lamaze panting. Jesse caught himself just before he burst out laughing.

Jesse glanced once toward the speedometer, caught himself edging toward eighty, and reminded himself the whole idea of him driving was to get Eli there in one piece. He eased off the gas, but they still reached Viroqua much faster than the speed limit would have allowed for. He was forced to slam on the brakes when, as they were rolling through the Emergency Room parking lot looking for a parking stall, Eli bolted.

Laughing, he leaned toward the still open door, and called after Eli, "Don't worry about me, I'll just park the car."

He found a parking space, then went inside and asked for directions to the maternity ward. After riding the elevator to the fourth floor, Jesse found Eli pacing in the hallway in front of a close door. He had that crazed look in his eyes again.

"Jesse! They're examining her. Told me I had to leave."

He frowned. "Is something wrong? Is she okay?"

"No, maybe. I don't know. The nurse said something about measuring something and pushed me out the door."

Relaxing now, Jesse dropped his arm around Eli's shoulder and steered him toward a small waiting room he'd passed. "Everything's going to be fine. How about we get some coffee and take a breather before you go back to Kendra? You don't want her to see you like this, do you? Man, you're falling apart at the seams. You'll freak her out. You don't want her to kick you out of the delivery room herself, do you?"

"Okay. Okay, yeah. Coffee." Distracted, his attention obviously on what was going on inside the delivery room, Eli followed Jesse. He accepted the steaming liquid, though he made little effort to drink it. Jesse figured that was probably just as well. He was already strung out on adrenaline as it was. But just holding the cup, having something to focus on, had the desired effect.

Please, Charlie, hurry up and get here.

As a homicide detective, he'd delivered death notifications…more times than he cared to remember. But he'd had precious little experience with this aspect of life. Birth. Had no clue how to handle a nervous, expectant father.

"Mr. Richards? You may come in now," a nurse called as she poked her head inside the waiting room.

Jesse barely caught Eli's Styrofoam cup before it hit the floor. Halfway out the door, Eli turned back. "Will you stay?"

"Yeah, absolutely! Go on, man. Go see Kendra."

Eli rushed away. One hour passed. Then two. Jesse paced in the small waiting room, flipped the TV on, flipped it back off. He should have told Eli that Charlie would be here soon. But, then again, it wasn't like he had a car to go anywhere. The sound of the elevator opening just across the hallway drew him.

"Hey!" Charlie greeted him with a huge smile. "Is Eli with Kendra?"

"Yeah, a couple hours now." He led Charlie to the waiting room, and pointed to the vending machine. Including Eli's cup, he'd already had three. "Want one? Could be a long night."

"Sure, thanks."

They sat together on one of the hard sofas in the sterile white waiting room. Candy and soda vending machines hummed softly near the door. He set his half-empty cup on the low coffee table, and leaned back.

"I told the others I'd call as soon as we heard

something," she said.

"That's fine. In the meantime, might as well rest up. It's going to be a long night. First kids always take the longest."

She arched an intrigued brow at him. "Oh, and you know this how?"

Charlie deposited her coffee cup next to his, and settled back. Jesse drew her against his side, tucking her head into the curve of his shoulder, catching her hand against his chest.

"Helped delivered one once," he murmured. He was treading into territory he usually avoided discussing. But, as he stared down at her, he found he didn't mind so much. Not this time.

"Really?"

"Yeah. Car accident in a snow storm. A real mess. It was the lady's third baby, so it came pretty fast. Good thing she knew what the hell she was doing, 'cause my partner and I had zilch for experience between the two of us, and her husband was out cold."

He and Demarco had been close by at the time, and responded to the call. Good thing, too, because that baby had decided not to wait for paramedics. It had been the one and only time something like that had ever happened to him. To this day he prayed he never had to play midwife again. *Ever.*

"You know that was a ploy, right? Getting you to sit down beside me?" Jesse whispered against her hair, desperate to change the subject all of a sudden.

"Was it now?"

"I've been looking for an excuse all night to get you back in my arms."

She blinked up at him, color flooding her cheeks.

His name slipped from her on a needful whisper.

Her fingertips curled into his shirt, smoothed outward, reminding him of how she'd clutched at him when they'd made love. He tipped his head and gently nudged her forehead with his cheek. She went completely still in his arms. He was pretty sure she'd even stopped breathing. Slowly, she tilted her head back, just enough.

Jesse brushed his lips over hers. Lightly. Over and over. The barest whisper of kisses, teasing them both. But he couldn't resist taking more, demanding more. He caught her lower lip between his, suckled.

Charlie moaned, soft and low, surging need straight through his veins. Unable to resist, he settled his mouth more firmly against hers, slipping his tongue between her sweet lips. Angling his head, he took her mouth, over and over until passion threatened to overcome good sense. She had a way of making him forget where he was. Yielding to his better judgment, doing his best to ignore his body's violent protests, he ended the kiss.

With a shaking hand, Jesse tucked Charlie's head against the side of his neck. He ran that same shaking hand up and down the side of her arm, trying to soothe them both. He shouldn't have let things get so far out of hand. Still, he kept her palm caged against his chest, so that she might feel the thud of his heart and know the way she affected him.

Even though he'd spent all night last night in her bed, he was already looking forward to spending another night with her. He'd just not imagined it would be spent like this. Soon, he promised himself. Tonight, they'd stay for Eli. But tomorrow, she'd be his again. For now, he'd just have to settle for holding her.

Chapter Seventeen

"Jesse."

He startled awake, blinked and began to sit up until he registered the weight of Charlie's head upon his shoulder, the press of her chest against his. Glancing down, he stifled a yawn.

They must have fallen asleep while waiting for word on Kendra and the baby. And, in doing so, they'd maneuvered around on the cramped sofa until Jesse had one leg up on the seat, one on the floor. Charlie was sprawled across his chest, angled between his hip and the back of the sofa, one leg thrown over his, sound asleep.

"The baby's here," Eli whispered from his perch on the coffee table.

He wore blue scrubs, a little blue cap, and had paper booties over his shoes. Dark shadows lined Eli's eyes. But his smile was a mile wide and radiant enough to blind a man.

"It's a girl. She's so beautiful, Jesse. Seven pounds, thirteen ounces. Twenty inches long."

"Congratulations, buddy," Jesse whispered back.

"Thanks!" His exhausted gaze dipped to the still sleeping Charlie. "You two should go on home. It's like four in the morning. Kendra's sleeping and the baby's in the nursery. Stop by and take a peek at her before you go."

"Will do." Jesse nodded his head, winced as a shot of pain scored the muscles on the left side of his neck.

Eli got up to leave, but at the door, he turned back. "Hey, Jesse. Thanks for sticking around. I mean it, man. And thanks for helping me keep my shit together."

"No problem," Jesse said. "That's what friends are for."

And he smiled. Eli was the first one he'd allowed himself in almost a year. It was good having friends again. It was good to belong somewhere.

Eli's gaze dipped once again to the woman sleeping on Jesse's chest. "Maybe I'll get to return the favor someday, huh?"

Jesse's eyebrows flew up, and he darted a look to Charlie, but she still slept. He turned back to the door, but Eli was already gone.

A baby. With Charlie.

Jesse stared down at her sleeping face as he cradled her in his arms. Eli's words kept running through his mind. He'd never really given much thought to having children. Always just assumed it would be a given for Molly and him. Eventually.

Then after she'd...

Well, he figured he'd buried the dream of children, of having a family of his own, the day they'd buried Molly.

Shockingly enough, Eli's comment didn't scare him as much as he'd though it would.

A baby with Charlie.

Not right away, of course. But someday, maybe. He could almost see it. And he didn't fear, didn't dread, didn't balk at the idea. Not one bit.

He knew it was because of her, because of Charlie.

She was the reason he'd begun to look forward to all kinds of things he'd given up hope of ever having.

He brushed a light kiss across her brow, smoothing her hair back with his hand. "Charlie. Baby, wake up."

She stirred, frowned, and burrowed closer.

Warmth blossomed in his chest, spread through him like a fever. He'd never been one to sugar coat things, never one to live in denial. He was falling for this woman, and he faced that fact head on now.

He was falling for her. Hard.

He pressed another kiss to her forehead, then nudged her head back, trailing soft kisses down the bridge of her nose, peppering them over her cheeks and her eyes. "Wake up." He dropped more kisses across her face, bathing her in the tender emotions bubbling inside him. "Come on, Charlie, wake up."

"Jesse?" Charlie murmured. She squinted one eye open, and scrunched up her face.

God, she was so adorable. Jesse couldn't resist. He captured her lips with his, stroked his tongue along the seam of her mouth, groaned aloud when she immediately yielded to him. She was so warm, so soft, so responsive. Within seconds, he was rock hard and knew that this situation could only end one of two ways.

Either he stopped this kiss—stopped it right now—and took her home, or someone was going to walk in and get one hell of an eyeful.

Wrenching his lips from hers, he sucked in a ragged breath. "You're killing me, woman."

Her sleepy, seductive smile tested his resolve.

"Unless you want to find yourself in a *very* compromising position—and, to be fair, I feel I should remind you we are in a public hospital waiting room—I would suggest you put that smile away and move off me."

She glanced around them, seemed to note the open door, and then turned back to him. Her smile hadn't slipped a notch. In fact, it had taken on a decidedly wicked tilt.

Jesse's eyes flared and a shot of adrenaline spiked through him. Oh, she was asking for it. He lowered his head to lay claim to her lips again, his hands skimmed her sides reaching the hem of her shirt.

Giggling mischievously, she scrambled up and out of reach.

"You're going to pay for that," he shot her a mock scowl as he sat up. After raking his hands through his hair, he extended both arms and stretched the stiffness from his muscles.

"Oh!" She gasped suddenly. "Eli! Kendra! We should go see if—"

"It's okay, relax. Eli was just here a few minutes ago and woke me." Her gaze flew to the sofa, and Jesse could all but see the wheels grinding away. *Had Eli seen them like that?*

Her blush was endearing.

"They had a girl. It's just shy of four in the morning, and mother and child are all resting. Eli just came out to send us home."

"Oh." Her disappointment was a tangible thing.

Grinning, he added, "Eli said we should stop by the nursery to take a peek at the baby before we go."

She brightened instantly. "Well, what are you waiting for? Let's go!"

They gathered their things, and Jesse trailed her

down the darkened hallway, passed the nurses' station to the wide bank of windows surrounding the dim nursery. Baby girl Richards was the sole child in the small room. The nurse seated at a desk in the corner looked up and smiled. Charlie pressed up to the glass for a closer look at the pink swaddled bundle, smiling in that goofy way women do around a new baby.

"Oh! Look, Jesse," Charlie whispered. "She's so beautiful. Just look at that face! She has Eli's chin, I think. Did he say what they named her?"

"No."

Jesse couldn't resist, he moved behind Charlie, slipped his arms around her waist and rested his chin on her shoulder, pressed his cheek to hers. "She's all wrinkly, like a big prune."

Charlie gasped, offended on the baby's behalf. "She is not! Well, maybe a little bit—but she's supposed to look like that. She's perfect!"

Chuckling, he held her tighter and rocked slightly side to side. "She's bald."

She nudged her shoulder against his chin in a playful rebuke. "Don't you listen to him, sugarplum," Charlie stage-whispered through the glass to the sleeping newborn. "You trust Auntie Charlie on this. You, my sweet one, are going to break hearts wherever you go."

They stood watching the baby sleep for a few more minutes in silence. At length, Jesse stepped back and took her hand. "Come on, let me take you home."

They exited through the Emergency Room and were on the road in short order, Jesse behind the wheel of Charlie's vehicle. He reached over, and linked their fingers together.

Charlie yawned. "Stay with me?"

"That's the plan." He raised their joined hands and pressed a kiss to her knuckles.

Jesse drove directly to Charlie's little cabin in the woods. Charlie reached up and pushed the garage door opener. Jesse guided the SUV inside and turned the ignition off. The door lowered behind them. Without a word, he followed her inside the cabin. They hung their jackets up on the hooks by the door. For a moment he froze in place. Such an ordinary, mundane thing to do. It was as if they were coming home after a long day, like they'd done this a hundred times together already.

"Are you hungry?" Charlie asked over her shoulder as she walked down the short hallway from the garage to the kitchen.

"Starving," he murmured. Then he caught her by the elbow, and spun her back into his arms.

He sealed his lips over hers, swallowing her gasp of surprise. She twined her arms around his neck, and melted into him. Jess was lost. He swept her off her feet, lifting her high against his chest.

Jesse's determined stride carried them to her bedroom. He paused just inside the darkened room to slap on the light. He wanted to see her when he took her. See the expression on her face, watch the way that lithe body moved against his.

At the side of the bed, Jesse lowered her feet to the floor and captured her face between his hands, held her there for a long, long moment. She was the most beautiful thing he'd ever seen. He realized, in that moment, he'd never get enough of her. Of looking at her, of touching her.

He wasn't falling for her.

He'd *already* fallen. Splat.

The sense of urgency that had been simmering inside him since he'd woken up with her on his chest had been tempered somewhat, replaced by these unexpected, nearly indescribable feelings of awe. When he finally lowered his head, he claimed her lips almost reverently. Stroking his tongue along hers, he savored her flavor, the textures of her, and each soft murmur of pleasure he wrought from her.

Again and again, he tasted her as the delicate scent of her perfume went straight to his head. His hands were by no means idle. He touched and caressed, exploring silken skin as clothing fell by the wayside, a temporary barrier to the treasures beneath. And when her soft hands found their way beneath his clothing to his own flesh, the fever burning inside consumed him.

With his hands on her hips, he steered her, guiding her back and up onto the bed. Mouths still mating, tongues tangling, breathes mingling. Charlie closed her hand over his straining erection, and Jesse's entire body jerked. She stroked the heavy, thick length of him, and it was nearly his undoing. His body shuddered, and a bead of moisture slipped free. The pad of her thumb captured it, spreading it round and round the sensitized, swollen head. Teasing, tormenting him.

Groaning, nearly out of his mind with need, he used his body to tip her back until she landed on the bed. He gripped her knees, spread them, and then wrapped those toned, smooth legs around his waist before he even realized what he was doing.

She drew him closer as he angled his head, sinking deeper into the kiss. Sanity was a very nearly lost cause the second her slick womanhood slid along the ridge of his erection, arched invitingly up to meet him.

A tiny kernel of awareness hit him, scolded him for not slowing down, not taking more responsibility before he worried about his own needs. Christ, he'd just spent the majority of the night at a hospital…awaiting the birth of a child. That should have been sufficient reminder to slow down and use his head. And, while yes, he might be open to the possibility of having a baby with Charlie someday, that someday wasn't now. Particularly not without having discussed it with her first. And certainly not this early in their relationship.

But she was already deliciously wet, and the breathy little moans gurgling in the back of her throat made it awfully hard to listen to that little voice. Nevertheless, he pulled back at the last second to hunt for the condom in his wallet. And then he was back, pinning her beneath him, poised at her entrance, kissing her senseless.

If he could just get inside her, just feel that tight heat close around him, maybe then he'd be able to slow down, make it last a little longer. Maybe he'd be able to grab hold of some semblance of control.

But the moment he sank himself deep inside her, Jesse was lost. His body took over, and his mind abandoned him completely.

He couldn't stop moving. The friction, the decadent sensation of her closing tight over him, squeezing him as her body slid against his was mindboggling. Her beaded nipples pressed into his chest. Her soft, full breasts rubbed at him with every stroke, making his mouth water for a taste. He ached to squeeze and pluck and caress those nipples. And so, he gave in to those urges, leaning the upper part of his body back so he could lavish them with attention.

And in doing so, he inadvertently changed the angle of his thrusting. His hips pushed deeper, pressed against her harder, grinding. He watched through hooded eyes as Charlie arched her back and tossed her head to the side, crying out. Her face was a study in passion.

He lowered his mouth to one nipple. Those delicate fingers of hers weren't so delicate anymore as they furrowed into his hair, fisting, drawing him closer, demanding he take more.

He was helpless but to obey, both his body's demands as well as hers. He drove his hips relentlessly against her, burying himself deep inside her as his mouth and hands alternated worshiping her beautiful breasts.

Charlie's body went taut beneath his. Her breath quickened. He dragged his lips up the ridge of her throat. His hands found their way to her head, and he tangled his fingers in her hair. Jesse dragged her head back, angling it for a soul searing kiss. And, as she hovered there on the edge, as her body cried out for his, begged his for release, he sealed their mouths together. He pounded his erection deep, deep inside her, sending them both spiraling to the stars.

Jesse slowly came to his senses. His head was nestled on the pillow near her shoulder, his heart hammering in his ears. Her arms and legs were still wrapped tight around him. With a satisfied groan, he nuzzled against the side of her neck.

Unable to form a coherent thought just yet, he did manage to slide his head back a bit on the pillow so he had a clear view of her face. She was pink, flushed from exertion and, he'd be willing to bet his next paycheck, embarrassment.

He brought their foreheads together, brushed his nose over hers. Then he dropped a kiss to the tip of her nose before sliding out of her. He made short work of disposing of the used condom, and then settled himself beside her on the bed. With a contented sigh, he pulled her into his arms.

"Thank you," she said, her voice languid and just a tiny bit hoarse. "For remembering to be safe. I, ah, I tend to lose my head a bit when I'm with you."

"I make it a rule to always use a condom. Which reminds me, I'm gonna need to restock. That was the last one I had in my wallet." Now she turned bright red. He couldn't resist. He leaned over and kissed her cheek. "Don't worry, I won't restock in town. I can about imagine how fast *those* rumors would start flying."

She looked slightly uncomfortable. Nevertheless, she asked, "What about…well, before?"

He knew she wasn't referring to where he'd purchased condoms. Yeah, discussing previous partners didn't exactly encourage the mellow afterglow to stretch on, but he had to respect her for pursuing this conversation. Most women might be too embarrassed, or too timid, to address safe sex with their partner. But it was something that should be done. Something that *needed* to be done. It was important.

This was difficult for him to talk about too, but not for the same reasons. Discussing his sex life brought back a lot of memories he'd just as soon leave buried right along with Molly.

"Used a condom then too." He paused for a moment and drew a deep breath. But—because he respected Charlie—he refused to take the easy way out and, instead, took the plunge. "I haven't been with anyone in almost a year. Before that, I was in a committed relationship for about four years. Before Molly and I moved in together, we were both tested, and we were clean."

Charlie studied his face for a long time, questions brewing on those beautiful eyes. He feared those questions, didn't know if he was ready for this conversation yet.

"I usually insist on protection too." She smoothed her hands along his shoulders, easing some of the tension. That she resisted pressing him for information about Molly, and why they were no longer together, went a long way toward easing the rest. "But I'm also on the pill, just FYI. More to regulate cycles than anything. It's been a while for me too."

He thought of her work habits, of the way her friends breathed a collective sigh of relief when she'd—however unintentionally—expressed interest in him. Jesse chuckled. "I gathered as much."

She frowned up at him. "What's that supposed to mean?"

"Nothing," he soothed, drawing her closer and rubbing her back. Mollified, she settled against his shoulder. "There's something else we need to talk about."

She stiffened, as if bracing herself for the worst. He tilted her head back so he could stare into her eyes. "I know you were worried before about when I plan to leave."

She immediately began to shake her head and pull away. "I know the score, Jesse. I'm not trying to put any pressure on you. I know you don't intend to stick around, long term, so I won't—"

"That's just it," he interrupted her, pressing a finger to her lips, cutting her off. "I want you to understand something, and I want to make myself very clear. Everything's changed now, Charlie. Do you understand me? I'm not going anywhere. I'm here. For as long as you want me."

He had so much to tell her. So many things he needed to explain. About his life before coming to Badger Creek. About Molly and his time on the force.

And the reason he left it all behind.

And he still needed to call Carver. He hadn't forgotten about that news report, or the uneasy feeling curling around his spine.

But he owed his attention to Charlie right now. No matter how badly he wanted to go chasing after what might be his last shot at the Chess Master. Old instincts were hard to ignore.

He was done letting the Chess Master own him.

She blinked, once, twice. He caught just the faintest glimmer of moisture in her eyes.

"I want you!" She threw herself on top of him, smothering his face in kisses. "Oh, I want you!"

Jesse laughed at her exuberant answer. But even as he kissed her back, something niggled at him. Something worrisome and uneasy. Something that hadn't been there for a long time.

Real fear. Would this—what he had going with Charlie—be snatched from him as his future with Molly had been? Could he keep her safe in a world where monsters like the Chess Master ran free?

God, he hoped so. Because he honestly didn't

know what he'd do this time around if Charlie was taken from him too.

****

Jesse ran through the night. Thick mist swirled around him, pulled at him like invisible hands, slowing him down. Somewhere out there, a woman's voice called out to him, begging him to find her, screamed his name. Jesse had to find her, find her and save her before the Chess Master left another note claiming checkmate.

The Queen needed him.

Jesse's Queen.

"Where are you?" Jesse panted.

Every breath seared his throat, burned his lungs. But he sucked them in, one after another, as he ran. He was frantic to find her, but he didn't know where she was, didn't know where to look.

And then, finally, he broke free of the veiling mist, the treacherous fog. He stumbled out into the middle of an endless room. A room with soft light and blood red walls. There were people everywhere, moving slowly, aimlessly, in every direction, their unblinking gazes focused on some point he could not see. Their tortured faces twisted in pain.

He reached out, intent on stopping someone, asking for help. Maybe one of these women could help him find his Queen. But his hand went right through her. Again, he reached out. And once more his hand misted through a solid body. Jesse was as insubstantial as the fog surrounding them.

"Help me," he shouted. But no one turned to look at him. No one acknowledged his presence in any way.

Almost hysterical, he jumped in front of one after

another of the women. Each of their foreheads held a brand. Pawns, Rooks, Knights, Bishops. But no Queen.

Where is the Queen?

The chess pieces walked right through him. Sinking his hands deep in his hair, Jesse gripped the damp strands in frustration as the screams grew fainter until they stopped all together.

The Chess Master had found her. Jesse had failed. He'd failed, and another woman had died.

Now the women around him changed. Each wore the brand of the Queen. Each had a crown on her head, a beautiful crown.

Oh, God, so many Queens.

He jerked his head from side to side, reaching out to grab the one closest to him. But, again, his hand went right through her.

How can I protect them all?

Jesse jolted up in the bed, his wide-eyed gaze darting around the dark room. His damp chest heaved, but he couldn't catch his breath. Terror was a hot ball lodged in the back of his throat.

God, he hadn't had that nightmare in months.

He dragged in a shuddering breath and tried to relax. But he knew he wouldn't be able to. Not after seeing that newscast.

He needed to calm down before he woke Charlie. But he couldn't make his mind obey, and insidious thoughts crept up on him. He hadn't spent a lot of time these last few weeks keeping tabs anymore, not like he used to do. And it wasn't as if he were exactly easy to get a hold of. He didn't even carry a phone anymore. Not since the last one had broken right before Sackville. And he'd not checked in with the station, nor had he checked in with DeMarco or SSA Anderson or Agent Carver since his arrival in Badger Creek. Yeah, he'd been flying below the radar.

Flying below it? Hell, he'd fallen completely off the radar altogether. It was time he corrected that. He'd call Agent Carver later today. Just to ease his mind and quell this irrational fear.

Charlie shifted in her sleep and mumbled.

"Shh," he whispered, smoothing his hand down her arm.

Curling himself around her, he pressed a soft kiss to the back of her shoulder.

"Jesse?" Charlie stirred, murmuring groggily.

"Shh, it's okay. Go back to sleep."

She burrowed into her pillow, and Jesse wrapped himself around her and tried to go back to sleep himself. It took a lot longer than it should have.

Chapter Eighteen

The Chess Master pulled the old truck alongside the curb. The sign in the front yard of a white Victorian advertised Thelma's Bed and Breakfast. He sat in the truck a moment longer, watching as a witch, a vampire, a fairy princess and Captain America ran down the sidewalk.

The princess paused beside the truck to dig in the bright orange plastic pumpkin dangling from her wrist. She pulled out a sucker, unwrapped it, and popped it into her mouth as she set off after the others. Farther down the street, ghosts and baseball players, zombies and Jedi raced from door to door beneath yellow streetlights.

I wonder what costume little Janie picked.

He chuckled as he climbed from the rusty green pickup and strolled up the sidewalk. His gaze, as ever, tracked his surroundings, taking in every detail. The house, a grand old lady, was well maintained. A small manicured yard. Strategically placed flower gardens. White picket fence.

How quaint.

He ascended the steps, crossed the porch and let himself in the front door. The foyer was spacious, dated but tidy and clean. He shook the tiny brass bell on the corner of an antique desk, then folded his hands in front of him and waited patiently.

A few short moments passed and then a tall, painfully thin, white-haired woman came marching through the wide double doorway to his left. She looked to be in her seventies, but age had not stooped her shoulders or dulled the shrewdness in her gaze. Those keen eyes were assessing him now, and he knew what she saw. He'd carefully constructed the image, after all. A slightly paunchy man in his mid to late fifties. Receding hairline. Thick glasses. Mole. Unassuming. Non-threatening. He smiled warmly at her, just a harmless, road-weary traveler looking for a safe place to rest his head.

"Good evening," she greeted him, extending her hand. "I'm Thelma Carter. May I help you?"

He stepped forward and gently clasped her hand between both of his, patting the paper-thin skin lined with blue veins in a friendly fashion before circumspectly releasing it.

"Good evening, Mrs. Carter. I'm Robert King." He affected a slight southern twang. "I'm looking for a room for the night. Perhaps a couple nights, actually. Please tell me ya'll have an available room?"

"You're in luck, Mr. King. We do." She smiled graciously and motioned him to the seat in front of the desk. Mrs. Carter moved behind the desk, tipping her head appreciatively when he remained standing until she'd taken her seat.

"Will it be just you this evening?"

"I'm afraid so," he smiled, affecting a touch of sadness in his tone and his eyes. "My wife, bless her, passed on six months back. We'd been planning this trip, you see, to see the sights in our retirement. But then she—" He dipped his head down, squeezed his eyes closed and drew a ragged breath. Squaring his shoulders, he lifted his chin, and pasted on a brave smile. "Well, I'm traveling alone now."

"My own dear Clyde has been gone twenty-three years this January. You have my deepest sympathies, Mr. King." Her expression was somber now, and he knew he had this in the bag.

"You have a lovely home, if I may say so."

"Thank you." She inclined her head. "We do try. Now then, may I see some form of identification and your credit card."

"Oh. Oh, dear," he said, widening his eyes. "I have my driver's license, but I'm so sorry. I don't have a credit card. I fear mine was stolen a few days back. A pickpocket." He shook his head as if deeply disappointed. "So sad, but you just can't seem to trust anyone these days. I did contact the credit card company, and I had my son wire cash to me, though."

She reached out to pat his clasped hands where they rested on her desk. "Please, don't trouble yourself so, Mr. King. Cash will do. I pride myself on being a very good judge of character. Besides, I deem it my Christian duty to help wherever I can."

"Oh, thank you so much, ma'am. I must admit, I made a mistake in not pulling over sooner, just the thought of staying in that motel I saw in Sackville," he pulled a face and shuddered, "well, I just couldn't bring myself to do it. But the thought of continuing to drive at this late hour on to another town in hopes of finding a motel…well, the very idea was a bit daunting. Badger Creek is such a beautiful town. Small, but beautiful. I was so happy to see your sign in the yard."

"I understand. We don't get many new faces in

town." She smoothed imaginary wrinkles from her cuffs, her expression aloof.

"Oh?" He tilted his head, inviting her to go on.

"As you said, we are a very small community, Mr. King, small but safe. Let me assure you, very safe. Why, I was close friends with the town's Chief of Police's mother, God rest her soul," she boasted. "Such a dependable man he's grown into."

Considering the woman's age, that left a pretty wide span of possibilities over the Police Chief's age. But he didn't comment.

Thelma accepted his license and carefully penned his forged information into a thick ledger. She quoted the price for a full week when he stated once more that he was rather tired of driving and might enjoy settling in for a bit.

"Breakfast is served promptly at seven a.m. I do apologize, Mr. King, but you just missed dinner." She adjusted her snow-white cardigan and offered him a benevolent smile. "Although, I could make arrangements to have something sent to your room if you've not eaten your evening meal yet."

"I do appreciate the offer, ma'am. But I certainly don't wish to put you to any trouble. Perhaps, if there's a restaurant still open in town, I might grab a bite there? Stretch my legs a bit. I've been cramped up in the truck for so long, a nice brisk walk would do me good."

"The restaurant has closed by now," she tsked. "The Irish Rose is probably the only place in town this time of evening that will still be serving food. It's just on the other side of town."

"The Irish Rose?" Oh, he knew all about the Irish Rose already. The moment it had come up in connection with Detective Reid, he'd researched the pub on the internet. But, once again, appearances must be maintained.

Her papery cheeks took on a pink hue as if she were scandalized to even be discussing the matter. "They serve spirits there, and play rather loud music on the weekends, too. But the food at the Irish Rose is actually quite tasty. Authentic Irish fare. Been there myself a time or two with friends," her voice dropped conspiratorially, "even though it is a bar, you know. We went there for the food, of course."

"Oh, of course." He nodded his head and thanked her. Once business was concluded, Mrs. Carter led him upstairs and ushered him to his room.

"Did you have a bag, Mr. King?"

"Yes, but I left it in the truck. I wasn't sure if there'd be room."

"Will you be needing assistance? My grandson—"

"No, no. Please, don't trouble him. I can get it on my own."

"All right, then. I trust you'll find everything you need."

"Thank you again, ma'am. Everything seems quite cozy." The place was a damned museum. He was afraid to breathe wrong that he might knock over some priceless heirloom. "I'm sure I'll be fine. But I do believe I'm going to slip over to the Irish Rose for a bite to eat and a stretch of the legs. I promise I won't be out late, and I'll be quiet as a church mouse when I let myself back in."

Nodding, wishing him a good night, she closed the door gently behind her. The Chess Master crossed the room and pulled the lace curtains to the side to peer out the window. Tidy houses as far as the eye could see. Such a restful little community. So innocent and peaceful. What a refreshing change of pace. Detective Reid had chosen well. This certainly would challenge him, though. Push his talents to their limits. No crowds of people to blend into, no faceless anonymity.

He'd have to be very vigilant to adhere to his identity.

Whistling softly, the Chess Master let himself out of the house and pocketed his room key. The groups of children on the street below were beginning to thin. It was time to get the lay of the land and go see an old friend.

And it was time to choose his players.

****

Charlie ducked behind the bar to see if Jesse needed a hand. The pub was packed tonight, but then they were always packed every Halloween Eve it seemed. Most wore costumes, though there were some still dressed in street clothing. Jesse, dressed as a dashing gypsy, was manning the bar like he'd been born there, and she was impressed. Not only by his adept skills as a bartender, but by his costume selection. Somehow, he'd managed to dress himself as her male counterpart.

Every time she looked at him, she found herself struggling not to giggle. He'd cornered her earlier in the walk-in and swept her into a kiss worthy of the cover of one of those romance novels Paula was so fond of reading on her breaks. Charlie's off-the-shoulder peasant blouse and thin kerchief skirt hadn't provided much protection against the walk-in's refrigeration system. But once Jesse had taken her in his arms, once he'd pressed his strong hard body up against hers and claimed her lips in a mind drugging kiss, she'd all but gone up in flames.

Heat crawled into her cheeks, and she began to devise ways of luring him to her office, or into the cooler again. Or out back. Anywhere they might steal a moment alone. Surprised by her less than professional intentions while on the clock, she cleared her throat and asked instead, "Need any help?"

He glanced up from the Eyeball Martini—a house specialty served only on Halloween—that he was pouring. He recited Georgia Ann's order from table thirteen. He added, "They have a running tab. John Carroll needs a refill, and Sean's drink is running low."

"Gotcha," she said, jumping right in.

They moved in tandem behind the bar, as if executing a choreographed dance they'd been performing for years. When they finally had a brief lull, Charlie glanced over to see Jesse deep in conversation with John Carroll, his elbow propped on the bar as they discussed John's apple crop. Charlie caught herself gaping and snapped her mouth closed.

Though John joked with her and many of their regular patrons, he was typically very reserved with new people. In fact, Caleb had been assistant manager for over five years now and John rarely said more than a handful of words to Caleb at any given time. Yet there he sat, telling Jesse all the ins and outs of raising a good apple crop as if Jesse were a long-lost grandson. And Jesse stood there smiling, absorbing every word.

Shaking her head, turning away with a silly grin plastered on her face, Charlie came face to face with Caleb.

"Oh! I didn't hear you come up." She pressed the heel of her palm over her racing heart.

"Sorry," Caleb said, his sullen gaze avoiding hers.

He'd been doing a lot of that since the employee picnic. Charlie was thinking it was about time to take that bull by the horns, so to speak. Shooting a quick glance around the taproom, Charlie made up her mind. She'd scheduled extra staff tonight, and they seemed to have things well in hand. For the moment, at least.

"Hey, Caleb, give me a second, would you?"

"Can't," he evaded with an unapologetic quirk of the lips. "I've got drink orders for three, four, and six."

She caught sight of one of the approaching waitresses. "Give them to Paula," she ordered, using a tone she'd never had to use with Caleb before. "I'd like a word with you in back. Now, please."

A muscle twitched along his jaw, but, thankfully, he didn't argue. He relayed the orders to Paula, who bobbed her head, memorizing every word, and Charlie breathed a sigh of relief. Thank heaven it had been Paula coming over, and not their new girl, Shelby. She didn't want to give Caleb even the slightest excuse to deny her. While Shelby was good with customer service, she sometimes got orders mixed up. Paula was a pro.

Turning, she led the way back to her office.

"Close the door and take a seat," she said as he followed her inside.

Uneasy, she sat down behind her desk. She hated confrontations, but it was a necessary evil in her position. How to approach this? As friend, or boss? She just didn't know. She opted for friend, figuring she could fall back on the boss routine, should friend fail.

She waited until he settled his lanky frame in the seat, and then just threw it out there. "What's wrong?"

He frowned at her and shrugged nonchalantly, but his guarded gaze never quite met hers. "I don't know what you're talking about."

He leaned back in his seat, propped his ankle on his knee, and plucked a speck of lint from his black sock.

"Caleb," she tried again, waiting in silence until he finally met her gaze. "What's wrong?"

He stared at her for a long, long time. She began to think he wasn't going to respond, but then he burst from his seat without warning and began to prowl the cramped office.

"Not tonight, Charlie. I don't want to discuss this tonight."

"Caleb, we've been putting this off for too long as it is. You've been walking around ever since the picnic like a wounded bear." But then she paused as something else clicked. Her eyes narrowed. "No, that's wrong. You've been acting like this ever since I gave Jesse a job. Why?"

"Just let it go, Charlie."

"I can't let it go. Because you haven't. I need to understand what's going on with you two. Don't you know your job is secure? I could never replace you."

"It's not *me* and him that's the problem," he snapped. Then, just as quickly, he looked as if he'd give anything to call those words back.

A deep frown pulled Charlie's eyebrows together. Lots of little things began to converge on her. Cryptic comments Doris and Georgia Ann had made. Comments she'd pushed aside as so farfetched as to be preposterous. Yet even Jesse had alluded to Caleb's feelings. Had she deliberately misread or ignored the situation? Perhaps in hopes of avoiding exactly this confrontation?

Her lips parted, but she couldn't quite fashion the words, didn't know what to even say, or how to handle the situation. Because this was *Caleb*. Her friend. Her right hand.

Something of her distress must have shown on her face, because Caleb slowly sank down on the chair. A look of resignation, of utter defeat settled upon his countenance.

"Caleb, I didn't—"

"Don't." He cut her off, shaking his head. "Just don't, okay."

"But, Caleb—"

"Charlie, I know, all right. I can see it every damn time you look at him. Christ, everyone can see it." His voice was strained now, and he didn't bother to keep the edge of bitterness from his voice, cutting her deep. "I knew it the second you stepped from the kitchen when he came in to apply for the job that first day, and you saw him sitting there."

Charlie didn't know what to say. Had she been so transparent?

Caleb raked his hands through his hair and rolled his eyes before finally settling his gaze on her. She wanted to disappear, to squirm in her seat, to look away. But she couldn't. She owed him that much, at least. And so, she held his gaze, though it was one of the hardest, most uncomfortable things she'd ever done.

"I always thought I'd have time, you know?" He didn't wait for a response, didn't seem to expect one. "Make myself indispensible around here. Make you see how good we could be together. And I guess all the while, I was hoping you'd start thinking about how good we could be together *outside* the pub too." He considered her, his head angled slightly to the side. "But it never even occurred to you, did it?"

"Caleb," she said, filled with anguish. "You are indispensible to me. I'd be lost without you. Both inside *and* outside of the pub. You're my best friend, Caleb."

Her final words deflated him, the last shreds of hope in his eyes slowly withering and dying. Slowly, as if he'd aged a hundred years in the last five minutes, he pushed to his feet.

"I'll get over it." His gaze caressed her face one last time, as if something inside him were saying goodbye. Charlie wanted to put her head down on her desk and weep.

"Caleb—"

"This conversation didn't happen," he interrupted, his voice taking on a stubborn tone she'd rarely ever received from him. "Leave me my pride, Charlie."

Without another word, his back stiff, Caleb strode from the office, leaving the door open behind him. Charlie sat there for a long minute, staring after him as the sounds of the taproom filtered through the kitchen to the office.

How could she have been so blind? So cruel? Caleb deserved so much more. But she couldn't help how she felt. Couldn't help who she loved.

Charlie sucked in a sharp breath, and her eyes flew wide.

Can't help who I love?

Love?

She loved Jesse.

Needed him as she needed air. And she'd be devastated if he didn't stay, despite all his assurances.

Oh, God! She'd fallen in love with a drifter. A man who hadn't stayed in one place in the last year—as far as she knew—for longer than a hand full of months. The pit of her stomach dropped. What was she going to do?

"You okay?"

She started, glancing up as Jesse stepped inside the office. "I just saw Caleb. He looks like hell." His gaze skimmed her face. "You don't look much better. What happened?"

Oh, God. She blinked up at him, unable to speak. *Oh, God.*

Panic began to squeeze her heart as she stared at Jesse through a sudden sheen of tears. He'd leave, no matter what he'd said. He'd leave. It was what he did. He'd leave, and she'd be left behind, devastated. Just as she'd devastated Caleb.

Karma was a bitch, and she was in for a whole heaping helping.

"Hey!" Jesse moved around the desk, pulling her up against him. Strong arms closed around her, dragging her closer, sheltering her as he pressed her head to his shoulder. "Shit. I'm sorry. I shouldn't have pushed. I—"

"No," she murmured against his shirt, wrapping her arms around him at last. Absorbing his strength, she leaned into him, drawing a lungful of his scent. Holding on to it, holding on to *him,* as long as she could. "It's not your fault. I should have seen this coming."

Whether she was referring to the situation with Caleb, or to her falling in love with Jesse and the subsequent, unavoidable heartbreak when he inevitably left, she honestly didn't know. But she'd deal with Caleb. And when the time came, when Jesse finally left, she'd deal with that too.

Do I really have any other choice?

Unwilling to hide in her office, Charlie moved out of Jesse's arms and returned to the rowdy Halloween crowd. Overwhelmed by not only the revelation of Caleb's feelings for her, but her feelings for Jesse, she couldn't meet either of their gazes. And though she pasted on a smile, judging by the concerned looks she was receiving from her staff as well as her patrons, she knew it didn't quite reach her eyes.

Unable to focus on drink orders, or any other task for that matter, Charlie picked up a tub of empties and the bulging trash bag behind the bar. The girls and Caleb had the tables well in hand, and Jesse was manning the bar like a boss.

Charlie needed a moment to herself, away from the noise. Away from Caleb's kicked dog expression and the jumble of emotions just looking at Jesse caused.

She quietly slipped through the door behind the bar into the dim kitchen, and headed for the freight door. The cold, dark night called to her. Just a minute or two. That's all she needed. Just a moment away to level herself out and get her emotions back under control.

Chapter Nineteen

"Hey, where'd Charlie go?" Georgia Ann called from the end of the bar. "Jack and Sylvia Becker want to say goodbye before they leave."

Jesse frowned, glancing up from the register. He scanned the crowd, but Charlie was nowhere in sight. His heart gave a hard knock. He set the pint he'd been building aside, his palms suddenly sweaty. He'd been trying to call Agent Carver all damned day, with no luck. To hear that Charlie was missing sent his already-strung-tight nerves right over the edge.

"Caleb," he called, giving a short, shrill whistle.

The assistant manager glanced over. He looked like he'd rather chew broken glass than talk to Jesse, but Caleb approached the bar nonetheless.

Jesse didn't give a flying rat's ass about Caleb's attitude right now. He had more important things to worry about. "You see where Charlie went?"

Frowning, Caleb shook his head and glanced around. "No. Did someone check her office?"

Paula sidled up to the bar. "Need a Capt'n and Coke, an Eyeball, and a Sex on the Beach, Jesse. Hey, what's up with the pow-wow?"

Jesse ignored the drink order. "When was the last time you saw Charlie?"

Paula peeked over her shoulder at the milling crowd behind her, and Jesse followed her gaze. Pirates and drag queens, witches and goblins. A multitude of costumes, but no gypsy.

"She's not back yet?" Paula asked with a frown.

"Back yet? Where'd she go?" Jesse couldn't shake the uneasy tickle crawling up his spine. "How long's she been gone?"

Paula gave a helpless shrug beneath Jesse's scowl. "I saw her grab the trash and some empties, I don't know, maybe ten, fifteen minutes ago. What's going on?"

But Jesse didn't bother answering. He was already slamming through the kitchen door. The room was empty, the lights dimmed as usual this time of night. He ran back to her office, but the lights were off, and she wasn't there. He even took a second to glance in the breakroom. Empty.

With his heart lodged in his throat, and Caleb dogging his heels, Jesse flew to the freight door. It was closed tight, and locked to the outside. Jesse threw the door open and charged outside, shouting her name.

There was no reply.

Overhead, the newly installed security lights had flooded golden light onto dark pavement. The area behind the pub was vacant. No one lingered near the fenced in area around the trash bins. Just to be sure, Jesse ran over, circled them, looking for evidence of he didn't know what, a struggle maybe?

Where the hell is she?

He found nothing. And that scared the living hell out of him. Terror closed his throat and swam in the pit of his stomach nearly making him sick right there on the dingy concrete.

"What the hell's going on?" Caleb demanded,

stalking after him.

Jesse didn't respond. Partly because he was in too much of a hurry to find her. Partly because he was afraid if he opened his mouth, he might vomit after all, so strong was his fear. Unfounded fear maybe, unreasonable fear, but fear nonetheless.

Caleb reached out as Jesse stormed past, trying to snag Jesse's elbow. But Jesse jerked from his grasp and jogged back inside leaving Caleb to follow, or not.

Jesse burst through the still empty kitchen and plowed through the door, the command for Georgia Ann to call the police right on the tip of his tongue when he spied Charlie coming in the front door.

He was around the bar and snatching her up in his arms in the blink of an eye.

"What the hell?" Charlie gasped, her voice muffled against his shirt.

He set her back on her feet, took her by the shoulders, and gave her a rough little shake, unmindful of the scene he was causing. "Where were you?"

Charlie stared up at him as if he'd lost his mind.

"I needed some air, so I took the trash out." She searched his face, frowning. "I forgot to brace the back-door open, and accidently locked myself out, so I came around. What's going on?"

Jesse forced a swallow, let his eyes sag closed, and dragged her back into his arms. "Don't do that again."

"Do what again? Jesse," Charlie demanded, pushing herself out of his arms. "Why are you freaking out?"

Shaken, Jesse stepped back. He glanced around the room. All over, people were staring. Shaking his head, he took another step back. "I need a break," he muttered.

Before anyone could comment or question him further, he hurried outside, his pulse still racing.

****

Charlie moved through the crowd, greeting longtime customers by name and introducing herself to a few new faces. She was determined to put thoughts of Jesse's strange behavior, his possible leaving despite his assurances that he didn't intend to go anywhere, and the pain she'd caused Caleb aside. For now, at least. Caleb was mingling with the crowd, and Jesse was back behind the bar. They'd all just have to get through tonight. Tomorrow they could deal with the fallout.

"Charlie!" She looked over to see who had called her name. A smile broke over her face, and she threaded her way through tables and customers.

"Henry," she said as she eased up to the middle-aged man's table. "I didn't expect to see you here tonight." Henry, the diner's owner and primary cook, was rarely seen outside his business. The few times when he was, Henry was usually running to the post office or the grocery, or doing some such errand for his restaurant. Or flirting with Doris in his own adorably awkward way.

"Got a date tonight," he beamed up at her.

Please, don't be Doris. Please. Dad will be so crushed.

"Hey now, Charlie, you ain't trying to muscle in on my date, are ya? Took me years to finally get him to ask me out."

A relieved sigh escaped her as she turned to smile at the woman sliding into the seat opposite Henry. Annabel Bellows had been a checker at the grocery store as far back as Charlie could remember. And right now, Charlie was so happy she wasn't Doris, that she leaned down and kissed the startled woman's cheek.

"I wouldn't dream of it, Annabel. Henry's far too much man for me to handle."

"Oh now," Henry blustered, blushing a deep shade of scarlet as he toyed with a small cork coaster. Annabel chortled with glee.

"Georgia Ann," Charlie called, motioning the nearest waitress over.

"Yep!" Georgia Ann had been flirting with a table of boys from the college a couple towns over, padding her tips no doubt. She hustled over to Charlie's side.

"Bring Henry and Annabel a bottle of champagne. On the house." Though she rarely made a habit of comping drinks, this was a special occasion. Henry had finally turned his attention to someone other than Doris. Now all she had to do was convince her father to step up to the plate. She turned back to the couple. "Enjoy your night, guys."

"Gee, thanks, Charlie!"

Smiling, she gave Henry's shoulder a friendly squeeze before moving on to gather up some empties from the next table.

"Is it always this busy?"

Charlie paused beside the man sitting alone in the next booth. "Not quite *this* busy. But it is Halloween, and Badger Creek likes to celebrate."

"I see that," the man chuckled as he watched Frankenstein, Little Bow Peep, and a guy dressed as the killer from a popular nineties slasher flick stagger by, holding each other up.

"Do you always have live bands?"

"Every weekend," Charlie raised her voice to be heard over the noise.

"They're quite good. Local boys?"

"Yes." She smiled as her gaze went to the raised dais in the far corner. "And the one playing drums? That's a girl."

"Oh!" The man's bushy eyebrows rose. "My mistake." He smiled up at her through thick, horn-rimmed glasses, and she had to make a concerted effort not to stare at the rather large mole beside his nose. "I saw you behind the bar earlier. You must work here?"

"I run the place." She offered her hand. "I'm Charlie McKenna. Are you new in town?"

"Just passing through." He reached out to shake her hand, but seemed to misjudge the distance. Correcting his mistake, he took her hand in his and shook it tentatively before letting go. His depth perception was probably bad, the poor guy. And with glasses like that, it was little wonder. "I can't tell you how nice it is to meet you."

His warm enthusiasm was charming. "Well, it's nice to meet you too."

He blinked up at her, but before he could speak again, the unmistakable sound of a table being shoved out of the way caught her attention. She quickly scanned the crowd.

Oh, crap on a cracker. Not again.

Turning back, she offered the gentleman she'd been speaking with an apologetic smile. "I'm sorry, would you excuse me?"

She crossed to the other side of the bar in a flash, stopping beside Caleb where he stood toe to toe with Dylan of all people.

Charlie took in Caleb's scowl, the group of men a short distance away trying to talk their buddy down, and Dylan's kiss-my-ass smirk. Before she could step in and try to diffuse the situation, Jesse was there. Dylan's buddies instantly shut up and took a healthy step back.

"Is there a problem here?" Jesse growled.

"I was just asking Dylan to leave," Caleb said, for once forming a united front with Jesse.

"Ain't done nothing wrong," Dylan drawled, leering at Charlie. "Just came in for a drink."

He didn't seem drunk, not yet anyway. In fact, he seemed entirely sober, which almost made the situation worse, given the way he seemed to be trying to pick a fight.

She glanced around the bar. Yep. Everybody was watching. Again.

A horrible sense of déjà vu settled upon her. *No*, she decided. *Not tonight.*

"Dylan, come outside with me," she invited.

His grin spread. "Now you're talking."

Caleb moved to follow, but Charlie quickly shook her head, laying a hand on his arm. "Call Stanley," she mouthed.

Caleb looked like he wanted to argue, but finally stepped back and, as Dylan turned away to follow Charlie, he pulled his phone from his pocket. Charlie pointed a finger at Jesse. "You stay here."

She just prayed Stanley wouldn't be too far away. And that Jesse would remain inside.

Once through the door, out of sight of the taproom, she rounded on Dylan and drilled a finger into his chest. "What the *hell* do you think you're doing here, Dylan?"

"I just—"

"Oh, cut the crap," she snapped. "You didn't come in for a drink, just like you didn't '*come to see your girl*' the other night, so don't even go there. You came here looking for a fight, and we both know it."

His charming façade slipped, and that old familiar glint snuck into his eyes. "Came to have a little chat with your new bartender."

Adrenaline spiked. She took a step forward, glaring at him. Surprisingly, he backed up a step. So, she took another step forward. And another. Until she'd paced him in a circle and her back was to the pub now. "You stay the hell away from Jesse, you hear me?"

"Or what, Charlie? What are you gonna do? Call Stanley? That old man can barely handle his wife. You think he's gonna arrest me? Haul me down to his little jail?" Dylan stepped closer, letting his lecherous gaze rover over her. "Why don't you try asking nice, sugar? I bet me and you could come to a mutually...*beneficial* arrangement."

Now she stepped back, but he was faster. He had his hands around her waist and was jerking her into his arms before she could move. His lips descended on hers in a punishing, angry kiss. She twisted her head, shoving at his shoulders, but she was gaining no ground. And so, she did what any smart woman in her position would do.

Bracing her hands on his shoulders, she rammed her knee up as hard as she could, her goal to make his nuts pop out his ears.

Mission accomplished. Choking, Dylan released her in a heartbeat. He grabbed his crotch and slowly sank to his knees. And once he was kneeling before her, she hauled off and punched him in the nose with every bit of strength she possessed.

"Don't you ever, ever touch me again you lying, cheating, disgusting pig," she spat. Scrubbing the back of her hand over her mouth to wipe away his filth, she stepped back. Only then did she realize she had an audience.

Caleb, Paula, Georgia Ann, Mark Peters from the local Co-op, Shane Martin from the power company, John Carroll and a few others crowded the entrance, gaping in astonishment. Even that nice man with the glasses and the mole that she'd been talking to was outside watching. And standing in front of them all—grinning with unmistakable pride—stood Jesse.

Stanley chose that moment to pull up, lights flashing. He got out of his car, adjusted his utility belt around the girth of his waist, and approached.

"Charlie?" He nodded acknowledgement in Caleb's direction, "Caleb said you might have a spot of trouble." Stanley's disgusted gaze dropped to the man still on his knees, moaning, blood gushing from his nose. "Looks like you took care of things well enough."

Only then did she become aware of the dull ache in her knuckles. Cradling her hand to her midsection, she smiled at Stanley. "I did, but thanks for coming."

"Want to press charges?"

She frowned down at Dylan. How could she have wasted a moment on the likes of him? Well, she wasn't going to waste another second, that was for sure.

"Do I need to, Dylan?" She waited for him to focus watery eyes on her. He shook his head. "Then you better listen up and pay attention. If you ever so much as step foot on premises again, I'll have you arrested on sight for trespassing. You hear me?"

He nodded, still cupping his crotch with one hand, his bleeding nose with the other, looking a bit green around the gills now.

"You know, I think I'll haul him in, all the same." Stanley stepped forward, pulling his cuffs out. Charlie blinked, surprised. Stanley yanked Dylan's wrists behind him and snapped the cuffs in place. "I've got enough to worry about tonight without wondering if he's gonna come back pestering you. This way, if he's in jail, I'll know right where he is."

"You ain't got no cause to arrest me," Dylan wheezed.

"No?" Stanley leaned close, took an exaggerated whiff. "'Cause it sure seems to me like you had one too many to drink." He cranked the cuffs tighter making Dylan flinch. "Yes sir, I'd say Public Intox is a darn good possibility. Course, me being the nice guy I am, instead of writin' you up, I'll just let you sleep it off in a special little bunk in the back."

Dylan staggered to his feet and jerked his arm from Stanley's grasp.

Stanley took on a whole new attitude. One Charlie'd not seen since Homecoming her senior year. Dylan had been involved that time as well.

"Don't be stupid, boy." He yanked Dylan back with surprising strength, and then smacked the back of Dylan's head with the flat of his hand. "'Less you want those charges, plus a few more, to stick?"

Scowling now, Dylan glared at the faces around him, lingering on Jesse. But he walked willingly to the back of Stanley's cruiser and climbed inside. Once the door was closed, Stanley turned back to Charlie, eyeing the way she was holding her hand.

"You change your mind about pressing charges, Charlie, you just give me a call. Get some ice on that hand."

She nodded. Stanley slid behind the wheel and drove away, lights flashing to announce Dylan's shame to the rest of the town. Charlie squared her shoulders and turned back to face her audience. The man with the glasses and the mole caught her eye. He gave her a broad smile, an approving wink, before allowing Caleb to usher him along with everyone else back inside. Everyone but Jesse.

Jesse closed the distance between them and wordlessly drew her into his embrace. She wrapped her arms around his waist, not caring if anyone lingered to watch this time. She needed this.

"You didn't come charging to the rescue."

"No." He kissed her hair, squeezed her a little tighter for a minute.

"But you wanted to, didn't you?"

"I did." He turned his head, smoothing his cheek along the crown of her head now as he held her close. "But I'm a smart man. I learned my lesson. Besides, you had things in hand."

"I did," she said. And she had. She'd handled herself just fine. "What if I hadn't?"

"Then I would have finished it for you," he said. And this time there was no gentleness in his tone.

She glanced up. He was staring down at her with such a fierce look, she caught her breath.

"We should go back inside," he finally said. "People will start talking."

"So, let 'em talk," she whispered, reaching up to

draw his head down. She initiated the kiss, but it didn't take long for him to assume control. And when he finally pulled back, they were both out of breath.

"Come upstairs with me tonight."

"I thought you liked my place."

"I do." He stepped back, clasped her hand in his and raised it to his lips. Pressing a quick kiss to her knuckles, he grinned down at her with heat in his eyes. "But my place is closer, and I don't know how long I'm going to be able to wait."

Floating on a cloud, Charlie followed him back inside. She glanced around the pub. The place ran like a well-oiled machine once more. Jesse relieved Caleb behind the bar, and Charlie joined him there.

"You come on out to the orchard sometime, Jesse," John Carroll invited. "I'll show you around."

"I'll do that, John. Thanks."

Wow, another first. She'd never known John to invite anyone to his orchard before. Oh, sure, he'd occasionally extended an invitation here or there on his wife's request. Always, *"Wanda says come on out."* But never on his own behalf. She blinked in wonder at Jesse. Smiling, Jesse moved behind her and wrapped his arms around her waist.

For a split second, probably out of habit, she stiffened, her eyes flying wide. But he held her tight, as if anticipating her reaction and refusing to be dislodged or brushed off. When she turned her head to peer up at him, to question him, he caught her startled lips in a quick, possessive kiss.

Releasing her mouth, Jesse continued to hold her in a loose embrace as he turned his attention to a customer who'd asked about the score of some game. And he kept right on standing there, holding her, until she relaxed in his arms and leaned back against him.

At first it was a bit awkward. After all, she'd never allowed this type of intimacy in the workplace before. Jesse's actions declared loud and clear to one and all that they were together. But the longer she stood there in his arms, the more she thought about it, the less she minded the very public display of affection. In fact, she found she liked the idea a little too much.

Content, she wrapped her arms around Jesse's where they rested around her waist. She let her gaze roam over the pub, pleased to see everyone having a good time.

She caught a flash of movement near the door and glanced over. Oh, that nice man she'd started chatting with before Dylan's little scene was leaving. She hadn't even thought to go back to apologize for cutting their conversation short.

He paused there by the door and turned back. Charlie smiled when she realized he was looking in their direction.

She offered him a friendly wave from the circle of Jesse's arms. She hoped the man came back before he left town. He seemed very nice, and she hated to think he might leave with the wrong impression of the pub.

But the man smiled and inclined his head, bowing at the waist, bidding her an old-fashioned *adieu*. And then he slipped through the doors out into the night.

"Who are you waving at?" Jesse asked near her ear.

"That man from booth sixteen." She thought for a second, and then frowned. "Hmm, you know, I never caught his name."

Chapter Twenty

The next morning, Charlie sat at the desk in her office adding up the previous night's receipts when there was a knock at her door. She glanced up and smiled at Paula.

"Hey, Paula. What can I do for you?"

"There's a kid out front, says he's got a package for Jesse. I sent him around and up to the apartment, but Jesse's not answering his door."

"I think he said something about going to the grocery store today before work." Frowning, Charlie stood and skirted the desk as curiosity got the better of her. Who would be sending a package to Jesse here?

As she entered the taproom, she caught sight of a teenager holding a large manila envelope. "Hi. I'm Charlie, can I help you?"

"I'm looking for Detective Reid," the boy replied. She didn't recognize him, but then she probably wouldn't recognize many kids his age.

"Um," she stuttered. The title had thrown her for a moment. "He went to the store but he should be back pretty soon. Can I help you with something?"

The boy looked to the envelope in his hand, and then to his watch. "Man, I'm gonna be late for class." He stared at her for a heartbeat, indecision etched on his face. "I guess it'd probably be okay to leave this with you."

"I can certainly hold it until Jesse comes back."

Relieved, the boy passed her the manila envelope, then spun on his heel and jogged out the door without another word. Charlie turned the package over in her hands. Large black lettering marked the front.

Detective Jesse Reid.

Slowly, she turned and made her way back to her office. She sat down behind her desk, still gripping the envelope, unable to get her mind to move beyond that one simple word.

Detective.

It wasn't like she didn't know he'd had a job, and a life, before coming to Badger Creek. But this was something solid. A tangible piece of evidence. Cold, hard proof of his life *before*. The life he was so careful to never talk about.

And the title was there. As if he'd never left the career behind. As if it was there, waiting for him. Waiting for Jesse to be done with her. A call back to his old life. A life that didn't include her.

And, God, how pitiful was that? Why did she keep waiting for the other shoe to drop? Why did she insist on borrowing trouble? Why couldn't she just enjoy the moment for what it was?

But what was *it* that was between them anyway?

Why did she always have to define things? Set labels and limitations on things?

She wasn't sure how long she sat there, surely an eternity by now, staring at the envelope, this reminder of Jesse's past. A past she knew precious little about. But then the thump of footsteps sounded overhead, and she found herself on her feet, envelope clutched in her hand before she'd had a chance to consider the questions she needed to ask, or the possible answers she might get.

At the top of the steps at the back of the pub, she paused. The wind buffeted her, chilling her to the bone as she hadn't thought to grab a jacket. And still she couldn't move.

Was this it then? The moment he would ride out of her life and never look back?

God, she'd thought she'd gotten past this.

For one moment, she entertained the idea of going back to her office, of not telling him about the package. Of hiding it, destroying it. She hadn't even looked at the contents, but somehow, she knew whatever was inside would change everything.

Detective.

And, even as she considered it, she discarded the notion. She couldn't do it. She couldn't pretend. She was a horrible liar, and the moment he looked at her, he'd know something had happened. That something was wrong. She couldn't betray his trust like that.

No, she had to do this. Now.

Without giving herself time to think it over, time to let the worry overcome her better judgment, she banged on the door. The muted thud of footsteps moved closer, and the door opened. She'd been looking down, staring at the envelope in her hands. When she looked up, Jesse's welcoming smile turned to a questioning frown. Charlie tilted the envelope so the name printed on it was clearly visible.

And she watched with mounting concern as all the blood slowly drained from his face.

****

Jesse paced back and forth across the apartment

living room. Charlie sat on the couch, holding herself perfectly still, perfectly straight. Her eyes following him, asking all the questions she had yet to voice.

He glanced down at the unopened envelope resting so innocuously on the old coffee table in front of the couch. Considered it as one might watch a bomb, its timer dwindling away.

Shit.

His pacing resumed with renewed vigor. It couldn't be. It was a joke.

A damned sick joke.

But who else would know about the messages? Who would know how they'd been delivered? That was one of the few details that hadn't been leaked to the press.

And how did the Chess Master even know where Jesse was?

Just like that, ice ran through his veins.

There was only one way to find out. He had to open the envelope. Had to look inside.

And then, he had to make the phone calls. The ones he'd been avoiding.

He dropped to his knees beside the coffee table and glanced up, thinking to suggest Charlie leave. In the past, the Chess Master had only ever sent his clue on a slip of paper, and one mundane snapshot of his intended victim.

But this envelope was thicker than the others, heavier. Jesse had no idea what to think. The look on Charlie's face changed his mind. She wasn't going anywhere. Besides, she had every right to know what they were facing.

She had a right to know what kind of monster Jesse

had brought to her door.

A fresh wave of icy fear ripped through him. So terrifying, he could barely function. What if this truly was from the Chess Master? What if he'd somehow found out about Charlie?

What if...

All these damned *what ifs* weren't doing him any good. And, judging by the way she was staring at him—the wide eyes, the compressed lips, and the pale skin—he was probably scaring her more now than the envelope was.

With shaking hands, he drew the envelope closer, handling it carefully. Jesse pulled a pocket knife out and slit the end. With one last apprehensive glance at Charlie, he slid the contents out onto the table.

Charlie cried out, and then slapped a hand over her mouth. Her eyes were huge as she stared at the horrific images. Without warning, she vaulted to her feet and ran from the room. Jesse pushed to his feet to go after her, until he realized she was only going as far as the bathroom.

The door slammed closed behind her, and Jesse turned his attention back to the small pile of photos, one after another, each one almost too grisly to completely process.

He'd witnessed scenes like this before. Carefully staged scenes. Bloody scenes. Scenes of death and mutilation that left hardened police officers puking in the bushes. He'd seen those images so many times, some in person, some through photos, that he'd memorized the faces of each and every woman.

He picked the photo up, held it to the light.

He didn't recognize this face.

But every photo was of the same victim, just different angles. As if to share a multitude of artistic views. Jesse wanted to be sick.

At the victim's feet lay a newspaper. Picking the photos up, he stepped closer to the window and peered at them in fresh light.

A staged newspaper clearly showing the paper's origin and the date. A very recent date, only a few days ago. And the town?

Sackville.

The room spun around Jesse, his world imploding.

No. No, not again.

A closer look at the snapshot of the Sackville victim revealed the mark branded onto her flesh.

A Pawn.

The game had started again.

Jesse moved back to the envelope, intent on shoving the damning photos back inside, when a sheaf of white paper fell out.

That single piece of paper terrified him far more than all the others had.

My Dearest Detective Reid,

I felt it behooved me to take a moment to send a special note to you. I wish to express my most sincere gratitude for making this the most exciting game yet. I've matched wits with many men in my time, and none have been such a pleasure to compete against. You are truly a formidable adversary, and I hold you in the highest esteem.

I would also like to congratulate you on promoting a new Queen. Please, give my regards to your lovely Charlie. She is a most pleasant young woman to converse with, full of courage and grit, and I look

forward to spending time with her again.
Yours truly,
The Chess Master

P.S.—I sincerely hope my opening salvo is up to your standards. I knew you would be at a disadvantage not being able to view the scene for yourself this time, so I took the liberty of enclosing a few photos for your consideration.

It's your move…

"What is all this?"

Jesse glanced up at the sound of Charlie's hoarse voice. Her face was damp, and she pressed the back of her wrist to her mouth. Though she peered at him through haunted eyes, her focus seemed compelled to return, time and again, to the envelope on the table. At least he'd thought to turn the photos face down.

"I need to borrow your phone."

"What?" She blinked at him as if in a daze. "I want to know what that's all about—"

"Please, Charlie. I swear to you, I'll tell you everything. But right now, I need your phone. And I need you to stay here. Right where I can see you. Do you understand me? I need you to stay right here."

He took a step toward her, but when she shied away he held his hands up, palms out, and said, "Please? This is very important. I'll explain everything. I promise."

She stared at him for a long time, then finally reached into her back pocket and took out her phone. She extended it in a shaking hand. Desperation had him by the throat. He couldn't resist. Jesse closed his hand over hers, phone and all, and drew her into the shelter of his arms. She resisted at first, stiff as a board while

261

she tried to push him away. But then she broke down, gripping his waist as she leaned into him.

"Please, Jesse," she whispered against his chest. "I need to understand."

"I promise," he said at last, cupping her cheeks in his hands to stare deep in her eyes. "Please, just sit down. Stay here. Okay?"

She peered up into his eyes, as if trying to discern his secrets. Finally, she sat down and clasped her hands between her knees while she watched him.

Jesse stared at the phone in his hand, debating whom to call first. Carver hadn't returned any of his calls yet. His former partner Demarco maybe? Or SSA Anderson? Taking a deep breath, he thumbed a number into Charlie's phone and waited for the call to connect. He got voicemail. No way was he leaving a message like this. Hanging up, he swore, then dialed the precinct.

A female voice he didn't recognize picked up.

"Detective Demarco, Violent Crimes Unit, please." His gaze went to Charlie. She stared at him with wide eyes.

"Hold, please." The phone beeped in his ear.

"Demarco," a deep voice answered.

He hesitated for half a second. The sound of DeMarco's voice overwhelmed him with emotion. He closed his eyes and turned from Charlie, could barely find his voice. "It's me," he said quietly.

A moment passed. "Reid?"

"Yeah." He took a deep breath.

"Damn, dude. Where are you? You okay? Where've you been all these months? I've been trying to get a hold of you, but even your brother had no idea where you were."

So many questions, but that was DeMarco. A detective clear to his DNA. And Jesse had questions for DeMarco too. But the only one that mattered right now was the one question he feared above all others.

"He's started again, hasn't he?"

"Yeah." Demarco heaved a weary sigh leaden with apprehension. Jesse's knees nearly buckled. As it was, he had to grab the kitchen counter for support. A blow to the midsection would have left him with more air. A chair squeaked from Demarco's end of the line.

"I've been trying to track you down. I warned Billy already. Told him to have you get in touch with me the moment he heard from you."

"I haven't spoken to Billy since…since Molly…"

"You see it on the news? Shit, that had to be a shock."

"He found me, DeMarco." Jesse's gaze went to Charlie. She was hanging on his every word. "I don't know how, but he found me."

DeMarco swore.

"He sent me another envelope."

DeMarco swore louder.

"And there are pictures. Jesus. Lots of pictures. All of the same vic. There's a new detail this time. He placed a newspaper at her feet showing the date and location. Demarco, the paper's less than a week old. And it's from a town nine miles from where I've been staying. And there's another note. But this one is more detailed. A full letter." He picked up the note and read it out loud to DeMarco, all too aware of Charlie's frown as it ran the gamut from confused to puzzled to horrified.

Demarco was silent for a long while once Jesse was done. Then he asked, "Listen, do you have a fax where you are?"

"Um, yeah. Just a sec." He asked Charlie for the number, and repeated it to his partner. Then he gave DeMarco Charlie's phone number and his location.

"Look, I know you're not officially in the loop anymore, but I'm going to send you everything I've been able to get my hands on for the last few murders. And, Reid, you need to call Anderson, like yesterday, man. You should probably bring the local boys in on this too."

"I will," he promised.

"Jesse," DeMarco said, paused, drew in an audible breath. "It's good to hear from you. Don't let this be the last time, got me?"

Jesse closed his eyes and savored for the moment, that sense of camaraderie he and his partner used to share. "I got you."

After disconnecting the call, Jesse looked to Charlie. She held the note from the Chess Master in her hands. Training had Jesse flinching over contaminating evidence.

"Don't," he said, rushing forward to take it from her. "Don't touch it, okay? Or the photos. They need to be checked for prints."

He knew they would find the same prints on these as that they'd found on all the others. But he just couldn't stomach the idea of her touching something so evil.

She turned a haunted gaze on him. God, it looked like she was going into shock, she was so pale. He reached over, took the throw blanket from the back of the couch and draped it around her shoulders.

"I have one more call to make, sweetheart, okay?"

She nodded, wordlessly pulling the blanket closer. She looked so fragile, so shaken. He wanted to hold her. Wanted to reassure her that all would be well. That nothing could hurt her. That he'd keep her safe.

But he honestly couldn't tell her that, now could he?

Sighing, he began to pace again as he thumbed in the next number. This time, as the call connected, his gaze locked on Charlie's. He asked to be connected to the appropriate field office.

"Supervisory Special Agent Vanessa Anderson, please."

"And may I tell her who's calling?"

Jesse stared at Charlie, licked his lips.

"Yeah," he said, loud and clear. "You can tell her this is Detective Jesse Reid, Minneapolis PD, Violent Crimes Unit."

Charlie's gaze dropped to her lap. She didn't make a sound, but she looked utterly miserable.

"One moment, please," the operator said.

He waited in silence for the call to connect. SSA Anderson answered on the third ring. "Detective Reid, SSA Anderson here."

In a matter of minutes, he filled SSA Anderson in on the package he'd received. Initially she was hesitant, but eventually she brought him up to speed on the Chess Master investigation. It was more than he'd expected given their last interaction. And worse than he'd feared. They were no closer to catching this killer than they had been when he'd been working the case.

"Do you have the next target, Detective Reid? Do

you know who the Queen is this time?"

Jesse turned to face Charlie. The bottom of his stomach dropped. Every fiber of his being screamed in denial. His gaze traced the features of the woman he'd come to love more than life itself.

More than he'd ever dreamed possible.

Jesse gritted his teeth against the raw fury and the sickening fear churning in his gut. "I do."

Chapter Twenty-One

Jesse dropped onto the couch beside Charlie. She was so cold all of a sudden, the bleak look in his eyes chilling her to the very marrow of her bones. None of this made any sense.

She needed answers. "So, you know who sent these pictures?"

"Yes." He dragged both hands down his face, his expression weary. "I'm...or I was, rather, a detective with the Violent Crimes Unit in Minneapolis."

She hadn't pushed him for answers before, figuring he'd tell her when he was ready. But considering the contents of that envelope and the phone conversations she'd overheard, she had a right—no, a *need*—to know. Sooner rather than later.

"Tell me why you left."

He took a deep breath. "It's a long story."

"I've got time," she snapped, finally reaching the limits of her patience...and her calm. She couldn't sit here and pretend she hadn't seen those pictures.

And *her* name had been mentioned in that twisted letter.

He reached for her. Charlie scooted back before she even realized what she'd done. She caught the flash of hurt in his eyes, and the resignation. She didn't want to hurt him, but she didn't want to be held right now, didn't want to be coddled.

She wanted the facts.

All of them, whether she liked what she heard or not.

"I was a homicide detective," Jesse said. He leaned back against the sofa and dropped his hands on his lap. "A little over a year ago, my partner and I were called to the scene of a murder. It was bad, like the stuff in those pictures. I'd never seen anything like it." Jesse shook his head, his gaze and his mind far, far away.

"The murder, the *details* of the murder, threw up a red flag in the FBI's database. It was the same M.O. they'd been tracking all over the Midwest. We had a serial killer on our hands. This guy typically killed a random number of women—three or four—in one location, and then moved on. He also preferred large cities. The people I was supposed to protect and serve became a target. Because of me."

"What do you mean, because of you?"

"For some reason, he made contact…with me. The Feds said it was the first time he'd ever reached out to anyone. We still don't know why he picked me. But this was all like a game to him. He'd send clues—a cryptic note and a single headshot of a nameless woman—addressed specifically to me. He'd then give me twenty-four hours to locate the woman before he made his move." Jesse pointed to the pictures on the table giving her a pretty good indication of what the killers "move" might be.

"He calls himself the Chess Master." Jesse gritted his teeth, and his expression tightened. "To him, these women are just pieces on the board. Pawns, Bishops and so forth in his game…all working up to his end game, the Queen."

Charlie wasn't happy he'd held out on her. Not that she'd expected him to spill something this traumatic during his interview...or even soon after. But they'd been intimate long enough, he should have shared this information. Particularly if this sadistic madman was still out there, still targeting Jesse in some way.

For a moment, Charlie doubted. Herself. Jesse. Her own judgment. But there was one basic certainty she clung to with both hands. Deep down, Jesse was a good man.

But, that didn't mean she'd be played for a fool, regardless of the fact she'd fallen in love with him. There would be no more secrets between them. Conflicted, she did her best to push all the rest aside and focus on the situation at hand. There had to be something they could do to stop this killer.

One thing she did know, Jesse beating himself up over something he had no control over wasn't going to get them anywhere. Besides, she couldn't stand to see the torment in his eyes.

"Jesse." Charlie finally reached out and squeezed his wrist. He flipped his hand over, laced his fingers through hers, and held on as if she were his lifeline. A jumble of emotions passed over his face. "Jesse, look at me. *You* didn't choose for these people to die. This wasn't your fault."

"People still died—"

"You said yourself, he'd killed before Minneapolis and once he played his game out, he moved on to kill again somewhere else, right?"

"Not this time."

Charlie cocked her head, frowning.

"The Chess Master stayed in Minneapolis after he

murdered…after he killed the Queen."

Now she was really confused. "How do you know?"

"Because he made one more kill." With his free hand, Jesse dug his fingers into the center of his forehead, rubbing hard. "Did you see the mark branded on the chest of that victim in the photos he sent?" At her nod, Jesse went on. "Well, after the Queen, he broke pattern. He took another Pawn in Minneapolis. Another player *after* the Queen. He'd never done that before. At the time, I wasn't…in a position to focus on the case. Looking back now, I think he was trying to start another game…maybe. Hell, who knows. Regardless, the Feds had taken complete control by then. I guess he didn't get what he was looking for, so he moved on to a new city."

"How many women has he done this to?" It made her stomach churn just asking.

"Honestly? I don't know for sure. I don't think anyone does except maybe him. Last positive ID, well, now including this woman in these pictures…over thirty. In all likelihood, there are a lot more out there that we don't know about. The only thing that matters is I couldn't stop him."

"The *FBI* couldn't stop him, Jesse, and they'd had much longer to do it than you did."

"But I had an advantage they didn't."

She frowned at him, silently urging him to go on.

"The killer communicated with *me*, remember?" He pointed at the envelope on the table. "Me, specifically. Just like this. Daring me to find them before he did. Find them and save them before he killed them."

He told her then of the sleepless weeks trailing a monster. Of the women he'd failed to save. Of the nightmares that haunted him still. Then Jesse grew quiet. Though he left his hand in hers, it was as though he were withdrawing into himself right before her eyes.

"There's more," she prompted. "What aren't you telling me?"

"All through his twisted, sick version of Queen's Chess he's always focused on the goal...the Queen. Could he capture her, or could his opponent...me...could *I* keep her safe?"

Jesse twisted around and captured both her hands in his. He held them tight between them. She'd never seen him looking so grave.

"Charlie, the last Queen he captured...the woman he murdered—" Jesse broke off, closing his eyes for a moment as if stealing himself against the awful truth he was about admit, and her reaction to that truth. "That Queen was Molly Bartlett...my girlfriend."

She froze, unable even tug her hands from his. Unable to speak. No. No, this couldn't be happening. *Oh, God, Jesse!*

"The Chess Master sent one of his clues to the station one night while I was on duty. There was a delay at the front desk, and I didn't get it until it was too late. And while I was sitting there, trying to figure this guy out, trying to get inside his head, he was...he was with Molly. He," his voice broke, and he had to stop and clear his throat before he could go on. "He did that," he pointed at the overturned photos, "to Molly. He killed her...in our home."

"Oh, my God, Jesse," she gasped. The raw grief on his face shredded her. She could only stare at him in shock.

"After…after I found her." he took a deep breath and visibly forced himself to continue. "I was officially taken off duty, put on administrative leave. But I followed the case, got tips from a sympathetic agent, pumped my partner for information. I used whatever I could…whoever I could…to get a lead. I was obsessed."

He closed his eyes again, as if reliving the horrors he'd recounted. Charlie sat in silence, almost numb with shock, chewing her bottom lip as she stared at those face down photos.

"SSA Anderson, the lead agent on the case threatened to have me arrested for obstruction. It's been almost a year."

"And now this Chess Master is here too?" Her voice sounded tiny, and very afraid, even to her own ears.

"He's here. And that envelope is another clue."

"The game's starting all over again." Cold sweat broke out on her brow, and she feared she might throw up again.

"It is," Jesse confirmed. "That was his first move. You saw the mark on that woman's chest. She was the Pawn. He's maneuvering pieces. That letter was to let me know he's after my Queen."

She shook her head slowly, blinking. *I don't want to hear this. I don't want to know.*

Jesse held her hands when she tried pulling away. He gave them a tiny tug and squeeze to make her look at him. When she met his gaze, the look in his eyes terrified her.

"It's you, Charlie. *You* are my Queen."

Comprehension slowly drained the blood from her head until the room spun around her. "You mean another innocent woman is going to die, and another and another…until he finally gets around to me?"

"No!" Jesse gripped her shoulders and jerked her into his arms. "I'm not going to let him get to you. I won't let you out of my sight. Do you hear me? Not for a moment. I won't let that bastard anywhere near you."

Her emotions were all over the place, spanning the full spectrum from deep, primal fear to the darkest anger. And beneath it all, a paralyzing sense of helplessness.

"Again," she whispered against his shoulder.

"What?" He leaned back and frowned down at her.

"Again," she repeated, pushing back out of his arms. She wiped the tears from her cheeks. "He's already gotten to me once, remember? It's there in the note, Jesse." She snatched the paper up, reading an excerpt aloud.

"Please, give my regards to your lovely Queen. She is a most pleasant young woman to converse with, and I look forward to spending time with her again," Charlie read. "*Again*. He says it right here. He's already made contact."

Jesse took the note from her. She couldn't even get up and pace, her legs too shaky to hold her. Her icy hands trembled as she clutched them in her lap.

His gaze flew to her. "You've seen him. Think Charlie. What did he look like? He's a master of disguise, can blend in anywhere. That's one of the reasons we had such a hard time finding him before. He was just another face in the crowd. But here, in this small town, he should stand out. Is there *anyone* you

273

remember talking to that you don't know? Anyone that might have acted or said something suspicious?"

Something nagged at her, but she couldn't quite put her thumb on hit. And then, as she rubbed the bridge of her nose in frustration it hit her. The nose…or rather, beside the nose. That big mole. And the glasses. The way he'd winked at her.

The man she'd been talking with before the incident with Dylan.

Her skin crawled. She'd touched a killer. Shaken his hand.

Charlie told Jesse everything she could remember about him. Jesse spent the next few minutes questioning her, picking her memory apart, but she couldn't come up with anything more than what she'd already told him.

"SSA Anderson said they'll have agents en route as soon as possible. They should be here within six hours or so."

"That's a long time to wait when he's already made his first move, Jesse." She touched his cheek. "Call Stanley," she urged. "Give him the chance to do his job too, Jesse. What could one more set of eyes hurt?"

"Okay, yeah," he promised. "Does Badger Creek have a sketch artist?"

"I don't think so, but we have Marlene Nesbit. She's the high school art teacher…or she was. I think she's retired now. She's pretty good."

"You'll have to meet with her, sit down and explain what he looked like with as much detail as possible."

"I can do that. But won't he have figured out by now that we know what he looks like? Won't he just change his appearance again?"

"Maybe, but the more people we have aware, the less chance he has of hiding in plain sight. We need to put pressure on him, find him before he can…"

His voice trailed away as he glanced to the photos on the table.

Shaking his head, Jesse looked at her then, really focused on her, and his expression was filled with contrite anguish. "God, Charlie, I'm so sorry. I brought this monster here. If I could leave, could get him to follow me before anyone else got hurt I would. You know that, right? I'd leave, and keep on driving to keep you safe."

"He'd just keep killing." She put her hands on his shoulders, slid them up to cup his cheeks. "Here, or somewhere else. He'd keep killing. You have the home field advantage here, Jesse…an even better one than in Minneapolis. You have us, all of us, and like you said, this is a small town. He *can't* get lost in the crowd here. You know him better than anyone. Use the knowledge. Let us help you. Please."

"I won't have you putting yourself at risk."

"He's already made me a target." She searched his eyes, filled with determination. Resolve to stop this monster was the only thing burning through the shock and the fear. She put as much feeling behind her words as she could without breaking down. "I trust you, Jesse. I *know* you can keep me safe."

He opened his mouth to argue, but she pressed her lips to his, silencing him.

"I trust you," she reiterated. Kissing him again and again until he responded by pulling her across his lap.

"I swear to you, Charlie." He tucked her head

against the side of his neck and held her tight. "I'll do whatever it takes to keep you safe. *Whatever* it takes."

****

The Chess Master parked down the block and sat in the idling truck, waiting. Watching. The Knight lived alone. No husband. No boyfriend. No roommate and no kids. He glanced at his watch.

Ah, plenty of time.

He could spend all day observing. He had the patience for it. But that would be unwise on this playing field. Someone would—not might—*would* notice here.

A middle-aged man came out of the house next door, dressed in a dark business suit and carrying a briefcase. He climbed inside a midsized SUV, the only vehicle parked in the carport, and drove away. And still the Chess Master waited. Like a spider with a fly hovering, hovering, hovering above its net. He was an expert at knowing the exact, perfect moment to strike.

Finally, just a few minutes after eight, a minivan pulled out of the Knight's other neighbor's attached garage. A harried mother tipped a silver coffee mug to her lips as three children in the back seats bounced and waved their arms animatedly. The fourth, a boy who looked to be in his early teens sat in the far back, his dark head tipped back against the seat and cords dangling from his ears.

The Chess Master gave it another ten minutes, just to be sure. When no one else peeped from the neighboring houses, he climbed from the truck and strolled down the street at a leisurely place, taking in the scenery. The Knight he'd carefully chosen last night lived in a nice neighborhood. Nothing too ostentatious, nothing too ritzy. But nice. Well-manicured lawns.

Tidy, maintained homes.

Usually he took more time in choosing his players, in positioning them. But he'd just had such a good feeling about this one, and he wasn't one to look a gift horse in the mouth.

Besides, everything had changed. The board...no longer a massive city, but a small intimate community instead. And the players themselves. No longer nameless faces in a crowd, but pieces in a community that would immediately be recognized and missed. Therefore, the rules had changed.

At first, he hadn't been sure he'd like this new game. He really wasn't one for change. But the more he considered, the more he strategized, the more he liked the possibilities. Anyone could be a player. The stakes were even higher. And all bets were off.

How clever of Detective Reid to add these new twists in the game. This just goes to show how right I was in choosing him. What a brilliant adversary he's proven to be!

He dipped his hand into the deep right pocket of his coat and fingered the pewter piece nestled there. His little Queen. His good luck charm. One he carried everywhere he went. But it wasn't the only thing in his pocket anymore. Smiling, he patted the tiny plastic horsey too.

No curtains moved as the Chess Master meandered along on the sidewalk. No one stuck a head out the door. Not even a dog barked. He couldn't have orchestrated a more perfect scenario. This was meant to be.

He'd turned up the collar of the long trench coat he'd found in the back of the truck as he'd been walking. Now he turned it back down to reveal his face as he walked up her sidewalk. A collar made a statement. A turned-up collar caused suspicion. Turned down, a collar exuded innocence and credibility. This is my face, open to the world…you can trust me, it said.

He knocked on the door and waited.

And waited.

He rang the doorbell, but he didn't grow impatient. He just needed to give the Knight time to wake up, time to answer the door. After all, she'd worked quite late last night. And he knew she was home. He'd returned to the pub in the wee hours of the morning to follow her home so he'd know right where to find her.

Shuffling on the other side of the door alerted him to her approach.

See? Perfect.

He affected a benign smile. The door opened a crack, and she squinted at him, her hair mussed, and her eyes heavy from sleep.

"Yes?"

"Oh, oh, dear, I'm so sorry!" He feigned distress. "I woke you, didn't I?"

She smiled at him, perfectly polite, even though it was obvious she wanted nothing more than to crawl back into bed. "Can I help you?"

"Well, um, yes, I hope so. I'm a bit lost." He ran a hand over his thinning hair as he glanced down the street, orchestrating a worried expression. He resettled the thick rimmed glasses on his latex enhanced nose. "I'm staying at Thelma's. The Bed and Breakfast? And, well, you see I went out for an early morning stroll, and I'm afraid I got a bit turned around. I know it's a small town, but I must keep turning the wrong way because I just can't seem to find my way back."

"Oh, that's no problem." She opened the door and stepped halfway out onto the step, tugging a thin cotton robe close around her attractive figure.

"Say, you look kind of familiar," he said, squinting at her face.

She frowned, tilting her head.

"Oh, I never forget a face. I've got it!" He smacked his forehead, rolling his eyes as if he couldn't believe his own forgetfulness. "I know. I must have met you at the Irish Rose last night. Did you eat there as well? What wonderful stew they have!"

Smiling, she shook her head. "I'm a waitress there."

"Ah. Well, I feel better now. Hate it when I recognize a face but can't pin a name to it or remember where I know it from. And oh, dear… Now I really do need to apologize for waking you. You must have been working quite late, and here I am, bending your ear."

"Really, it's no problem at all." Pointing to the west, the Knight said, "You want to go to the end of this block and turn right. Go…" she bobbed her head with a severe look of concentration on her face, as if she were mentally tabulating the distance, "six blocks. Turn left at the old feed mill, and go two more blocks."

"End of the block, left, and six blocks after the feed mill. Right, got it. Thanks so much. And I'm sorry about waking you—"

"No, right then the six blocks and a left—wait. You know what? Just stay here a minute. Let me grab a pen and a piece of paper, I'll draw you a map. I'll be right back, okay?"

"Sure, sure. I'm sorry to be such trouble. Take your

time."

She turned away and slipped back inside, leaving the door ajar behind her.

"Take your time," he murmured again.

The Chess Master eased his hand inside the left trench coat pocket, passed the roll of duct tape hidden there, and he gripped the small hypodermic needle. Smiling, he stepped inside the entry way and gently closed the door behind him.

Chapter Twenty-Two

Jesse had spent the better part of the afternoon in the Badger Creek Police station with Charlie at his side. He'd flat out refused to allow her out of his sight. They'd gone over every detail, every note, every photo, until Jesse was sure the small-town Chief of Police had properly assessed the severity of the situation.

Then they'd called in the artist Charlie had recommended. The Nesbit woman had rendered a remarkable likeness. Still, having done everything he could think of to get a step ahead of the Chess Master, Jesse couldn't shake the lingering sense of unease. SSA Anderson had called earlier to inform him something had happened with another case and they wouldn't be arriving until much later than previously planned. Jesse never thought he'd see the day, but he found himself admitting he'd feel much better once the Feds arrived.

Hell, who was he kidding?

He wasn't going to feel better until the Chess Master was out of commission. Out of commission for good, not just locked up behind bars. Charlie wouldn't be truly safe, and Jesse wouldn't rest easy, until the bastard was dead.

Charlie guided the vehicle into the parking lot and turned off the ignition. Jesse didn't know if it was his preoccupation with the Chess Master, or if he'd just become used to Charlie's driving, but he'd hardly minded the ride that time. The pub was beginning to bustle with activity for the evening. Before she could reach for the door handle, Jesse grabbed her hand.

"Charlie, I don't like this. I think maybe you should...I don't know, take the night off or something. Maybe we should go back to the station, hang out there until—"

"Jesse, I'm not going into hiding until this killer is caught. You have to be reasonable."

"I have a really bad feeling about this."

She squeezed his hand, comforting him despite the fact she had a target on her back. The woman amazed him. Once she'd gotten over the shock, Charlie had pulled herself together and been a rock all through Stanley's interrogation. She'd been calm and collected with the artist. Anyone else in her shoes would have been a hysterical mess by now.

"You're going to catch him this time. I know it. You'll keep me safe, and you'll catch him." She reached over and tugged his coat to draw his attention from his fears and regrets, from the past. "Hey. I trust you," she reiterated emphatically. "Trust yourself, Jesse. You're better than he is."

He stared at her a long moment. And then he cupped the back of her neck and pulled her closer, pressing his forehead to hers. Tilting his head, he captured her lips. But the kiss wasn't enough. He needed her to understand. Everything. And he'd learned the hard way not to let important things go unspoken.

Because you just never knew.

"I've fallen in love with you, Charlie," he whispered against her lips. Then, he pulled back a little and peered hard into her eyes. "I. Love. You."

Her lips parted, and her eyes widened with unmistakable surprised pleasure. She blinked, then blinked again as moisture pooled in her eyes, threatening to overflow.

"I love you too."

Smiling, he sank his hands into the silk of her hair, cupped her head, and kissed her again. Joy, pure and overwhelming, burst through him. He'd hoped. But he hadn't been sure.

Soon he wanted more, needed more. Taking hold of her waist, he dragged her out from beneath the steering wheel, over the center console, and across his lap. He cradled her in his arms and kissed her with all his heart, refusing to let thoughts of the Chess Master taint this moment.

He slipped his hand up beneath her sweater, and trailed his fingertips over skin soft as silk. And then he cupped her breast, groaning at how perfectly it filled his hand. He rubbed his thumb in slow erotic circles around her nipple through the lace until she arched her back, panting.

"Come upstairs with me," he whispered against the side of her neck.

"Oh," her head tilted back when he tweaked her nipple. Her eyes closed, and she gasped. "But I should go inside. They'll be needing help and—"

"They lasted this long. They can wait a little longer. Caleb's here, he'll keep things running till you get back. Come on," he fervently encouraged, nipping at her earlobe.

He wasn't lying. He did need this, very badly. Needed her. Knowing that a killer was stalking him, was hunting her, lent urgency to his movements and desperation to his voice. He couldn't take the chance that something might happen, to either of them, and he'd let this moment pass them by. "Please, Charlie. I need this. *We* need this. For us. Come with me upstairs. Just you and me. Just for a little while."

She turned her face to his, captured his lips. "Stop talking, Reid, and take me upstairs," she whispered between drugging kisses.

That was all the encouragement he needed.

Fumbling with the door, he managed to get them both out of the vehicle, across the parking lot, and up the backstairs undetected. They'd barely cleared the threshold, when Jesse spun her around and right into his waiting arms. He slanted his mouth over hers and kicked the door closed behind him with the back of his boot. Jesse swept her up in his arms with every intention of carrying her to the bedroom. But he only made it as far as the couch before her questing fingers and enticing kisses made him lose his head.

Lowering her feet to the floor, he made short work of stripping them both. Their legs tangled, and the breath left her lungs in a giggling whoosh as he tumbled her onto the sofa and followed her down. He touched and kissed and caressed her…everywhere. And she did the same to him. Charlie writhed beneath him, moaning, arching her hips up to him, inviting. And she was so slick, so hot. God, she was ready for him.

That wet heat was his undoing. He gave up any last semblance of control and lost himself in her.

****

Charlie couldn't catch her breath. Leaning over her, Jesse braced himself on his elbows, sparing her as much of his weight as he could. But she needed him so much, needed to feel him inside her, moving with her. And when he touched her, she almost came undone right then and there.

Moaning encouragement, she gripped his hips and urged him closer, practically begging him to take her. His movements were less than gentle as he positioned himself above her and drove himself inside her, deep inside. His urgency fueled hers.

"God, I love you, Charlie," he groaned at her ear as his hips pounded against her.

Lifting her legs higher, taking him as deep as she could, she gripped his hair in her fists and kissed him with greedy need. Her body had taken on a mind of its own, writhing beneath his in a primal rhythm. And above her, his powerful frame rocked into her, pinning her, caging her, holding her captive for his fierce desire. His hand slid beneath her hip, cupping her bottom, squeezing, angling her as the intensity of his thrusts increased.

And suddenly she was flying, her body convulsing as wave after wave of pleasure rolled through her. Throwing her head back, she screamed his name, clutching him tighter. Above her, Jesse's body bucked, every muscle locking tight as he groaned aloud.

She came back to her senses as Jesse trailed nibbling kisses along her jaw and over the curve of her lips. A fine sheen of sweat slicked their skin, and their chests heaved in sync with each other.

"Thank you," he whispered in her ear after a while. "Thank you for coming up here with me."

"Goof," she teased, pushing at his shoulder, until she saw that he was serious. "Jesse," she said, cupping his cheeks. "Being with you is…it was important to me too."

He kissed her then. A long, lazy mating of tongues that said far more than words ever could. After fumbling their way through dressing and more stolen kisses, Charlie managed to drag him downstairs. And just in the nick of time, by the looks of things.

Utter chaos reigned.

The dishwasher wasn't working, the truck had shown up late, Doris had cut her palm on a broken glass and gone to the emergency room for stitches. Caleb was flustered, becoming curt with staff and customers alike, and two of the waitresses were late for their shifts. Her two, most dependable waitresses, of all people.

Charlie glanced around the rapidly filling pub. Noting which tables had been helped, and which were still waiting for service. "Has anybody tried calling Georgia Ann or Paula yet?"

"I tried Georgia Ann, but I went straight to voicemail. Haven't had time to try Paula," Caleb called over his shoulder as he made change for a customer.

Jesse shook out an apron and tied it around his waist. He shot Charlie a lingering grin that said, loud and clear, he thought their little tryst had been more than worth it. And then he jumped into the thick of things behind the bar.

Charlie caught her lower lip and tried to ignore the heat stealing into her cheeks. On a mission, she darted behind the bar and quickly dialed first Paula, and then Georgia Ann. Not getting a response from either of them, she made a snap decision and called several part-timers for reinforcements.

"Any luck," Jesse asked the moment she hung up. He slid a shot glass in front of a regular, and made change.

"No. Neither of them is answering. I'm getting worried, Jesse." Despite the bustling crowd, Charlie lingered behind the bar and turned concerned eyes his way.

Caleb dropped a tray of empties on the bar and gave Jesse two more drink orders. "Heard anything yet?"

"No. Not a peep," Charlie said. "It's not like either of them to no show, not without a phone call at the very least."

A large group came in then, and began pulling tables together. Caleb and Charlie shared a concerned look. Charlie grabbed a spare apron from a peg behind the door, snatched up an order pad and a tray and jumped in to help. Almost an hour passed before she had time to try calling again.

Still no answer for either of the waitresses.

Jesse frowned. "This isn't typical, is it?"

"No, not for either of them. Georgia Ann can run late for a shift now and again, but she always calls. And Paula hasn't been late for a shift in three years." Caleb said, addressing him perhaps for the first time without rancor. Charlie was just too frazzled to be hopeful things had changed on that front.

Jesse's expression filled with apprehension.

A chill skated through her. "Jesse?"

"I don't know," he said, shaking his head.

Caleb looked back and forth between the two. "What's going on?"

"He needs to know now. It can't wait till later," Charlie insisted, her tone brooking no argument.

Jesse stared at Caleb for a moment, then finally

relented. He shot a glance to Charlie. "Can you handle the bar for a few minutes."

"Yeah, go ahead. Use my office," she instructed, stepping behind the bar as a grim Jesse and a suspicious Caleb slipped into the back.

A short while later, they returned. Jesse, if anything, looked even more apprehensive. Caleb's face was chalk white.

"I think we should call Stanley," Charlie said. "I'd feel a lot better if he went by to check—"

"Charlie," Jesse interrupted, nodding toward the door.

Georgia Ann flew through the front door, juggling her purse with one hand, dragging her coat off with the other.

"I'm so sorry, Charlie, Caleb," she panted. "I, ah, I lost track of the time, and I headed over as soon as I realized I was late. I tried to call to tell you I was coming, but my phone was dead."

A relieved breath slipped from Charlie as her shoulders sagged and she closed her eyes. Thank God. One of her chicks was safe, at least. Now she only had to find Paula.

"It's okay. Just, do me a favor, don't leave the building again until I can talk to you, okay." Charlie reached over and squeezed her shoulder, grateful the girl was all right.

Georgia Ann frowned as she tied on an apron. "What's wrong?"

"Everything's fine," Charlie replied, shooting Caleb a warning look. "Table thirteen is ready to order."

She watched as Georgia Ann made her way to the

table Charlie had indicated. "I'm going to run to the back to call Paula again…and maybe Stanley," she told Jesse and Caleb.

Jesse caught Caleb's eye. The assistant manager slipped behind the bar to take his place while Jesse followed Charlie to the back. Paula still wasn't answering. A cold knot of fear twisted in the pit of Charlie's stomach. After calling Stanley and requesting that he drive by Paula's place right away, Charlie and Jesse returned to the taproom. But Denise and Ginny, the two part-timers she'd called earlier, had already arrived and things were beginning to level out.

Charlie stood at the end of the bar, jumping every time the door opened. And she prayed. Jesse came up behind her, settling his hands on her shoulders and smoothed them down her arms. He drew her back against him. But he didn't offer any words of comfort. He must know they'd be empty until Paula walked through that door.

The phone beneath the bar rang, and they both started. Caleb snatched it up. "Irish Rose."

He listened in silence. Without a word, he turned, his lips pressed in a thin line.

"It's Stanley," Caleb said, holding out the receiver. "He wants to talk to Jesse."

Chapter Twenty-Three

"I'll take the call in Charlie's office," Jesse told Caleb.

Charlie followed him. There was no way she was missing out on this.

After closing the door behind them, Charlie watched as Jesse picked up the receiver. "I got it, Caleb." Once the definitive click of the extension hanging up sounded across the line, he said, "Go ahead, Stanley."

All the color leached from his face, and he dropped heavily onto the chair behind her desk. Closing his eyes, he bowed his head and passed a hand over his face.

And when he looked up at her, Charlie knew.

Her knees buckled. She crumpled onto the remaining chair, too distraught to cry. Too shocked to make a sound.

Paula…

Charlie thought of Paula as she'd stood at the bar, joking with customers, laughing along with Charlie and the others. Or the way she liked to pop quarters into the old Jukebox in the corner after closing time so they could have music while they cleaned. She remembered the way Paula had come early with Doris to help decorate for the employee party. And how she always left a half-empty glass of Dr. Pepper behind the counter to sip on while she was on shift.

Dear God, not sweet, lovable Paula!

"I will," Jesse said into the phone. "Did you speak with SSA Anderson yet? Uh-huh, and her eta?" A moment of silence, and then he glanced up at Charlie and replied, grim and determined. "I'm not letting her out of my sight." Another moment passed. "We'll be there."

Jesse dropped the receiver back onto the base and stared at her for a long moment. Without saying a word, he got up, came around the desk. She didn't realize how cold she'd grown until he drew her into his warm embrace. Jesse held her gently and murmured apologies to her as the numbness wore off and her emotions exploded.

She shook her head, trying to push him away.

"No. No!" She struggled against him as her mind, and her heart, rebelled. Frantic not to face the truth, desperate to put off the inevitable, she shook her head, her body stiff. "It's a mistake. It's not her. Stanley made a mistake. You saw those pictures. You can barely recognize what's left of the...of the..."

And then she began to tremble. Her legs went weak again, and her stomach rolled. She clutched his shirt in her fists for support, for something to anchor her. "Oh, God, Jesse! Did he do that to her? Did he...did he do those terrible things to Paula?"

Jesse held her closer, shushing her. He pressed his cheek to the top of her head. A sob hit the back of her throat, choking her, erupting before she could stop it. And then came another. And another. Before she knew it, the tears were flowing, falling like rain. She couldn't contain them. Couldn't stop them. Her grief, her horror was too strong.

Jesse sat down and pulled her onto his lap. She curled around him, seeking comfort in the shelter of his hard body. At length, he pressed a wad of tissue into her hands, and waited as she blotted at her face and blew her nose.

She was exhausted. Completely wiped out. Her puffy eyes burned, and her nose was stuffy. But, far worse, was the horrible empty ache in her chest.

Paula…

Jesse shifted her in his arms, forcing her to sit up. Carefully, he brushed the loose hair back from her face. "We have to go, baby."

"Go? Go where?"

"Stanley needs me at the scene—at Paula's house." He smoothed his hands down her arms, and his touch calmed her as nothing else could. "He needs me to help process the scene. They aren't really…equipped to deal with this."

"Then you should go," she nodded, moving from his lap, swiping both hands across her cheeks. She could do this. She had to. Somebody needed to be strong, and she was the boss. The others would look to her now, take their cues from her. When they found out—

"*Us*, Charlie, we're both going."

"No." She shook her head, taking a step back. "No, *you're* going. I have to stay here."

"I told you, Charlie," he argued adamantly. "I'm not letting you out of my sight."

"Jesse, please." She turned grieving eyes on him, praying he'd understand. She couldn't go there, couldn't see Paula's house. Even if she didn't go inside, she'd seen the pictures of those other women, what the Chess Master had done to them. She couldn't sit outside, knowing what had happened within. No, she just couldn't face it.

Because her friend was dead.

And the monster intended to do the same to her.

Besides, she needed to break the news to the others about Paula. There was so much that needed to be done. She had to stay here, had to stay busy.

"Charlie—"

"Jesse, no. I can't go there. Can't you understand? I just can't."

His expression softened, just a bit. But that steely glint of desperate determination lingered in his eyes. "Charlie, I can't leave you."

"I won't be alone, I promise. I swear it to you. I'll stay here, surrounded by people. I'll be with Caleb the whole time you're gone. I won't leave the building. I won't even come back to my office alone. I promise. You go, do what you need to do." He didn't like the idea of leaving her, that was plain as day, but neither did he want to force her to go to a crime scene.

"Please?" she pressed.

"Charlie, you don't understand how dangerous this is," Jesse growled.

"Yes. I think I do." She forced herself not to think of Paula, or she'd break down all over again. "I swear I'll stick with Caleb the whole time."

She remained silent as she watched Jesse wage a fierce internal battle. When he spoke at last, he looked vaguely ill. Definitely not comfortable with his decision in the least.

"You stay directly in Caleb's line of sight at all

times. You don't leave the taproom without Caleb. You don't even come back to your office without him attached to your hip. You don't go to the bathroom unless Caleb's standing right outside the door. And don't you even so much as *think* about taking the garbage out, do you hear me?" He pointed a finger at her, his expression as serious as she'd ever seen it.

Charlie slipped her arms around his waist and pressed her cheek to his chest.

"I swear," she whispered.

He stood there for moment, rigid in her arms. As if he were still arguing with himself about the sanity of caving to her pleas. Finally, his arms came around her, and he buried his face against the side of her neck, inhaling deeply.

"You stay safe, Charlie," he whispered fervently. Tipping her head back, he caught her lips, his kiss just shy of painful. Touching his forehead to hers, he stared into her eyes. "Please, *please*, stay safe for me."

****

A sickening ball of unease churned in the pit of Jesse's stomach as he surveyed the crime scene. He hadn't been joking earlier tonight when he'd said he had a bad feeling. At the time, though, he could never have anticipated *this*.

Paula's house was…

He shook his head, closed his eyes, and then opened them again to examine the wreckage. Never before had the Chess Master displayed this level of violence. Usually he'd contained himself to one room, to the victim herself. This looked like a war zone. And not just the living room where her body had been discovered. No, the kitchen was in shambles. Her bedroom a nightmare.

Paula had put up one hell of a fight.

And she was still dead.

For the last hour, he'd desperately searched for some clue as to how to find the Chess Master. He could just as well have been searching for the proverbial needle in a haystack.

It would probably help if he could focus. But all he could think about was Charlie, and whether she was safe. Whether Caleb had taken his direful threats to heart. He'd already called twice to check on her. She was fine, she'd assured him the first time. The second time, she'd spoken through Caleb as she'd been neck deep in some problem with the pop dispenser.

"Were they all like this?" Stanley asked, drawing Jesse's attention back to the here and now. The Police Chief tucked his thumbs into the utility belt of his blue uniform, his demeanor subdued as he nodded toward the body bag being lifted onto a gurney by the county medical examiner and his assistant. Jesse had to give the small-town cop points. While his face was white as a sheet and beaded with sweat, the cop had held himself and his crew together admirably.

"Yeah, pretty much," Jesse said, turning back to study the living room one last time. "The body, at least. The house, that's different. Worse now. Like he—" He paused, shaking his head, trying to get a handle on his thoughts. There was something off this time. Something nagging at him like unfinished business. He shook his head. "It's worse this time. Even by his standards."

"You think it was because she fought back?"

"Could be." But he wouldn't bet on it. If anything, he'd wager the level of destruction had more to do with whatever was going on inside this bastard's head than anything Paula may have done.

Chapter Twenty-Four

Charlie shivered as she aimed the SUV's heat vent toward her chest. Grimacing, she peeled the sticky, soda-soaked shirt from her skin. Loathed to soil her jacket as well, she'd opted to just drape it over her shoulders and rely on the vehicle's heater for warmth. Unfortunately, her plan wasn't working very well in the face of the sudden turn in the weather and the unexpected freezing drizzle. She worried about Jesse out on the slippery roads, but at least he was driving her vehicle and not his motorcycle.

"Jesse's going to kill me," Charlie muttered beneath her breath for what must have been the hundredth time.

"It can't be helped," Caleb assured her. He gripped the steering wheel with both hands. His eyes never wavered from the slick roads. "We'll only be gone long enough for you to shower and change and then we'll head right back. I'm with you, and we'll be careful. Besides, no other nut-jobs but us would be out in weather like this."

Caleb's weak attempt at humor fell shy of the mark. Grief for Paula still sat heavy in her chest. And fear that the madman that had murdered Paula would eventually be coming after her was just too much for her to see the humor in any situation right now. Though, she did appreciate Caleb trying to lighten the mood. While he and Paula had never been particularly close, she knew he must be suffering from the shock of her death as well.

"I should have called him, told him where we were going." She plucked at the clinging, cold material on her thighs. Of all the times for the soda machine to go haywire, tonight had not been ideal.

"We'll be back before Jesse is. No sense in worrying him for no good reason. Besides, right now he should be concentrating on..." His voice trailed away as the weight of his words, at the reminder of their loss sank home. "I can't believe he brought that monster to Badger Creek." Anger laced his tone.

"Caleb, we've been through this already," Charlie snapped, her patience worn thin.

God, she was suddenly so tired of his attitude where Jesse was concerned. After Jesse had explained the situation to the assistant manager, Caleb had been silent with shock. But that silence had quickly worn off, and the shock had turned to anger. It hadn't taken long at all before Caleb had begun blaming Jesse for Paula's death, and for putting them all at risk. As if Jesse had known the Chess Master would follow him here.

Charlie had staunchly defended Jesse. She knew he would never purposefully do something to put someone else at risk. He'd done his part to apprehend this killer, done everything within his power to put this Chess Master away where he wouldn't be able to hurt anyone else. Jesse couldn't have possibly known that a madman would track him here.

But Caleb was a dog with a bone. "Look, Charlie, all I'm saying is—"

"I've already heard what you're saying.

Repeatedly. And I don't want to hear it again. You're wrong, Caleb." She turned to glare at him. "This isn't Jesse's fault. And if you were being honest with yourself, you'd admit it and stop trying to make him look like the bad guy in this horrible situation. You and I both know the real reason you're riding his case so hard, and I have to say, Caleb, I'm pretty disappointed. I thought we were both on the same page. I thought you understood that how I feel about you has nothing to do with Jesse."

Caleb said nothing; instead, he continued to stare fixedly at the road ahead. But his knuckles whitened on the steering wheel, and the muscle along his jaw began to tick.

Charlie instantly regretted taking the hard line, but she reminded herself it was time to stop coddling him. This needed to be laid out there in black and white. Obviously, his plan of pretending things were fine, of pretending she'd never found out about his true feelings for her wasn't working. For either of them. She couldn't go on like this any longer. It was hurting their personal relationship and, eventually, it would begin to erode their working relationship as well.

She softened her tone, but she refused to pull punches. "Even if he had never come to town, Caleb, you and I still wouldn't ever be anything more than friends. You understand that, right?"

She regretted hurting Caleb. And she was, it was more than obvious. He'd been her best friend for a long, long time. But she couldn't regret setting things straight between them. It would only hurt him more in the long run if he thought there was a sliver of hope for something more serious between them.

"I got it," he said, his voice held an edge that made her cringe.

"Caleb, please." She tried one last time to mend fences. "I don't want to hurt you. You have to believe me about that."

"I said I got it," he snapped. But then he finally glanced her way. His expression softened, and he offered her a sad, disappointed smile. In a less harsh tone, he added, "I got it. Just friends."

"Thanks," she said, reaching over to touch his shoulder.

He nodded, and for the first time since her confrontation with Caleb in her office, he seemed more himself. The Caleb she'd trusted and relied on for so long.

He cleared his throat and glanced back to the road. "Jesse did say this killer always has downtime between murders, right?"

Back at the pub, Caleb had sounded so convincing when he'd suggested a quick trip home to change after the soda machine mishap. But now he didn't sound quite so sure of himself. He sounded as if he were justifying, trying to reassure them both that they were operating within a window of safety.

From what Jesse had explained to her, there were no scenarios in which anyone was safe as long as the Chess Master was on the loose.

Regardless of Caleb's rather rational sounding arguments earlier, or his less than convincing assurances now, Charlie's gut instincts were screaming at her. She shouldn't have left the pub without letting Jesse know what was happening, end of story.

"I should call Jesse," she murmured again, resolved

this time as she pulled the phone from her pocket. And, for once, Caleb didn't argue.

Jesse, not wanting to be out of touch even for a short while, had borrowed Doris's cell phone, informing Charlie that come first thing in the morning they'd be making a trip to Viroqua to get his broken phone replaced. Charlie quickly dialed Doris's number.

The call went straight to voicemail and recorded female voice answered. "Hello. You've reached Doris Hanselman. Please leave a message, and I'll get back to you."

Frowning, Charlie disconnected and blinked at the phone. Maybe he was trying to get through to her? Then she noticed her own reception bars were flickering. She glanced up as freezing rain pelted the window. Had a tower gone down somewhere?

Chewing the inside of her cheek, she tucked the phone away and held both hands up to the vent, shivering again. This time, however, she wasn't sure if it was from the cold, or from some deeper sense of foreboding.

Whatever it was, she just wanted to hurry and get back to the pub. She jumped when a pair of headlights fell in behind them and tailed them all the way out of town. Nerves strung tight, Charlie held her breath until Caleb took the turn off to her house and the headlights behind them kept right on going down the highway.

As darkness filled the rear-view mirror, and her little cabin came into view, Charlie took her first deep breath of relief since leaving the safety of the pub. She fished the keys from the bottom of her purse, and then she and Caleb climbed out and scurried toward the front door, feet slipping and sliding, heads down and shoulders hunched against the biting sleet.

Once inside, Charlie flipped on the lights and locked the door behind them. Chilled to the bone, thinking only of showering quickly and getting back, Charlie motioned absently toward the living area. "I'll hurry."

Nodding, Caleb flipped the lid open on the redwood box on her coffee table and picked up the remote, aiming it at the TV above the fireplace. Then he dropped onto the sofa and propped his feet up, as much at home here as he was at his own place.

Charlie stood there for just a moment longer, staring at the back of his head. Everything about the way he behaved while in her home, the way he knew just where to find the remote, the way he plopped down screamed brother, not lover.

How can he not see that?

Shaking her head, she turned and hurried down the darkened hallway toward her bedroom. She paused at the half-closed door and frowned. All the hair on the back of her neck stood on end. Why was the door half closed? She'd left it all the way open when she'd left this morning, hadn't she?

She couldn't remember.

The room beyond was pitch black. She strained to hear movement beyond the door, but could detect nothing beyond the voices from the TV down the hall. With a trembling hand, Charlie reached out and gave the door a push, prepared to leap back at the first sign of trouble. Nothing moved but the door.

Shaking her head, she reached around the corner to flip the light on. All was as it should be, just as she'd left it this morning. She hadn't made the bed, but she'd been pressed for time this morning. The curtains were still drawn. And the closet door was slightly ajar, which reminded her she'd have to work on that latch this weekend.

Charlie hurried to the closet and jerked the door open. She reached up into the shadowed interior, and grabbed the chain to turn the light on. But one tug, then a second yielded no results. Her already frayed nerves nearly snapped. Gritting her teeth, she snatched the first thing she came to and moved back from the closet. She knew she was probably being paranoid, but she couldn't help but keep a wary eye on the closet as she left the room.

Holding the change of clothing well away from her body, Charlie crossed the hall to the bathroom. The sound of a sports announcer's excited voice echoed from the living room. She could just see the back of Caleb's head from here. Closing the door to the bathroom behind her, she stripped and showered in record time.

Once out of the shower, she ran a brush through her hair, but didn't bother drying it. She took ten seconds to apply a quick coat of mascara, then scooped up the wet towel and wrapped it around the ball of her soda-covered clothing.

"I'm almost ready," she called. Caleb grunted, but she couldn't understand him over the TV. Charlie shook her head, well-acquainted with the utterly male preoccupation. Sports news was still broadcasting, and light from the TV flickered at the end of the hall.

Charlie hurried to her room and dropped the dirty clothing into her hamper. She grabbed a pair of sneakers from the bottom of her closet, sat on the side of the bed to put them on, and then flipped the light off.

"Okay, Caleb, I'm all set," she said as she entered the living room. Frowning, she looked down at the empty couch. The TV was still on, but Caleb wasn't in there. Frowning, she rounded the corner to the kitchen. "Caleb?"

****

"Why?" Stanley asked in a hoarse voice. "Why like this?"

Jesse had said it once a long time ago to DeMarco when his partner had asked pretty much the same thing. Now he repeated those words to the Badger Creek Chief of Police.

"Crazy's got its own set of rules."

Jesse walked to one corner of the room, and then the other, carefully studying details, aware Stanley watched his every move. Jesse examined blood splatter patterns and an overturned recliner, a shattered lamp. A toppled, broken TV. Mail that had spilled off an upturned end table.

"She put up one hell of fight before he brought her down," Jesse remarked.

"Paula would have. She could be a scrapper when she wanted, but she's a good kid," Stanley said, his voice thick with emotion. He cleared his throat, and when he spoke again, anger held reign. "She *was* a good kid. Too damned good for this."

His time in the academy and his many years on the force had taught Jesse not to take his work personally. He'd seen many a good officer, many a good detective burn out because they hadn't been able to separate themselves from the job. But all too easily, Paula's smiling face came to mind, her kindness and patience as he'd been learning the ropes at the bar, her warm welcome at the picnic at Charlie's house. Aside from Molly, Paula had been the only other victim Jesse had known personally.

And that's how he was taking her murder. Personally.

Very, *very* personally.

Because that's exactly how it had been intended. As a personal jab at Jesse himself.

See how close I am.

See what I can do.

"Think any of that blood's his?"

"Usually, I'd have said no," Jesse shook his head as he squatted down and used the tip of a pen to turn over a porcelain shard coated with blood. "As a rule, the Chess Master strikes like a snake, fast and vicious, attacking his victims before they've even had time to realize they're in danger, let alone to fight back."

Once again, those dark tendrils of guilt begin to tangle around him. Those useless *what ifs*. What if he'd taught Molly even the most basic self-defense moves? What if he'd taken the time to make sure she knew how to defend herself in the event of an attack? Would she have stood a better chance of surviving?

And what if they'd called Paula sooner, warned her to be on the lookout?

What if—

He'd learned a long time ago; *what ifs* wouldn't bring someone back from the dead. But he could do something about it now. He'd teach Charlie. He'd show her how to spot dangerous situations, teach her how to break holds so she could escape. He'd even teach her how to shoot a gun. In fact, he'd start tonight. He'd give her the fighting chance Molly and Paula never had.

"This time, I wouldn't be so sure. Lot of blood this time. I'm betting money some of it's his." Glancing up, Jesse said, "I'm praying she got him good. Scratched him up at the very least. Best case scenario, she gouged him deep enough for stitches. Put a call in to local clinics and hospitals to keep an eye out for anybody fitting his description—hell, make that any male age 30 to 70—that comes in needing stitches."

"Will do," Stanley nodded. "And our M.E.'s a good guy. Never had any cases like this, but Dr. Granger's solid, knows his stuff. He'll follow the letter of the law. He's a real stickler for procedure, so you won't have to worry about evidence being inadmissible."

But Jesse's mind wasn't on evidence. Wasn't on making a case stick. A guillotine was poised over his head, waiting to drop. Promise or not, he should never have left Charlie.

He dropped the shard back in place. He hadn't found anything more that what was expected. He had to get back to her. Had to see with his own eyes she was safe.

Grim, his mind made up, Jesse rose. But as he did so, he caught a glimpse of something beneath the edge of the sofa. Just the stingiest little tip of yellow envelope. Striding over, he bent down and lifted the ruffle on the bottom of the sofa. His breath left him on a whoosh.

"What is it? What'd you find?" Stanley peered over his shoulder.

****

"Oh, my God!" Charlie gasped. She froze for half a

second. Her throat closed on a scream. Caleb lay on his side in the middle of the kitchen floor. Garish scarlet blossoms marked his shirt high on one shoulder, and in two spots on his abdomen where his life's blood slowly drained into a pool beneath him.

"Caleb!" she cried, scrambling to her knees beside him. "Caleb, open your eyes. Look at me. Oh, my God, Caleb. Stay with me!"

Frantic, she jerked open a nearby drawer and ripped out dish towels. Her hands shook so badly that she fumbled them. Snatching them up from the floor, Charlie pressed the towels to his wounds, and he moaned aloud, only half conscious.

"Stay with me," she kept muttering, her breathing rapid and shallow. She had to get help. She held a towel in place over what seemed to be the worst of his wounds as she dug in her pocket for her phone. *Get help. Get help.*

He was bleeding so much. Had any vital organs been hit?

And then cold realization settled upon her like an icy blanket. Caleb hadn't had an accident. He hadn't slipped while opening a soda and nicked himself. He'd been stabbed. Deliberately.

Multiple times.

She went completely still, didn't even breathe, suddenly aware of the unnaturally silent room. She couldn't hear the sports announcer anymore. Her thumb carefully depressed the number nine—God, that beep had been so loud—before inching over to the one.

Had the killer heard?

The Chess Master is here.

Oh, God.

Slowly, she depressed the number one once.

And that's when she knew. There were no footsteps to mark his arrival. She doubted if she would have been able to hear them over the pounding of her own heart anyway. But she knew with some inner awareness, like the fine hair standing up on the back of your neck when you know you're being watched. That creepy-crawly feeling you get when your car breaks down along some shadow-filled, unnaturally quiet road in the middle of night. Or that oozy feeling that slithers down your spine when you step into a dank, pitch black basement.

He's right behind me.

A lone tear slipped down her cheek as Charlie stared at Caleb's unnaturally pale face.

Oh, God, please, please let him live. Let someone come in time for him.

And, just as she knew *he* was behind her, she knew what would happen the moment she pushed that number one for the second time. The question was, would she be able to stall him? Could she distract him, or fight him long enough for the call to connect? For the police to trace the call back to her cabin?

Could she hold him off until help arrived?

I'm so sorry, Jesse. I should have listened to you. I'm so, so sorry.

Charlie pressed the button, instinctively ducking at the same moment. The whoosh of something heavy skimmed past her hair, narrowly missing the side of her head. She let her momentum roll her to the side. And at the same time, she shoved the phone beneath Caleb's hip, hopefully out of sight.

Please, please, let the call go through.

Charlie didn't waste time. She vaulted to her feet and came up swinging. But she missed, hitting only air. Wheeling, she searched for him.

And there he was.

Her mind struggled to reconcile what her brain knew about this man with what her eyes and her memory were telling her. *This* was the monster that had killed Paula and all those other women? *This* was the sadistic bastard capable of unspeakable atrocities?

This was the man she'd chatted with in the pub on Halloween Eve. The man with the thick horn-rimmed glasses and the huge mole beside his nose. With his receding hairline and the beginning of a slight paunch beneath his brown plaid shirt, he looked so normal. So mundane. So…likable.

Completely harmless.

Harmless, but for that soulless, emptiness in his eyes.

And the trail of dried blood at his hairline, the scratches down his cheek.

Crouched, ready to dodge, she held her hands up in a conciliatory manner. Only a spare eight or nine feet—and Caleb's prone body—separated them.

"You don't have to do this," she coaxed, fighting not to show fear, fighting to keep her voice level. They say predators could smell fear. Well, she must stink to high heaven of it, because she was utterly terrified.

"But I do, I'm afraid," he replied in that calm, reasonable tone she remembered from the pub. "You see, it's the next logical move."

"This isn't a game!" She forced a swallow, forced herself to calm down and level out her tone. "This isn't a game. People are dying. Real people."

"Regrettable, I know. But necessary." He glanced down when Caleb moaned again, and one side of his mouth quirked up as he shook his head regretfully. "He wasn't supposed to be part of the game though. I hadn't anticipated a second Knight."

He frowned then, looking a little confused. Tilting his head, he stared at Caleb for the longest time. And then, slowly, a smile—a really frightening smile— edged the corners of his mouth up.

"Of course, the desperado!" He said in an *ah-ha* kind of way. "How *clever* of Detective Reid. I must admit, I would never have guessed he'd be willing to sacrifice a player like this." A queer sort of admiration filled the Chess Master's gaze as he looked back at her. "Oh, he must value you much more than the last Queen."

The Queen. The last player to take the field before the final checkmate.

She glanced to the doorway. Could she make it? Where were the keys to the SUV? Had Caleb left them inside the vehicle? Or were they, even now, in his pocket. She couldn't remember.

Even if she couldn't get inside the vehicle, even if the doors were locked tight, somehow it felt safer being out there in the woods, in the sleet and the dark, than in her own kitchen with this psycho.

"I think that's about enough time, don't you?"

She couldn't help herself. "Enough time?"

Without taking his gaze from her, he knelt and pulled the phone from beneath Caleb's too still body.

Holding it up, he shook it slightly from side to side. "Enough time for them to trace the call, don't you think? Or shall we give them another minute or two?"

He lifted his brows, all thoughtful consideration. "Would you like to say something for the recording? Offer Detective Reid some bracing, motivational speech? Or, perhaps a tearful goodbye? You don't seem the type for mewling, thank heavens. I must admit, whining and pleading does tend to wear on a body's nerves. Hmm, I've never allowed this before, you know, a last message. But somehow, it seems…*appropriate*."

He held the phone up to her, as if he expected her to accept his offering in good faith.

Her throat went dry as wave after wave of horror washed through her. There would be no reasoning with this man. No pleading, no bargaining.

And no hope.

He was absolutely, irrevocably insane.

She bolted for the door. The sound of heavy boots followed her through the living room, across the porch, and down the steps. They trailed her across the damp driveway, splashing through the puddles of slush. Charlie raced on, feet slipping and sliding, arms and legs pumping, heart pounding so hard she thought surely every next beat would be her last. Biting cold sliced at her lungs like razor blades as she darted toward the dark tree line.

She wasn't sure how long she ran, or how far. Barren branches ripped at her clothing, slashed at her face and hands. Slush and mud were solidifying beneath her soaked tennis shoes, turning into an icy, slushy soup, making traction impossible. Still she struggled on, because she knew what awaited her if she stopped.

And then something hit her from behind,

something big. Something panting. She went sprawling, face first, onto the ground, a heavy weight on her back pinning her down.

"Exhilarating," he huffed near her ear as he pressed her into the frigid, muddy leaves and sharp twigs. And then, louder as he mastered his breathing, he said, "I must tell you, I have to thank you for that. I never expected you to run, leaving your friend behind. You should feel proud of your accomplishments, my dear. None of the other Queens have lived up to your standards. Detective Reid chose very well this time."

His weight lifted from her, and then *she* was being lifted to her feet. He subdued her struggles with surprising ease.

"There now," he said, carefully brushing clinging leaves and mud from her clothing. "You didn't hurt yourself, did you? That would be so unfortunate. Must conserve your energy, you know." He dusted his free hand along his thigh, as he held her by the elbow, and she thought she caught a glimpse of a tear in his jeans and a smear of blood in the stingy moonlight. She struggled, but it was no use. He spun her off balance, and then caged her from behind before dragging her toward an old truck he'd parked in her back yard, out of sight from the driveway. She struggled. She kicked and squirmed. Scratched and bucked.

But she didn't bother to cry or beg. Knew it would be a waste of breath.

He was stronger than he looked. Winded, but unmoving. She couldn't shake him, no matter what she tried.

The Chess Master's voice, when he spoke to her, didn't give away an ounce of anger or a bit of strain as he tugged her along in his wake.

"I'd tell you not to worry," he said conversationally, so calmly that his next words sliced twice as deep, "or that it won't hurt a bit...but I'd be lying through my teeth."

He smiled back at her then, as he forced her onto the floor of the truck and pulled a syringe from his pocket, happy as a kid with a new toy.

Charlie screamed.

****

Squatting, his latex-covered hands trembling, Jesse pulled the manila envelope free. His name was scrawled across the front in big bold script. Fear and anger made him lightheaded. This was new. The Chess Master had never left an envelope at the scene before. Then again, he'd never been quite this brutal before either.

He was escalating.

Flipping the envelope around, Jesse showed Stanley the front before carefully peeling open one end. A single white sheet slid free, all the more stark because the single word it contained had been smeared there in fresh blood.

"Checkmate."

At the exact same moment, a young deputy came smashing through the door, completely ignoring crime scene protocol.

"Chief," he shouted, out of breath. "Chief, dispatch just called." He skidded to a halt in front of Stanley and Jesse. "Got a 9-1-1 from Charlie McKenna's cell phone. Mindy said the phone pinged from Charlie's cabin."

In a single heartbeat, in one sickening moment of

clarity, Jesse understood. Paula had been a diversion. He was on his feet in the blink of an eye, one hand jerking Doris's cell phone from his pocket, the other knocking technicians out of his way as he ran for the door.

Chapter Twenty-Five

"In the cruiser," Stanley barked, puffing as he ran behind Jesse. Jesse didn't argue. Whatever would get him to Charlie faster. He darted through the sleet and threw himself into the passenger seat of Stanley's police car.

"He has her," Jesse rasped.

Stanley moved behind the wheel with a speed that surprised Jesse given the man's girth. Panic flooded him. He was too horrified to pray, too beside himself to beg the powers that be for her safety. Fear like he'd never known ripped at him, shredding his composure.

"Damn it, *hurry*," Jesse yelled. "He has her!"

Stanley revved the engine, flipped on the lights and slammed the car into gear in one seamlessly choreographed move that attested to decades of service.

Jesse raked both hands through his hair, forcing himself to draw one breath after another, forcing himself to calm down and think like a cop.

No, I need to think like a killer.

"He won't be there anymore, at the cabin. He'll know we're on our way, and he needs to take his time with her. He's going to take her someplace else. He wanted me to know he has her, to live every moment from now until she dies to know exactly what he's doing with her."

"So the 9-1-1 was a what? A distraction?"

"Send an ambulance to the cabin anyway," Jesse said.

"If they ain't there, why send an ambulance?" Stanley demanded even as he snatched up the cruiser's radio.

"Caleb would have been with her. She wouldn't have gone home alone. If the Chess Master has Charlie now, either Caleb's hurt...or he's dead."

Stanley paled even more, but he spat orders into the radio as he guided the cruiser toward the oncoming intersection, lights flashing as sleet pelted the windows. But they had no destination, therefore no direction, and Stanley let off the gas.

Jesse had to figure out where the Chess Master would have taken her. Quickly. Charlie was running out of time.

Stanley eyed him, fine beads of sweat visible on his brow and upper lip despite the cold. "You said he's never killed a man before, always stuck to women."

"He's making up the rules now as each situation comes to him." Damn it, *where* would he take her?

"Where do we go?" Stanley repeated his thoughts aloud.

"Someplace that would hold meaning to Charlie, someplace besides the cabin," Jesse said, racking his brain for the slightest detail. He recalled one of the briefings the FBI profilers had given the Minneapolis PD on the Chess Master. "Killing is psychological for him, just as much as it is a physical act. It's just as much about her as it is about me. I'm the King, but Charlie is the Queen. He needs to violate her sense of security, to kill her in the one place she should feel the safest. Where would Charlie feel the safest?"

"The pub," Stanley announced with dead certainty. "She grew up there."

"The pub's still open," Jesse argued. "He won't want to take her someplace public."

Think like a killer. Think like a killer, he reminded himself.

He forced himself to say the words, knowing Charlie might be, even now, living the nightmare he was describing. "He needs someplace where he won't be interrupted. He likes to take his time while he plays. From previous victims' ruptured vocal cords, he lets them scream. *Likes* it when they scream. So, it's got to be someplace she won't be heard. He feeds off her terror. But he won't want anyone else to hear, won't want to risk anyone coming to investigate."

"What about that apartment above the pub? It's live band night. Lots of noise. It'd muffle the sound of a lone woman screaming."

"Would the apartment have special meaning to her?"

"When Charlie was a little thing, that's where they lived, Quinn, Sheila, and Charlie. When Sheila ran off, Quinn and Charlie continued to live there. Quinn only bought the house over on Portage Street after Charlie graduated and went off to college. When she first moved back to town, before she got her own place out on the river, Charlie moved back to the apartment over the pub."

"Would that be common knowledge? Information the Chess Master would be able to obtain easily from someone in town?"

"This is Badger Creek. *Everything's* a matter of public knowledge."

"Go," Jesse shouted, making a snap decisionhe prayed wasn't wrong. Prayed he wasn't taking them in the wrong direction.

God, please let me make it in time.

"*Go!*"

****

Charlie came around slowly. Her head thumped in time with the deep bass thundering up through the floor beneath her bare feet. Her shoulders screamed with the pain of bearing her weight. She struggled to move, struggled to stand to relieve the stress on her joints. But she couldn't move much. Her arms and legs were spread wide, her wrists and ankles bound securely to huge railroad spikes that had been driven into the wall.

Just like those poor women in those awful photos.

Panic overwhelmed her, and Charlie struggled against her restraints. Her first reaction was to scream for help. An instinct she swiftly bit down on as she peered around her with wide, tear-filled eyes. She couldn't catch her breath.

Where is he? Where is he?

If he didn't know she was awake, she certainly didn't want to alert him. And then her surroundings slowly sank in. He'd brought her to the apartment.

Why?

Why would he bring her here of all places? Why had he allowed her to call 9-1-1 at the cabin?

The answer, vying for room in her pounding head, dawned on her slowly. The police would be focusing on her cabin. Miles away from here. Who would suspect he'd bring her here? So close to all those people below.

No one, that's who.

Her frantic phone call for help had sealed her fate.

She'd unwittingly helped the Chess Master, drawing everyone's attention elsewhere, giving this murderer plenty of time to toy with her before he killed her. She jerked and wiggled, twisting her wrists, but gained not the slightest bit of freedom.

Tears began to roll down her cheeks, unchecked, uncontrollable. A sob ripped at her throat.

No! No, he can't kill me here. Not here. Not in this place.

Not where she'd spent most of her life, first as a child then as an adult coming home. It would destroy her father.

And Jesse…

Oh, God, what will this do to Jesse?

The slight sound of fabric shifting caught her attention. Her head snapped around, and she spied the Chess Master lurking in the shadows. Once her gaze locked on him, he stepped into the light.

A boogey man waiting only for her to notice him.

"It's true what they say." God, how could he be so calm? Sound so rational? "The stages of grief?" he prompted. "They hold true even when one is considering his or her own mortality. Oh, maybe not in a particular order—doctors don't have quite *everything* right, you know—but those stages certainly exist. And I must say, watching the emotions flicker over your face just now was so poignant." He frowned, tilting his head.

"You know, the other pieces each experienced their own stages of grief too, I suppose. But they were never so noticeable, not through the fear. Not as much as yours were just now. I wonder why?" He seemed to ponder this conundrum for a moment, as if he truly wanted to know. He sounded almost academic, maybe even philosophic about it, about her death and how the knowledge of it affected her.

Is he serious? Is he actually asking me?

"Perhaps I didn't take the time to truly note it in the past? Hmm, I'll have to make sure I take more time going forward."

He was already looking ahead, plotting his next kill. She wanted to be sick.

She bit the inside of her lip to keep from railing at him, to keep from begging him for her freedom. She knew it would be pointless, and she wouldn't give him the satisfaction.

"Please, don't get me wrong. You *are* special, Miss McKenna." He smiled at her. "Such a puzzle. Such a prize. I think I could learn a lot from you. You seem to hold some key to Detective Reid. Something about you brought him back. Made him tick again. The answer is somewhere inside that brain of yours. You don't mind if I pick at it for a while, do you?" He rocked back on his heels, crossing his arms over his chest as his smile took on a sly edge. Had there been some hint of a double meaning?

"You see," he went on. "I'm naturally very curious. And one doesn't find an opponent as gifted as Detective Reid every day. I'd like to figure out what makes him so unique. As sad as it makes me, I understand I'll have to look for a new opponent soon. And Detective Reid has spoiled me, set the bar quite high. I fear I won't be content to challenge just anyone now. So, tell me, what were you thinking of just then, when the tears started coming? Were you thinking of him? Or of that young man that got in the way at your cabin?"

Caleb! How could I have forgotten him? Oh, God,

please let him be alive. Let him survive.

When she refused to respond, refused to feed into this monster's delusions, the Chess Master pressed, "Come now, Charlie...you don't mind if I call you Charlie, do you?...seems awfully stuffy to continue with such formality in light of the intimacy of what we're about to share here." He blinked up at her, courteous and inquisitive. Waiting for her to give her permission? "Oh, dear me, forgive my atrocious manners. You may call me Jeffrey, of course."

Nodding, apparently content that matters of etiquette had been properly addressed, he prompted, "Your emotions, please? I imagine they must be quite turbulent." He made a mew of his lips beneath the thick beard. His big mole was missing now, as were his glasses. And his nose looked different. Smaller. His paunch was gone too.

"You know, I've never asked before. Not any of the other pieces. And, come to think of it, not the last Queen either." A frown tugged his brow, and he shook his head. "How rude of me. Terribly rude."

"Let me go," she said, striving to stay calm. *Keep him talking*, she rationalized, hoping someone would figure out where they were. But her voice trembled with terror, and the tears continued to roll.

"Now, you know that isn't going to happen. Won't you tell me what you're thinking of? And if you would be so kind, would you describe your emotions?"

"Go to hell, you disgusting bastard," she snarled, jerking at her arms again. And finally, the anger came. Flooding her. Liberating her. Blocking the fear, at least for the moment.

His frown was aimed at her now, and he drew a

Brenda Huber

deep breath, disappointment shadowing his features. She didn't care. He was going to kill her anyway. That didn't mean she had to play along with his sick game first.

He ignored her for a while after that, behaving as if she hadn't spoken at all, hadn't demeaned herself somehow in his eyes.

Moving serenely around the room, taking all the time in the world, he rearranged the furniture, positioned the battered coffee table near her, stood back, then readjusted the angle. Next, he retrieved a large duffel bag from the floor beside the sofa.

Setting the bag beside the low table, he dropped to his knees and pulled open the long zipper. The Chess Master glanced up and smiled at her once more. That same friendly smile he'd offered her that night in the pub when she'd thought him just another harmless customer.

"Oh, I think this will be the best one yet." He cocked his head, considering her carefully. Excitement sparkled in his eyes. "Shall we try something new? It's all well and good to stick with the tried and true, but perhaps it's time to branch out a bit, so to speak."

As he spoke, he tugged the opening off the duffel bag wider, and Charlie caught a glimpse inside. Her anger faded in the face of brutal, paralyzing fear.

She watched with growing horror as he reached into the bag, over and over, pulling out random items. A hammer, a hack saw, pliers. And still he kept going, positioning dozens of items carefully on the table in a precise order. A small acetylene torch joined the vast array of tools on the table. Next came a pair of thick gloves.

And a small gray pouch. He hesitated a moment, his expression altering slightly as he regarded that pouch for a moment. Then, with exquisite care, he opened the pouch and extracted a pewter chess piece.

A Queen.

Oh, God, he's going to brand me like the others.

She struggled not to gag.

The Chess Master rose then and approached her. With great care, he began unbuttoning her shirt, careful not to touch her skin. She recoiled from his hands, fearing what any woman would. But he kept at his task until her shirt hung open. He didn't bother with her bra or her pants, not yet. She might have breathed a sigh of relief, if it hadn't been for that table covered with his ghoulish tools.

He wordlessly adjusted the collar of her shirt so it draped farther open on her shoulders, even going so far as to carefully reach around her to tuck her shirttails into the back of her waistband, leaving her chest and stomach exposed. And then he stood back, tilting his head this way and that, an artist considering a blank canvas, and the potential therein.

He returned to his bag and pulled out a small wooden box. He glanced up at her one more time and winked, excitement wild in his eyes now. Eagerly, he opened the box and held it up for her inspection, revealing an extensive set of shiny blades.

She'd seen what those knives could do. Charlie bit the inside of her cheek to keep from screaming, but she whimpered despite her resolve to show him no fear.

He set the box on the table, carefully positioning it. Then, he donned one of the thick gloves and picked up a pair of silver tongs. With the tongs, he carefully lifted the pewter queen, held it aloft as, with his free hand, he turned on the torch.

Using the same conversational tone one might use if asking her preference of tea or coffee, he glanced up at her and offered politely, "Go ahead and scream if you feel the need, I promise I won't mind."

Chapter Twenty-Six

"The lights are on up there," Jesse blurted, gripping the dash as Stanley skidded the cruiser into the parking lot.

Jesse vaulted from the vehicle before it came to a full stop. He slipped and slogged through slush as he raced across loose gravel, unmindful of the stinging slash where sleet pelted his face and arms, soaking his T-shirt. His took the stairs three at a time, his hand instinctively going to his hip. He cursed when he came up empty. No gun. Just like he had no badge. Damn it!

Didn't matter. He was still going in.

Stanley swore from somewhere behind him near the middle of the steps, and the railing shuddered and cracked from the force of a heavy impact. Jesse didn't slow down, didn't look back. Charlie was up there with a killer.

Crouching low, he shoved the door open and went in. The lights were on, a harsh glare compared to the driving darkness outside, but his eyes adjusted quickly. Scanning the room, he hugged the wall, keeping low. Easing along the hallway, he peered around the corner into the tiny galley kitchen.

Empty.

A nearly crippling sense of déjà vu washed over him, but he ruthlessly shoved it aside. Charlie needed him.

He wouldn't fail. Not this time.

The floor vibrated beneath his feet in time to the muted music and noise filtering up through the floor boards. He moved down the hall and peered into the bathroom. The music below was so loud, nearly drowning out all else. Even so, there was no screaming, no crying. No pleading or whimpering.

Not a sound from Charlie.

Jesse approached the living room on cautious feet. The killer could still be in there with her.

But Jesse also knew what else he might come face-to-face with. The Chess Master might already be gone, his work here finished.

A sound behind him turned his head. Stanley, red in the face and breathing hard, joined him in the hallway, his gun drawn. Jesse motioned, and Stanley fell in line behind him.

They moved into the room as a unit. Jesse nearly collapsed at the first sight of Charlie hanging there on the wall. It was all so eerily similar to his first glimpse of Molly that he was momentarily paralyzed.

But there were differences, and he clung to those differences like a lifeline. There had been so much blood back then. And Molly had been so still.

Molly had already been dead.

Though Charlie sagged against the wall, her chest still moved with each breath. Her head hung down, long hanks of damp hair obscuring her features. Blood smeared her wrists where she'd brutally fought her restraints, but there wasn't any blood anywhere else. Her shirt had been opened and hung limply from her shoulders. And on the tender pale skin of her stomach—

"*Holy Lord Jesus Almighty,*" Stanley whispered, clearly shocked.

The livid red design branded upon her delicate skin sent so many emotions whipping through Jesse, he didn't know how to react. An elaborate, flourishing brand of a chess piece, the Queen, marred skin that had once been flawless. Skin he'd once stroked and kissed. He could only guess at the excruciating pain she must have experienced, at what she must still be able to feel.

What he wouldn't do to take that pain from her.

Losing all sense of his surroundings, all awareness of the danger that still lurked like a coiled snake waiting for one moment of inattentiveness to strike, Jesse rushed to Charlie's side.

With excruciating care, Jesse clasped her face between his trembling hands and lifted her head. He forced a swallow as he saw for the first time the telltale bruises circling her neck like a garish collar.

"Charlie," he whispered. The lump in his throat made it difficult to speak, and his voice was raw with emotion. He smoothed the pad of his thumb across her bloody lower lip, willing her to be okay. "Charlie, open your eyes, sweetheart. Open those beautiful eyes for me."

As if dragging herself from somewhere deep, deep inside, Charlie moaned. Her eyelashes fluttered. And in an instant, her body went taut as a bowstring and a hoarse scream ripped from her chest. She thrashed and jerked at her restraints.

"Charlie! Charlie, it's me. You're safe!"

He held her face in a gentle grip until her wild, wide, bloodshot eyes focused on him. His fears were confirmed by the burst blood vessels in the whites of her eyes. The bastard had choked her. Choked her nearly to the point of death, then brought her back so he could torture her some more. Toying with her. Prolonging her pain, drawing out his pleasure.

But she was alive.

Her screams subsided, turning instead to heartrending sobs.

"I'll get you down, baby. Just hold on."

Jesse turned to the table beside her. He forced a swallow when he realized what he was looking at. The Chess Master's instruments of torture. The FBI had not, in all their studies and educated guesses, realized the extent of the Chess Master's collection. Was this the same bag of tricks he'd used on Molly? Would they find DNA from all those other women the Chess Master had killed on these...these *tools*?

Picking up a knife, Jesse turned back to her, dying a little inside as she flinched away at the sight of that blade.

Dimly, he registered the sound of Stanley's voice speaking into his shoulder radio, demanding dispatch send back up and an ambulance. Before Jesse could reach up to cut the ropes anchoring Charlie to the wall, however, Stanley's voice gurgled off midsentence.

Charlie screamed. Jesse spun around in time to see Stanley crumple to the floor, his throat slit ear to ear. The Chess Master stood over him, a dripping hunting knife in one hand, Stanley's gun in the other and a gleeful smile plastered on his face.

"It's so good to see you again, Detective Reid," the Chess Master greeted him.

"'Fraid I can't say the same," Jesse said, easing his body between Charlie and that deadly gun.

The Chess Master cocked an eyebrow at the knife in Jesse's hand. "Isn't there some expression about bringing a knife to a gunfight?"

"You know me," Jesse said. "I work with what I've got."

He kept his tone conversational even as he rapidly cataloged the room, making mental note of his assets...and his weaknesses. The biggest one being Charlie tied to the wall behind him. Exposed. Vulnerable.

"I'm so glad I have this chance to express my gratitude, Detective Reid."

Jesse's guarded expression faltered as a frown slipped into place. "You're gratitude?"

"For making this such an enjoyable match." The look of fanatical adoration suddenly twisting the Chess Master's face sickened Jesse.

"Why me?" Jesse hadn't meant to ask that. Hadn't wanted to give this guy any kind of power. But the question had been riding him ever since he'd received that first manila envelope.

"Oh, come now, Detective Reid. You don't have to be so humble, not with me."

"No, really. I'd like to know," he pressed. He knew he shouldn't be feeding into or encouraging the killer's psychotic game, but he'd already strayed into muddy waters. He was driven now, wanting answers, right or wrong. This killer had touched every aspect of his life. Damn it, he deserved to know why.

"I knew you were the one the moment I saw you at one of your crime scenes. A domestic shooting at a motel. I happened to be staying in the next room at the time. Imagine my surprise! I bet you don't remember, but you even questioned me while you were interrogating everyone in the area. Fate has a way of placing players in your path, you know, and I was lucky enough to observe you in action. You were so focused. So dedicated. I did a little research." The Chess Master's tone became conspiratorial for a moment. "You, my dear detective, have an *impressive* conviction rate."

Jesse was at a loss. That was it? That was all it had taken to become the object of this killer's obsession? A solid track record? One moment of being in the wrong place at the wrong time? His life, his future had been shattered all because he'd done his job? His mind screamed protest. That was insane.

"Playing with the FBI had lost its luster by then. You revived me, and I must thank you for that. I have to say, your reaction to that first Pawn in our game was, truly, all I'd hoped for and so much more."

"The first Pawn. You mean, Darlene Davies?" Jesse remembered every name. Every face.

"Was that her name?" The Chess Master shrugged. "I'd forgotten. But it doesn't matter. She was just a Pawn. The opening move in a new game. No one else has proven to be as much of a challenge as you have."

Jesse's blood turned to ice. "You stayed close? You watched us at the crime scene."

"I did. Every one, in fact. Rather difficult to enjoy the game if I'm not there to see it."

Jesse couldn't even begin to wrap his mind around that kind of evil. To have had the Chess Master so close, all those times, and not even realized it.

"I have to congratulate you on a commendable choice for Queen this time, Detective Reid." The Chess

Master beamed at him. Then his gaze turned briefly to Charlie, and Jesse bristled. "She's displayed great courage and fortitude, detective. Great spirit. She's held out much longer than the last one. You should be proud. I am."

Anger coursed through Jesse. He tensed and took a threatening step forward.

"I see I've upset you. Ah-ah. I'm afraid I'm going to have to ask you to drop the knife, detective." The Chess Master waved the gun toward the direction of Jesse's hand.

Gritting his teeth, holding one hand up in a false offer of peace—a magician's sleight of hand, distract with one hand so they don't notice what you're doing with the other—Jesse bent slightly at the waist to lay down the weapon. The tip of the knife touched the floor, and slowly Jesse peeled his fingers from the handle.

The Chess Master's shoulders relaxed, just the tiniest bit. Jesse knew it would be the only chance he got. He straightened with deceptive slowness. At the last second, he lunged for the table containing the Chess Master's tools of torture.

He didn't have any specific item in mind, just grabbed the first thing his fingers brushed. The wooden grip was smooth in his hand, the weight on the end hefty as he spun and threw at the same time.

The Chess Master reacted instinctively, just as Jesse had been counting on. He ducked to avoid the hammer, giving Jesse slim seconds at best. Jesse closed the distance between them at a dead run, not giving the Chess Master time to aim. He blocked the upward arc of the knife in the Chess Master's hand, hissed as the blade sliced into his forearm. With his fist, Jesse knocked the gun from the Chess Master's hand, and kicked it away. Then he plowed his shoulder into the killer and tumbled them both to the ground.

Jesse grappled for the upper hand, and gripped the Chess Master's wrist. But the killer stubbornly held on to the knife. Jesse slammed the Chess Master's wrist repeatedly to the floor. A knee rammed into Jesse's ribs, and pain knocked the wind from his lungs. And then a boot heel slammed into his thigh, bruising bone deep. But Jesse clung to that hand, knowing it would be over for him, and for Charlie, if the Chess Master won the fight for possession of that knife.

They rolled, each struggling for the upper hand. The back of Jesse's head hit the edge of the coffee table, and pain lanced his scalp. Planting his boot on the floor, Jesse shoved his hip up, twisting his waist, rolling until he had the Chess Master flat on his back.

But the killer used his momentum against him and kept rolling. The Chess Master tried to head butt Jesse, but he missed and whacked his forehead against Jesse's collarbone. Jesse's grip on the knife slackened for a split second, and the Chess Master shoved at him.

But Jesse swiftly tightened his grip on the knife. That moment of distraction cost him the upper hand. The Chess Master managed to roll Jesse beneath him, and he straddled Jesse's stomach, preventing them from rolling farther by bracing his knees on the floor. Using both hands, angling the blade toward Jesse's throat, the Chess Master used his weight to push down.

Jesse's arms strained and trembled as he fought to keep that blade from piercing his skin. His breath seared his throat. He grunted as he pushed back with all his might. His body ached, and his ribs screamed protest from where the Chess Master had kneed him.

For a split second, Charlie's stifled scream drowned out the muffled music from below. Jesse, still working to keep that knife from his throat let his gaze slip to Charlie. She was wide awake now, and she was watching them with terror in her eyes.

That glance gave Jesse the jolt he needed. He twisted, jerking the knife down and to the side, planting the tip deep in the floor beside his throat. A thin ribbon of dampness accompanied the sting along the side of his neck where the blade had drawn a shallow slice. Jesse brought his elbow up, smashing it into the Chess Master's neck.

The Chess Master fell back, grabbing his throat as he wheezed. Jesse arched his back, throwing the killer off balance. But the Chess Master wasn't done. They went rolling across the floor yet again, elbows and fists flying. Though his face was bright red now, and tears of pain welled in his eyes, the Chess Master fought like the madman he was. They crashed into the table, and the Chess Master's implements came crashing down all around them. Jesse caught a flash of silver as the killer swept up another blade.

In the slim space between their stomachs, Jesse grappled for control of the knife. Once, twice the blade skimmed his abdomen, tearing through his shirt, slicing flesh. The point dug in, just below his sternum. Jesse, his grip wet with blood, fought to twist the blade away. The angle of the blade moved, wavered, spun.

And then, a sudden gush of wet warmth soaked his hands, drenched his forearms, poured over Jesse's chest.

Above him, the Chess Master's eyes widened, filled with surprise and shock. His lips parted and blood bubbled past his teeth.

Jesse couldn't stop himself. He shoved the knife deeper into the Chess Master's chest, as deep as it would go, scraping bone, sinking it to the hilt. And then he gave that long, wicked blade a brutal twist. The Chess Master gasped. He tried to speak, tried to form a word. Nothing but a hiss of air escaped him. His eyes glazed over, and his lips, dripping blood, slackened. Shoving at the dead weight above him, Jesse scooted and rolled from beneath the Chess Master's body, knocking the killer to his side.

Jesse dragged himself backward on his hands and heels until he kicked himself free. And then he turned to crawl away. He paused for a second, swaying on his hands and knees, hanging his head as he fought to recover his breath. His blood roared in his ears. He wanted to puke his guts out, wanted to pass out, but Charlie needed him.

Jesse sucked in another breath. He spied Stanley's gun a few feet away. His cop's instinct had him crawling to secure the weapon first.

Charlie's scream hit him like a bucket of ice water. He dove the last two feet, snatched the weapon up in shaking hands, and rolled. The Chess Master was almost on top of him, staggering and weaving on his feet, that gruesome, blood-drenched hunting knife clutched in one fist while he gripped the ragged, gory hole in his chest with the other.

In the next heartbeat, Jesse raised the gun and pulled the trigger, marking the center of the Chess Master's forehead with a lethal red dot. The Chess

Master dropped to his knees before toppling the rest of the way to the floor.

Holding one hand over the long shallow slashes on his abdomen, Jesse climbed to his feet. He hobbled across the short distance to stand over the Chess Master's body, wincing with every step. Jesse stared down at that face, the face of a monster…at sightless eyes and slack features.

Expecting…

What?

Was it finally over? He had trouble processing it.

This bastard had hunted him, *haunted* him for so long. An evil fiend that had shattered Jesse's world and made his every waking moment a nightmare. The Chess Master lay there, unmoving, unblinking, not breathing.

Dead.

It finally hit Jesse. The nightmare was over.

"Checkmate," Jesse rasped.

An overwhelming sense of relief washed through him. He was free at last. Truly free. The Chess Master would never terrorize another innocent woman again, never destroy another life.

Charlie was safe.

After pushing the weapon into the back of his waistband, Jesse hobble-stepped over to Charlie. He whipped his blood-soaked shirt over his head and tossed it away.

Charlie hung there, sobbing, her head drooped to her chest. He didn't waste time soothing her, didn't bother with words at all. He snatched up another knife and made swift work of slashing her bindings. He caught her up against him as she sagged toward the floor, unable to stand.

"Shh, it's over. It's over now," he whispered against her hair. She only sobbed harder. Her hot tears bathed his skin as he held her in his arms. He cupped her cheeks between his hands, tipping her head back so he could look into her red, swollen eyes. "He's dead, Charlie. I'll never let anyone hurt you again. I swear it. I'm so sorry, baby."

Charlie finally nodded. She peered up at him, searching his face with damp, blood-shot eyes. The ugly circle of bruises around her neck reminded him again of how close he'd come to losing her. Her wrists were bloody where the rope had torn her delicate skin. Her hair hung in messy, tangled knots all around her.

But she was alive, and the sight of her, living and breathing, was such a beautiful thing that it made his chest ache and brought tears to his own eyes. Holding the center of his world in a tender embrace, Jesse slowly sank to the floor, his legs giving out on him at last as the distant sound of sirens grew louder.

"I love you," Charlie croaked, her voice hoarse from being choked.

Closing his eyes, Jesse dropped his forehead to hers. She still loved him. After all she'd been through…because of him, and she still loved him. A hot ball of emotion burned the back of his throat.

Lifting his head, he stared hard into her eyes and cupped her cheeks. "I love you too."

Epilogue

Charlie placed the hot mugs on the kitchen counter and stirred the creamy cocoa one last time. The phone in the living room rang, and she jumped, rattling the spoon against porcelain. She had to take a moment to steady her hands, and her nerves. Shaking her head, Charlie grabbed a dishcloth, dampened it and mopped up splatters of hot chocolate from the counter, then she wiped the streaks from the side of the cup.

She picked up both mugs and carried them into the living room in time to see Jesse dropping the phone onto the end table.

"Here you go." She handed him one of the cups. "Be careful, it's hot."

"Thanks," Jesse said. He took a tentative sip. But, as he leaned forward to set the cup on the coffee table in front of him, he flinched and sucked in a sharp breath.

"Careful," she scolded, taking the cup from him and placing it on the table herself. "You don't want to tear anything open again." The Chess Master's blade had left wounds all over Jesse. Some deeper than others. His forearm, his shoulder, across his abdomen, the side of his neck. Thankfully none had done serious damage, nothing several dozen stitches hadn't fixed. But Jesse had already tried to do too much too fast and ripped several open a couple days ago.

"They itch," he grumbled. Being an invalid did not sit well with him.

Through the material of her T-shirt, Charlie fingered the bandage covering her stomach. She knew all about the itching. The place where the Chess Master had branded her was healing well, but sometimes the itch nearly drove her insane. Her wrists were still healing, her throat was still sore and bruised, but she was alive, so she wouldn't complain.

She refused to give in to self pity or some misguided sense of damaged self-esteem. She would bear the brand of a killer for the rest of her life, a constant reminder of the night she'd survived a monster. But she wouldn't let how she'd received that brand define her.

No, she would view it as a badge of courage, and a mark of Jesse's bravery.

She was alive. Jesse was alive. That's what mattered. That's what she chose to focus on.

And Jeffrey Michael Huffman, AKA the Chess Master, was finally dead. The Fed's had been able to identify him at last. A single, forty-two-year-old dentist who'd just walked away from his practice one day without a word and never returned. He'd been treated from the time he was a small boy for some kind of attachment disorder, they'd been told. She couldn't remember the exact wording of SSA Anderson's explanation, didn't really care. Huffman had been a cold, heartless murderer. Nothing excused his behavior.

He'd never be able to hurt anyone else ever again. She didn't care about anything beyond that fact.

Nevertheless, the Chess Master had left his dark mark on Badger Creek. He'd claimed his final victims, leaving the small community grieving, their sense of security shaken.

Paula. Stanley. Their loss left a hole that would never be filled.

Jesse had changed as well, though his change had been far more welcome. He was no longer secretive. No longer did he bristle or change the subject when asked about his past. He'd overcome a nightmare, conquered his demons, bested the monster.

He'd moved into the cabin by the river with Charlie, and he told her every day how much he loved her. He no longer held a part of himself back. Rather, he embraced every moment, and took every opportunity to make her feel cherished.

He'd also, she was pleased to note, rekindled old relationships. He'd spoken to his former partner several times on the phone this past week. And Jesse's younger brother Billy had promised to come for an extended visit soon.

The future looked bright, full of hope and promise.

Jesse had even been offered the position of Badger Creek Chief of Police, once he'd recovered fully from his injuries of course. The jury was still out on whether he'd take the position, as he'd refused to commit himself until he'd had time to fully think it through. But if Charlie were a betting woman, she'd be putting her money on him taking the job. Jesse was a cop through and through, right down to the depths of his soul. He might drag his feet about it a bit. But he couldn't deny the way his eyes lit up whenever they talked about it.

As far as Charlie was concerned, there was nothing to think over. She'd seen him in action. Badger Creek would never find another who could protect and serve better.

"That was a quick call," she said. "Who was on the phone?"

"Your dad. He wanted to let us know Caleb will be released from the hospital tomorrow." Before she could say anything, he continued, "I already told him we'd pick Caleb up and take him home. He also wanted me to tell you everything is running smoothly at the pub and the three of us are not to show our faces there for at least another week *'or else'*. His words, not mine."

Smiling, she settled into the circle of Jesse's arms and propped her feet up on the coffee table beside his.

"We'll see," she murmured.

"And I'm also supposed to tell you that Doris will be bringing groceries out this evening, so we aren't supposed to go anywhere. Just stay home and relax."

Her father had cut his trip short as soon as he'd learned of the attack. He'd also finally stopped riding the fence where Doris was concerned, to Charlie's everlasting relief. The two had been behaving like moon-eyed lovebirds since Quinn had returned.

As for Charlie, she was champing at the bit to get back into the thick of things. She'd never been one to sit idle, and all this down time was making her a bit stir crazy. Jesse shifted his hold on her a bit. Sighing in contentment, she snuggled in.

On the other hand, times like this, snuggled up with Jesse in front of a roaring fire with the snow piling up outside the window could be awfully good for her too.

"Hmmph," Jesse grunted, clearly not happy with her response. But he didn't argue. If she knew him— and she was beginning to think she knew him very well—she'd say that instead of arguing, he was already scheming interesting ways of keeping her occupied right here at home.

He was silent for a long time. And then he asked, "Think you're up to planning another party?"

Turning, she looked up at him and frowned. "I guess so. Are you thinking about having Thanksgiving out here for everybody?" She began mentally ticking off all the details that went into planning a Thanksgiving feast when he shifted in his seat again.

"I had something else in mind."

Jesse carefully balanced a small black, satin covered box on her thigh. Charlie sucked in a sharp breath, her gaze shooting up to meet his smiling eyes.

"Open it," he encouraged.

Her eyes went damp, and her hands trembled. She lifted the box into the palm of her hand. She'd never expected anything like this, at least not so soon. Then again, maybe she was wrong, maybe it was just earrings or something. Still, her stomach fluttered.

As if he could read her mind, he kissed the side of her forehead and said, "I realize it's kind of early. But I didn't want to wait to let you know how I feel. I couldn't leave it sitting in my sock drawer, waiting for the right moment. We don't have to do anything with it yet if you're not ready. But I wanted you to have it. To know that it's there...if, or when you want it."

She stared at the box a moment more, her heart in her throat, and then finally opened it. Nestled inside was the most beautiful ring she'd ever seen. A square-cut, sparkling sapphire that matched Jesse's eyes, surrounded by tiny twinkling diamonds.

"I love you, Charlie. I want you with me always. Marry me," he said softly. And then, as if he feared pressuring her, he added, "You don't have to say yes now." He paused, then rushed on, "But a *maybe* wouldn't hurt my feelings either."

She stared at the ring, emotion clogging her throat. So many things swirled through her mind. So many things she wanted to say. But she couldn't seem to form words.

Beside her, Jesse held himself perfectly still. He was even holding his breath. She turned to look up at him, to stare into his eyes, needing to be sure this was what he truly wanted, and not something he felt pressured into because of the trauma they'd both shared.

What she saw in his eyes made the decision for her.

"Yes," she whispered, tears filling her eyes as she nodded. Then, louder, "Yes!"

"Really? You're sure?" His eyes widened. He looked so happy, so excited, and yet still the tiniest bit nervous.

She nodded, giving him a big, wet, sloppy smile.

"We don't have to rush into anything. I don't want you to have any regrets," he blurted. "I mean, I don't want you to think I'm putting you off or anything. Because I want kids, someday I want kids. And the white picket fence and all that. But maybe we could start with a dog or something? And—"

Charlie silenced him by pressing her fingertips to his lips. "Yes to the ring. Yes to the kids…someday. And definitely, *definitely* yes to the dog."

Unmindful of his stitches, Jesse pulled her up against his chest and captured her lips, sealing their future.

Oh, yes. The future looked bright indeed.

A word about the author...

Keep up with Brenda Huber's upcoming releases at:

www.brendahuber.webs.com
www.facebook.com/Brenda-Hubers-Author-Page
Twitter: @b_hubie
www.amazon.com/author/brendahuber

~*~

Also look for these books by Brenda Huber:
Mine
Shadows
Cravings
Texas Bride
Texas Blaze

~*~

Coming Soon from Brenda Huber:
The Seer
The Slayer
Temptation
Vengeance

Thank you for purchasing
this publication of The Wild Rose Press, Inc.

If you enjoyed the story, we would appreciate your
letting others know by leaving a review.

For other wonderful stories,
please visit our on-line bookstore at
www.thewildrosepress.com.

For questions or more information
contact us at
info@thewildrosepress.com.

The Wild Rose Press, Inc.
www.thewildrosepress.com

Stay current with The Wild Rose Press, Inc.

Like us on Facebook

https://www.facebook.com/TheWildRosePress

And Follow us on Twitter
https://twitter.com/WildRosePress